A
MODERN DAY
LYNCHING

A
MODERN DAY
LYNCHING

SHY RICHARDS

TABLE OF CONTENTS

DEDICATION

For those who are with me
always in spirit and
In my heart

Norma J Davis &
Casandra Renee Davis

A RUDE AWAKENING

The day was hot; the sun beamed in the sky without a cloud in sight. It went on record as one of the hottest days in Georgia. The heat index reached 125 degrees. The news warned the public not to engage in outdoor activities, but the day was heavy and dreary for Chayanne Carter-Parker, a mother of two. A severe thunderstorm warning should have been on the horizon by the way she felt. Chayanne pulled her new S-Class Mercedes through the black iron gate that protected her three acres of property. It was a rather peculiar day at Smith & Dallas Law firm; a high-profile case hit her desk that would be any mother's nightmare. She called the workday fairly early compared to most, to be in the company of her daughter Lilly whom she hadn't spent much time with. She was a bit uneasy as she pulled the car around the U-shape of her cobbled stone driveway. She parked and admired the way the sun beamed on the five-bedroom, four-and-a-half bath home, her heart filled with sadness as she thought about the sacrifices she made to get to where she was, her marriage at the forefront of the list. As she sat there sulking, she questioned if her sacrifices were worth being mildly happy.

She sighed exasperatedly and grabbed her black leather briefcase filled with case files from the back seat.

She exited the car to stretch her small frame in her tight, blue, power suit to allow her blood to flow through her limbs; she was exhausted from her forty-five-minute drive across town. The clacking of her designer Louboutin heels kept her company until she reached the front entrance. The lingering smell of pot roast and the scent of home greeted her at the door. A grin set across her face; she hadn't felt this revived in a while. Her divorce, although not so recent, was draining and sent her into a tailspin of deep, manic depression that she was in denial of. She refused to take the prescribed Prozac and Trazodone anti-depressants her Psychiatrist Dr. Folly recommended.

She winced at the sound of her mother's voice in her subconscious. "Those mental cases are for the privileged folks; those kinds of things don't exist for our people," she said. "When you get to feeling down, you have to ask the lord to step in baby. He'll fix it for ya, all you have to do is pray." Chayanne shook her head as if she freed her mind of her mother's logic.

Chayanne lived with Lilly, her nine-year-old daughter. She occasionally housed her seventeen-year-old son Ashton when he visited home from Georgetown University. Ashton graduated two years ahead of his class thanks to Charles's strict guidelines for academics.

Chayanne ascended the long staircase heading to her master suite. "Hey Klara, I'm home. I'll be down for dinner shortly," she called out to the nanny as she continued to her bedroom.

Chayanne was winded when she reached her destination. She hadn't been to the gym in a while, which was a part of her early morning regime.

She stopped going when the divorce proceedings began and hadn't found the will to pick back up on her fitness. She sat at her vanity taking a long, hard look at herself. Her smooth peanut-butter skin was glowing; her long reddish-brown hair shimmered in the light while she brushed it back into a loose ponytail. She screwed her face in distaste at the small bags forming under her wide, green eyes.

"I need a spa day," Chayanne admitted aloud to herself as she rubbed her face.

She opened the vanity drawer to search for her eye cream. Regretfully, she found an old family photo with Charles. She slammed the drawer shut. The picture was triggering, taking her back to her therapy session earlier that week.

"Chayanne, do something for yourself," his baritone voice bellowed. "You're always giving and nurturing others, it's time to do something for you."

A smirk set across her face as she thought about the new Mercedes she purchased. She bought the car with the alimony funds that collected dust since the ink on the divorce papers dried. A sense of satisfaction crept in.

The loud buzz of the room's intercom system distracted her from her thoughts.

"Ms. Carter?" Klara called out with her heavy Bogotá accent. Chayanne scrambled from the vanity to answer her call. "Ms. Carter, please pick up. AYE!" Klara said frustrated.

Chayanne pushed the talk button before Klara could call out once more. "Yes Klara, what is it?" she responded flustered.

"The calls from your office line are coming to the house line," Klara said. "It keeps ringing, non-stop; a woman is demanding to speak with you. She calls every five minutes, and I am trying so hard to finish supper. I know you just got home, but can you please talk with her?" Klara urged.

Chayanne sighed heavily, not wanting to deal with office work on a Friday evening, "Sure, patch her through upstairs." she responded with irritancy.

The cordless phone that rested on Chayanne's nightstand rang loudly; on the second ring she answered, "Ms. Carter speaking."

"Oh, I was trying to reach Ms. Parker, do I have the wrong number?" A woman with a thick southern accent said.

"I am Ms. Parker; however, I prefer to be addressed by my maiden name. How can I help you, ma'am?"

"Oh, thank God, I've been trying to reach you for several days now. Every time I get a break from work, I call your office. My name is Miss Yvette Baxter, my son's case is with your office and I've personally requested you. I know you're a busy woman, but I don't see anyone else fit for the job. I'm using all his life insurance money to pay your retainer fee Ms. Park... I mean Ms. Carter, I..."

"Miss Baxter," Chayanne called out interrupting her rant. "Your son's case just hit my desk this morning. I haven't looked over the details of the case in depth and I don't know enough about the case to tell you if I'm interested in taking it or not..."

"PLEASE, MS. CARTER! I am begging you. I am down on my knees at this payphone begging you to at least consider my boy's case.

He's gone Ms. Carter and he ain't coming back." She paused briefly trying to fight her tears away, "He needs someone that has a strong voice to seek justice for him, the way they've ridiculed him in the news... He ain't do nothing but be black." she inhaled shaking her head trying to find reason in all of the chaos. "I'm working triple shifts tirelessly Ms. Carter to make sure I have enough money to pay you. I even took a second mortgage on the house my daddy left for me. I need you; I don't want nobody else!" She demanded, "I've done my research on you and you win ninety-three percent of your cases, you've been named one of the best black lawyers of our time. I ain't got much, but what I do got I will give it all to you." She sobbed heavily on the receiver.

Chayanne put her hand to her heart silently pleading with Miss. Baxter's loss. "Miss Baxter, I can't make any promises; I need to review the file before rendering a decision. I promise, no matter the outcome..." she inhaled deeply holding back her tears. "I promise you; I'll be in touch."

"I understand you have a job to do," said Miss Baxter. "You do it well to be praised the way you are. Please, just do all that you can, that's all I'm asking. If you have children, I'm sure you can't imagine what it's like to lose one of them," She paused sniffling her pain. "My break time is up Ms. Carter, I pray to God I hear from you soon."

The phone clicked; the dial tone buzzed in her ear as she hung onto Miss. Baxter's last pleading words. Chayanne slid the phone down on her chest and let a tear slip from her eye. It was unbearable to imagine life without one of her children.

She groaned then hung up the phone, "I just don't know what to do on this one." She admitted to herself aloud as the acoustics of the room echoed back to her. There were a lot of office politics involved in Miss Baxter's case and because Chayanne had yet to make partner, it just wasn't her call. She felt helpless and her heart hurt for Miss Baxter.

Chayanne showered longer than usual; the steam engulfed her nakedness. She hoped somehow the answers would pour out of the showerhead as she scrubbed the day's stench off her; for some reason, she couldn't wash her feelings down the drain. She crouched in the corner of the shower, biting down on her towel weeping. She screamed, biting down harder, still unable to feel an ounce of relief. When the water ran cold, she composed herself and resumed her day.

She smeared the fog on the mirror to clear a space to peer at her. She dried her damp, curly hair with a bath towel; her green-hazel eyes puffy, tender, and redden. She'd become accustomed to the look, crying many sleepless nights after Charles left her and the children. She wore a mask for the world, never letting anyone see the wounds that lingered below.

She took a deep breath, "Snap out of it!" she demanded of herself. "You can't keep letting Lilly down. Be present, be in this moment," she reminded herself the way her therapist instructed her to do in her time of weakness.

She got dressed and headed for the long C-curved staircase. As she descended the stairs, a pile of mail slipped through the mail slot and hit the marble floor. She read each piece as she collected it. She noticed an unmarked manila envelope; she rushed to the window that hugged the door to see what the mail carrier delivered. No one was in sight. Confused, she fumbled to open the unmarked envelope.

"I AM SOMETIMES WHITE, BUT USUALLY
BLACK. I WILL TAKE YOU THERE, BUT NEVER

BRING YOU BACK... WHEN I KNOCK, THERE
IS ALWAYS A SOUL TO ANSWER."

Chayanne studied the riddle that was strung together with magazine clippings. She looked out the window again to reassure herself there was no one there. She scratched her head and flipped the card over in search of an answer.

~ KNOCK, KNOCK, KNOCK, 46 HOURS REMAIN.
REJECT THE CASE OR I WILL BE THE JUDGE
AND THE JURY.

Lilly laid in the grass, enjoying its softness and comfort while looking up at the sky. She enjoyed the sun's warmth on her face as she listened to the sound of Mary Elizabeth's voice ramble.

"Lilly, did you hear me?" Mary Elizabeth paused, awaiting Lilly's eye contact through the iron bars that separated their yards. "I said I want you to come to my sleepover next weekend. All the girls from our class are going to be there; my mom even made me invite Lexi." Mary Elizabeth sighed in disgust at the thought of her name.

"What's wrong with Lexi?" Lilly questioned pretending to be oblivious. "She's nice to me; she even gave me her favorite pen in English class because I forgot mine in my locker." Lilly explained, pretending to defend Lexi.

"Gross, I hope you gave it back! Lexi isn't pretty and she always wears that nappy Afro. Her teeth are bucked because her parents can't afford braces." Mary Elizabeth shot back.

An uninvited moment of silence intruded the girl's conversation. Lilly just laid there in the soft, vibrant, green, Bermuda grass staring up at the sky. She admired the hues the sunset decided to paint that evening; the pink faded into the purple and the purple faded into a soft orange. This was her favorite spot in the garden next to the Gardenias. Mary Elizabeth reached through the iron gate and tapped Lilly's shoulder. Lilly turned her head, looking into Mary Elizabeth's sparkling blue eyes. For a moment, they just gazed at one another. Their energy was awkwardly entangled; Lilly felt like Mary Elizabeth always came down on Lexi too hard, but she couldn't quite pin Mary Elizabeth's frustration with her. Before Mary Elizabeth could speak, Chayanne's soft voice called out for Lilly.

"That's my mom, I'll see you tomorrow Mary Elizabeth. I'll meet you at the gate after lunch tomorrow," Lilly said pulling herself off the ground, dusting her butt from derby. She collected the books she brought down to the garden to read. Mary Elizabeth's expression was uneasy; she looked a bit sad. It seemed as though she had an epiphany at the moment and wanted to extend an apology to Lilly, but she was uncertain why she felt that way. She refuted the way she felt, so she lied.

"I can't meet you tomorrow, I... I have to help my mom shop for my slumber party."

"Oh... well I guess that's a good way to kick off the summer vacation. Well anyway, I'll see what my mom says about coming to the party." Lilly smiled to cover her undecided feelings. Chayanne called out for Lilly once more. It was difficult for Chayanne to see over the garden that sat at the rear of the property.

"See ya!" Mary Elizabeth said disheartened. Both girls retreated and headed for their homes. It took Lilly longer than usual to make it to the freshly stained deck that wrapped around the sides of the house. Her head hung low; beads of sweat gathered by her brow. Her brown, thick, silky curly hair was like a wool hat on a cold winter's day. Her light skin was stinging from the sun's rays, her small petit body heavy from the day's play. Chayanne stood at the patio door with a sour look on her face, the look you have when you bite into a wedge of lemon. Lilly hung her head lower knowing her mother was unhappy with the timing of her response to her call. She used the rest of the energy she had left to muster into the cool air-conditioned house. As she was passing Chayanne to enter, Chayanne grabbed Lilly to embrace her long and hard. Lilly's guard dropped as she felt the love inside her mother's arms, something she'd longed for since the divorce. Lilly reminisced of how things used to be, when her mother actually made time for her, taught her things, took her shopping, and had sleepovers with her in the den. Lilly melted into her mother's arms; an overwhelming flow of tears slid down her face slowly. Chayanne knew she'd buried herself with work and had become neglectful with her motherly responsibilities, but she was overwhelmed and disoriented with her new normal. Charles was her first love; he was all she had known since her younger years. She confided in him about everything, there were no secrets. He was her best friend through twenty years of marriage. She wasn't sure how to start over, but she was figuring it out slowly. Chayanne squeezed Lilly tighter apologizing with her embrace. A tear rolled down Chayanne's cheek feeling Lilly's emotional agony.

She released Lilly and looked into her large, hazel, almond-shaped eyes. Lilly peered into her mother's eyes that mirrored hers.

"I love you, mommy," Lilly whispered as she wiped the tear from Chayanne's cheek. The gesture made Chayanne more emotional, and a floodgate of tears poured out.

She gasped, "Oh my sweet girl, I love you more than you know. Now go wash up for dinner." Chayanne instructed. Lilly ran up the stairs to put her things away and prepare for dinner. She was thrilled it had been months since her mother was home in time to eat supper with her. She had a bounce in her step as she approached the dinner table.

Lilly's eyes searched the room, "Mommy, where is Klara? She never misses dinner with me."

Chayanne sighed heavily, "It's just you and I tonight honey, like old times. Klara's been taking care of you so much lately her own children must have forgotten what she looks like." Chayanne chortled. Lilly returned a smile and began to eat with ease.

"I love it when it's just us—I... missed you mommy, I really missed you." Lilly spoke with relief.

"Yes, me too honey, you have no idea how much I miss spending time with you." Chayanne expressed her affection by rubbing Lilly's back and holding her small hand in her palm. They ate in silence; their company was enough for one another. Chayanne finished the last of the soft California Merlot in her glass. With the lingering finish of white pepper still on her palate, she cleared the dinner table. The sound of the glass plates and dishes clinking together drew Lilly's attention from the television show she was watching in the family room. She abandoned the TV to assist her mother with the cleanup. She was ecstatic that it was time to spend with the person she adored most.

"Mom..." Lilly hesitated, "may I go to Mary Elizabeth's slumber party?" Lilly asked while rinsing the dishes and placing them into the dish rack. Chayanne stood quiet; she reminisced on the email from Lilly's teacher a few weeks ago.

Dear Parents, it is my duty to inform you of an incident that took place between two students in front of the class. I apologize in advance to all parents for the racist, stereotypical remarks to follow, and the students involved will remain anonymous in this email. Today, a student was referred to as a nappy-headed pica ninny. Student 1 further disclaimed that student 2 could only afford Goodwill clothing. Student 1 was upset about a purple-shell necklace that resembled their own. Student 1 furthered their disapproval by writing the word NIGGER on Student 2's desk with a red sharpie. I am embarrassed by Student 1's handling their dislike for Student 2. Neither the school, nor I condone or tolerate the bullying of a student based on their skin color. Student 1 is subjected to immediate disciplinary action for their outburst. Please feel free to contact the Dean of Academics or I for more information on the matter.

Kindest Regards,

Mrs. Dyer

"Mommy did you hear me?" Lilly pushed.

"Yes honey, I heard you. Why do you want to go?" Chayanne asked with curiosity.

"Well of course Mary Elizabeth is my best friend, and besides, all the girls from the class will be there. I have to support my friend." Lilly responded in a matter-of-fact like tone.

"Even Lexi?" Chayanne said puzzled.

"Yes, Mary Elizabeth's mom made her invite Lexi." Lilly sounded annoyed.

"What? You don't like Lexi?" Chayanne pushed gently for more information.

"No... I mean she's not that bad, but Mary Elizabeth doesn't like her. Why would her mom even her invite her?"

"Honey why do you like Mary Elizabeth? Is she nice to you?" Chayanne asked baiting Lilly.

"We are the same, we both have light eyes, we both have long hair, we go to the same private school, we live in big houses next to each other, her dad is a judge and you're a lawyer, we both like pink, we both have white skin..."

Chayanne taken aback interrupted, "Honey, your skin is light brown like an oatmeal cookie when it's baked at perfect temperature..." she held her tongue and then continued. "Lilly, you do know mommy and daddy are black?"

A look of skepticism appeared on Lilly's face. "Mary Elizabeth said I'm white, she said I wasn't like any of the black people her daddy sends to prison, so I'm not black... I'm like her mommy I am." A look of despair spread across Lilly's face as tears welded in her eyes. "You and daddy aren't bad people so how could you be black?" Chayanne placed her hand over her heart. She never felt such a grave feeling of failure in her life. Her face turned flush red, her chest tightened, and her throat got hot and parched. Chayanne, in disbelief, questioned motherhood. How could she allow her daughter to grow up and not teach her the disadvantages society had given her and all people of color?

"Mommy, is everything alright?" Lilly questioned with concern. Chayanne nodded yes. She sat at the breakfast bar and continued to watch Lilly load the dishes. The sound of the running water filled the room. Lilly completed her task and headed for the stairs. She mounted the staircase and turned back to speak to Chayanne.

"Mom, you never answered me. May I go?" Lilly insisted so she could call and inform Mary Elizabeth.

Chayanne hesitated, unsure of how she wanted to answer. "I want you to go get ready for bed. I'm going to tuck you in tonight and I'd like to share a story with you. After you've heard the story and ask questions to comprehend, you have the choice to decide whether or not you want to attend Mary Elizabeth's party." Lilly screwed her face in uncertainty. She was curious to know what a story had to do with Mary Elizabeth's sleepover. Chayanne shooed Lilly away before she had an opportunity to press her for information. She sat at the breakfast bar, pouring herself another hefty glass of Merlot. Her heart was heavy with concern for Lilly; she recalled having the racial profiling debate with Ashton when he was nine. Chayanne couldn't understand what she had missed with Lilly. She felt terrible; a mother's job is to show her child how to navigate through life, she thought. Is it Lilly's privileges that make her believe she's equal or the innocence of being an adolescent? Maybe if I had spoken with her about the classroom incident, she would have had a firm comprehension of her racial identity. Chayanne combatted back and forth with herself, helping herself to another glass of Merlot.

She sat petrified, sipping rapidly as she prepared herself to relive the horror story she was about to share with her naive daughter. Lilly saw the world through rose-colored lenses. Hatred boiled within Chayanne for having to alter the way Lilly saw the world. She grabbed the bottle of Merlot, not realizing it was emptied on her last glass, and set it down gently on the white and gray marble counter. She was so upset that she was unable to feel the slightest buzz from the wine. How does a mother explain to her child that society hates her because of the color of her skin? Her light skin tone and eyes are the product of a slave master raping her great-great-grandmother. How does a mother soften the blow of reality? Chayanne paced across the kitchen floor hoping to kick up the answers.

Lilly called down, "Mommy, I'm ready."

Chayanne nervously attempted to buy more time. "Baby, did you brush your teeth?"

"Yes mommy, I did, I'm ready to be tucked in."

Chayanne put her sweaty palms on the counter as the tension inside her stewed. Chayanne slowly contemplated if her childhood memories would be too graphic for a young child's mind. Could this possibly damage her? Would she need therapy to deal with arising issues? Chayanne reached the dark gray wooden landing at the top of the stairwell. She swallowed hard; her footsteps bounced off the wall echoing loudly as she approached Lilly's doorway. Lilly turned the dimly lit night light on and it illuminated the room just enough to keep the monsters at bay. She sat on the edge of her powder pink bed as she swung her legs impatiently waiting for her mother. She dressed in her favorite pink unicorn pajamas, the ones she would wear when she had a sleepover with Chayanne in the den downstairs. It was obvious she was on the verge of outgrowing them; the pants rode up her leg hugging her lower calf and the shirt revealed the bottom of her belly button.

Chayanne laughed softly, "Honey, we need to get you some new pajamas; you've outgrown those things."

Lilly joined in on the laugh, "I think you're right; do you think they have these in my size now?" She asked anxiously.

"Tomorrow is my off day," said Chayanne. "We can go to the store and check it out." Lilly smiled; things were starting to feel normal. Her mother seemed to be returning to her a minute at a time.

Chayanne pulled the covers back and placed Lilly's feet under the pink sheets. She pulled the fluffy white duvet up to Lilly's chest. She climbed into bed next to Lilly and allowed her to snuggle underneath her bosom. Lilly adjusted slightly then rested gently in Chayanne's arms. Lilly inhaled deeply, closing her eyes to allow her senses to hold on to Chayanne's scent. She had to make sure what she was experiencing was real. She had longed for a night like this; just the two of them.

Chayanne cleared her throat and spoke in a soft, warming tone.

"I want to tell you a story about when I was a girl your age."

CHAPTER

2

CASTING STONES

The heat was stifling to Chayanne in the back of her uncle's shinny green Ford Falcon. Her damp sunflower sundress drenched from her sweat. Chayanne begged him to roll the window down from a tiny crack to a full breeze. Chayanne loved Saturdays; it was her favorite day of the week. Momma would let Uncle Anthony take David and her to the park. Afterwards, they got ice cream while she worked a double shift at the hotel and the hospital. Chayanne looked over at David, who was older. He was passed out asleep on the backseat next to her. Chayanne winced, noticing the grass stains on David's school jeans. She knew Momma was going to get him for it.

She heard Momma's voice play in her head, "I work so hard washing laundry for those white folks down at the hotel," she said. "You don't do me any justice wearing your good school clothes out to play."

She knew Momma's speech all too well when it came to keeping things nice and clean. She was leant with daddy, who worked in the coalmines. His job required him to smell weird and get dirty all day. When Momma couldn't get the funk out of his clothes, she would throw them away and exclaim, "Poor James." Chayanne noticed the tape was coming unraveled on David's glasses. The Collins boys roughed him up earlier in the school year and cracked them into two pieces. Momma tore him a new backside and instructed him to stay away from the Collins family, as if he were the one attracting trouble.

"You leave those good old boys alone," she said. "There ain't no place for a black man in this world when he messes with whites. I need you to come home to me every night, and you can't do that messing with them boys." Chayanne didn't comprehend because she wasn't picked on. The dark-colored girls envied her light skin, light eyes, and long, fine curly hair. Her assets drew attention from all the boys at the school, as they would smile and ask to take her books and walk her to class. The white girls were even more accepting of Chayanne. Not to mention, they wanted a black friend that wasn't so tinted. David's mocha skin and shiny, thick, jet-black curly hair made him stick out like a sore thumb. Fifteen percent of the school's population was African American. Momma wanted the children to have a great education so they didn't have to work as hard as the older generations.

Chayanne traced her knee under her dress with her small index finger, growing impatient by the second.

"Uncle Anthony, are we almost there yet? We've been in this car for days now." Chayanne exclaimed with an antsy attitude. She didn't have a real concept of time; they had only left the park ten minutes prior to her complaints.

Uncle Anthony laughed, "Oh baby girl, calm your horses, we're almost at the ice cream parlor." Chayanne sat quietly with excitement. She always got vanilla and chocolate scoops mixed and she could hardly wait. She could feel the coolness and creaminess that coated her tongue every time she licked the cone. Her toes danced in her white open-toed sandals as she sat daydreaming about it. Ice cream was the treat of the week because Momma never allowed David or her to indulge in the sweeter things in life. She wanted them to be levelheaded, grounded, and humble.

"Ain't nothing in life easy and sweet for a colored person." Momma's voiced echoed. But of course, Uncle Anthony always broke the rules when Momma wasn't looking.

Uncle Anthony was a banker; he owned the town's only black credit union. He was the one who helped Momma and Daddy get a house in a good neighborhood to help send David and Chayanne to one of the best white public schools. Uncle Anthony was a mathematician and he wasn't shy about his accomplishments. He had a brand-new fancy car every month. He was the Jones that every colored family attempted to keep up with. Uncle Anthony had his way with all the ladies, which was the reason he never married or had children of his own. He was a rolling stone and wore the title proudly.

He instructed David to never settle down to early. "David, there are always plenty of fish in the sea my man," he said. "Never settle, always keep an option or two." Anthony laughed thinking of all the women he'd come across.

He always gave Chayanne the opposite advice, "Suga, you settle down with the first Jack in town that's willing to give you nothing less than the world you deserve. You're truly special baby girl, and if he's coon enough not to see it, leave him right where he stands." Uncle Anthony was so overprotective of Chayanne. He knew all kinds of men would be at her tail when she was no longer a prepubescent girl.

The car finally came to a halt in a front parking space at the ice cream parlor. Uncle Anthony combed his short, reddish-brown relaxed hairdo. He looked just like a white man if you glimpsed at him for a second and not a minute longer. His eyes were dazzling gray and his skin was slightly lighter than Chayanne's. Lots of town folks referred to him as red considering his redbone complexion. His six-foot-three-inch muscular frame exited the car, causing the shocks to spring into their places waking David. He stood well-dressed, adjusting his purple collared shirt and tucking it into his brown slacks that were held by a darker brown belt. He reached his long, lanky arms into the passenger seat grabbing his brown-straw fedora that matched his slacks. All sorts of women smiled and greeted him, blushing as they pushed their children's strollers passed the car.

"Hello ma'am," or "Good afternoon miss," is what his reply was to the smiles.

Chayanne stomped her feet in anger; her patience burned out, "Uncle Anthony, let me out!" She screamed.

"Now Suga, cool it, you're too pretty to act with such foolishness." Chayanne straightened up before he could finish his sentence; she knew how to work Uncle Anthony for what she wanted. She was only throwing a temper tantrum to make him feel bad and coerce him into getting her three scoops of ice cream this week. Uncle Anthony lifted the back seat, allowing Chayanne and David to break free. Chayanne clung to Uncle Anthony's leg. She was very coy at public forums. Besides, he was the only father figure she'd known since her daddy spent most of his days in the coalmines. When her daddy was home, he'd sleep and wasn't very interactive with David or her. Before they'd leave for school, he'd come in and grab a canister of coffee, his brown bag lunch, a slice of toast, and nod to them and close the door behind him. Chayanne couldn't recall the last time her daddy held her on his lap and conversed with her. When he did, it was a rare occasion.

David ran off to meet the other colored boys on the basketball court that neighbored the ice cream parlor. David would see his fourteenth birthday that summer and didn't want a nine-year-old white look-alike to cramp his style. He loved his Chayanne, but at times was harsh because of his unfair treatment due to his complexion. David looked of Dominican decent, but most children didn't notice the difference. He was very popular amongst the colored children. He was too cool for school, especially after adhering to the advice Uncle Anthony gave him. His natural, athletic abilities aided him in being picked first for all the playground sports. He was so good the high school wanted him to play varsity while he finished his junior high classes. Uncle Anthony knew David had the talent and skill to play professional baseball. He wanted David to achieve something he didn't get to accomplish in his lifetime.

"Come on Suga, let's get you that cone you've been dying for." Uncle Anthony said, dragging Chayanne to the line with his leg.

"Uncle Anthony, since you made me wait for forever, can I have three scoops today?" She asked with a charming smile.

He looked down smiling back at Chayanne. "You sure know how to sweet talk your way Suga. These fellas need to watch out; you'll have them working the lemonade stands for ya, huh?" He said chuckling.

Chayanne remembered clear as day; they stood in the line so close to her Saturday treat when the blue-eyed, blond-haired lady approached them. Chayanne mistook her for a model on a magazine cover. She looked at her while waiting for Momma at the hospital. Her porcelain skin was so radiant and smooth; the lady was glowing.

"Well hello red, long time yeah?" Her voice was harmonizing when she spoke. Chayanne couldn't help to stare with her mouth gaped open in awe.

Uncle Anthony, who was distracted looking in another woman's direction, finally took notice of the drop-dead gorgeous lady model in front of him. He was startled at first, almost like he'd seen a ghost.

Anthony swallowed so hard he was barely able to piece a sentence together. "Rebecca Sooner...is that really you?" Anthony's face went pale. Rebecca's presence made Chayanne uneasy; she clung to Anthony's leg a bit tighter.

"Wow, your daughter is beautiful. How old is she?" Rebecca asked, hoping it wasn't true. She looked down admiring Chayanne's features that resembled Anthony's. Chayanne admired the large diamond glistening in the sun that rested on Rebecca's ring finger.

"Ahem, no this is my niece Chayanne; she's nine," Uncle Anthony responded without hesitation. "I can't believe it's really you. How long has it been, fifteen years since you moved away?"

"Yes, it's really me silly," she responded softly. "Only it's not Sooner anymore... its Tomlin." An awkward pause inserted itself between the two; the laughs, screams, and cries from the playground seemed to mimic what they both were feeling internally. Chayanne interrupted, tugging at Anthony's pant leg. It was their turn in line to order. Without looking away from Rebecca, Uncle Anthony reached into his pocket grabbing for his money clip. He unknowingly peeled a crisp twenty-dollar bill out and handed it to her. Chayanne thought she was rich; her eyes lit up and her heart fluttered. She skipped merrily to the window knowing she could have whatever her heart desired. Chayanne ordered and stood by the pickup window patiently. The nineteen dollars and twenty-five cents crumpled up in the palm of her small right hand. She stood observing Anthony and Rebecca, but she wasn't the only spectator. The women scrunched their faces in distaste.

Chayanne heard a woman whisper, "A married white woman, flirting with a colored man; now there is something you don't see every day," The comment made Chayanne's stomach turn. All the ladies were friendly with Uncle Anthony. "Why was this woman so different?" she thought. Soon, the answer would find her.

"Here ya go, darling!" the lady said, handing Chayanne her three layered scoops of ice cream on a cake cone.

Chayanne shrilled with joy, "Thank you!" she said politely before indulging. Chayanne wandered around aimlessly and found a wooden bench to sit on nearby. She enjoyed her ice cream at a distance, still watching her uncle engage in conversation with this marvelous woman. She noticed the way he peered deeply into the Rebecca's eyes; it was intoxicatingly seductive, but for a nine-year-old girl, it appeared to be love. Chayanne hoped one day a man would look at her with the same intensity. The ice cream began to melt all over Chayanne's hands; the neck of her dress stained brown from the chocolate. This was the reason she was never allowed to get a three-scoop cone; she was incapable of eating it before getting filthy. She swung her legs as she licked as fast as she could to enjoy the deliciousness of the half-melted cone. The chatter amongst the crowd that witnessed Anthony and Rebecca grew.

"Sue Ann, it looks like the town whore is back," one of the ladies remarked in anguish. "I thought the Sooners were out of here for good, especially since Mr. Sooner discovered Rebecca was pregnant with that boy's nigger baby."

"Oh my gosh, her body though, how did she fit into that dress? It looks painted on. Lord I hate that I had these babies, they done thrown my body all out of whack. I can barely squeeze into my girdle anymore. My tits done went to hell, they're saggy as all shit. Wait, is that why the family moved?"

"Well, gee Sue Ann, we've only lived in this shit-hole town for all of our lives. Yes, Rebecca used to sneak around with that boy there all the time. Everyone knew, but when her father found out, he tried to rally the Klan claiming she was raped. The Klan was put under strict order not to set fires to the Carter house, his nigger daddy was with the NAACP. He was protected by some order or some crap by Senator Collins that threatened anyone who deemed to mess with the family. Rebecca was with child. Mr. Sooner packed his family up and headed to the outskirts of nowhere to break them apart. That little girl that was with them earlier is probably the baby she delivered; she looks just like em."

"Shut up, is it really true, Merry Ella? I never knew niggers to have such power. They must have known some of Senator Collin's secrets. What a twisted old bastard, I'm surprised he still running things."

"He won't be for long once the cat's out of the bag. I hear he's having an affair with some call girl that works down by the docks in the colored part of town."

Chayanne immediately lost her appetite and felt nauseated; it wasn't from all of the sweets. She didn't care for the way the lady spoke of her dear Uncle Anthony. She turned to face the overweight lady and the gossip girl, Sue Ann, that sat under the Dogwood tree behind the bench she occupied. Chayanne glared at the lady, flaring her nostrils. She waited politely for the lady to make eye contact with her. Chayanne's angry glare startled Merry Ella, causing her to dislodge from her seat and hit the ground full force. Chayanne stuck her tongue out mocking her yelping cries.

"My mother says you shouldn't say anything if you don't have anything nice to say at all, FATTY!" Chayanne blew a raspberry and exited the bench leaving the puddle of her melted ice cream behind. She tossed the remainder in the wastebasket nearby. She looked over her shoulder at the fat lady struggling to get up. Chayanne went to fetch David from the basketball courts. On the way, she stopped at the water fountain to cleanse her palate. She stood on her tiptoes to reach the spout where the water spurted. She pursed her small pink lips, gulping down the cool water. She felt like she drank five oceans by the time she finished. Her heels barely met the ground; she was forcefully pushed from behind. She planted on the rough hot cement face first. The money she held in her palm scattered. She laid there for a moment contemplating how to respond. Her fiery temper could get her into a whole world of trouble, as Momma would put it. She rolled over onto her backside sitting up, her knees were scuffed and bleeding. Her hands had a derby of tiny stones imbedded into them while blood trickled into her eye from the gash on her forehead. She looked up and noticed the overweight Merry Ella from the Dogwood standing over her with an evil snarl on her face.

The gleeful sounds of playing ceased, the crowd grew near the fountain. Chayanne noticed Anthony sprinting over; Rebecca followed close on his heels. Chayanne picked her small body off of the ground a palm-sized rock in hand. She never had prior dealings with bullies, and she never understood why David never stood his ground. Chayanne knew how she was going to manage Merry Ella ensuring she got what she deserved. No tears in her eyes; fury boiled in her blood. Chayanne squealed in rage, she drew her right arm back above her head and readied herself to cast the stone. Her hand was in full motion forward with all her might to back it. Her body jerked up from the gravel and spun around; Anthony made it there just in time. His strong arms embraced her tightly.

Rebecca, furious with Merry Ella, could not manage to hold her tongue. She exploded with anger and drew the crowd's attention, "You should be ashamed of yourself for attacking an innocent child!" her voice bellowed with passion and conviction. "If you'd done this to a white child, you'd be behind bars before sundown. I understand that you have low self-esteem — look at how you've let yourself go. By God, you stoop so low to hurt a child to make yourself feel valid. This is a child that you should protect and set an example for; not all of us hide behind the capirote to burn crosses in our yards. Instead, we stand with them taking every blow society hits us with. All youth is your future; so, treat them with respect!" Rebecca huffed attempting to breathe; she was red in the face with flared nostrils. She dared anyone to bring a rebuttal or an excuse in the light of day for Merry Ella's behavior. The oversized lady retreated to the Dogwood tree to gather her things, mumbling under her breath. Anthony's heart sank into his back as he bent down to retrieve the crumbled monies stained with speckles of Chayanne's blood. There wasn't much he could do to protect his beloved niece; he'd never felt so weak or little as a man. His body trembled with anger as he held Chayanne close to his chest—this would be a lump in his throat he could never swallow. His ego and pride bruised on display for the townspeople to bear witness. The crowd murmured amongst themselves and slowly disbursed back to their activities.

"Thank you!" Anthony mouthed to Rebecca. "David, let's go!" Anthony called out with all the bass he had in his voice—a warning to David not to give any lip. Chayanne laid her head on her Anthony's shoulder finding some comfort. She quivered furiously, upset at the fact she wasn't able to defend herself properly.

"Baby girl, you're shaking, are you okay?" he asked in a soft tone.

"I just want to go home." Chayanne responded in a daze. David followed behind Uncle Anthony closely. He looked up into Chayanne's eyes; he noticed her chin had several small cuts; she bled out on Anthony's shirt. David's eyes redden; the warm tears filled them. He too shared Uncle Anthony's anger and helplessness. David opened the car door and lifted the back seat to climb in. Chayanne, half asleep in her uncle's arms, clung to him tightly and resisted being put down.

"It was a pleasure seeing you Rebecca," he said ashamed. "My apologizes about the circumstances."

"You can't apologize for bullshit like that Red. All you did was be born colored, and that ain't nothing to apologize for sugar." She kissed him lightly on the cheek. Anthony retreated before she could wipe the smudged lipstick off of his cheek.

"Are you wanting to kick the hornets' nest? You're giving these folks more to talk about." He responded hastily. "Think about your husband!"

"If I cared what people thought of me Anthony, I wouldn't have returned." she remarked matching his hastiness. "People could never forget our past, not the way my daddy stormed us out of here after you and I…" she paused—something she thought about struck a nerve. She discontinued the conversation. She touched his shoulder, gently smiled, and disappeared into the sunset. Anthony sat Chayanne on the driver seat to once her over. His heart hurt at the site of his battered beauty; he clenched his chest kneeling down to Chayanne's eye level. She blinked slowly, barely able to keep them open.

"Sorry Suga, I should have never left you alone." Anthony said as he gently kissed the side of her forehead that wasn't bloody. To make up for it, he let her ride home in the front seat. Chayanne barely enjoy the privilege; she was asleep before the buckle clicked.

The wind entering through the window was the only sound that comforted both David and Anthony as they cruised home. A white salt trail from David dried tears stained his face. Anthony knew there wasn't a word he could utter to David to ease the agony he felt. Anthony gripped the steering wheel in anger peering into the rear-view mirror at David. The car came to a slow roll under the huge red cedar tree that sat in the island of grass nearest the road in front of the small, light-blue bungalow house. Anthony slammed his palm into the steering wheel, and then yanked at it in a fit of rage. He acted like a mad man, ripping the luxuries apart that made him feel accepted by his oppressors. At that moment, Anthony loathed what he'd become. His reality check set in;

he'd never be one of them. This was only the beginning of the summer of sorrows.

As Anthony carried Chayanne into the house, David ran ahead to draw her a bath with Momma's secret ingredients—Epsom salt and witch-hazel. It seemed to help soothe his cuts, scrapes, and bruises when he had unfortunate incidents.

Chayanne bathed herself in the steaming, murky water; her cuts burned and stung and she tensed up from the pain. As moments passed, she got accustomed to the feeling.

Anthony sat on the back porch smoking a cigarette to calm his nerves. The darkness of the night swallowed him. The red cherry that burned on the tip of the cigarette was all that could be made out. David treated his grass-stained jeans, hoping Momma wouldn't take much notice. He knew so much of the day had to be explained to her, but for now, everyone coped with the heaviness of the day the best they could.

CHAPTER

3

DON'T POUR SALT IN THE WOUND

Momma cursed Anthony for not calling her away from work to deal with Chayanne. She was in a fit of rage when he rattled off the day's events nonchalantly. Anthony attempted to calm Momma, not wanting to her to wake David and Chayanne.

David laid awake, listening to Momma's soft whimpers from the living room. Anthony had long gone home. Momma whispered prayers to herself in between her sobbing episodes. David wanted to comfort her, but he stayed put and stared at the glow in the dark constellation of stars he putty-glued to his ceiling ages ago. The world didn't seem so simple to him anymore, unknown dangers lurked behind every corner.

Momma pulled open Chayanne's curtains to let the sunlight beam in. She was anxious to examine her baby; she paced the family room all night waiting to do so.

Chayanne put her hands up, covering her eyes to block the intrusive light. "Momma, I'm not ready to get up, I'm tired," she whined turning over. Chayanne was oblivious to Momma, drinking a pot of coffee and counting the hours until she could wake her. She couldn't be patient any longer; she yearned to see the damage done.

"Sweetie, I just miss your face, that's all. Get up and let me have a look at you." Momma pleaded nicely.

Chayanne huffed and puffed with annoyance. It was hard enough to wake her for school, Chayanne knew Sunday was the one day she could sleep in if Momma was working. When Momma was off, she insisted on going to church as a family. Chayanne pulled her slender legs from underneath her covers. She stood up rubbing her sleepy eyes; her long nightgown covered her legs. Momma waited anxiously for Chayanne to move her hands from her face so she could have a good look. Chayanne dropped her hands to her side and looked into Momma's face. Momma gasped and covered her mouth with her hands. Tears poured from her eyes as she sobbed quietly biting her knuckles, rocking back and forth on the foot of Chayanne's bed. Momma was in shock looking at Chayanne who was half asleep and didn't care what was going on. Momma sat in awe. Chayanne's eye looked much worse than it felt—a blue and purple ring stood out against her complexion. Thin, long cuts gathered on her cheeks and chin making a larger cluster. Momma grabbed Chayanne's head by the chin, turning it side to side, she pulled her nightgown up revealing her scrapped knees. It was too much for Momma to take in at once; she left the room fanning herself for air. Daddy was lurking quietly by the door observing. Chayanne went to crawl back into bed, but the voice of her father startled her awake. She stopped in her tracks with widened eyes.

"Baby girl, are you alright?" he asked taking a seat at the foot of her bed. Chayanne was afraid she was in trouble for allowing the lady to hurt her.

She swallowed hard, "Yes sir." she responded shying away from him. Daddy picked Chayanne up and put her on his knee. She tensed up, anxious about what was to come.

"Baby girl, why are you all scratched up?" Daddy had a method; he wanted to measure the emotional damage Chayanne was experiencing from the incident. He was curious if she understood why it happened. David now lurked by the door. His sleep interrupted by the commotion stirred by his parents. David, intrigued by his father's handling of Chayanne, drew him in more.

Chayanne hesitated to answer, afraid that trouble was in store for her with her father.

He could feel her nervousness intensify by the second, "It's okay to talk to me, you're not in trouble," he reassured her. He felt the need to establish she was in a safe place. "What happened to you wasn't your fault." He continued to disarm her internal guilt.

"Yes... yes it is, daddy. The lady was talking bad about Uncle Anthony and Rebecca. I told her that Momma said she shouldn't say things if they weren't nice or true. I was just so angry that she called Uncle Anthony a nigger and..."

"Shhhh," he interrupted her. He knew her innocence was tainted. He bounced her lightly on his lap and hugged her tightly while she cried on his shoulder. Momma rushed back to the doorway nearly knocking David over.

"Baby girl, who did you say the lady was bad talkin'?" Chayanne sucked her tears away immediately; she knew Momma had very little patience when she wanted an answer. Daddy mouthed "Rebecca" to Momma while he soothed Chayanne a little longer. Momma's yellow complexion turned pale, she rested her back on the wall, clasping the neck of her robe. She stared blankly into space, tormented by the memories of Rebecca. David's face turned up as he tried to figure out who this lady was and the significance she had to their family.

Anthony spent every Sunday morning at Bert's diner. He loved Bert's coffee and home-cooked recipes—it reminded him of his upbringing. It was his kitchen away from home. He always sat in the corner booth by himself reading the Sunday paper; he browsed for real estate sales, auctions, or estate sales. This is how he built the credit union's revenue. An unlit cigarette hung loosely from his lips as he highlighted the ads of interest.

"More coffee, Red?" the waitress asked with a twinkle in her eye.

"No thanks, darlin, I think I had my fill for the day—unless you want me to run wild through this here diner." he replied without looking away from his task. Anthony was so in tune with his process he didn't notice Rebecca at the diner counter stalking him from afar.

Rebecca contemplated disturbing him from his work, he was more handsome than what her memories could convey. She sat, biting her lip, admiring how he'd grown into his features. She crossed her long slender legs to smother the growing throb for him. "Excuse me," she looked down at the waitress nametag, "Carmen, do you mind serving my breakfast over there?" she asked politely, pointing at Anthony's table. The paper sprawled in front of his face.

The waitress shot Rebecca a dirty look, "Sure ma'am, why not?" Heavy tones of sarcasm accompanied her response. Rebecca smiled and waved her oversized wedding ring that danced and dazzled in the light at the waitress.

"Don't worry, you can have em, just don't spit in my eggs." Rebecca chortled, excusing herself from the counter. The look on the waitress' face was priceless. Rebecca struggled to contain her laughter; she giggled all the way to the opposite side of Anthony's table.

Anthony, consumed in the paper, could smell a soft, floral fragrance intrude his space, "Can I help you, darlin?" he asked unbothered by her presence.

"I don't know Suga, depends on whatcha have to offer a lady of my status," Rebecca spoke in her bouncy, southern tone. The sound of her voice enticed him. A smile spread across his face as wide as the Mississippi River revealed his perfectly placed white teeth accompanied by his dimples. He pulled the paper down slowly.

"Aw shoot woman, I thought you were somebody important," he laughed. She joined in laughing until her face turned red and her vein protruded on her forehead.

"Wow, I never could imagine I'd see your face again Anthony Reid Carter; it sure does feel good. I thought you would be long gone by now. You have a city boy's personality," she admitted flirtatiously, throwing her million-dollar smile at him.

"The way you smiling, honey, makes me feel like high school all over again. I suppose some things will always remain familiar." He paused taking all of her in with his eyes. He shifted in the booth fighting the temptation of arousal. "Yeah, I thought about city living, but I have to be here to tend to my nephew and niece." They both sat silent remembering the events of yesterday. "Uh, thank you again for handling that lady for my little Suga." he said palming her hand showing his genuine gratitude. He immediately snatched it away as the Carmen approached the table with both breakfast platters in hand. She had a smug look on her face, placing the platters in the appropriate places.

"Uhm, don't look too married to me." Carmen returned Rebecca's sarcasm; she rolled her eyes, slapping the checks on the table. Rebecca blushed in embarrassment.

"Yeah, about that, what's his name?" Anthony asked with a grin.

Rebecca darted her eyes, breaking their eye contact. She spoke in a low tone, "William Tomlin, and that's that, I suppose." she said, frustrated with the short-lived honeymoon. She took the unlit cigarette from Anthony's lip—placing it in her mouth. "Do you mind?" She motioned for a lighter. They both cupped their hands to protect the flame as Anthony held the lighter in place. She stared long and hard into his eyes as she drew on the cigarette and exhaled the smoke into the air, fanning it away from his face.

"You were always a rebel, weren't you?" Anthony asked with a bit of sadness in his heart. "Of all of the places in the world to go, why come back here? Wearing a rock like that seems like your old man can afford to go anywhere." Anthony folded the new paper, setting it aside. He wanted to enjoy his steak over medium eggs while he listened to the woes of his old flame.

"He wants to run for sheriff next year since the current Sheriff is set to retire. He thinks laying the groundwork this year as deputy will give him the edge he needs to win." She drew on the cigarette again. She held the smoke in her lungs, enjoying the euphoria smoking made her feel. She exhaled slowly then continued, "He thinks this is a great place to raise children. He's ready to start a family." Rebecca's demeanor turned cold.

Anthony refused to keep up the fake-it-till-you-make-it charades. He didn't want to hear about her fake happy life; he was thirsty for the truth. He stopped while cutting his juicy Ribeye.

He stared Rebecca in the eye, "What really happened to you that night? I waited at the back of that gas station in my Pontiac Streamliner until sunup, high on the thought of us running away together." His face was painted with disappointment.

Rebecca hastily put out the half-smoked cigarette; she clasped her hands together, unable to wrangle her anger. "He caught me sneaking out of the window. He pulled me in by my hair and beat me until I was black and blue." Her eyes watered, her nose snotty, " I could barely move when he finished with me. He had a sour smell of whisky on his breath; I'm surprised he didn't kill me, although I prayed for it. I knew if I couldn't be with you, Red, I didn't have the desire to live anymore." A sea of emotions swept over her as she broke down in tears. Knots of regret in her stomach, "I didn't need to go to the doctors; I knew I'd lost the baby. The blood clots and bloodstains on my sheets were my confirmation. The next morning before dawn set in, the old pickup truck was packed with our bags and minor belongings." She paused, staring off into the distance, "When we left, things got so much worse." Her brow wrinkled in pain as she briefly relived the torture of her father. "The drunken bastard came to visit me in the night more often. He thought our baby was his." she said disgusted. "He didn't know what the hell sterile meant, and by some act of God, I was blessed with his baby." She swallowed the vomit in her throat. "He apologized for beating me like it was going to be enough for all the perverted shit he'd put on me; he said he'd never forgive himself. My mother continued to ignore the signs, she just wanted a fucking fairytale, a happy fucking ending." Her breath grew shallow, the thought of her stepfather made her sick to her stomach.

Anthony sat in dismay. His hand stroked his red goatee. All these years, he had it wrong; he thought she lost the courage to run.

Chayanne's palm pilot buzzed violently on Lilly's nightstand, interrupting the story. Chayanne peered at the screen—gauging the importance of the call. Charles' name flashed on the screen, giving Chayanne an eerie feeling. She looked at her wristwatch and noticed it was a quarter 'til midnight.

"Honey, we have to finish the story tomorrow—you need to get some rest. I didn't realize it was so late." Chayanne said tucking Lilly in.

Lilly, upset, poked her lip out and folded her arms. "Mommy, I need to know what happened; I don't want to wait!" Chayanne kissed Lilly's forehead.

She walked to the room door, "I promise to tell you more tomorrow, goodnight sweetheart."

Lilly rattled off questions, not allowing Chayanne to close the door, "Where did the word nigger come from and why did the fat lady push you down? Did uncle Anthony run away with Rebecca?" Chayanne pressed her index fingers to her plump lips, shushing Lilly. Lilly's mind danced anxiously as she pieced the story together anticipating what happened next. She yawned as she laid there staring at the ceiling playing detective in her mind. A few moments passed by her eyes heavy like blankets; she closed them, drifting sound asleep.

Chayanne was skeptical of Charles's call; it was close to the middle of the night. The last time he called this late, she relapsed, having a night filled with intimate pleasure at her expense. It only peaked her hope of them reconciling their marriage. She hated herself in the morning when he coldly climbed out of bed without saying a word. He dressed frantically, leaving her alone with her self-sabotaging thoughts. It briefly satisfied her soul to feel wanted and desired by the man she built a life with a feeling that was drained from their marriage after Ashton was born.

Chayanne plopped down on the side of her bed; her body weighted like a ton of bricks. The emotions of the day finally caught up to her. She mulled, returning Charles's call over in her mind. The feeling of rejection sat in the pit of her stomach. Chayanne sighed while she berated herself silently; she finally mustered the courage—dialing Charles's number slowly from the cordless phone. Her anxiety grew with every ring, making her more nervous. She pulled the phone from her ear, placing her finger on the send button.

Charles's voice, as subtle and soothing as Berry White, reeled her back in. "Hello?"

She cleared her throat, pushing her nerves at bay. "Ahem, hello Charles, I'm returning your call." A strange, awkward tension between them inserted itself.

"Yeah of course, your name popped up on the caller I.D. Um, I... I was calling because it's Lilly's summer vacation and um I think it's time for her to experience life... Quentin and I are planning a trip to Denmark. Ahem, he's adamant about having a ceremony to form our civil union over the summer and... I... I'd like for Lilly to be there." A long period of silence "They legalized same-sex unions about a year ago and we don't want to wait any longer... I called Ashton, but he still isn't answering my calls. Maybe you could convince him to come; he was always his mother's son." He chuckled, attempting to ease things over.

Chayanne's dinner crawled up her esophagus and rested in the back of her throat, "umm... married... wow, that's great Charles! I'm so happy for you guys." she exclaimed, lying through her teeth pretending. She was learning to cope, thanks to months of therapy. She understood co-parenting was more important than her personal feelings.

"Uh thanks, I guess... I wasn't expecting that from you. It's kind of weird, but it reminds me of when we were friends." He said with a half-smile. "You take care Chayanne, and I'll speak to you soon." The phone disconnected, and the dial tone echoed in the darkness. Chayanne gently placed the phone on the base and sat quietly, piecing her thoughts together. Her briefcase caught the corner of her eye; she huffed, trying to silence the chatter in her mind. She knew grabbing her briefcase and heading downstairs to her office would be a deflection of dealing with her emotions, something she'd become damn good at. Chayanne got up and retrieved her briefcase; she made it to the door before the house phone rang. She rushed over to her tableside, hoping it didn't disrupt Lilly.

"Hello!" she said with irritation. She wondered who would call back so late. She didn't get a response. "Hello?" There wasn't a response the second time; she hung up and hurriedly checked the caller I.D. that read blocked call. Chayanne shrugged it off and headed for her office. The phone rang once more.

"Argh, goddammit!" she said aloud to herself. She aggressively snatched the phone, answering the call. "HELLO!" she could hear someone breathing heavily on the other end. "Who is this?" she asked impatiently, growing more and more agitated with the interruption. The ticking of a clock replaced the heavy breathing; three knocks accompanied. Before she could speak a word, the dial tone protruded her ears. The ticking of the clock reminded her of the anonyms letter that was stuffed in the mail slot. She rushed down to her office to retrieve it, to look for more clues. Chayanne searched high and low, the letter was nowhere to be found. She remembered placing the letter in the top right drawer of her desk before she called Lilly in. She slammed her fist in anger, allowing it to get the best of her. Her office phone rang; she let the answering machine intercept the call.

"Tick tock, tick tock, knock, knock, knock." a creepy voice recorded on the machine. Chayanne dashed to answer the call, but it was too late.

4

THE DEVIL WEARS LIPSTICK

The chirping of the birds and the smell of bacon filled the morning air. Chayanne had her blackout curtains drawn, still asleep. Lilly was in the kitchen with Klara assisting with breakfast; she wanted to make Chayanne a big feast, hoping she could bait her to spill more of the story. It was a quarter after nine when Lilly approached her mother's door with the breakfast tray. Lilly thought it to be unusual that her mother wasn't awake yet; she was always busy with work, even on a Saturday. The door was closed; Lilly carefully set the tray on the ground, not spilling a drop. She turned the knob and pushed the door open; she retrieved the tray and entered. The slow creep of the door woke Chayanne. She rolled over—lifting her eye mask—unaware of the time.

"Honey, is everything alright? Why are you out of bed?" her dry voice cracked.

Lilly was tickled by her mother's level of awareness, "Mommy, it's morning silly." she said, bringing the breakfast tray to her bedside table. She placed it there then looked up at her mother. She noticed Chayanne's puffy red eyes. "Did you have trouble sleeping?" Lilly asked concerned.

43

Chayanne pushed her body upright—freeing her arms from the covers; she took the ceramic steaming cup of coffee from the tray and sipped it with caution. She looked at the alarm clock in disbelief.

Chayanne disregarded Lilly's concern, changing the subject, "My, my... how'd you know how I like my coffee?" she teased lightheartedly.

Lilly laughed, "I've only seen you make it a million times, mommy." she said, nudging her over and sliding underneath the covers with her. Chayanne's body warm, soft, and inviting, the right level of comfort for her precious Lilly. Chayanne smiled in a way she hadn't in a while. She felt cared for and nurtured by her small child; a level of care she didn't know her child knew existed.

"Would you like for me to hold my questions until the end of the story, like my English teacher Mrs. Dyer requires, or may I ask now?" Lilly asked excitedly.

Chayanne burst into laughter, "This whole time I thought you were treating me, but that's foolish of me to think. You just want more of the story." she said, tickling Lilly with her free hand. Lilly laughed, shrilling a scream of joy, enjoying her mother's affection. Klara heard the screams from the kitchen; she rushed in the door, her heart racing frantically. She knew how agitated Chayanne could be when interrupted.

"I'm sorry Ms. Parker, is she bothering you?" Klara asked timidly.

"Oh no! Klara, she's fine, we're just messing around. Thanks for helping her make breakfast, I had a late night of work, and oddly I didn't know I slept in." Chayanne paused permitting her thoughts to catch up. "You know Klara, you can actually have the day off. This little flower and I have a story date." Chayanne smiled widely. Klara's face seemed pleasantly surprised; Chayanne's mood swings weren't the slightest bit pleasant lately. Klara had a flashback of last weekend when Chayanne raised her voice in a gut-wrenching tone, "If you can't care for Lilly and keep her occupied and out of my office, I will hire someone who can!" Chayanne slammed the heavy office door in Klara's face.

Chayanne interrupted, untangling Klara from her thoughts, "Klara, you don't have to worry, I'll still pay you for the day." Klara nodded yes with an expressionless face, unsure if she was dealing with the same woman.

"Thank you, Ms. Parker." Klara replied happily. Klara tidied up from breakfast and packed her things and left for the day.

Chayanne crunched on the crisp bacon and sipped her coffee delighted; Lilly laid next to her patiently.

"I think you should do what Mrs. Dyer instructed; you may find the answers to what you seek if you're patient." She looked down at Lilly still chewing on her bacon. "Is that fair?" she asked.

"Yes, mommy, that's fair. Now can you please tell me what happened?" She pleaded; her patience was wearing thin.

"Of course!" Chayanne paused, thinking of where she stopped.

Momma kept Chayanne home the last week of school. She didn't want any attention drawn to her appearance—raising questions amongst the school. She was weary it would stir a whole lot of trouble, considering the devil Rebecca Sooner was back in town. Momma didn't let Chayanne feel the sun on her skin that entire week, keeping her inside and occupied, Momma made Chayanne start her summer reading list early. Chayanne began to get stir crazy by Friday; her cuts and bruised eye faded with each day that passed.

She begged Momma to take her to the bank to visit Uncle Anthony; she really hoped he'd give her a dollar to buy penny candy when Momma wasn't looking. Her secret stash was running low since she'd been home all week; it was the only thing keeping her sane. It was a little after noon when Chayanne emerged from her book and decided to bother Momma again.

"Momma please, can we go now?" Chayanne begged—tugging at the bottom of Momma's housedress. Momma was putting the finishing touches on the pound cake she baked.

"Chayanne, I told you to let me finish this cake for the bank tellers, and then we'll go," she shot Chayanne a look warning her she was close to wearing her nerves down. "Now go put on your dress and brush your hair." Momma demanded.

Chayanne skipped happily into her room to follow Momma's instructions. She was relieved knowing she would finally get out of the house. She sat down at the small, white wooden vanity Uncle Anthony bought her for the past Christmas. She retrieved her brush from the top drawer and attempted to detangle her hair. She brushed the long strands of silky curls that easily sprung back into place.

"Chayanne, you've been meddling with me all day. This isn't playtime, put your dress on and hurry here now!" Chayanne hurriedly brushed the other half of her hair and rushed to put her dress on; she was determined not to meddle too much with Momma, getting on her bad side with Saturday being so close. She put the long lien powder blue dress on as Momma wanted to hide the lingering scrapes on her body. She met her mother at the door, smiling from ear to ear. Momma grabbed her hand while balancing the cake in the other. She put Chayanne in the back of the jeep wagon, buckling her in and placing the covered cake on her lap. Chayanne's feet danced to the sound of Mr. Henry's struggling lawnmower. Momma smiled, waving at Mr. Henry and then got into the driver's seat.

Momma was an anxious mess when she drove; she would listen to the political news station to help her focus. She started the car and turned the radio up.

Radio Announcer: Doctor King and his supporters are set to march the streets of Birmingham, Alabama this weekend...

"Momma have you ever been called a nigger?" Chayanne asked, interrupting the radio program. Momma kept her poise, turning the radio dial and clicking it off.

"Chayanne, I don't want you to use that kind of language. It is not ladylike, but most of all, it is a derogatory term used to offend us colored people. The slave masters of our ancestors degraded our people with that kind of language." She paused to look in the review mirror at Chayanne's face. Momma with all seriousness said, "Yes, I have been called a nigger, it was an unpleasant experience. Your father and I used to protest and march with Dr. King in the 50s; this was just a little time ago before you and your brother were born. I was hosed down and thrown in jail for the night. The jailer said, "Nigger's in the world should rot for the way we conduct ourselves; No nigger would ever be equal to white folks," and he spat at us and smacked the bars with his club.

"What is dero-gi-tory?" she asked, butchering the word; Momma spelled the word out to help Chayanne with the proper pronunciation, " D-e-r-o-g-a-t-o-r-y, now you spell it."

" D-E-R-O-G-A-T-O-R-Y," Chayanne spelled it out. "What does it mean?"

"It means to lessen a person's or thing's reputation, it's very demeaning and rude. It's something that we don't practice in our household. You're a young woman that respects herself and others, ya hear?"

"Yes ma'am." She responded sitting back from the window.

Anthony sat in his comfortable chair in his office at the bank with his back to the door. The sun peaked through the wooden blinds, embellishing the dust particles that floated freely.

A stern knock echoed throughout his office; the door opened slightly "Mr. Carter, you have a visitor." His receptionist called gently through the small, cracked door. Anthony paid her no mind, waiving her away; he was making his yearly contribution to the NAACP, a tradition of his father's that he upheld in his memory.

She left a small crack and hurriedly approached the porcelain model in the red dress with the red painted lips, "It'll just be a moment; he's on a very important call. May I get you some water while you wait, missus?"

Rebecca ignored her; the décor of the bank engulfed her attention, "My, the owner has fine taste in art." she said, acknowledging the famous Monet Water Lily Pond painting and then admiring a black and white photograph of Louis Armstrong playing his trumpet.

"Well thank you missus, I will let Mr. Carter know you've taken a liking for his expression in art... Are you from city hall?" the receptionist inquired, pushing her curiosity. She knew many whites didn't wander in the colored parts of town. Rebecca shot a nasty glance at the receptionist, letting her know she was overstepping. The receptionist lowered her eyes to the floor and rushed back to guard her desk.

"Lucile, send them in." Anthony called out, covering the receiver of the phone. He turned his attention back to his conversation.

Rebecca didn't wait for Lucile's direction; she barreled through Anthony's office door, closing it gently behind her. She sat in one of the custom-made leather armed cigar chairs. His lingering cologne intoxicated her; she crossed her legs, fighting her constant crave for him. She was moved, erotically, seeing Red in a position of power. Her urges cultivated within as she listened to his soothing jazz-like voice. His back to the door—still unaware of Rebecca's presence—he promptly finished his affairs.

"Good day to you sir...Absolutely, of course, I look forward to it... Yes, you take care too, sir." He placed the phone gently on the hook without turning his chair. He stood to stretch and propped himself up on the edge of his desk with his back still facing the door. "Are you here to open a new account with us?" he asked, politely fixing his tie.

"If opening an account is required to have a moment of your time sir, then of course," Rebecca responded in a seductive tone.

A malicious grin set over Anthony's face; he quickly removed it, turning to face her. She squirmed and adjusted in the chair, her silky panties moist. Anthony walked to the other side of the desk; he leaned back on the edge, a few feet away from where she sat. He tapped his right fingertips lightly on the desk.

Anthony kissed his teeth, "You keep making your face familiar, what am I supposed to do with that?" his tone sly as a crook, "You're making this rather difficult for me to adjust to you being back."

Rebecca smirked, "You're like a magnet Red, it's hard for me to stay away. Besides, you're the only one who gets me around these parts."

"Interesting fact, now what would your beloved husband say to that darlin?" he pried.

"I didn't marry him for his love sweetie; truth be told, I only ever loved one man." She teased, having an honest moment. "He is setting to get into politics. If I want to make change; it should start at home. What do you say to that?" she asked, seductively biting her lip.

"Well, darlin, I see you have a plan, kudos to you! Besides, it's not legal for us to integrate and marry; the anti-miscegenation laws took care of that. I hope you have a plan to fix it." He turned his face up. He walked to his liquor table and poured the decanted bourbon in his crystal glass. "Too early for you to drink, darlin?" he asked raising his glass to her. He went back to his desk, leaning on the edge.

"There you go getting all political on me. It's never too early for this lady to let her hair down." The air thickened, their eyes locked. Rebecca stood from the chair and walked to Anthony, inserting herself between his legs. Rebecca ran her hands gently up his inner thighs, arousing him in the manner his presence aroused her. Anthony closed his eyes—imaging all the intimate things they previously shared.

Her hands neared his manhood; he grabbed her wrist, stopping her in her tracks, "you're a married woman, I don't want to compromise you." She positioned her lips close to his without touching.

"You're the one compromised between us, Red." She freed her hands gently, massaging his groining. He exhaled into her parted lips exhilarated with every touch. "I see a lot has grown for you over the years." She laughed softly, teasing him with her lips the anticipation of her kiss drove him wild.

Chayanne was bouncing off the walls as she raced to the entrance of the bank.

"Baby girl, slow down, don't go running through this bank like you don't have any home training!" Momma demanded trying to keep up with Chayanne, who was minutes in front of her. Chayanne bolted past Lucile not stopping to say hello. She was happy to finally see Uncle Anthony who purposely hadn't been by the house for supper all week. She burst into his office unannounced; Chayanne startled Rebecca and Anthony. They jumped away from one another as if they were two-school kids caught misbehaving. Anthony, shocked by the intrusion, immediately headed for his office restroom to adjust his erection.

He called out to Chayanne behind the wooden door. "Suga, I am so happy to see you! I'm so glad you came by today. Are you feeling any better?" Chayanne, face blank, tried to piece the situation together.

"Hey sweetheart, it's so nice to see you. You heal pretty darn fast." Rebecca said, kneeling down hugging Chayanne. Chayanne stood limp as Rebecca embraced her. An uncanny feeling made the hair on Chayanne's neck stand.

"I wasn't expecting to see you, Mrs. Rebecca." Chayanne said bluntly as Rebecca released her.

"Yeah, I guess I have a knack for popping up unwarranted. Anyway darlin, it's a pleasure to see your smile." Rebecca tugged Chayanne's chin gently.

Momma approached the office door after she spoke to Lucile and dropped the cake she baked to the tellers. Momma's mouth gapped open, and her stomach dropped to the floor when she noticed Rebecca displaying her affection to Chayanne.

"Well, if it ain't the damn devil in his own flesh. I heard you were back in town, but I couldn't believe it until I saw you with my own two eyes, Rebecca Sooner." Momma exclaimed hastily.

"Oh, my word Evelyn!" Rebecca responded nice nasty, "It's Tomlin, now maybe that's why it was unbelievable, my husband is the new deputy sheriff in town. How on God's green earth have you been? Rebecca said, standing to her feet to patronize Momma. She knew that Momma's hate for her started in her soul. Momma chased Rebecca off plenty of times when she caught her sneaking into Uncle Anthony's room or when she caught them finishing the act while their parents were at work.

"What kind of trouble are you stirring up for him now, Rebecca?" Momma said with tight lips, "Anthony has worked too dog on hard for you to come back in and tear it all down!" Chayanne could feel the hatred Momma had running in her veins for Rebecca; Momma's face only turned that color red when she was going to skin David or Chayanne for breaking one of many rules. The tension was thick and unbearable between the women for Chayanne; Anthony quickly emerged from the bathroom to diffuse the commotion. When he caught a glimpse of Momma, he hurriedly dismissed Rebecca and walked her to her car. Momma was so angry she'd gotten dizzy, and a tiny stream of blood dripped from her left nostril.

"Momma, you're bleeding." Chayanne gasped, taking a wad of Kleenex from the box on Uncle Anthony's desk to assist her.

"Baby, go on and get Momma some nice cold water please." Momma asked, fanning herself with her hand.

Chayanne ran to Lucile's desk, "Hi Miss. Lucile, Momma needs some water. Will you assist me please?" she asked politely.

"Well, there are your manners." Lucile said poking fun, "of course baby girl, I will assist you," Lucile got up from her desk and took baby girl off to the lounge area to retrieve water.

Uncle Anthony re-entered the bank, scurrying to get back to his office. He was quite embarrassed at Momma's explosion. He braced himself for the tongue lashing Momma had been holding for him. He walked into his office with a deep sigh of exasperation. He placed himself behind his desk as if it was a fort to defend him against Momma's words.

Momma dapped the rest of the blood away, "If that woman EVER touches anyone of my children again, I will put that devil into the grave myself; the lord knows I will." Momma said between her clenched teeth. Anthony nodded, confirming he understood her feelings as he took mental notes. "Why is that women still sniffing your drawers if she married?" Momma asked rhetorically, "Mark my words Anthony Reid, Rebecca Sooner, or whatever the hell she goes by is going to be the death of you!" Momma exclaimed with fear in her voice, "I thought you took notes the first time; she almost took you out when her family left storming the town like there was no tomorrow. You're smart and I don't understand why you can't leave well enough alone!" Momma was furious, she was the one who cared for him and helped him pick up the shattered pieces of his heart when Rebecca vanished. When he didn't leave his room for an entire month, Momma was the one to feed him and clean up after him. She nurtured her brother back to his sanity.

"Now Evelyn, you poking around making something out of nothing. I'm not wooing Rebecca. We were merely shooting the breeze." Anthony explained defensively.

"Shooting the breeze, you must take me for a fool, if the night ain't as black as day." Momma fused, "She's crazy about you, so damn crazy she's going through a bunch of hoops and hurdles to come across into the colored parts of town to see you. I can see that from a mile away; you get the fuzz, poking round here if you want. She's married to one Anthony, don't go getting messy causing trouble for yourself. You best stop letting her show her face in the likes of you. These white folks are looking for any reason to take you down. You're a successful businessman; you made something of yourself. Be a role model for these children, don't be another lost cause, boozing and lying up with these jezebels. You're a threat to their existence; tread lightly. Wake up and smell the damn coffee, Anthony! That woman hadn't thought of you; if she had, why didn't she come back when she could will her way in the world? That woman is foible to your existence, and you have not a clue." Chayanne intruded on the conversation when she opened the door to give Momma the water she fetched. The weight of the room was heavy; Chayanne studied Momma's and Uncle Anthony's demeanor from the doorway; she adored them most in the world and knew in her spirit, something wasn't right.

CHAPTER

5

THE SEARCH IS ON

Three Saturdays had come and gone since Momma had words with Uncle Anthony at the bank. There hadn't been a clue as to when he'd come back around. Chayanne missed him dearly; she'd eaten all of her penny candy. In addition, she didn't get her ice cream and she was a sugar junkie without a fix. She'd grown bored with her summer routine already. David was busy becoming a young man, ripping and running through the neighborhood on the new bike Daddy got him; he didn't have time to entertain her. He was headed to high school when the new school year began; his spot was already secured on the varsity baseball team. Daddy said the bike was for him to get home faster after practice; he didn't want him lingering around on the opposite side of town for trouble to find him.

Chayanne moped on the front stoop; it was the fourth Saturday and no Uncle Anthony in sight. She cursed Momma in her mind for that day at the bank. She wondered what was said to keep him off for so long; Uncle Anthony never stayed away this long even when politics were debated and got heated amongst the adults at the dinner table. The adults could never agree on Dr. Martin Luther King Jr.'s non-violent approach or Malcolm X meeting violence with violence. Of course, Momma and daddy sided with Dr. King and Uncle Anthony sided with Malcolm's movement of taking things back that belong to the colored community. Although they didn't agree, oftentimes it would end with Uncle Anthony leaving, cursing Momma and daddy slamming the front door behind him. He would always find his way back home a week or two later.

She sat there and policed the neighborhood, looking for a group of girls to play hopscotch or jump rope with. Everyone was enjoying small intimate circles of friendship that she never received an invitation for; Chayanne felt like an outcast. When she made friends, it was brief as a fashion trend. Chayanne wanted to debate like the grownups or talk about the books she was currently reading; she was a child wise beyond her years. The sun beamed down; it was at the highest peak of the day. Chayanne observed Mr. Henry headed her way with a small boy.

"Hey Chayanne, how are you today young lady?" Mr. Henry asked politely. Chayanne looked the frail boy over—his clothes dirty and tattered and his tiny Afro matted. He smelled like he hadn't bathed in weeks.

"Hello Mr. Henry, I guess I'm managing. I'm bored; I read all my summers list. I'm supposed to be with my Uncle Anthony today, but I don't know where he is." she sighed disheartened.

"Well, that's alright, I brought you a new friend. This here is my nephew, Charles. He's going to be staying with me for a while." Mr. Henry introduced Charles, placing his hand on his shoulders.

Chayanne looked at Charles once more, "Uh, Mr. Henry, I'm not accepting applications for new friends right now. Maybe tomorrow." she declined; her nose scrunched up from his smell.

"I had a feeling you might say that. Well, I guess I have to take these fudge pops on to some other kids that have open applications." he said peering at her out of the corner of his eye, pretending to walk away. "Come on here boy, let's go." he instructed Charles.

"Did you say fudge pop?" her face lit up with joy.

"Why yes, of course, how else do you make friends, besides the occasional application process." Mr. Henry chuckled.

"Oh, well in that case, I have an opening. He can sit with me on the stoop. I can't leave here until Momma gets home from the hotel." She patted a seat next to her. Charles quietly climbed on the stoop and sat with her. Henry opened the fudge pops for the two before heading across the street, back to the brigaded of people that crowded his home. They sat in silence, each of them enjoying their fudge pop.

They finished in unison, Chayanne biting on the left-over wooden stick asked nicely, "Would you like to come in and get some water?"

"Sure okay," Charles responded in a low, croaky voice. He followed her into the kitchen where they both enjoyed a drink of refreshing water.

Chayanne broke the ice the best way she knew how, "why do you smell like that?" she asked curiously.

Charles smelled himself before responding. His face appeared unpleasant once he got a whiff. "I guess it's because I haven't had a bath in a while. My mom left me in the house and never came back. She told me not to move or touch anything, so I didn't."

"Where did she go? Haven't you eaten?" her eyes widened; she could never imagine Momma leaving her alone for days.

"Um, I'm not sure, I sat there for six days, I think. I peed on myself a few times," he admitted in embarrassment, his cheeks redden. "My Uncle Henry came to get me… Uncle Henry made me a sandwich earlier."

Charles was relieved to talk to someone his age. He spent the morning talking to the police and court-appointed affiliates about his mother's whereabouts.

"How old are you?" Chayanne asked, leading him to the stoop.

"I'm ten." he said proudly.

"Oh wow, you're puny, I thought you were seven. Why are you so small?" She looked at him confused; she touched his small, matted Afro. "Maybe you would look taller if your hair was combed; would you like me to comb your hair?" she asked, twisting her body side to side.

"Um, that's okay. My uncle Henry said once all the people leave, we can go buy me some new clothes and I would finally bathe." excitement rang through his voice.

He was so unfortunate; the simple things brought him joy. Chayanne was sure a good meal and a warm bed meant more to him than she could ever fathom. The house phone rang, interrupting Chayanne's gentle interrogation of her new, adopted friend.

"That's probably my Momma calling to make sure I'm near the house. I'll be right back." she touched him on his shoulder to reassure him of her return.

"Hello, this is the Carter-Rice residence, how may I help you," Chayanne spoke gently into the transmitter.

"Hello, young Chayanne, this is Dr. George at the hospital. I work with Mrs. Evelyn, your Momma. May I speak to your father?"

"Daddy's not home; he's down at the coal mine where he works. Momma will be here soon," she said looking at the large analog clock that hung above the dining room table; it read 2:34 p.m. "She just got off from the hotel four minutes ago. It takes her twelve minutes to drive across town. Can I take a message for her?"

"Dear, your mother is down at the hospital, she's not on her way home. Is there another adult present for me to speak with? It's rather important that I talk to someone."

"Not at the moment, Dr. George. I can give you my Uncle Anthony's telephone number, but I'm not sure if he's home. He hasn't picked up the phone for me in days."

"Okay yes, that would be great if you'd give me the number." he said, taking a pen out to write on his prescription pad.

"8-3-1-2-7-5-7. If he isn't there, you can try the bank at 8-3-1-6-7-0-0." She was proud to be of assistance to the doctor, just like Momma. "Is that all, Dr. George? I have a new friend that needs me, I don't want him to think I've abandoned him like his mother."

Dr. George's face was puzzled. "Yes dear, that will be all, thank you so much for your help. Bye, now."

"You're welcome Dr. George, goodbye!" Chayanne placed the phone on its base, disregarding the severity of her conversation with Dr. George. She thought Momma decided to work an extra shift at the hospital; she knew she would call and check on her later. Chayanne knew not to question Momma's motives if she didn't want a fat lip. She skipped out of the screened door, back to the stoop, where Charles sat patiently.

"Oh great, you're back." He pointed to the cars exiting Mr. Henry's, "I get to finally take a bath and change clothes." He picked at the dirt patch on his filthy jeans.

"I'm so happy for you Charles, you deserve a bath." she confirmed his feelings, patting him on the back. They watched all five cars leave, one by one. Mr. Henry walked the deputy sheriff to his car pausing to converse with him just a bit longer in his yard. Mr. Henry pointed over to the stoop where Chayanne and Charles sat; then headed over in their direction.

"Afternoon kiddos." Deputy sheriff greeted them in unison, nodding his head. "I am deputy sheriff Tomlin. "He extended his hand to them both.

"You sound funny deputy, you aren't from around here, are you?" Chayanne asked for confirmation.

"Well gee, you're absolutely right little missy. I came up here from the swamps of N'Olearns. I can't put anything past you, can I? His accent was thick as his full, blond hair on his head. "What's your name sweetie?"

"I am Chayanne, and this is my friend, Charles. He's Mr. Henry's kin," she said, taking his large palm into her small fingertips to shake it. "It's a pleasure to meet you Deputy Tomlin."

"Awe shooks, now if you aren't the true definition of Southern hospitality young lady. Do you mind if I take your friend Charles to speak with him?"

"Well, let me check with him first." Chayanne insisted. She turned to whisper in Charles's ear. She asked if he felt comfortable leaving and if he needed her to come along. Charles shook his head yes to being comfortable and no to needing her assistance. "Deputy, you may borrow my friend. Charles, I will see you tomorrow. I should go call my Uncle Anthony anyway." she said getting up from the stoop, dusting her yellow dress off.

The deputy brow raised, "Mr. Anthony Carter your uncle?" he asked with a suspicious nature.

"Why yes sir deputy, and he's the best uncle a girl could hope for."

"Hmmm, well alright now sweetie… you take care." he said, tipping his hat and escorting Mr. Henry and Charles back across the street.

Chayanne waived goodbye and disappeared into the shadows of the house.

Chayanne called Uncle Anthony's phone three times before she tried the bank. The bank's answering machine picked up, informing her it was after operation hours for Saturday. Chayanne locked up the house using the spare key that Momma kept in the flower vase. She headed down to the quarry to search for David; she knew that was where the older kids hung out and swam. It was after 3:00 p.m. and Chayanne knew Momma wasn't scheduled for a shift at the hospital, but curiosity sat in; she wondered why Dr. George called instead of Momma.

The sun beamed on her back as her face drenched with sweat. She reached the quarry twenty minutes after she left home; it always took longer on foot and her bike was locked in daddy's shed. They wanted to make certain she wasn't trying to keep up with David when they weren't home. She searched the group of boys for David, who wasn't at the quarry. She'd seen the boys hang around with David before, especially his best friend Sticks. Chayanne tirelessly approached the boys.

"Hey Sticks, have you seen David?" Chayanne inserted herself amongst in the group of chattering teenage boys that didn't know she was there.

"Chayanne, what are you doing wandering out here by your lonesome?" Sticks asked frazzled. "If David were here, he'd get you skinned."

"If you didn't hear me the first time, I'm looking for my brother." she snapped back in a sassed tone.

"He's down at the town square, hanging out with Denise." he said hostilely.

She knew heading into town on foot could be dangerous; she had to walk through the white neighborhoods that David consistently warned her about. If she had her bike, she could cut through the trails, embedded in the woods behind the neighborhoods undetected, but she didn't. She thought of the next best thing.

Chayanne sighed heavily thinking about the thirty-minute walk, "Sticks can you ride me on your bike to town please?" her toned lightened now knowing she actually needed a favor. Chayanne looked at Sticks like a second big brother; he had been David's best since diapers, and she knew she could trust him. He was the only one of David's friends that didn't stare at her with a skeevy grin, making her feel uncomfortable.

"Chayanne, I don't feel like going to town right now. It's hot; I just want to swim." he said, removing his t-shirt. He readied himself to jump into the cool waters of the quarry.

Chayanne kissed her teeth in annoyance; she kicked up dirt with her sandals, trying to find a bribe he would jump after. "Sticks, I will give you a dollar to take me I need to get David." She asked again, removing the dollar from her white socks with the fluffy shear.

"Arrrgh, if I didn't need more baseball cards, you'd be up shits creek without a paddle," he picked his shirt off the ground and put it over his head. "Come on, you're so annoying." He directed her toward the mound of bikes the boys created.

"Hey Chayanne, you're looking mighty pretty today." one of the boys shouted and laughed.

Another boy shushed him with a warning. "David will kill you for talking to her like that. He almost drowned Kevin in the quarry for whistling at her. That's why he doesn't bring her up here anymore."

Chayanne turned back and stuck her tongue out at the boy who complimented her, "Stop being gross!" she shouted, climbing on the back of Sticks' red Micargi bike.

His frail frame struggled to take off, but he got the hang of it; she wrapped her arms around him, hoping he would be enough to hold onto, his nickname came from his long, lanky, skinny body; he looked like he barely ate.

Chayanne enjoyed riding without all the work of pedaling. The wind in her hair and the sun on her back, she rode enjoying the blue sky. Sticks rushed through the backwoods trail that he and David made to make their commute to town inconspicuous and timely; they reached the town square in a matter of minutes. Sticks stopped to let Chayanne off of the bike.

"Dollar, please!" he demanded.

Chayanne rolled her eyes, "duh, you don't get the dollar until we find him. This isn't for charity, you know!" she said with all the sarcasm she could muster. Sticks sighed heavily; walking his bike to park it by the square's playground.

"You know, if you weren't David's annoying little sister, I would've left you to fend for yourself. You need to show some appreciation." he said with agitation in his voice.

They searched the town, high and low, turning over every rock, but David wasn't in sight. Two hours had passed Chayanne weary and exhausted from the day's heat collapsed on a bench; Sticks, not far behind, followed cue.

"See, if you would've left me here, I would be stranded." she rolled her eyes, annoyed she couldn't find her brother.

Sticks plopped down famished, "He said they would be here." he said, sucking his teeth agitated.

A nice breeze blew through town square, cooling them off; Chayanne wiped the sweat that gathered from her brow. She sat there, hoping Sticks would have a clue of where David could have gone next.

Anthony's voice shook Chayanne, "Suga, what on earth are you doing out here? Where's your Momma?" She jumped from the bench, turning around to face him.

"Uncle Anthony, I've been calling you all day!" she said furious, "Where have you been? You haven't been to the house in weeks!" she responded with fire, forgetting a child's place.

She looked over the brown-skinned woman that smiled aimlessly on Uncle Anthony's arm.

"Chayanne Carter-Rice, where on earth is your Momma, and who is this boy?" Uncle Anthony was on the verge of losing his chill.

"Hello sir, I'm Sticks, David's friend." If looks could kill, the look Uncle Anthony shot Sticks was enough for three deaths.

"Son, I wasn't speaking to you!" he shot back at Sticks, "I am talking to this little bag of sass right here." he exclaimed, turning his attention back to Chayanne. "Chayanne, if I have to ask you one more time where your Momma is, you will be in a world full of hurt missy."

Chayanne sighed, being the first one to break, "She's at the hospital, Dr. George called looking for daddy. He wasn't home, so I gave him your number. He said it was important and he needed to talk to an adult. Momma wasn't supposed to work at the hospital today, so I don't know why she's there. Some time passed, and I got worried because Momma wasn't home; now, I'm looking for David and Stick is helping me." she placed her hands on her waist when she finished.

Worry spread over Anthony's face. He tapped his chin with his index finger, piecing together Chayanne's story, "Suga come on here we need to go find out what's going on. Uh Twig, if you see David, you tell him to come down to the hospital where his Momma works." Uncle Anthony scooped Chayanne up and headed for his car.

"Yes sir, I will let David know." Sticks called out after them. Sticks went to fetch his bike to continue the search, now he knew the real reason behind Chayanne needing to find him and not just to annoy him.

Uncle Anthony raced down the roads to drop his lady friend home, before racing to the hospital. His foot stayed glued to the gas pedal until the hospital came into view. Uncle Anthony slammed on the breaks in the parking lot, bringing the car to a screeching halt. The engine still running, he grabbed Chayanne out of the back and rushed through the emergency room doors. His heart racing, a loud, high-pitch tone intruded his ears as he tried to think of whom to ask about his Evelyn Carter-Rice.

CHAPTER

6

JANE DOE

David had emerged from the woods that sat adjacent to the quarry. He adjusted his dark, denim pants and tucked his white t-shirt in them. Denise fixed her hair and reapplied her lipstick, looking into the compact mirror. Denise, older than David, finished up her sophomore year at all colored high school. She believed fooling around with David was a sure ticket out of the poverty. Everyone knew he would end up playing professional baseball, but her life was much different than his. In those fifteen-minutes, she had taken the last of his childhood innocence. They walked down to the water's edge quietly with a gap of distance between. David, unsure of himself, mulled over if she was pleased with his performance. He couldn't help that he was a perfectionist with everything in his life. He picked up a stone to skip out over the water; he cast the stone and it skipped, danced, and disappeared. He noticed a bright, red flowery dress floating nearby.

"Hey, someone lost their clothes," He called out to Denise laughing. "She's not going home without this I bet. Ooowee, her Momma is going to skin her good." He grabbed a long, thick branch from the edge of the woods to fish it out. The garment neared the surface, so did the silhouette of a woman. She was face down in the water. "HOLY SHIT, it's a lady!" David said in a fit of panic.

He rushed into the water to help her; Denise rushed in after helping him drag her out of the water. They went in knee-deep, each grabbing an arm, pulling her to the dry dirt surface. They turned her over, positioning her face up; Denise regurgitated her lunch at the unsightly corpse. She had been beaten to death; her left eye detached from the socket, but still attached to her body, her right eye swollen shut. A gash split her face in half diagonally with meat hanging from it. She'd been in the water for some time now; her body was swollen from the absorption of water. David sat inches away from the foul-smelling lady in shock; his skin grayed, pupils dilated, and body cold. He could not move. The image of the woman would be burned in his mind forever.

Sticks approached David and Denise; he'd known all along where David really was but wanted to throw Chayanne off his tracks. He didn't know what Chayanne's motive was for finding David until Anthony made her spill the beans. He knew Chayanne antics all too well; he knew she held on to information until she needed to turn the tides of power on David.

"DAVID!" he called out from the bike trail making his presence known in case they were still in the groove. He smiled knowing his friend wasn't a virgin anymore. Sticks saw Denise, her face covered in tears. The hairs on his neck stood up; he sensed something heavy was going on. He skidded in the dirt inches away from David's back.

Sticks was so focused on David, he disregarded the dead body he sat next to, "David, your uncle said…" his words stuck in his throat when he inhaled the stench the dead woman's body gave off. His face turned white and his nose tracked the smell to the dead woman.

"GO GET HELP PLEASE!" Denise screamed in fear, clinching the collar of her dress; she crouched down on her knees. Sticks backed away, stumbling falling off his bike. Sticks pulled his focus together picking up his frail limbs from under his bike. He hopped back on the trail, pedaling as fast as his legs allowed.

Chayanne and Anthony sat in the waiting area waiting for Dr. George. Anthony reached Daddy at the watering hole; Anthony knew that's where he unwound with the fellas on Saturday evenings after work. He urged him to gulp his last round and get down to the hospital. Chayanne grew worried; she didn't understand what the fuss was over Momma. She worked at the hospital five days a week; she couldn't figure the difference about today. A troubling feeling grew in the pit of her stomach as Anthony paced the waiting room feverishly.

"Suga, you did right coming to look for someone. I am proud of you. You even got someone older person to tote you around, to look after you." he said praising her.

"What is Momma doing, Uncle Anthony? Why are we here?" Her stomach rumbled loudly; she'd only eaten breakfast that Momma made the family—A PB&J for lunch and a fudge pop Mr. Henry gave her. She wasn't allowed to touch the stove or oven unsupervised, but she was certain Momma would have had supper on that evening.

Anthony heard the rumble pains in her stomach, "Evelyn is going to be alright; we have to wait for Dr. George to tell us what's happening. Let's go to the vending machine." he said, picking Chayanne up into his strong arms and cradling her. At that moment, Dr. George appeared; his was face blank and hard to read. He waived Anthony over; he placed Chayanne down on the chair, handed her a couple of dollars and walked over to Dr. George. Both men stepped behind the swinging doors to shield their conversation. Chayanne studied Anthony's face through the glass of the door. His face flushes red as he listens to Dr. George. He brushed his left hand through his hair and appeared to be unraveling at every word that Dr. George's mouthed.

The ambulance cries grew louder, approaching the quarry area where David and Denise were waiting. David—still frozen in his frame of mind—hadn't budged; Denise tugged at his shirt, trying to snap him out of it before the heat approached. The colored medics entered the scene accessing the situation; they immediately tended to David, placing him on a stretcher and loaded him in the back of the ambulance.

Deputy Tomlin addressed Denise, "Miss, are you alright?" she cowered back in fear; the neighborhood she lived in wasn't too fond of the fuzz. "Now miss, I'm not going to hurt you; I just need to ask you a few questions." he pleaded, sympathizing with her. "We can do this here or down at the station, that is your choice. If we go to the station, you will need a parent to come and sit in." He wearily handed her his handkerchief to wipe her face; he'd hoped his gesture would mend a bridge of trust.

She accepted his gesture; "I'll… do it here, if that's okay? My mom works late and would kill me if she got called out of her shift."

Denise gave Deputy Tomlin an account of events that helped them discover the body.

She omitted the truth, thinking her mother would get wind of her spreading her legs. "We um… were walking down to the water to take a swim, and that's when we found her floating in the water face down, um… David went in first to grab her, and then I helped. It wasn't until we helped her to the dirt that we noticed she was gone already." She knew if her mother knew she wasn't a virgin anymore she would have to be to church every Sunday, attend every bible study, and be forbidden to see David. Denise put the hysterics and waterworks on to stop Tomlin from prying.

"Okay…okay, if I have more questions, I'll be in touch." He clicked his pen, placing it back into his neatly pressed pocket; he flipped his notepad closed. He dismissed Denise; he radioed into the station as he walked away.

"Dispatch, can you get a deputy over to Henry Miller's, I think we've found his sister and we need a positive I.D. I will meet them down at the morgue in about an hour after I wrap up the crime scene. Over." He was unfazed by Jane Doe's unsightly appearance. He motioned the deputies to wrap the scene as he plowed into his cruiser.

The dispatcher replied, "Copy that deputy sheriff. Over and out."

The ambulance reached the emergency entrance minutes after leaving the quarry. They wheeled out David, who laid motionless blinking. Daddy arrived simultaneously to David; he hurriedly jogged into the hospital right behind the medics.

"We have a boy—13 years of age—in shock; we need the doctor right away." One of the medics called out to the receptionist; it caught Daddy's attention and he noticed David lying there stiff as aboard.

He panicked, grabbing for David, "That's my boy, what happened to my boy? If he's hurt, it was those Collins boys." Daddy cried out helplessly; the medics pulled at him to restrain him.

"Sir, calm down, he's in shock; we need you to stay here." the medic demanded, pushing the bed David was lying on through the double doors. Daddy waited, pacing near the doors to get the okay on David.

His pacing was a distraction to the receptionist, "Sir... excuse me sir, you can't stand here. You're stopping the flow of foot traffic for the medics. Please have a seat in the waiting area; a doctor will be out to speak with you shortly." Daddy complied with the receptionist's order. He headed down the well-lit hall to the waiting area.

Chayanne called out for him when his lanky and tired figure appeared. "Daddy, daddy, what are you doing here?"

He lifted his head from the floor, "Baby girl, what...what are you doing here? You should be at home." He said surprised. She pointed with her small index finger to Anthony behind the double doors with Dr. George. Daddy bolted toward the men in curiosity. Chayanne sat patiently, watching the men in her life radically debate with one another and Dr. George.

Boredom quickly found her, Chayanne wandered off, sneaking past who was on a call. At first, there wasn't much to see; she would go in and out of rooms until she wandered into the room where Momma laid with her eyes closed.

Chayanne walked to her bedside. "Momma?" she called out softly, she thought Momma was taking a nap. Chayanne stood deliberating the details of Momma's pale face. Her lips dry and cracked, she laid unresponsive. Chayanne reached her small hand up to grab Momma's hand; Momma opened her eyes, looked at Chayanne, and weakly smiled.

She swallowed hard "Hey baby girl!" her voice raspy and speech slurred. "Where'd you come from, sweetheart?" she asked, closing her heavy eyes.

"Uncle Anthony brought me. Momma, do you have a cold? Why are you in the bed?"

"Oh baby, Momma's not feeling too well. I've been here since early morning; I didn't even make my shift at the hotel. The doctor says I need to rest if I have a chance of fighting this cancer." she wheezed as her breathing continued.

"Well momma, I can make you soup, the kind you make me when I'm sick. Will that help?"

"Aw, you're sweet baby, that'll be a good start. A real good start."

"How long does cancer last, Momma?" Chayanne was anxious to know if it lasted longer than a regular cold.

Momma laughed, "Well sweetie, it depends on the stage of the cancer and the treatment. Dr. George says we caught it early." Momma dozed off.

Chayanne felt down that Momma was ill, "Momma I'm sorry for being mad at you about Uncle Anthony. If you get better, I won't be mad anymore." Momma squeezed Chayanne's hand gently smiling.

"I love you, my sweet girl, I will always be with you no matter if you're mad with me or not." A tear slipped out of Momma's eye when she closed them.

She was in pain and she was fighting it with all her might. Chayanne climbed into bed with her and nuzzled up under her arm; Chayanne quietly hummed the lullaby Momma sung to her when she was afraid, Chayanne hummed the tune until they both were fast asleep.

David snapped out of his trans, he was gasping for air and tears poured from his eyes. He cried loudly for Momma.

The nurse motioned for daddy to come into the room " If you can't calm him Mr. Rice, we will sedate him." She warned.

Daddy nodded, he wrapped David in his strong arms. Daddy held his tears, knowing he couldn't hug the parts of him that really hurt, or the part of him that would begin to hurt when he found out about Momma. He held his son—rocking him and holding back his pain. David calmed himself; his sobs eased, feeling safety in the comfort of daddy's arms.

David listened to the rhythm of daddy's heartbeat to calm him further. "Daddy where are Momma and Chayanne? Why haven't they come?" Through all the chaos and bad news, daddy forgot about baby girl.

Daddy decided in that moment it wasn't the right time to break the news about Momma. "They're fine. They're here waiting; they want you to be okay. They want you to get better." Daddy embellished a bit. "So, what happened to you, son? David clenched daddy tightly, not wanting to see the woman's face in his mind.

Daddy soothed David, "It's okay son, I'm here whenever you're ready." he patted his head, dying to know what happened to David.

Daddy sat with David for a few hours; he wasn't prepared to face the truth about Momma. David was asleep when Dr. George entered the room.

Doctor George spoke in a low tone, "Mr. Rice, I've prepared David's discharge papers, he's good to go. I would like you to schedule a follow up visit for next week so I can monitor his progress."

Daddy nodded blankly, acknowledging Dr. George's request; He felt the noose of life strung him up to a poplar tree, leaving him for dead.

"Mr. Rice, you should take some time off and give your body some time to rest. I won't cut Evelyn's pay; she's done a lot for this hospital and her family has done a lot for this town. I know you'll need every penny to pay for the treatment she'll need.

"Thank you!" Daddy replied with a gracious heart. Keeping food on the table while he cared for Momma would be one less thing he would have to worry about.

"The sheriff told me to let you know they want to speak with David. They have some questions for him at the station, any time you're available tomorrow." Dr. George informed him.

Dr. George looked at daddy's bloodshot eyes; he could only imagine the laborious work that the coal mines would have on a man's mental. Daddy nodded once more, exhausted with his thoughts.

Daddy skimmed through, signing David's release paper. David dressed himself and daddy went to search for Anthony. He found him in the waiting room; Anthony's face buried in his palms. Daddy placed his strong hand on Anthony's shoulder.

"We have to be strong for her, that's all we can do. We have to help her through it, Ant; she's going to be alright, she has to be alright." Daddy said consoling him.

Anthony groaned, "I know." He replied dully; without Momma, he would never feel whole, and that is what scared him most.

Daddy grabbed his chin and thought, "I need you to take the kids home for me. I've been putting off seeing her." Daddy looked down, ashamed that he couldn't be strong in this situation, "David doesn't know; Dr. George said he's in some kind of shock state and telling him could make it worse. I don't think baby girl…" he stopped to look around the room for her. "Where is baby girl?" he asked with growing concern. Anthony sprung up, looking under chairs and tables for Chayanne.

"I'll check the vending area; she said she was hungry, but Dr. George came in with news when we were stepping away. You go check with the receptionist." Anthony demanded distraughtly. They searched high and low, turning the hospital upside down. Ten minutes into their search,

Dr. George informed them, "Chayanne is asleep with Mrs. Evelyn." he said, taking them to her room, "The staff was transporting her into the extended patient room when they found Chayanne curled up next to her."

Daddy placed his hand on his chest in relief, "Anthony, can you go check on David, I need a word with baby girl." Anthony, without reply, left the room. Seeing his sister so lifeless and not herself shook him to his core. He threw up in a nearby wastebasket; he wasn't able to hold his nerves.

"Baby girl, how did you get in here?" Daddy asked, nudging her awake.

Chayanne rubbed her tired eyes. "Daddy, I'm sleepy," she whined, "Momma needs me here to hum songs to her; it helps her sleep." she explained rolling back over.

He smiled, knowing his baby could comfort his wife when he couldn't; he could no longer fight his tears looking at his daughter, lying on her dying mother. Momma had stage three-breast cancer; it spread to one of her lungs. Dr. George informed both Daddy and Anthony that her only option was to remove her breast and lung and undergo chemotherapy. If Momma decided not to do the trail of therapy, she would only have three solid months to live.

The moon settled high in the sky when Anthony pulled into the driveway. With the children sleep in the backseat, he sat there with the engine idling, sobbing, hoping not to wake them. His fit of grief lasted briefly; he wiped his face, composing himself. He carried Chayanne to the door, entering the house. David lagged behind; his body felt like cinder blocks. The steps of the stoop looked like Mount Everest. The rattling leaves of the bush caught his attention.

Sticks waited in the bushes for an hour after he ate supper, "Psst David…" Sticks called out quietly.

"Sticks, what the hell? It's after ten; your mother is going to kill you." David whispered aggressively. He looked up the stairs to make sure Anthony wasn't watching.

Sticks waived David off, "Cool it, I went home when the streetlights came on, I snuck out because… Are you okay?" David stood silent looking into the dirt like it had the answer to Sticks question. He couldn't even mutter a response. Sticks revealed himself from behind the bush, shaking his head side to side in disbelief, "That was her, wasn't it? That was the lady, that's why you can't say nothin."

CHAPTER

7

MISPLACED EMOTIONS

Uncle Anthony managed to doze off seconds before Daddy arrived from the hospital. Anthony had Momma's medical books sprawled on the coffee table; he was researching and looking for answers. He refused to let her sink without a fight. The jingle of Daddy's keys entering the lock woke him. He stood stretching his limbs yawning.

"Morning James." he gathered the books neatly placing them on the bookshelf.

"Mawnin Anthony, how are the children?" he looked just the way he sounded, exhausted and weary.

"Suga is fine, she went right to bed when we got in. She doesn't seem to be worried; maybe she doesn't understand what's going on. The kids never had to deal with death—our parents passed away long before they arrived." He pinched the top of his nose where his eyes met, attempting to rid his tiredness. "David seems strange, not like himself. He was out whispering to his friend Twigs in the bush when we got in. I just didn't have the fight in me to figure out what the hell was going on. I'm sure it's because it's that weird phase in a boy's life, the things he needs to figure out before becoming a man." Anthony filled Daddy in as much as he could; he knew Daddy was a familiar stranger to his children. He stayed away; always working to provide a better life. Daddy scratched his head; Anthony could tell he was overwhelmed mentally. "If you need anything, just call me. I'll be around the house for a bit... James, we're in this together." Anthony said assuring him.

Daddy moaned "Thank you Anthony! Evelyn's awake; she asked for you to come down to the hospital. I need you to come back; the boys at the station want to talk to David about whatever happened yesterday."

Daddy disappeared into the dark hallway entering the bathroom. Uncle Anthony gathered his things and headed out of the door, the sun barely peeked its head over the tree line.

Chayanne woke to the sound of sizzling in the kitchen; she was thrilled thinking Momma was home. She sprung out of bed, sprinting full speed down the hall.

She came crashing into the kitchen, "Momma!" She said her heart bursting with excitement that soon turned to disappointment. It was Daddy making breakfast; the smoke filled the room while the food was burning. "Where is Momma?" she said, frowning her hands placed on her hips.

Her words surprised him; he was focused on trying not to burn the house down. Grease popped from the stove burning his hand, he jumped back a few feet.

He fought the popping grease with the hand towel, "Baby girl get back!" he demanded, swinging wildly like a mad man.

Chayanne's patience thinned; she hated being ignored, "Daddy please, where is Momma?" she grew angry.

David approached the kitchen standing behind Chayanne. He rubbed his eyes, still trying to wake himself. It took him a few minutes to grasp what was taking place.

David's mouth dropped in awe, "dad what are you doing?" he asked hysterically. "Did you miss an anniversary, or did you make Momma mad?" he joked looking around the room for Momma.

He wandered down the hall to their bedroom and scratched his head in confusion. He returned to the kitchen.

He tapped Chayanne on the shoulder, who was impatiently tapping her foot waiting for daddy to answer, "Chayanne, where is Momma?" he asked concerned. "Did she have to go to work? I thought this was her Sunday off?" he questioned rubbing his head.

He went to look at the calendar Momma kept on the wall with her schedule and work numbers. That Sunday was blank, indicating she had nothing to do. Daddy placed his version of breakfast on the table. He opened the back door giving the smoke an escape route.

"Go on and have a seat." Daddy instructed. They both did as they were told. A look of disgust swept over Chayanne's face as she looked down at the blackened crispy items of food; she couldn't manage to identify what each item was. She looked across the table at David who shared the same expression. Daddy joined them with plates and cutlery in hand.

He sat in Momma's chair, "Let's dig in." Daddy insisted with a smile, proud of his attempt.

Chayanne pushed the empty plate away from her, "Daddy, Momma's cooking doesn't look like this, are you trying to poison us?" she asked with all serious.

David joined in, "Dad, where is mom?" David asked again. He could no longer negate the truth with his curious children. He knew they wanted answers.

Daddy's eyes danced around the room, "I know this feels abnormal, but this is what it has to be for a while. Momma... Momma isn't feeling well; she's at the hospital."

David adjusted his glasses, "What do you mean she's not doing well? I was at the hospital yesterday; you said Momma and Chayanne were fine. Chayanne's fine, but Momma is sick?" his jovial tone was now flat; his body language wasn't light with laughter.

Daddy's face looked concerned, the energy in the room shifted, "I made a choice not to tell you yesterday, so I'm telling you now! Momma ain't doing too well, Dr. George wants to give her treatments down at the hospital and she'll be there for a while." Daddy said sternly, asserting his authority.

David shifted in his chair not satisfied, "Doing well could mean lots of things daddy, what's wrong with her and when can we see her?" David asked, annoyed with his father's half made answer.

Chayanne sadly chimed in, "Daddy, she just needs soup. I talked to her yesterday and she said that would make her better. Seeing as you can't cook, I'll have to do it." Chayanne said innocently.

David was livid, "Wait, so baby girl knew Momma was there yesterday and she spoke with her?" David stood up away from the table, his tone more aggressive.

Daddy looked at David across the table accessing his mood. The tension thickened like the fog on a wet dreary day.

Daddy stood from the table towering over them both, "Chayanne went looking for you yesterday all over the town. Where were you?" Daddy shot back.

David stood quietly—not prepared to answer the question—but wanted answers to questions of his own.

Chayanne twirled her hair, "Ummm… she said it wasn't a cold, but cancer. Momma said she needed treatment to beat cancer for us." Chayanne answered softly.

A small knock at the front door gave Daddy the perfect excuse to excuse Chayanne from the conversation; he needed to be alone with David.

"Baby girl, go answer the door please!" Daddy said, not breaking his gaze from David. She got up from the table, merrily skipping off to answer the door in her nightgown.

"It's Deputy Sheriff Tomlin, Daddy." She called from the front room. "Do you want me to answer the door to let him in?"

Daddy's brows rose in curiosity, he walked to the entrance of the kitchen to look at the front door.

"We will finish whatever you think this is later." Daddy said to David sternly.

David angrily responded, "This is bullshit, you can't answer my questions but you want to ask me a million." David slammed his fist onto the tabletop causing a plate to topple over the side and break.

Daddy calmly retreated and stepped back into the kitchen; he twisted his mouth and squinted his eyes.

He cornered David, "I put clothes on your back, food in your stomach, and a roof over your head. I taught you how to navigate life so you can become a decent man. I make sure you live in a safe neighborhood to go to a good school. I gave you life—If you ever disrespect me in my home again—you better pray to the lord and savior that you can outrun me because boy, I will break your ass! The last time I checked, I was still the God damn parent; you answer the questions that I am asking and you speak when you're spoken to. You and Chayanne have the privilege to mouth off, but boy I wish you could have met my daddy; you'd be picking your teeth off the floor. Now, where the hell were you yesterday? Why the hell is the sheriff deputy so pressed to see you?" Daddy didn't bat an eye as he hemmed David in the corner waiting for a response.

David lowered his eyes to the table in embarrassment, " I was at the quarry, sir."

Daddy's grip tightened on David's collar, "So why come when Chayanne went down to the quarry looking for you, she couldn't find you?" he wanted the truth, and he wasn't going to let up until he had it.

"I..." he paused, nervous to tell his father his dealings with Denise.

Chayanne came fumbling into the kitchen, "Daddy, may I go outside and play with Charles?" Chayanne intruded, giving David sometime to contemplate on what to tell his father. Her eyes widen, she stood there wincing, waiting for an answer; she hated when they got in trouble.

Daddy turned his head slightly to acknowledge her, but never took his eyes off David. "Baby girl, who is Charles? Where does he live and who are his parents?"

Chayanne cleared her throat softly before rattling off her knowledge of Charles, "Charles is my friend I adopted yesterday over fudge pops. I didn't want to because he smelled funny and was dirty, but I got to know him a little more. His momma abandons him and now he lives with Mr. Henry, his uncle across the street."

Daddy smiled and nodded, "Make sure you brush your teeth and make your bed before going out baby girl. Stay near to the house and we will go see momma in a little while. Is the deputy sheriff at the door still?" he asked sternly.

Chayanne froze in her tracks, "No sir, he was across the way at Charles's house and saw your truck. He said he needed David at the station. I told him you were busy and would be down soon."

"Thank you baby girl, you did great!" Daddy turned his full undivided attention back to David, "That is how you answer my questions. Stop making me interrogate you like these white folks; I can't protect you if I don't know what to protect you from."

David sighed deeply; Daddy's hand felt like a ton of bricks on his chest. "I was in the woods with Denise at the quarry on the far side. Chayanne isn't allowed over there when we go because of the deep drop-off, so she wouldn't have thought to go there... Denise and I found a woman's body floating nearby. I panicked, I've never seen a dead body before, and I was unsure of what to do."

Daddy didn't need to ask what happened between David and Denise; he could sense David's newfound confidence wasn't by accident.

Daddy let go of David and stepped back, allowing him some breathing room. He cautiously observed David's mood.

"Is that all you know about the lady?" Daddy pushed, sensing David's uneasy tension.

"Yes sir." he lied through his teeth.

David saw the lady before on the boardwalk a week before finding her in the quarry with the same dress on, but he didn't want to share that with him.

Daddy sensed David's dishonesty about something, but he didn't know what. "Mmmmh, are you sure that's all?"

"Yes sir!" David said, breaking eye contact. He felt like his father could see through his lie by staring into his dark eyes.

Daddy let up, "Go clean up and get dressed, we need to be at the sheriff station by noon. David, like I said... I can't protect you from things I don't know. You're becoming a man and you will have to reap the consequences of your actions... I hope you wore a condom with Denise; women that see you now see a one-way ticket into your life if they are with child. Your Daddy don't raise no fools, so don't be taken for one." Daddy exited the kitchen, coldly leaving David with his messy thoughts and a kitchen to clean. David exhaled, relieved that his father's interrogation was over.

Chayanne rushed to do what she was told; she was excited to see her new friend awaiting her company on the stoop outside. She felt important and like she belonged. She pulled her denim jeans over her long skinny legs; they were hand me downs from David. Momma refused to buy a young lady a pair of pants. She put on an old, white t-shirt of David's and some of his worn-down Chuck Taylors. She hightailed it to the door; Charles sat—waiting on the stoop swinging his legs—humming a light tune.

"Hey Charles, want to ride bikes?" she asked startling him.

"Uh, I don't have a bike yet, maybe some other time. I was hoping you could show me the neighborhood." he replied easily.

Chayanne sat next to him, "I have to take one of those rainchecks the grownups take; my daddy says I can't go far, and I have to go see my momma later in the hospital."

"Oh... is she dead like my momma?" his mood changed. Sadness loomed over him; he wiped a tear from his eye, "My Uncle Henry took me to the morgue to see her yesterday. She was in the water for a long time; he said she drowned swimming at the quarry. My Uncle Henry said she died peacefully." A bit of doubt spread over his face. "I know what it feels like when I get water up my nose... that's not a peaceful feeling." he admitted with slumped shoulders.

"Charles, what does it mean to die?" she asked, emerged by his conversation.

"It's like they are asleep forever; they can't wake up no matter how hard you try. I called out for my momma while we were there, but she never talked back. My Uncle Henry wouldn't let me say goodbye." Tears slipped from his eyes silently. He swung his legs to numb his pain; his heart never knew loss. Chayanne cupped his small body with the arm closest to him, bringing him close to her.

"Well... I don't mind sharing my momma; she's really sweet, but she's strict and has lots of rules." She joked, looking at his face covered with tears and snot.

He was hysterical and angry at the world; he didn't understand the pain he was going through. "You don't have to be lonely anymore, I'll never leave you, I promise." she said trying to ease his pain and understand his hurt. His breath stuttered; he breathed through his sobs. She sensed in the pit of her stomach it was something more that bothered him.

CHAPTER

8

TREACHEROUS WATERS

Daddy and Anthony escorted David into the police station; their heads held high, unapologetically. They were prideful men; they had nothing to hide and just like any white man, they felt they too had a place in this world alongside them. They didn't scare easy—never did and never would. They were uncompromising to set that example for David, a growing man. The chatter of the police station muted itself when they walked through the door. They could feel the hatred in the room when they approached the front desk.

Daddy spoke in a low, bellowing tone, "James and David Rice, to see Deputy Tomlin." Daddy said, adjusting his cufflinks under his black suit jacket.

Anthony's face went empty; he was coming face-to-face with the man he felt sorry for but envied. The officer manning the desk ignored Daddy, never looking up from his paperwork. Uncle Anthony fidgeted in his stance—his irritancy grew—he loathed being ignored. Daddy tapped his fingertips on the counter.

Daddy inhaled to stay calm, "Sir, do I need to repeat myself?" he asked with a little more bass in his voice.

"Frank, can you let Tomlin know these boys are here to see him." The officer said staring daddy in his eyes, daring him to correct his use of the word boy.

Daddy smirked and nodded; he wanted this to be a peaceful interaction. He knew if things escalated, Anthony would be difficult to manage. Seconds after Deputy Tomlin was informed of their presence, he appeared from a back office in full uniform.

"Gentlemen, please come this way." he said smiling pleasantly directing them.

They all walked into the back office in single file. David followed behind Tomlin, leading the others; Tomlin shook each man's hand as they entered the room. He was unaware that he was amongst familiar company. He allowed the men to seat themselves. Anthony refused a seat, not wanting to give Tomlin the upper hand or think they were equal. Tomlin sat and began with the interview.

"Gentlemen, my name is Deputy Sheriff Tomlin, I would like for you all to introduce yourselves for my tape recording please."

David was about to do as requested, but Daddy held his hand up, silencing him.

Daddy spoke in a deep monotone voice, "What exactly is this recording for, deputy sheriff?"

Deputy chuckled, clicking off the recorder. He's never come in counter with such an intuitive black man, "The department would like this incident on record. Of whom we are speaking with and the information of the discovery of Miss. Parker's body. David isn't in any type of trouble here, we just want to know how he found the body and what he saw. It's that simple; his cooperation will be noted when we find the person responsible." Daddy lowered his hand, allowing the others in the room to speak.

Tomlin smiled friendly, he started the recording over, "My name is Deputy Sheriff Tomlin, I am interviewing with?" He motioned for them to speak.

"My name is David Carter-Rice."

"My name is James Rice."

"My name is Anthony Carter."

Anthony couldn't help his smile when Deputy Sheriff Tomlin's face vacated its expression. He stopped the recording to compose himself.

"Ahem, gentlemen please excuse me," he said, removing himself from the room. When he cleared, Daddy turned to face Anthony who stood in the corner grinning like a tomcat ready to pounce on its prey.

"Ahem, Ant, what in the hell is that about?" Daddy asked with concern.

Anthony adjusted his suit and tie, "Oh nothing worth sharing, we just have something in common, that's all. I didn't think he expected to meet me in this light." Uncle Anthony made his remarks, removing a cigarette from his jacket pocket. Daddy was baffled—he had not a clue how Anthony was acquainted with the deputy sheriff and he sure as hell wasn't about to pry. Anthony sparked a match—lighting his cigarette—taking a long draw to calm his sordid nerves; he exhaled the smoke to further eradicate his emotions. Deputy Tomlin reentered the room, his poise intact.

"Ahem, gentlemen, I apologize about that... I... um... needed some water. My throat was parched." Deputy Sheriff Tomlin looked like he wanted to puke, thinking about a young Anthony penetrating his sweet Rebecca. He adjusted in his chair uncomfortably, "So let's continue the recording, shall we?" David's statement took all of thirty minutes for him to reencounter the events of yesterday. He finished his statement, but Tomlin wasn't done.

Tomlin sat upright in his chair, "One last question, David. Did you know Ms. Parker?" Tomlin asked with suspicion.

Daddy put his hand over David's mouth, "Is there something you're wanting to tell me deputy sheriff?" Daddy asked rhetorically, "It sounds to me like it's time for us to seek counsel." Daddy's nostrils flared; the feeling of betrayal prowling nearby.

Tomlin waived his hands, disarming the room, "No, no that is not at all what's happening, we just want to be able to cross David's name off the list of suspects." He responded defensively.

"Why would he be a suspect... because he's black? Black folks like us don't hurt our kind. You need to go after the Klansman, I'm sure they can give you a full account of what happened to that there lady. You might as well put this on your unsolved case pile because you all refuse to convict your own for killing poor innocent blacks. We didn't ask to be here deputy sheriff; I think you need to self-correct. If you want to ask my boy any more questions, you can contact our counsel. You should be ashamed of yourself trying to place blame. He fetched the lady from the water. If he were a suspect, why return to a scene of the crime? That just doesn't make sense." Anthony's hand firmly gripped Daddy's shoulder; he applied pressure to get daddy off the edge. It was easy for Anthony to distinguish that Tomlin wanted a scene giving him a reason to throw them all in a cell. "Deputy, you have a good day sir." Daddy removed his hand from David's mouth and motioned for him to exit the room.

Tomlin clapped his hands, "My, my, my Mr. Rice, looks like you missed your calling. You sir should have been a lawyer. I commend you for coming in and allowing David to give a statement. My apologies if I over stepped. You gentlemen are free to go... Oh, one more thing, tell that pretty little daughter of yours, Chayanne I said hello." Deputy sheriff winked at Anthony. "I'm sure this isn't the last we will see of one another; you take care now Reeeeed!" Tomlin said tipping his head.

Uncle Anthony balled his fist in his pockets. "Deputy, I would hate to believe that's a threat on my family?"

Tomlin smiled, "Oh no Mr. Carter, I'm just merely getting acquainted. Like I said, you all are free to go, unless you have a problem, son." He said, enticing Anthony's anger.

Daddy pushed Anthony toward the door, freeing him from the hasty environment. Anthony was fueling with anger, but he collected his cool before he exited the office.

Anthony turned in his tracks, "You don't seem like the type to carry the majority's opinion of your people, especially not marrying pretty old Rebecca Sooner; I just hope you don't become a product of your environment, deputy. Good day to you, sir." Anthony had to have the last word; he couldn't let him think he had him cornered. He closed the door gently, leaving Deputy Sheriff Tomlin to himself.

Lilly laid her head on Chayanne's shoulder, "Mommy have you ever seen a dead body?" Lilly asked interrupting the story.

Chayanne giggled softly, " I thought we agreed to hold all questions until the end, young lady." She said deflecting the question.

Lilly looked up at Chayanne, "Yeah I know, but Daddy's mommy died when he was so little. He didn't see her body, but Uncle David did."

Chayanne rubbed Lilly's forehead, pulling her hair back kissing it. "I know honey, life has mapped out all experiences for people differently; we may not know what we face, but our job is to understand the obstacles, and come out better people after the experience." She sat there holding Lilly in her arms, hugging her firmly. "Let's go shower and get ready for the day; we can make lunch together." Chayanne said, hearing Lilly's stomach rumble loudly.

Chayanne looked at her bed clock. Most of the day passed; it was late afternoon pushing the boundaries of the evening. Lilly enjoyed listening to Chayanne's interpretation of life; it spoke to her soul and eased her worries. Lilly couldn't hide her excitement; Lilly was astonished at how quickly she regained a connection and a sense of belonging with Chayanne once more. She took time to tell her about her upbringing. This was all the comfort Lilly desired. Lilly peeled herself from her mother's side getting out of bed. She skipped joyfully to her bathroom to do as she was told.

Chayanne, fully emerged in her story, took notice to Ashton's two missed calls hours ago. Chayanne's gut feeling told her Ashton was on the verge of a mental break since Charles's decided to remarry. Ashton struggled much more with the divorce than Chayanne. Charles concealed his sexuality initially from Ashton—who was fifteen at the time—when

Charles came forth and admitted his sexual desire for men. Ashton felt it to be an excuse for Charles to walk out on the family.

Chayanne returned Ashton's call at his dorm after a few minutes of non-stop ringing. She tried him on his emergency cell; she patiently waited for his answer.

Hello... hello mom?" he answered, unable to hear much; the sound of falling beer bottles, loud music, and laughter were in his company.

"Hey honey... I can barely hear you, is everything alright?" Chayanne listened to the roaring crowd of people enjoying themselves. "Ash, I just noticed I missed your call." she spoke loudly, screaming over the crowd.

Ashton rustled through a crowd of people finding a quiet spot in the den. "Mom, hello?" he said, checking the screen to make sure the call was still live. "Sorry for the noise, I'm at a day party at the frat house. How are you mom, are you okay?" he slurred into the receiver.

Chayanne tapped her fingertips on her knee, accessing him as he spoke. "It's alright honey, you're only young once, no need to apologize. Yeah, I'm doing okay. The kiddo and I are hanging in there." It was a brief pause; Chayanne wanted to muster up the courage to fulfill Charles's favor. "Have you talked to your father?"

Ashton fidgeted with the phone, "I knew you were going to ask that. He called me nonstop at the dorm yesterday, and then four times on the cell. He left a sappy message saying how important it is to him for me to come... Did he ask you to convince me to go to his fucking wedding?" he babbled. It was apparent to Chayanne that Ashton had been drinking; the way he slurred his words was her indicator. "How dare he try and make you a pawn in his match with me!" Ashton grew enraged, "You know mom, this is bullshit, I don't see why you didn't take his sorry ass for every penny he had."

She calmed her nerves, pissed that he'd been drinking underage. She held the phone to her chest, muffling his rant. She knows there was little to nothing she could do being so far from him. She inhaled deeply and returned her attention to the call.

"ASHTON!" She yelled for his attention, "Are you still seeing Dr. Green?" She wanted him to focus his attention elsewhere; she didn't want him to go into a downward spiral. It was difficult for her to manage his mood swings; through time she learned that inserting a temporary distraction would bring him down a notch.

"Yes ma'am, I've been seeing him twice a week now." he replied. She could hear him doing his breathing exercises through the phone to recenter himself in the present. " I'm sorry, I know I can... I can go a bit overboard. I'm just not ready to deal with him, honestly."

Chayanne collected her theory, "Ash... it has been three years since you've spoken to him, and I know you're upset and hurting, but he's your father. No matter how you slice it kiddo, those are the facts. I don't want you to take things for granted; he's here now living and breathing, give him his flowers while he can smell them. Just because we aren't married anymore doesn't mean he loves you less. I know you're angry, but don't let there be a day you live with the regret that you didn't reconcile your differences."

Ashton sat on the sofa, her words began to sober him, "How could you just forgive him like he hasn't hurt you?" he said, dying to know her secret, "He moved on, simple. Quentin is so pressed for dad to start another family that he's trying to use dad's money to adopt a baby! He has two kids he barely sees. Just because he writes a fat check for child support and tuition every month doesn't mean we are cared for, mom, and you know that." Ashton's voice huffed through the phone.

"Baby, you have to let some of that anger for your daddy go. If I can do it, so can you. There are some things you may never understand about him, but don't ever for one second question his love for you and your sister. You're the only family he's truly ever known." Tears swelled in her eyes as she pictured young Charles in his tattered clothes on the day she first met him. "You have to learn to let go, Ash, life changes every second, and you can either change with it or let the change weed you out; adaptation is what keeps us alive." She wiped her tears with the bed of her fingers. "I think you and Lilly should go support your father, don't abandon him, he doesn't deserve that. I know I raised a better man than what you're pretending to be. We're all scared, and we carry fear in our hearts, but don't let the intangible things you carry piled on your back stop you from being the bigger man."

Ashton let his mother's words sink in. He had no rebuttal.

He rubbed his freshly cut hair, "I love you, mom. I'll call you later." He disconnected the call with his heart in hand. He never allowed himself to feel sadness, but today, it reared its ugly head eating away at him like rot.

Chayanne and Lilly met in the kitchen not long after they both tended to their hygiene. Chayanne got a pot of hot water, placed it on the stove, and prepared to make Lilly her favorite macaroni and cheese.

Lilly sat at the breakfast counter watching Chayanne like a spectacle, "Mommy, what happened after the police station?" she asked, pushing for more of the story.

Daddy and David walked through the small maze out of the sheriff's station. Anthony lagged behind taking his time; he'd hoped Tomlin would give him reason to be stricken with the knuckles of his fist, but Tomlin didn't give one. Anthony made it to the front doors. Rebecca entered her head down, digging in her pocketbook for tissue. His cologne—warm, pleasant, and inviting—greeted her first, then the strength of his broad chest. Rebecca unintentionally bumped into him. They traded glances, undressing one another in public with their eyes; they both smiled blushing. Rebecca bit the tip of her index finger diving deeper in her intimate thoughts.

"Excuse me, missus." Anthony apologized with a smile.

His heart filled with satisfaction as he exited the station. Rebecca in a daze, allowed her eyes to follow after him; her feet cemented in place.

"REBECCA!!!!!" Tomlin screamed, startling the entire station that was occupied in other work.

A COMPROMISED WOMAN

The mixture of white lilies and pansies that filled Momma's hospital room wilted. This was the third week of her treatment. Chayanne faithfully sat by Momma's side, daily, reading aloud to her; she was currently reading, To Kill a Mockingbird by Harper Lee. Chayanne had read the book five times since its release and it was her favorite. She wanted to share with Momma; Chayanne was convinced that the book was making Momma better.

Daddy entered the room, "Chayanne gather your things, it's time to go." he said, grabbing for her book.

She pouted close to tears. "Do I have to leave momma? She sleeps here all alone." Chayanne didn't like her mother's absence. The first week, Daddy gave her all the sweets in the world to distract her, but the lackluster wore off when she ate too much and got sick. The second week, she ate PB&J sandwiches for dinner, and she would gag if she were made to eat another. The third week was lonely, Daddy went back to work and David was never around. Being home without Momma didn't seem much like home to Chayanne anymore.

Daddy packed her things, "Yes, baby girl, Momma has to stay here to finish her treatment. You see all of these flowers; it's a lot of people depending on her to get better. She needs her rest baby girl; we have to go. I've been in the mines all day and I just want to rest." He said, kissing Momma on the forehead.

Her pouty, bottom lip hung close to the floor as she followed Daddy out of the room in tears.

David avoided the hospital; he'd ignored momma's sickness altogether. He thought of it more like an ailment that she would recover from and be better soon. He tried not to think much of it and he used any and everything as a distraction. He spent most of his days down at the ballpark playing pickup games with some of the colored children from various neighborhoods. He was in his element; he was free from life responsibilities in those moments.

David was up to bat next; he prepared for the plate warming up his swing.

Sticks anxiously jumped up and down waiving, "Yo David… psst David." Sticks whispered subtly trying to get his attention. David was in the zone and focused on hitting the ball over the fence to end the game. "David…David!!!" he continued, trying to remain inconspicuous. Sticks attempted to warn David that the Collins boys and a small group of spectators were approaching the field. "God dammit, DAVID!" Sticks blurted loudly, unable to hold his tongue any longer as the group closed in.

David looked over his shoulder at him, "Goodness Sticks, what the hell, I'm trying to focus." he replied annoyed.

"The Collins boys are here." he said pointing in their direction as they audaciously approached David.

David inconspicuously looked in their direction, "Fucking shit! I just don't have time for this bullshit today." He exclaimed in frustration. David never was afraid in his heart, Momma always instructed him to cool his temper and keep his attitude in check. She was aware that his fiery side would kill one of the Collin's kids and she believed they had a death wish the way they meddled with David. David dropped the bat, bracing himself for impact. Dougie—seventeen—was the oldest of the three Collins boys. He pushed David into the fence, striking him in the face with an open palm. David's glasses flew into the sand.

"I heard a gang of you monkeys were at the station talking to the sheriff. What's that all about, boy?" David collected himself from the blow; he picked his chin up staring Dougie in the eye.

The Collins crowd egged Dougie on. "Teach that coon a lesson Dougie, show him his place."

The kids who were playing baseball formed a crowd on the opposite side of the white kids. Tension sprouted in the atmosphere; the loud crackling thunder set the tone and the storm clouds gathered as a violent storm set in.

David looked Dougie dead in his grease-ball eye, "I didn't tell them anything of importance if that's what you're asking." David responded, licking the blood that ran from his lip and spitting in the sand. "I have a game to get back to that you interrupted, if you don't mind."

Dougie crouched down close to David's ear. "If you tell anyone and I mean anyone you saw me with that nigger bitch on the boardwalk,

I will beat you until you're black and blue, and I will personally gut you open. Then, I will make your sister my whore; she's a pretty little thing." He spoke out of range from the crowd. David clenched his fist tightly, the rage bubbled within him. Dougie was four-years older, but David had size and muscle mass on him and only stood an inch shy of Dougie's 5'7 slim frame. Dougie slung David to the ground, ripping his t-shirt clean from his body.

Dougie howled, "See that there boy, I own you! All ya'll niggers get before you bite off more than you can chew." He instructed, Dougie's crowd of people backed away slowly, retreating to their cars.

David picked himself up out of the dirt with his chest poked out; his pride bruised more than his body. Some girls in his grade stood nearby admiring his nice, chiseled chest and bravery. They waived in the distance, fighting for attention.

"Way to go David to not punk out to those motherfuckers." one of the older kids in the crowd commended him.

"Let's get back to our game." another kid called out. David realized the monuments of support he had within the community of young and older kids. He felt proud to be fearless in that instance. The sky darkened and grayed; the thunder rumbled as the storm rolled in but still a few miles out.

"Aw shit, we have to call it guys." Sticks said disappointed. David collected his equipment and loaded them onto his bike.

Sticks rushed to catch up to David, "Hey David, way to step up, man," he said, patting him on the back. "I don't know why that punk ass put on the façade of being tough, everyone knows if he wasn't Senator Collins's son, he would have disappeared off the boardwalk."

David picked his glasses up. He nodded acknowledging Sticks's kind words and pushed off, pedaling home shirtless. His jeans stained with dirt and grass; he missed the sound of Momma nagging him about wearing his good jeans. His heart felt heavier the closer he got to home.

Charles counted as streaks of lightning illuminated the sky, "One-one thousand... two-one thousand... three-one thousand... four-one thousand... five-one thousand." The cracking of thunder stopped his count. "See Chayanne, it's five miles out." he explained. They stood under the tin covering on Mr. Henry's porch. Mr. Henry asked Daddy permission for Chayanne to keep Charles occupied while he ran to the market. Daddy agreed to let Chayanne play, he needed a break; in addition, baby girl needed a distraction from her hospital visit. Daddy noticed the longer Momma stayed away, the harder it was to pull baby girl away. Charles and Chayanne watched the clouds get thicker as they rolled in, dimming the sunlight.

Chayanne sat on the porch, "Charles, come and sit with me." Chayanne patted a seat next to her. Charles looked uncomfortable as he stood close to the screen door. "Come on, I'm not going to bite you silly." she teased.

He frowned, "I can't... I can't sit down, my bottom hurts." he informed her close to tears.

Chayanne's face was befuddled as she navigated her mind to figure why his bottom was hurting. "Did Mr. Henry skin you with a switch?" she probed.

"I can't tell you… I won't tell you because… because I just can't okay." He opened the screen door aggressively letting it slam against the house.

He stamped, throwing a tantrum all the way to his room. Chayanne noticed Charles was a bit off from the day they first met; she didn't pay any mind because he had just lost his mother. She got up from her seat and followed him in the house, closing the screen door behind her.

Chayanne pushed through Charles's slightly opened bedroom door, "I didn't want to say anything, but you have an attitude." Her lips pursed out at him; she mimicked his behavior. "I'm your best friend… well I'm your only friend and you shouldn't be rude. I adopted you, you know." Charles laid on his stomach with his face buried into the pillow. "You can tell me anything, I don't understand why you're so secretive lately, gosh!"

Charles talked into the pillow; his voice muffled, "If I say anything he's going to hurt you and make you dead just like my momma. You're the only person I have in the world, and I can't lose you too. So drop it!" He pushed himself out of bed with his weak arms. "You know what, just go wait on the porch until he comes back. I don't want to play anymore." he rolled his eyes, crossing his arms, turning away from her.

She sat on the bed, "I'm not going anywhere! No one can make me dead but God, that's what Daddy tells me about Momma. You can't believe everything people say." she sassed him, "If you don't want to be friends anymore, fine, but don't make up lies."

He hesitated, "I'm afraid, I don't want to live here anymore."

"Yes, I got that you're afraid, but why?" Chayanne insisted he talk.

He began sobbing softly. "You wouldn't understand. I just miss my momma; I want her to come back. Why did she leave me, Chayanne?" He questioned, rubbing his wet eyes.

Her heart sank, she didn't have the answers. She wasn't prepared to experience the pain Charles felt if Momma died.

She embraced him; rubbing his back the way Momma did for her when she felt blue. "It'll be okay, we will figure it out. My Momma will be home soon to take you away from here. You will have a real mom again Charles, please don't cry." She sobbed with him unable to believe her own lie; she had no clue if momma would be home at all, then she too would need saving.

The rain poured fiercely; Uncle Anthony sat on his sofa in the darkness enjoying his whisky and the sound of the rain pattering against the house. The only light was from the rose of his cigarette tip, the rain soothed him, his mind opaque with worry. A light knock echoed through the front room, freezing him in mid-sip; he attempted to read his wristwatch, but he had no luck. He knew it was well past midnight; he walked through the back door half-past ten a couple hours prior. He shot up, worried it was James or one of the children to inform him his Evelyn took a turn for the worst. He adjusted himself, buttoning his shirt. He rushed to the door and swung it open with worry. Relief quickly found him and his face dully surprised when he noticed Rebecca. She stood—dolled up and drenched— with her hair wet and stringy. She could have just stepped off the runway if her left eye wasn't painted black and blue. She was shivering from the cold rain; Anthony stepped aside, allowing her in. He stepped onto the covered porch, surveying the pitch-black night to see if she was tailed. He took one last puff of his cigarette, flicking it into the yard. He sighed, exacerbated with her presence, and retreated into the house, closing the door quickly. He returned to his seat on the sofa; his glass of whisky rolling in his fingers.

He smacked his lips, "To what do I owe this lovely surprise?" he sardonically asked.

Rebecca trembling took a few pieces of the neatly stacked fired wood for the fireplace, "Where would you like for me to go, Red?" her irritancy was at its peak, "Most of the town thinks I'm a harlot. I don't have any friends remember; I gave that life up to be with you!" She was on edge;

she picked up his pack of lucky cigarettes off the coffee table, helping herself to a smoke. She threw the burning match onto the wood; the fire came alive, illuminating the room dancing.

Rebecca retrieved an empty glass and poured herself a double whiskey neat, "He beat the living shit out of me for looking at you the way I did in the station. It's fine, his fist doesn't have shit on my daddy's," she paused, taking a drag of the cigarette, "He thinks we're sleeping together, that I'm spread eagle for you every night. He's pulling a double shift. He said I ain't ever look at him with the intensity I look at you... I didn't marry to be put through the hell of my childhood. I swear, I will kill him dead if he puts hands on me again; I promised him that, and that's a promise I intend to keep!" She walked the room uneasy, gulping down the glass contents.

Anthony sat up; the light from the fire glowing on his face, "Yet, you come here, putting me and my family in danger. He threatened me while I was down at the station, making some sick pedophile comments about my Suga..." He paused, staring through her soul, "If he ever comes near my niece, I will kill that motherfucker!" His voice filled with so much vexation; his jaw clenched tightly."

He raised his glass, giving the floor back to her; he sipped the whiskey, enjoying the smooth burn while he listened.

Rebecca poured another glass, "I told him he was crazy to think I was sleeping with you. I know what that could expose your family to; I fight myself over my urges for you every night. I don't want us to be estranged, Red." she tapped her chin, "I explained to him how you're my only friend in this hellhole where he wanted to be! You're the only person that understands me for who I truly am. You treat me with the delicate desire and passion that every woman requires. You don't treat me like I'm some procession that can be controlled, manipulated, or sold. You better my existence, I feel like my purest self when I'm with you." she knocked the shot of whiskey back and went back to pacing franticly. She repeated herself, "Red, I'm gonna kill him, I swore it; that I would never be with a man that was anything like that bastard. Here I am, pretending to be a fucking housewife!"

The thunder sent vibrations through the house; the loud boom gave the impression the storm was ripping the sky in two. The lightning danced, teasing the thunder as it crackled again. That calmed Rebecca enough to make her sit.

The effects of the alcohol set in for her; her shivers disappeared as the firewood cackled in the fire. She grabbed the whisky bottle on the coffee table and helped herself to another, enjoying the way the first made her feel. Anthony slouched back onto the sofa; he let the sound of the rain calm him once again. Rebecca joined in listening, the rain was like a smooth jazz song with all the right notes. Rebecca put her cigarette out in the ashtray; she picked up on the vibe daintily sipping the whiskey like a lady should. She sat back on the couch, staring at the ceiling.

Anthony fiddled with his glass, finishing the last of his whiskey, "How'd you know where to find me?" he tapped her exposed knee with his middle finger.

She turned toward him, their gazes met, "I knew you could never sell your father's land. I guess it was a hunch. Some things will never change about you, and that's what I love most." she commented, fingering her strawberry blond hair that dried from the heat of the fire.

The whisky masked Rebecca's pain; it also gave her the courage to do what she yearned to do the moment she saw Anthony again.

She leaned over close to his face, her palm touching his cheek. She blinked her large blue eyes, staring into his soul. Her lips partly opened. She gently pulled his face, pressing her soft, plush lips into his; he coyly pulled away. Rebecca couldn't resist her urge any longer; she pulled herself onto his lap by his half-buttoned shirt. She straddled him, giving her dominance. He wasn't going to get away from her that easily. She cornered him, trapping him beneath her body and the sofa. She peered into his mind knowing exactly what he craved. She kissed him once more, gazing into his eyes; he could no longer resist her enticing foreplay. He indulged in her kiss, the softness of their tongues intertwined; it was a guilty pleasure. He wrapped his muscular arms around her, his large hands rested on her body. He pulled her into him, wanting all that he'd missed over the years in that instance. Lustrous passion filled the room, each of them drowning in one another's kiss. Rebecca ripped his shirt open, the buttons found a resting place on the floor. She roughly kissed his neck biting down softly; she wanted to unleash her built sexual frustration. Her tongue made a trail onto his exposed chest over his harden nipple, down to his torso, resting underneath his belly button. He hung his head back, aroused more and more with every flicker of her tongue. His erection growing, she felt his hardened bulge against her breast. She slowly kissed her way back to his mouth; her silky panties moist with her juices. She pulled him into her kisses passionately by the nape of his neck. With her free hand, she unbuckled his belt, unzipped his trousers, and unbuttoned them. His boxers exposed, she reached in, feeling him flesh to flesh. She stroked him—arousing him to full attention—he exhaled a moan onto his lips, satisfied with what she discovered.

She smiled, "I bet I know what you've missed most." she teased seductively. She seduced him with her words as she whispered a gentle breath into his ear. She planned to use the wetness inside her mouth to further coerce him to penetrate her, touching the place of pleasure buried deep inside her that only he could reach. She gathered herself like a composed dancer; she slid down his body like a pole. She pulled his clothes from underneath him exposing his well-toned thighs. She pressed the tip of his head against her lips; his eyes enlarged in anticipation. She rubbed his tip over her lips then lunged all of him into her throat, suckling every inch of him that went down. He tossed his head back, biting his knuckles as he gripped the sofa's cushion with the other hand. His body tensed and slowly relaxed, no one could satisfy his filthy needs the way she could. Rebecca worked her magic, reminding him of his addiction to her. His hips thrust, slowly pulling him in and out of her firm lips. The back of her throat is where he melted, it unraveled the most pleasure. His knees weakened, the euphoria overtook his body; she felt his orgasm nearing. His strong hands firmly griped the nape of her neck. She pulled away, dapping the excess wetness of her mouth with the back of her hand; she leisurely mounted him, pulling her panties to the side. She felt the tip of him pulsating for more, she enticed him more letting the tip rest against her opening; his hands tightly wrapped around her small waist, he wanted her to feel every inch of him. She slid down with ease, gasping loudly to catch her breath, he was much larger than she remembered. She slowly worked her hips grinding into him back and forth, then in circles. He was in sync with her rhythm. He bounced her lightly by her waist, wanting it a bit rougher. The longer he stared into her eyes, the more his old wounds perturbed. The pain she made him feel surfaced. He picked her up, still thrusting inside of her. He cleared the coffee table with his free hand and everything crashed to the floor; he placed her on the tabletop and tore her panties off. He wanted her to feel his power uninterrupted—his love, hurt, and lust for her in every stroke. He pushed inside her with force and their eyes locked; she could feel every heart-wrenching emotion he wanted her to. Tears escaped her eyes as she neared her climax. His hips churned; he pulled out just enough to tease her and thrust back in, leaving her breathless. She wrapped her legs around his waist and arched her back; he knew how to make her body moan for him.

"Don't stop... Don't stop... I want it, I want you." Her nails gripped deeply into his back, leaving track marks as he thrust in and out of her. "I love you Anthony... I'm sorry I left you... I'm sorry Anthony... I'm sorry," she cried in blissful pleasure as she exploded her silky creaminess covering him. "Oh, oh, oh Anthony... I love you... mmmh." Her moans filled the space, her legs trembled; her body quivering and shook uncontrollably as she orgasmed for a second time. Anthony's thighs smacked violently into her buttocks. His climax built quickly with the sound of her soft moans humming in his ear. She felt he was close; the familiar look in his eye that made her melt instantly gave her butterflies. A tear slipped for his eye as he pulsed and plunged into her wetness, giving it all he had. He attempted to pull out to ejaculate on the table, but she used her strong leg muscles to push him back inside of her throbbing wetness; he jerked and twitched exploding inside her. He came to rest on her bosom, his heart beating sporadically; he pushed up off the table collapsing back onto the sofa, exposed.

CHAPTER

10

EVERYONE IS DIFFERENT

Lilly ate her Mac and Cheese quietly, wondering what happened after Uncle Anthony and Rebecca had their grown-up talk. Chayanne stepped away to take a call from Mr. Dallas; Lilly overheard him saying the firm decided to pick up the Baxter's case for publicity. She sat there wondering what it was like to be in love. Uncle Anthony risked everything for Rebecca; it intrigued Lilly that the two never stopped loving each other after fifteen years but couldn't be together like normal people. She'd seen plenty of interracial couples, especially when Chayanne took her shopping at the mall for school. A stream of thoughts flowed through her mind; she couldn't wrap her head around the hatred white people carried for blacks. She couldn't comprehend how humans could consider other humans degrading because their skin was tan, but what bothered her most was the legality of blacks marrying whites. She stopped eating and spooned the cheesy noodles instead, she suddenly lost her appetite. She had a different feel for her Charles, since he appeared in the story; she never would have guessed his life was filled with tragedy and trauma the way he carried their lives present day. Her heart hurt for him. The wheels of her mind turned back the clock; Lilly followed Ashton's lead and decided to disown their father since he filed for divorce. Charles made several attempts to take Lilly for weekends shortly after. The first weekend, Lilly locked herself in her room, screaming at the top of her lungs,

"YOU FREAK! YOU'RE A FAGGOT! You'd be better off dead; you've disgraced our family." she exclaimed hastily, impersonating Ashton's points of view.

Her words were too much for his heart to handle; he tried eight weekends in a row, hoping she would have a change of heart.

During the court proceedings, the judge questioned the children over custody; both Ashton and Lilly requested Charles's visitation rights be terminated. Ashton again spearheaded their feelings; he believed that Charles's choice of lifestyle was unfit to raise them. The judge thought Ashton's words were harsh considering all that Charles provided for them. The judge considered the children's testimony and granted Charles every other weekend with supervised visitation. Charles had always been a good father, he wanted nothing more than to be involved in Ashton and Lilly's lives but they resented him. They didn't fully understand why he chose to leave the marriage.

Lilly retrieved the cordless phone from the kitchen wall; filled with sorrow, she returned to her seat at the breakfast counter. She slowly dialed Charles's house number. As the phone rang, she squeezed her eyes shut, hoping he wouldn't answer so she could leave a meaningful message on his machine.

"Hello, this is the Parker residence." An unfamiliar male's voice answered.

"Um, maybe I have the wrong number. You don't sound like my dad." Lilly said disheartened and relieved at the same time.

"Oh wait, is this Lilly?" the man asked surprised.

Lilly confused answered, "Yes, and you are?"

"I am Quentin, Charles's partner; your father is out right now, would you like to leave him a message?" he asked bubbly.

Lilly became irate, disconnecting the call; she had a lot of unresolved feelings for Charles and wanted to sort it out before she could accept someone new in his life.

Chayanne returned to the kitchen with a lingering worry from her call, "Hey honey, who are you on the phone with." Chayanne asked.

"Uh no one, wrong number." she lied. Lilly wanted to make certain she was ready to make amends with Charles without involving Chayanne. "Is everything alright at work? You were on the phone for a while." Lilly asked, combing through her long hair with her fingers awaiting an answer.

Chayanne blew a gust of air, "Yeah, I suppose." she twisted her mouth knowing that wasn't true.

She tried to reason with Mr. Dallas on the case; she didn't want to reveal that she'd received threats on her life about the case. She knew he wouldn't too much care; he was more concerned with the free promotion of the firm when they nailed the case with a W. He'd never spoken to the victim's mother or made plans to; Mr. Dallas wanted to capitalize off the misfortune of Miss. Baxter and was willing to exploit Chayanne to meet his bottom line. Chayanne traced the lines of the countertop vexed with her brewing emotions.

Chayanne played tug a war in her mind; she didn't want her feelings to pour unto Lilly's mood, "Are you feeling okay? You seem a bit off from when I left… you didn't even finish your lunch." she said, pointing to the full bowl of macaroni and cheese.

Lilly too played tug a war within, "Mommy…who's Quentin? He said he's dad's partner… does that mean business partner?" she needed clarification.

"Is that who was on the phone? He called looking for your father?" her perplexed look confirmed to Lilly that Chayanne was familiar with Quentin.

Lilly was unsatisfied with Chayanne response, "Mommy, who is he?"

Chayanne walked around the countertop sitting next to Lilly; she took Lilly's hands into hers, unsure how to explain Charles's choice to remarry.

Chayanne's mind briefly visited the day Charles came out to the children, weeks after he filed.

Chayanne thought for a second longer, "Hmmm, Quentin is your father's lover…" she paused, allowing Lilly to ask for clarification.

"Like Rebecca and Uncle Anthony?" her face bemused.

"Similarly enough, people don't want them to marry, just as much as they didn't want whites and blacks to marry. Charles's deals with a lot of scrutiny for his sexual preference. It's unfair treatment, mostly from those who aren't accepting." she braced herself for Lilly's reaction.

Lilly retorted, "I HATE HIM! He's ruining everything for our family." her lip quivered, "It's not fair, all the kids in my class parents are together, and I'm left out!" Chayanne rubbed Lilly's back until she calmed herself. She wanted her to feel free to express herself, unapologetically; it was important for Lilly to discover her feelings without influence. "I wish him dead, like his momma; that would be easier to explain than him loving another man. Kids are going to tease me if he shows up with him." Lilly turned flush in embarrassment, thinking of the kids in her class making fun and outcasting her like a leper.

A light bulb went off in Chayanne's mind, "Do you feel that is just to hate a person because of their skin color." Chayanne asked eagerly.

Lilly jumped to answer, "No, of course not!"

Chayanne nodded in agreeance, "So why is it fair to hate someone because they are different than everyone else? Their wants and needs are just a different color than your own, wouldn't you agree?"

Lilly sat quiet, Chayanne had a valid point, "Am I racist?" she murmured.

Chayanne held her laugh in, "That's not the proper word, but I'm happy you made that connection. Lilly, what do you think of your father? Forget about what Ash, all of the kids, and their parents think, what do you think of him?"

"I think he's a coward for leaving his responsibilities. I think he's not a man for leaving you, making you cry for months. I think he doesn't deserve you or us. I think his morals as a man are grotesque..." Chayanne gently pressed her index and middle finger to Lilly's lips to shush her.

Lilly's words played a familiar tune, "That's plagiarism, you're taking Ashton's words. Ashton sat at that dining table and spewed those same things. It isn't fair for you to plagiarize someone else's feelings for your own, so shall we start again?" Chayanne challenged.

Lilly thought about Charles for a moment, "I don't know what to think of him. He's always been a great dad until he decided not to be a dad anymore." her finger traced the gray lines on the countertop.

Chayanne nodded, she was making good progress, "Honey... you're father never decided not to be your dad; you decided that you didn't want to be his child because of his sexuality. You saw how much it hurt Ashton, so you mirrored your brother's feelings instead of finding your own. You have a mind and it's important as a black woman that you use it. You may think the world is on a silver platter for you, but it's not..." she inhaled deeply as she explained, "You sweetheart are a double minority, and it doesn't get any realer than that; you may think you have white privilege, but the world is cruel. You have to be twice as good as Mary-Elizabeth for someone to notice you, or your efforts. Most little black girls have never met their fathers; they grow up in single-mother homes attaching themselves to men that abuse them and belittle them; they follow patterns that their mother's set. You're fortunate enough to have a father that loves you, cares about you, and provides for you. You and your brother take that for granted; I see what the other side is like every day I step into that courtroom. I tried to protect you from the world, but instead, I've blinded you from the truth. I've never wanted you to see the things I've seen, live through, or share the pain that I have. I blame myself for being absent-minded with you after the divorce; instead, I showered you with gifts and pampered you because I wasn't mentally apt. Society wasn't built for us baby, it was built against us; we have to learn how to survive and thrive in systems that were designed to destroy us." Chayanne surprised herself with the courage she displayed to be honest with Lilly.

Chayanne was relieved she was undoing the damage she caused by being absent-minded. There wasn't a book written on how to parent a black child. Her confidence beamed, nailing one of the many lessons a child of color needed to learn.

Lilly began crying and climbed into her Chayanne's arms. She was overwhelmed at the thought of fighting daily just to belong or fit in. Her mother had never been more honest with her to the degree of that emotional gut-wrenching moment. Chayanne rocked Lilly, kissing her on the forehead and humming like she used to do when Momma was in pain. Lilly had a newfound respect for her; she admired her, although Charles hurt her to the core by leaving. She still demanded respect for him. Lilly thought it took tremendous strength to stand up for someone that wronged you. Lilly sniffled, wiping her eyes with the back of her hands; her mother's humming soothed her and filled the emptiness she felt inside.

Lilly's voice crackled, "Can you tell me more now mommy, please?"

She inhaled, smelling Lilly's freshly washed hair, "Sure honey." She responded continuing the story.

Tomorrow eventually turned into weeks for Chayanne every time she'd ask when Momma would be home. It was July already; they were well into summer vacation. Chayanne hadn't refused to speak to daddy. She was furious with his lies; she couldn't bear to hear tomorrow, as tomorrow never came and momma was still alone in the hospital.

Chayanne and Charles were playing Rummy with a deck of old cards she found under David's bed; the same place he kept all of his sexy magazines. This was her first time seeing Charles since he told her to leave his room. Chayanne stayed with Momma at the hospital from sunup to sundown; most days, she was exhausted from crying and couldn't muster enough energy to play. She slowly plummeted into a mild depression, not really eating or interacting much, not even with David. It felt good to feel the warm sun on her face. Sweat poured from her body reacting to the heat. She enjoyed the smell of fresh cut lawns.

Chayanne spread her cards, "RUMMY! I win again." She said with enthusiasm, rubbing her fifth victory in Charles's face.

He shook his head smiling, and he refused to admit defeat. "I let you win because I missed you." He pushed her arm gently, "Chayanne, I'm sorry I was so mean to you the last time I saw you." His eyes lowered to the cemented stoop, "I thought I lost you too because... He stopped coming in the night. I thought you told your daddy, I thought you'd figured out..." The truck approaching grabbed their attention. Daddy pulled into the driveway slowly; Momma was sleep in the passenger seat, slumped over on the window. Chayanne stopped dead in her tracts watching. Momma looked unrecognizable, most of her hair was gone and the patches she had were gray and unkempt; her skin washed out. Momma was lifeless and her energy was dim and dull. Daddy helped her from the truck as she struggled to walk on her own. She was too weak. Charles opened the screen door as they approached the house; Chayanne was frozen in disbelief; momma looked awful outside the hospital room. As momma passed Chayanne on the stoop, she reached out and caressed her face, smiling weakly.

"I'm so happy to be home, to finally wake up to your pretty face every day." Momma said softly, out of breath. Her and Daddy disappeared into the house; Charles shut the screen door softly behind them. Chayanne lowered her head, placing herself back in front of the card game.

Charles confused by Chayanne's lack of enthusiasm, "Are you not happy to see your momma home?" Charles asked joining her.

"I just realized how sick she is, that's all." She said with a low sorrowful tone. "She's just skin and bones." she crossed her legs Indian style and placed her chin in her palms.

"She's home now, so she must be getting better." He placed his hand on her arm. "It's going to be okay; I promise." She slightly smirked at his efforts to comfort her.

Chayanne changed the tune from her frivolous issues, "Have they found out who hurt your momma yet?" she changed the subject, not wanting to subdue to her overwhelming emotions.

"No, my uncle said the sheriff has a new lead, but no suspects yet. We have to go to the custody courts tomorrow. I can't get into school without some papers. My uncle said it was just another tactic to rob a black man of his education." He had an epiphany, "Maybe that's why he stopped." Chayanne looked at Charles's amused expression, trying to figure out who stopped what.

"All these codes you talk, just speak English; that's the only thing I know how to speak." she said, scratching her face from a mosquito bite.

"Chayanne, I will tell you later, I have to go get ready for court tomorrow." he said, bursting with energy as he leaped from the stoop into the grass, sprinting across the street. Chayanne set there watching him from a distance. She sat on the stoop until the streetlights started glowing like fireflies. She dreaded what she would discover if she went into the house.

11

UNSPEAKABLE ACTS

Chayanne awoke a little after 10:00 p.m. The bass in Anthony's raised voice vibrated the wall that neighbored the family room. He was upset with Daddy; she could hear Daddy trying to reason with him. Chayanne put her ear to the wall; their voices muffled. She quietly got out of bed and slightly opened her door to listen in.

"It doesn't make sense James, why would you bring her home away from her treatment?" his voice filled with conviction with maim running through his veins.

Daddy replied, "She wanted to be with the kids. She's tired of the hospital, Ant; you aren't there day in and day out. It's time for her to be comfortable." Daddy fought back.

"James, she needs to get better, she can't get that here. You can't afford an in-house nurse; I would know, I've been covering the hospital bills. You need to take her back!" Anthony demanded, drool hanging from his lips; he looked like a mad man.

"I can't do that... I won't do that, that's not what she wants." He responded, standing his ground peacefully.

Anthony shook his head side to side as he paced back and forth.

"Well, if you can't do it... I will. She's going back, kicking and screaming. I don't care anymore." The creek of Momma's bedroom door startled Chayanne. She jumped back in her room closing the door to a crack. Momma emerged from the shadows slowly, using all the strength she had.

"It's not nice to eavesdrop baby girl, if you want to be noticed and apart of the conversation insert yourself unforgivingly. It's better to ask for forgiveness than for permission." Momma smiled, knowing she was there; she used the walls to prop her up and help her get to the living area. She couldn't take the fussing between the two men she loved dearly; it was time for her to play peacekeeper. She made it to the edge of the hall; both men noticed her presence.

"Baby, what are you doing?" Daddy rushed to help her.

"Evelyn, you need to get back to bed, clearly there aren't any adults in this house for you to know better!" Anthony helped by grabbing the opposite side of her from daddy.

"SIT ME DOWN!" she demanded, using all the wind her one lung could carry.

Chayanne knew that tone and it meant business. She cracked her door open a little more.

The men placed momma on the sofa, "Baby girl, come on in here. You might as well have a say so, since everybody seems to know what's best."

Chayanne did what she was told, ascending from her bedroom. She stood nervously at the edge of the hall; she wanted to spectate and not deliberate.

Momma dapped the drool from her lip with her handkerchief, "Where is David? He needs to be here too." Momma requested.

David tiptoed pass Chayanne's her a little after nine; the house was resting. He'd snuck out quite a bit; Daddy was too occupied with his selfishness to notice. Chayanne stood quiet, she allowed Daddy to go to his room to discover what she already knew.

Daddy hurried back to the family room, "He's not here." Daddy said, looking surprised.

Anthony deliberated on Daddy's awareness, "This is too much for you to handle, James, the kids, and Evelyn. You have to go back Eve; this just proves my point." Momma raised her hand to silence Anthony.

Momma turned her head slightly looking over her shoulder at Chayanne, "Baby girl... where is your brother? I want you to think real carefully before you spit out a lie to me. I will not tolerate dishonesty in this state of health, just like I won't tolerate it on my best day, ya hear!" Chayanne looked around the room with her eyes bouncing from object to object, avoiding eye contact with the adults. Chayanne shrugged her shoulders, not wanting to get David in trouble. Momma grew impatient, "Cat got your tongue?" She pushed for an answer; Chayanne stood quietly staring at the floor, swinging her body nervously. "Well how about this; since you won't say, how about you take David's punishment for him. Go outside and get me a switch down." Momma said, waiting for her decision.

Chayanne got nervous, "Momma, I don't know where David is. I heard him sneak out, but I don't know where he goes at night." she answered honestly.

Momma looked Daddy in the eye and nodded her head, signaling him to take care of the problem. "Well, back to the matter at hand. I am tired of being a science experiment for those people at the hospital. I just don't have any more fight in me; if the good lord is ready to take me, so be it, but I refuse to lay down and die. I don't even believe the treatment to be working. I am worn out, waking up in the middle of the night to spit up the little that I ate; alone, with no family to comfort me. That's not how I picture my last days; if I'm going to go; I want to go in the comfort of my home. I am done taking the white man's treatment Anthony Reid Carter, and ain't a damn thang you or anyone else can do about it. You can't fight me on what's best for me; I know you scared to lose me, but you will always have me." Momma established her position very clear and firm. "I'm in my children, so ya'll best to start taking better care of them." she adjusted her headscarf, pulling her house robe snug.

Anthony upset, "So you're giving up, just like that? What about the kids, how do you expect them to live without a mother?" Anthony shot back; her reasoning was outlandish to him.

Momma was wheezed, "I could die walking out of the market, I could die in my sleep, and I could die whenever God decides, but what I decide to do with my time while I'm here is my business. You can choose to spend my last days bickering and holding a grudge; all that will do is leave you with is regret, not me, you. It'll soon eat away at you and God knows what else. This is how I am choosing to fight my battle; its mine to fight, alone. I'm the only one that is in constant pain and aching. Now, if you don't mind; I have grown weary and I am very tired. You done sucked all that I had out of me, Jesus," She excused herself, dissolving with the darkness. "James, you need to go and find my boy and bring his black ass home!" she commanded, shutting the door behind her. Daddy grabbed his hat, jacket, and keys and headed for the door. Anthony, hot, was on his tale, still filled with complaints.

"Please just convince her to get well James. This is unnatural for her to just give up. Dr. George said she was taking to the treatment just fine." he pleaded.

They climbed into the car and Anthony continued his rant. He was heard nagging him until Daddy pulled from the house. Chayanne watched wearily from the window; no one cared to explain in children's terms what was actually going on; was Momma better or not? She sat on the sofa and twilled her thumbs until they hypnotized her to sleep.

Daddy arrived home a few hours after he and Anthony departed. David wasn't in clear sight, wandering the streets in the colored parts of town where the nightlife came alive. They walked the strip, searching and questioning his whereabouts; no one knew where he could be. Daddy even went over to Sticks and still not a clue. His keys rattled in the keyhole stirring Chayanne in her sleep, but not waking her. He took notice of Chayanne asleep on the sofa and placed her in bed where she belonged. His melancholy sigh broke him; he sat in his rocking chair while the feeling of defeat clouded him. He sobbed quietly to himself as his world caved in on him one day at a time.

David crept around the side of the house as dawn swept in. He thought his absence went successfully unnoticed. The air felt sticky and humid and sweat dripped from his face. He ran home from the other side of town. He'd fallen asleep and lost track of time. Denise's mother was working the graveyard shift as she did once a week and he wanted to take advantage of their alone time, practicing his adult moves. He pulled the black milk crate as close to the house as he could and stood on it to give himself a boost into the window. He lifted himself quietly into the window; his feet hardly touched the floor. His eyes met Daddy's. Daddy sat on the edge of David's bed, waiting on his arrival. David's eyes enlarged, his heart pounding like djembes. Daddy's face was empty with emotion. He sat quietly, giving David the opportunity to explain. David, timid and afraid of daddy's actions, said nothing. Daddy shook his head in disgust, exiting David's room. David in dismay of Daddy's reaction, plopped down on the bed, panting in relief.

He lied awake not wanting to close his eyes in fear of daddy breaking down the door for his behind. He swallowed hard, not knowing what the day would bring.

The breakfast table was filled with clanking plates and loud crunches of bacon. Momma prepared breakfast, and everyone's heart filled with joy, enjoying the delicious meal. The house felt normal, although she'd only been home throughout the night. Daddy sipped his coffee; he hadn't said a word the entire morning. David brimmed with happiness; Momma's company meant her treatment was a success. Momma sat at the table, unable to eat a bite of food; the admiration of her family filled her in that instance. She permitted David some time to bask in her presence since she hadn't seen his face in months.

Momma dapped her mouth, "Where did you sneak off to last night and how long have you been doing it? David froze; he could barely swallow the food in his throat.

Daddy shifted, resting his right ankle on his left knee. David knew the ridicule was coming, but his defense was down as he inhaled Momma's cooking. The children hadn't had a decent meal since she'd been gone.

He gulped some orange juice, clearing his throat from derby, "I was at a friend's... They've been having a hard time since we discovered the body at the quarry; I just wanted to be there for them."

Momma dissatisfied with his answer, "If that were true, why be sly and sneak out?" she pressed, "Is it because you think you're a man— because you're committing the act of one?"

His eyes lowered to the table; he was ashamed Momma knew he was having sex. He refused to be dishonest with Momma so he nodded yes; unable to pick his eyes up to meet hers. Chayanne ate the rest of her breakfast in amusement wondering when the fireworks of punishment were to start.

"I figured that was the reason you missed a very important discussion last night; doing things you have no business doing at that age will lead to a lot of disappointments in life." she pursed her lips, rocking her body in the dining chair to subside the pain she was feeling. She directed Daddy for her pain medication. She was unable to speak, gasping to catch her breath; her breathing rhythm caught up; she sipped some water. "I need to go lie down for a while." Daddy helped her from the table, placing her into the bed. A feeling became apparent to Chayanne and David as they stared at one another across the table; momma wasn't getting better.

Early in the afternoon when the sun reached its highest peak, Charles appeared, disrupting Chayanne, who laid on a blanket in the front lawn reading. She was in search of solace within herself.

"Hey." He greeted her dryly—clumsily lying on her blanket, looking up at the sky.

She paused her reading to give him her attention. She knew he'd just arrived home from court; she vaguely noticed Mr. Henry pulling his old, beat-up pick-up truck into the driveway.

"How'd it go?" She asked, reaching for his hand. Their fingers intertwined and locked into one another.

Charles moaned unfavorably, "It was kind of weird, the lady took me into a room without my uncle and asked me if I was happy living with him?"

Chayanne's heart stopped, and she sat up to look Charles in his eye, "What did you tell her?"

"Well, last night, my Uncle Henry warned me what would happen if I was honest with her; that they would take me away and I would never see you again... It came down to choosing me or you." He rubbed his face; he sat up to meet her eye to eye. "I will always choose you; you're my best friend. You're the only good thing that's happened to me since my momma died."

They sat, hand and hand, "You're so unhappy with Mr. Henry, that's a lot at stake."

"I know, but it's something that has to be done." He squinted his right eye as the sun's rays met it. "He'll get his one day; when I'm big enough I will take care of him." he said with an evil look to follow.

"Why are you so angry at Mr. Henry? He seems like a nice man; he gives us treats." she remarked naïve of the truth.

Charles's breath shuttered; he closed his eyes tightly. "He comes into my room at night and does things to my private. He puts it in his mouth, he plays with it until it's empty." His body grew tense describing the things that were done, "The day my butt was hurt... he repeatedly jammed his finger in it until his private was emptied on my leg; my bottom was bleeding when I used the bathroom." A trail of tears made a journey to Charles's shirt. "He does all sorts of things to me. They make my stomach hurt; I puke my guts out every time."

Chayanne's mouth gaped in awe; she couldn't believe that Mr. Henry was perverted, but she knew Charles wouldn't lie to her. Her heart broke in two, Charles trusted her with his ugly truth.

Chayanne's imagination drifted, "Do you want to kill him?" she asked hesitantly, not wanting to know the real answer. "We can ask him to take us to the quarry to swim, then push him over the cliff."

Charles thought about Chayanne's plan for a moment, entertaining the idea of killing his uncle, "Then, where would I live? I can see it in your face that something is wrong, that your momma won't be able to save me like you promised. It's okay though; I know she would if she was better."

Chayanne removed her hands out of his and laid on her stomach, playing with a blade of grass. "Well, it was a lot of fuss over Momma being home last night. I didn't know what it meant, but today after she made breakfast, she could hardly speak without losing a lung from coughing. I know whatever the grownups were talking about yesterday was bad, real bad. My Uncle Anthony was really upset with my daddy."

she pulled another blade of grass, playing with it in her fingers. "I'm sorry that Mr. Henry is hurting you, I want to help you take care of him. We don't have to wait until we get bigger to do it." Before those words slipped from her lips, Charles had a plan.

12

STRANGE FRUIT

The dial to the car radio clicked off; Anthony was unable to bear the news any longer, the death of Medgar Evers was just announced. He sat there in his car outside the bank, spiritless on Wednesday evening. Any black man wanting to make a change had a target on his back. His stomach turned over uneasy, making him nauseous. He'd spoken to Edgar weeks before his death, the day he made his yearly contribution. He peaked his head outside the car door, regurgitating his breakfast, which was the only thing he'd eaten that day. He took his white handkerchief dapping his mouth. Anthony sat numb, incapable of gathering his emotions. He imagined Medgar's body lying cold in the morgue; the hairs on the back of Anthony's neck stood up, the surface of his skin tingled. Something wasn't sitting right within. He started the car, it idled just like his heart. He pulled away slowly, heading to visit with his sister.

Momma and Daddy sat on the sofa; Chayanne and Charles laid on their bellies passing notes in front of the black and white television, barely listening in on the events surrounding Medgar Evers. David hadn't been home since the sun peaked its head through the clouds. Daddy and Momma were in a heated debate; they had opposing views on how the courts would prosecute the man that shot Medgar. Uncle Anthony strolled through the door with the smell of death greeting his nostrils. Momma been home for a week and death made itself known more each day. The air sour and unpleasant, Anthony stepped back onto the stoop for fresh air. He coughed to clear his passages. Chayanne and Charles joined him on the stoop, not discerning themselves with Anthony. They were consumed in Charles's plan to rid the world of the pedophile, Mr. Henry.

Chayanne distracted by the coughing, "Uncle Anthony, are you alright? Are you getting sick like Momma?" Chayanne asked with a frown on her face, looking him over long and hard.

Anthony replied with tears in his eyes from coughing so hard, "No Suga, I'm just catching my breath. A lot has happened today." his face surprised that she was immune to the smell.

Charles concerned, looked him over and asked, "Are you sure? Your face looks like you had a meeting with the dead."

"How ironic, I was thanking the same thing, Charles." Chayanne chimed in.

Anthony sat on the stoop; his emotions outweighed his body. "Where's David? I knew for sure he would be tuned into the Medgar Evers talk."

Chayanne looked away, "Well, he hasn't been home all day. Daddy's been looking for him. Momma is worried; he's been sneaking out to see some girl." she shrugged.

Anthony stood and stormed into the house, "What in the hell is going on around here? Why am I never consulted when things go awry?

How long has the boy been missing?" Momma stopped mid-sentence, she gave her undivided attention to Anthony.

"You were a young boy once... may I remind you of Rebecca Sooner who you would go weeks missing for? I don't think we have to be alarmed just yet. He knows I'm dying, hell, the stench alone tells you that. How do you figure a boy should handle that?"

Anthony kissed his teeth, "God damnit Evelyn, don't you see what the hell is going on around you?" Anthony replied incandescently, "They are out here lynching us with bullets and you let the boy disappear. Hell, his daddy should be teaching him how to deal since he pulled you from the doctor's care!"

Daddy rose from the comforts of the sofa, "Anthony... I beg you, watch your tone. We may have differences, but there is no need for them to divide us; not during times like these." He adjusted his pants, "Please don't disrespect me in my home, in front of my wife, and while my children are in earshot." Daddy said calmly. Momma grabbed at Daddy's side striving to defuse the situation between the two men, once again.

"Well now, dammit James, you don't seem that bright to me in light of all this, now. You let your children run wild; you should have punished him the night we had to go searching for him near the promenade. If you were present a little more often, maybe the boy wouldn't be a lose fucking cannon!" Daddy's lips pursed and his head bobbed. Anthony still hadn't struck the right nerve to invoke Daddy to act out of character.

"Anthony, I beg your pardon! James is a good father to those children and there is no need for you to try and challenge him. It's clear, you're just as upset about Medgar and you fearing what will happen to us blacks in the midst of his death, but I will not tolerate you speaking to James in that manner." Momma barked from the sofa too weak to stand, but she still had fight in her.

"See James, that's another problem right there… You let your woman fight your battles instead of being a man and standing up for your own. No wonder the Collins boys put a knot upside David's head every week. If I had a father as weak as you, I'd be half the man you are standing here. No wonder David is so troubled; he might need to come stay with me for a while since he ain't really got a daddy to show him how to be a man!" Anthony huffed his chest out, picking a fight with Daddy; he was the kind of man that didn't know how to properly deal with his emotions or grasp what he felt at the moment.

Daddy reared toward Anthony; he was finally drawn in. Anthony's provocative words cut deep. Anthony stood his ground, not flinching a muscle; he would finally feel something else other than internal pain; the kind no medicine known to coloreds could cure.

Daddy reared back to take a swing… The loud thud on the screen door drew him out of his fit. Sticks tripped over the last step at the top of the stoop; he ran headfirst into the screen, causing the weak tin to dent.

He gathered himself dizzy, barely standing, " They got David, they have him and they are going to kill him!" Daddy and Anthony jumped in unison to grab the door handle. Sticks was out of breath; he was drenched in sweat. He'd rode his bike as fast as the pedals could stand from the quarry to summon them for help.

Anthony grabbed Sticks, helping him find his balance, "Who has him? Twigs, what in the damn hell is going on?" Anthony asked, trembling in his skin.

Sticks panted, attaining his breath; "The Collin's two youngest boys have him. They are convinced David went to the sheriff about Miss. Parker, the dead lady he found at the quarry. David saw Dougie with her at the promenade that night; he was drunk, pulling on her, and smacking her with his fist. David knew they were sleeping together in secrecy. He was giving the lady money like she was a nightwalker. Now Dougie is in lock up, the sheriff is questioning him, and they are all convinced David told." he paused to catch his breath. "The Collins and some of the Varsity team is wailing on David; you can barely recognize his…"

Uncle Anthony flew off the stoop like he had wings attached to his back; "Twigs, show me! Get in the car and show me where they are!" He demanded without an ounce of fear in his voice. Sticks ran down the steps, hopping in the car with Anthony. Daddy hopped in the truck to follow behind. Momma watched from the living room window with her heart pounding. Chayanne and Charles mouths open in awe, quavering uncontrollably. A stream of warm urine trickled down Charles's legs; his eyes blurred and burned as tears met his cheeks.

Momma prayed quietly; she asked the lord to take her life instead. She wanted to bargain, knowing she wouldn't be courageous enough to bury her child, if necessary. She begged for mercy and forgiveness as she asked the lord to take her. Chayanne and Charles watched from the doorway; they'd wandered inside to ask Momma for clarity. Chayanne, in denial, heard the truth from momma's mouth, confirming her illness hadn't banished. She realized Momma was dying and couldn't be strong for anyone anymore, not even herself. Chayanne's misery and grief burden her; Momma felt her and she looked up, catching a glimpse of her before she vanished out the door and into the night. Charles ran in stride with her to find comfort in one another.

The tires screeched; the car slid in the dirt as it came to a halt. Anthony leaped from the car, still in motion. The headlights of Anthony's car beamed on David's naked body that swung from the strong tree branch; his legs kicked while he dangled, trying to free himself for air. The noose tightened with every attempt. His eyes were puffy and swollen shut. His face was bloody from his nose. A gash sat above his right eye. His body swayed, almost lifeless.

Uncle Anthony reached for his pocketknife; cutting the twine that was braided into the thick rope, "DAVID... DAVID, I'M HERE FOR YOU!!! HANG ON. DON'T YOU DIE ON ME, MAN... DON'T YOU DIE ON ME, YOU CAN'T DIE ON ME." he expressed through his tears, pouring from his soul. His heart galloping out his chest. David's body dropped from the branch; Daddy swooped in, catching him before his body hit the ground. Daddy was more frantic than Anthony. He had difficulty removing the rope from David's neck; his breath shallow.

"COME ON JAMES, SNAP OUT OF IT! WE NEED TO GET HIM TO THE HOSPITAL!" Anthony screamed, jerking David from Daddy's arms, knocking him over. He rushed him to the backseat of the car. "Twigs, hold his head, talk to him, and don't let him sleep." He jumped in the driver seat and floored it. The dirt spat out from underneath the rear tires. They spun until gaining traction and they sped off. Anthony hit eighty down the dirt roads.

Daddy was left behind on his knees in a pool of David's blood under the truck's light. He struggled with his sanity; his fist balled ready for war.

Chayanne and Charles climbed into the treehouse that sat in Mr. Henry's backyard; the family that inhabited the space before Mr. Henry had built it. It had become their recent hangout since conspiring a plan to rid Charles of Mr. Henry. Chayanne curled up into a ball and sobbed, unable to focus on Charles's pain. Charles found his favorite corner; he rocked himself crying silently—his mind fragile.

He knew his momma had a different boyfriend every night. The name Dougie shot chills up his spine and goosebumps all over his body. He would visit Momma often and he was by far her favorite boyfriend; Charles knew the way Dougie looked at his momma, he was head over heels for her; it reminded him of the way he was with Chayanne. Dougie would often go on a drunken rage—becoming violently jealous when he found Momma snuggled up with other boyfriends. Charles couldn't fathom that Dougie would be the one who made his momma sleep forever. Charles came too when Chayanne's sobs grew louder; he spooned her on the old wooden floorboards that creaked and smelled moldy. He placed his arm underneath his head and the other over Chayanne's body.

He rubbed her hair gently, coddling her, "Shhh, it's okay, don't cry. Everything is going to be okay; we can fix it." Chayanne's heart was lodged in her throat and she was unable to convey her hurt to him. She continued sobbing until the sun broke the clouds for dawn, sending a harmonizing ray of hues throughout the sky. Her eyes puffy from the tears, her eyelids drew a heavy shade. She found comfort in Charles's light snore. She dozed off to sleep, where her distress didn't exist.

WHITE LIES

The sirens wailed in the distance and amplified as the ambulance approached. Chayanne peaked out the treehouse window, following the truck through the grid of the neighborhood. She was still missing from the night before. Charles climbed down five minutes earlier to freshen up his piss-stained clothes and prepare sandwiches for lunch.

Chayanne was confused, as more turmoil built inside her; she felt a seed of resentment being planted for Momma and Daddy. She sided with most of Anthony's progressive viewpoints on the operation of life. The ambulance finally came to rest in front of her residence; she watched from a bird's eye view as two medics wheeled Momma from the house. She held Daddy's hand and conversed with him. Momma fainted when she heard the gory details of David's dangling body. At first, Chayanne felt compelled to climb down and poke around for information. She was curious and needed an update on David, but she refused to give her hiding spot away. She watched the lights twirl as they drove away with Momma. Daddy stood in the yard, watching the truck disappear as fast as it came; he removed his hat, scratching his head. He took a small whiskey bottle from his back pocket and took a long, hard sip to subdue his rattled nerves. He took his folded blue bandana from his other pocket, dabbing his forehead from sweat. He walked toward Mr. Henry's house in search for his daughter. Chayanne crouched down in the tree house, hoping she wasn't spotted. Her face tuned in anger; she pulled her knees into her chest, sitting still. Daddy skipped the front door when he saw Charles running outback. He walked around the house.

Daddy whistled, "Hey little man, have you seen my baby girl? She's been missing and we have to go over to the hospital, her momma and brother are there." Daddy's eyes were bloodshot; he reeked of booze.

Charles stopped dead in his tracks; he knew how upset Chayanne was, "No Mr. Rice, I thought she was home. I was waiting for her to come out and play. Are you sure she's not hiding in the house?" he fibbed, hoping he lured him away from the house.

Daddy scratched his head in confusion. "Her momma said she ran out the house with you last night, when all the commotion was going on." Daddy's words jumbled and slurred.

"Yes sir, that is true, however, Chayanne left a little while after we ran off; she said she was going home and would see me today."

"Alright, if you see her, tell her to call Momma's hospital work number. It's a lot of strange things going on around town." He stumbled away back across the road into his truck. Charles waited until he pulled away and disappeared. Charles climbed the tree with a knapsack full of goodies in between his teeth.

Uncle Anthony stood guard outside of David's hospital room. He was sweating profusely; the flashbacks of David's body swaying haunted him. Dr. George, fortunately, stabilized David. Anthony's hands lodged deep in his pockets. His left hand caressed his pocketknife; he was ready to kill. His hair sweated out and his clothes were stained with blood and splotches of dirt. Fresh coffee stain on his trousers, he dropped his cup when he saw Evelyn being wheeled in. She calmed him from a distance; she explained that she fainted bumping her head on the kitchen counter. Evelyn ensured him she was okay and that she needed him to stay put with David. Anthony—trembling like a leaf in a windstorm—stepped into David's room to be certain that the machines beeped continuously; his life depended on them. The breathing tube was lodged into his throat to ensure he got enough air; he was fortunate that his larynx didn't collapse when they strung him up to the branch. His neck was bandaged from the deep lacerations the rope caused while his left hand rested in a cast. Sticks said they used a bat to crush it. They'd hoped to end his pitching career for the upcoming season. He had twenty-eight stitches in the gash above his eye, both eyes blackened and swollen shut. Dr. George said it was a miracle they'd gotten him there in the nick of time; David was seconds away from DOA status. Anthony's lip quaked uncontrollably as his eyes bounced from injury to injury; he wanted to kill the boys that were so brutal and unkind, he knew hatred was deeply embedded in the towns DNA. He slouched down against the wall. His eyes were red from the tears, lack of sleep, and stress. His body was tired and weary, but he had to be strong for everyone; they all seemed to be unraveling.

Sticks slept in the waiting area; his lanky body stretched out over three chairs. His arms were tucked in his shirt for warmth. Two deputies approached him giggling amongst one another. One of the deputies took out his club and jabbed it into Sticks' body.

"Hey boy, wakie, wakie!" he demanded, still jabbing at him. Sticks groaned in pain, falling to the floor half asleep. He smugly looked up into the deputy's face. "Who the hell you eyeing, boy?" The deputy swung the club into the side of Sticks' face. The impact of the club sent Sticks' head in the opposite direction; blood splattered onto the white walls and gushed unto the tiled floor from his mouth. "Now, we hear you have a statement to make about the Collins boys, is that true?" Sticks held his hand up, asking for a moment to gather himself to speak. "We can't hear ya, boy!" Sticks eyes searched the room before he spoke, no escape route in sight.

"Please sir, I would like to make a statement involving Ricky Collins, Timmy Collins, and some of the varsity baseball team. I am sorry I upset you for sleeping." Sticks pleaded on his knees, still bleeding out. The second officer kicked him, causing him to fall on his chest. He kicked Sticks in the side once more.

"Deputy Dickens, I don't think this nigger received your message with the nightstick. How about we throw this son of a bitch in the wagon and teach him what happens to niggers that talk out of turn." the deputy said rowdily, intimidating Sticks.

Officer Dickens crouched down, "Listen hear you fucking tar piece of shit, you ain't see nothin or hear nothin. If we so much hear you fixed your filthy nigger pie hole to speak about the Collins, we sure gone fix you good. We're going to pay a visit to your mammies house and burn that som-a-bitch to the ground." he spat his tobacco juices in Sticks' face. Both deputies laughed in unison, as they exited the hospital. The nurse watched the incident through the sliding glass an recorded the officers' threats on her patient's pocket recorder. She planned to use it for reference. As the officers cleared her line of sight, she rushed, calling for a doctor to help the poor boy.

Daddy visited the liquor store, buying himself another bottle of whiskey. He chose to self-medicate to deal with the issues life threw at him. He visited his best friend Peter, a white man who ran the butcher shop in the colored part of town near the promenade.

"Welcome to Chops…" his words fell deaf, as he saw the well-respected James Rice stumble into his shop, unable to stand. Peter scrambled to Daddy's side, aiding him to stand. He flipped the open sign closed and locked the shop doors. He dragged Daddy's limp body back into his office, placing him in a chair. Daddy sat upright long enough for Peter to fetch him some water. He drank the water willingly, falling into a dizzy spiral, fading into darkness.

Daddy awoke and the sun was going down. Peter sat across from him, waiting patiently.

Peter ticked away at his calculator under the small lamp on his desk, "James, what's going on? Over the eighteen years I've known you, I've never seen you down a bottle; you have enough respect for yourself to go on and do that. Talk to me, brother." he requested, pushing his silver-rimmed glasses up his nose.

Daddy's throat dry, he spoke with difficulty, "I need a box of twelve-gauge shells." He adjusted upright into the seat, swallowing his saliva, trying to lubricate his vocal cords. He grabbed the cup of water from the desk, finishing it in one big gulp. "Ahhh!" he said, sounding revived from the murky shadows of the dead, "I sawed-off my shotgun, I just need more ammo. I have a bullet for every last one of those crackers that hurt David."

Peter confused, scratched his head full of hair, "James, what in Jesus' name are you talking about?"

Daddy cupped his head with both his hands, "It'll never reach the papers, Pete. You know good and well most of our news is word of mouth. They been harming and killing us black folk for years, it is never publicized because it's like going hunting for game; it's just like killing a damn buck and putting it on the mantel for show. I'm sure you haven't even gotten wind of the Parker lady..." he sighed frustrated, "Them damn Collins's boys strung up David to a poplar tree down by the marsh of the quarry. They beat the shit out of em." he sobbed as a picture of David's bloody, naked body flashed in his mind. "I'm tired of sitting around like a duck, waiting for them to kills us off. I have to protect mine Pete, and Martin's theory ain't savin us. I have to rid of this threat, I'd rather be the one dying, knowing my family is safe."

Peter was in disbelief. David's story didn't make the morning papers; he knew the word would soon travel spreading like wildfire and send the colored part of town in an uproar.

He sighed reaching for his bottom desk drawer to retrieve the shells Daddy requested, "James, I'd be a fool not to warn you what this will cause. I need you to think of Evelyn and Chayanne, you playing right into the hands of the crooked laws by taking justice into your own. You need to be careful; think long and hard on this. Think of how much your ladies are going to need you. You killing off those boys aren't changing the unjust ways of the judicial system, nor the constitution that these racist motherfuckers built the country on. Making change is bigger than squeezing that trigger; it's better than a short-lived victory. You kill them off and there will always be another white man with his knee on David's neck, slowly denying him of his human right to breathe. This is bigger than that brother; we need to stand together in battle. The tide is slowly changing; don't give them the satisfaction to kill another black man." Peter placed two packages of shells in Daddy's hands; he gripped them tightly, drawing Daddy's eyes to his. He hoped his words got through to him.

Chayanne enjoyed her ham sandwich; Charles and her didn't exchange many words; they both were trapped in their mental prisons, navigating through the truths they witnessed. Chayanne finished and climbed down the boards embedded into the sycamore's sides. Charles peaked through the doorway, watching her climb down. She leaped, not touching the last three boards and landing upright on her feet. She looked up at him, waived and ran home to bathe. She wished she could wash what she knew away. She was much more tranquil being blissfully ignorant to the adult's lives that seemed to pull her under like quicksand. She entered the house, happy to be alone. The phone rang out, crying for attention. She hesitated to answer, thinking Momma or Daddy was calling to check on her whereabouts, but she answered anyway.

"Hello, this is the Carter..."

"Tell your coon boy to keep his mouth shut or we will shut it for him, permanently." An unknown voice said, followed by a scream, hurting Chayanne's eardrums. She dropped the phone and stepped back; it wasn't until she heard the dial tone that she felt safe enough to hang it back on the base. She shook her head in disgust; she hated when people picked on David.

She turned the faucet knobs, watching the tub fill with water. She swirled her hand back and forth, helping mix the hot and cold together.

She removed her worn clothing and stepped into the steaming water, wincing. She adjusted the temperature and submerged herself while holding her breath. She opened her eyes, peering through the clear waters.

CHAPTER

14

FRIEND OR FOE

The day was spread out, filled with unruly heat waves. Chayanne woke in a pool of sweat; she sprung out of bed, nervous that she'd pissed herself. She soon realized her nightgown wasn't stained yellow. She propped her window open with the boxed fan, turning it up high. The gushing wind blew her long, curly hair and gown. She pranced around the room like she was Miss. Marilyn Monroe.

It was the third day Momma and David were in the hospital; Daddy was nowhere to be found; he hadn't turned up since she spotted him from the treehouse. She moved through the house pretending she was an adult and answered to no one. Charles came by daily to keep her company; he brought her leftovers so she didn't starve. Mr. Henry was a better cook than Daddy. The death threats for David increased as the days went on, but she disregarded them. Sometimes, she'd take the phone off the hook for hours and forget to put it back on. This was disturbing, because when momma called, she couldn't get through. Momma begged Anthony to go to the house, but he refused to leave David's side. He assumed that James was taking care of his Suga, as a father should. He thought at any second, James would tote Chayanne through the hospital doors, putting both Evelyn and his mind at ease. The analog clock ticked loudly; he was unable to free himself from watching the time.

A high pitch rang in Anthony's ears, he hadn't slept or eaten much for that matter. David got stronger by the day, and Anthony felt his strength slipping away. The chair he'd been glued to became uncomfortable. Midday rolled around and he decided to ring James. Anthony was puzzled as to why he wouldn't check on his family.

The phone rang and rang and he prepared to hang up, "Will you please stop calling here, no one here cares. You hate black folks, we living and breathing just like you! We even bleed the same color, if you call here and threaten my brother one more time… I'm going to find you and…"

Anthony ghastly to Chayanne words, "Suga, what in the world is going on?" Anthony interrupted.

Chayanne changed her tune when she heard his voice, "Hello, this is the Carter-Rice residence, how may I help you?" she laughed maliciously on the other end.

"No…no, you don't pretend with me young lady, what is going on?" he demanded answers.

She covered the phone and laughed loudly, "I've been taking care of myself. I'm an adult now, no one has been here for three days; you're the first to call to check on me. Ugh, these stupid clowns keep calling saying they're going to kill David, Momma, Daddy and all that nonsense. Honey, I'm just tired of the phone ringing nonstop." she imitated Momma on the phone, gossiping with her church friends.

Anthony tried to shake the sleep to make sure he was following her, "Suga, are you sure James hasn't been home?" he asked persistently.

"Like I said, he ain't been here. The last time I saw him he said bye to Momma in the ambulance. He pulled something covered in an old, oily tattered rag from the tool shed on the side of the house. He got into his truck and drove off. He abandoned me like Charles's momma did, but I ain't mad. You said he wasn't even half a man, ummhum, I heard you the night you rushed out to get David… How is he by the way? No one tells me anything around here." she pursed her lips with a smile on her face and her hand on her hip; she had Momma down to a science.

Anthony tried not to laugh to antagonize her impressions, "Suga, I need to come and get you. It's not safe for you to be in the house alone with all those death threats… Listen to me carefully, you are in danger; go to Charles's house and wait there for me. I am sorry that you've been there alone. I've missed you and everything is going to be okay, I promise." He attempted to appeal to the things she was missing lately.

"Lawd honey child, I am far from scared of them crackers calling here." She smacked her lips. "If you tell me where to find them dog on keys to the tool shed; I can get my bike and ride down to the hospital myself." she replied pleasantly, how she always did when she wanted her way.

Anthony covered his laugh, "Baby girl, please go to Charles's and stay put. I will be there as soon as I can." he pleaded with her, "If you do as I say, I will give you… fifty dollars and I will take you to get an ice cream cone on Saturday. What do ya say?"

She put on her business face, "Um, give me a second to think this over Mr. Carter." she said, imitating Anthony when he'd talk business over the phone at the bank. She only saw a fifty-dollar bill in the bank vault; the offer was very enticing, but she had to raise the stakes. "I will take the fifty, but I also want you to purchase five dollars' worth of penny candy for my stash; Jesus knows I've been out for months now. I want two scoops of ice cream, and you have to promise to get me from Mr. Henry's tonight… He gets weird after the lights go out and I just ain't got time for that, honey. I will die a virgin." she said snapping her fingers.

Uncle Anthony screwed his face, what in the hell is she talking about, he thought, "Well Miss. Carter-Rice, I think you drive a hard bargain, but you have a deal. ONLY, if you go as soon as we get off the phone. Write Mommas work number down. When you get to Mr. Henry's, call the hospital and ask for room 307. Do you understand?"

"Yesum, I suppose I do." She hung up the phone and followed orders. She wrote the phone number and room number down on a note pad Momma kept next to the phone.

"Charles, come on here honey. We have to go to Mr. Henry's; some bad stuff is going on chile, and we can't be here when the shit hits the fan." Charles, unclear of what was happening, jumped up following Chayanne out the door and across the street to his house.

Anthony tapped his leg as a distraction while he waited for Chayanne to call; he fought to keep his eyes open.

THUMP! Uncle Anthony shook the sleep off of him—grabbing his pocketknife and switching the sharp eight-inch stainless-steel blade out; the light gleamed on it. He crouched back in a stance, ready to pounce. The door opened slowly; Momma wheeled through the door in her wheelchair. She ran into the door, struggling to get it open. She hadn't quite got used to how they worked.

Momma wheeled herself in, "Anthony if you don't put that thing away, you're going to hurt yourself." she hissed.

He relaxed his tension, folding the blade back into the knife when he heard her voice. He sat back in his chair eyeing the phone.

She took notice, "Why you sizing up the phone like it's one of your women?" she teased.

He chuckled, "I'm waiting on Suga to call me back. I gave her clear instructions."

"You got through, oh thank you, Jesus!" She rolled her chair close to the phone, eyeing it waiting for it to ring. "Are they okay? I haven't heard from James in days now. This ain't like him." She held her breath, for gruesome thoughts that led her mind astray."

The telephone rang; Anthony snatched answered faster than lightning.

"Hello...Hello?" He said impatiently.

"Yes, hello, this is Henry Miller, I have Chayanne in my care. She's requesting me to drive her to the hospital. I'm just calling to confirm."

He was relieved, "Yes Mr. Henry, if you don't mind, I will pay you for your troubles. We haven't been able to leave the hospital and we didn't know that she was home alone all this time." Momma's face tensed, she grabbed for the phone. Anthony fought her off with his free hand.

"Yesum, no problem sir, I'll bring her down right away." he said disconnecting the call.

"Whew, what a relief." Uncle Anthony sat back in the chair—flopping his arms to his sides letting them dangle—his knuckles grazing the tile. He didn't pay Momma's angry face much mind.

She poked at him with her index finger, "You mind telling me what the hell is going on with my child at my house?"

Anthony smirked like a sly fox, "Well Evelyn, that's how it feels to be left out; you're finally getting a taste of your own medicine. You can ask Suga all the questions you want when she gets here. That husband of yours left poor Suga alone for three days now." he shook his head having the last laugh. That's all I'm going to say, for now." He clasped his hands on his stomach and closed his tired eyes.

Momma knew Ant was right, "Oh Anthony Carter, you go to hell being petty like that." She chuckled, relieved to know that Chayanne was enroute. She wheeled herself closer to David's side—he laid unresponsive—the monitors beeping. The swelling in his eyes had gone down a bit, thanks to Anthony icing them every few hours. She groaned, imagining the pain he felt; she regretted telling him not to fight back. She cupped his hand in hers and hummed the song she used to when he fussed as a baby.

Anthony sought an opportunity, "Evelyn, I need to go change and get some food in my stomach. DO NOT leave this boys side. He's been getting all kinds of death threats at the house." He looked at his wristwatch, "It's about a quarter till three, give me until five and I'll be back."

"Death threats?" she asked, confirming she heard him right.

Anthony shook his head, "Just don't leave him, no matter what anyone comes in this room and say to you. You don't leave him until I get back."

Momma nodded. Anthony exited the room, surveying the halls; he strolled casually down to the nurse's station in search of his ally. He approached with a heap of confidence in his stride.

"Hey darlin, did you take care of what I asked?" he flashed his charming smile.

She blushed and fluttered her eyes, "Well of course, Red, did you think I would let you down?"

"That didn't cross my mind for one second, honey, I promise." He assured her, tracing her small, petite, manicured hand with his index finger.

She handed over the tape recording; Anthony knew how the law worked and he needed insurance that things would be handled in the right light.

"How's Twigs, he holding up okay?"

She laughed, "His name is Sticks, yes he did just like you told him, he sure didn't back down. I don't know what you giving these children to think you're some kind of superhero, I know whatever it is, I need some."

"Twigs or Sticks, hell its all the same for that matter. I'm glad he's doing okay. Did you call his mother and let her know to go down to the station and file a complaint?" he pressed his lips on the palm of her hand.

"My, my, my Anthony, are you this curious in bed when you're trying to please a woman?" she squirmed in her chair. "Yes, I did as you asked. Now go on and get I have work to do." She smiled flirtatiously as she twirled her hair. He returned a tom-cat grin and headed out of the exit door.

THE TRUTH HURTS

Anthony made it home in one piece. The attempted lynching on David, a rising youth baseball star, made the daily papers headline published by an anonymous journalist. The streets flooded with mobs of angry coloreds. The town's Mayor got wind and was up the sheriff's ass with a microscope. A copy of the waiting room tape recording made it on the mayor's desk in an unmarked manila envelope.

Anthony pulled his car around back; he didn't want anyone bothering him in the few minutes of peace he bargained for himself. He jingled his keys in his hand, bouncing them around in search of his door key. A small draft of wind pushed it open to a crack. He looked at the mud to study the footprints of those who'd come and gone. Nothing stood out to him, so he retraced his steps backward, down the small set of wooden steps.

"Dag on it, I forgot something in the car!" he said aloud to distract the uninvited guest. He watched the rear windows for movement and snuck into the worn-down garage that sat in the back of the house. The garage housed his father's tools; he neatly organized them. It was damp, dark, and smelled of rotting wood; it needed to be rebuilt before winter set in. Anthony reached under his father's old pickup, retrieving the Ruger-hunting rifle. Anthony cocked it; he reached into the tool bed grabbing the shells. He loaded it—his head on a swivel. He draped an old jacket from the truck over the gun to conceal its existence. He peaked out from the shed; no one was in the line of sight of the windows. Anthony walked to the car and opened and closed the door. He walked the small set of steps and entered the house. He listened attentively for a creak in the floorboards. Anthony heard the draft entering through the cracks in the floor; he meticulously placed his footing to move through the house. He knew what boards creaked and which ones didn't; it was his make-shift alarm system he'd learned as a boy. He smelled sulfur from a match that was struck; cigarette smoke lingered into his nostrils; a woman's scent greeted him warmly. He moved cautiously toward the bedroom. Her long legs glimmered in the sunlight. He paused, admiring her for a moment, and then checked the mirror to see if anyone was hiding in the shadows of the room.

He called from the hallway to see if he could stir a movement from an uninvited guest, "Who's in here?" his head turned in the opposite direction from the opening doors.

"Red, it's just me Suga." she responded, putting her cigarette out. He backed away from the door, allowing her to exit freely. He stood by the mantel with his back on the wall and rifle in his shoulder pocket. He aimed, ready to fire; he waited for someone to appear from the hallway.

"I came as soon as I heard about David in the papers." she creaked down the hall stepping recklessly on the boards. Her sporadic movements calmed him; she was a concerned lover. Anthony swiftly hid the gun behind the plant that neighbored the mantel. He didn't want to stir her with worry; he moved closer to the sofa. "Is he alright?" she asked, stopping dead in her tracks when she scanned over Anthony's bloody clothes. She clasped her hands around her mouth and nose, "Did he make it?" she asked trembling.

Anthony leaned over, propping his tired body up on the back of the sofa, "There is a war stewing, I think you best get home Mrs. Tomlin. May I remind you, your husband is the puppet master that sicced them no good hounds on my nephew. He knew good and well David didn't point the finger in the Collins direction. His temper flared, "THE GOD DAMN FACTS DID! He convinced those boys he got David to back his story. How the hell does that mysteriously lead to him being hung naked from a tree? The damn town talks, and when you know the right people and lined the pockets of the mayor, you best to know everything that goes on, even an ant pissing on cotton." He removed his shirt, tossing it into the wastebasket.

"Red…" she was shocked; his response was cold and brutal. She stood offended that he used her marital name to address her. "Now you're judging me like everyone else? I always do what needs to be done. Don't you ever disrespect me like I'm one of them, again." she huffed, "I'm about to draw you a bath God damnit! You can catch me up on what's happening after you've rested."

Anthony rolled his eyes in annoyance; the harder he tried to push Rebecca away, the more she latched on. They saw each other several times after she showed up on his doorstep drenched and beaten. He penetrated her deeply with passion: in the car, his office, the restroom, the theater, and the pool after hours. Rebecca, carefree from guilt, wanted to be punished for the truth, not for Tomlin's assumptions.

He climbed into the steaming water; it soothed his aching muscles. He sat with a hot rag draped over his face, falling asleep instantly.

Chayanne gave Mr. Henry a compelling argument to persuade him to let Charles tag along; she would do anything to protect the fragile boy. Mr. Henry nodded and drove away, telling Charles to call him when he was ready to be picked up.

Chayanne rushed to room 307, ecstatic to see Uncle Anthony. He was the only person she felt love for besides Charles.

"Come on Charles, move those little nubs." she called back to him, dashing down the halls.

"Awe, come on Chayanne, you're really fast; you're making my asthma flare up again." he said, stopping to take a puff of his inhaler.

Chayanne looked back and laughed at Charles, he couldn't even be a normal kid. Chayanne made it to the room and she busted into the door, filling it with her intense energy.

"Uncle Anthony, I'm here… I need my fifty dollars!" she said, searching the room for him, disregarding Momma's existence.

"Well baby girl, you made it." she wheeled over to the door, blocking her view of David.

"Oh, hey Momma." Chayanne replied dryly, unbothered by Momma's existence. A sassy look pressed upon her face.

Momma sat back in the chair with her feelings hurt, "Baby girl, what's gotten into you?" she asked close to tears.

Chayanne folded her arms, leaning against the wall, "You mean besides the fact you and Daddy left me alone for three days, turning me into an adult without my permission; or the part where everyone talks over my head, not really explaining things in kid terms about your health? Or the fact that you're choosing to die on your own terms not taking treatment; or the fact that you're trading your life for David's, or the fact that daddy is a coward and has no backbone?" she asked sassily, rolling her eyes.

The back of Momma's hand met Chayanne's cheek. Chayanne unstirred by momma's response touched her cheek, a trail of blood trickled from her lip. Her green eyes glowing with hate met Momma's hazel eyes that bared hurt. Chayanne stared at Momma, wiping her mouth with the palm of her hand; she smacked her lips and stormed out of the room. She ran over Charles, who was running into the room. Unable to keep his balance, he flew into the wall.

"Baby girl, you come back here!" Momma demanded wheeling herself after Chayanne. Charles picked himself up and walked into the room, his eyes fixed on David's bandaged face. Charles, like a moth to a flame, cautiously approached. A black boot caught the door from closing behind him.

Peter's words replayed in Daddy's mind while he tailed the younger Collins boys here and there. Every time he thought he was ready to spring into action and make a move, he would hear Peter's voice in his mind, reminding him of what was really at stake if he followed through. The sawed-off shotgun rode next to him on the passenger's seat, keeping him company. Daddy learned the boy's favorite hangout was a cottage clubhouse near the quarry marsh where David's body swung in the summer breeze. Daddy parked his pickup near Peter's butcher shop; he would later use this as an alibi. He walked through the front of Pete's shop and out the rear door undetected; Peter was too busy with customers to notice. Daddy dipped off into the woods with the shotgun strapped to his back. He hiked three miles to stand ten yards away from the small cottage. The young boys laughed and boasted amongst one another, they were reenacting the lynching of David. Daddy got closer; he pushed his body against the wooden panel under a small open window for a closer listen.

Ricky, the youngest of the Collins, expressed his frustration, "Timmy, if you didn't go all bat-shit crazy when Dougie told you he wanted to leave town with the Parker lady, we wouldn't be in all this mess. Dougie is in trouble for something he didn't even do because he won't rat you out." He shook his head and cracked open a can of beer. "You really fucked things up when you didn't put David's bat back alongside of their tool shed. I don't know why on God's green earth you would carry that thing around like some trophy."

Timmy eyed Ricky distastefully; the audacity to blame him for the mess Dougie made, following in their father's footsteps, sleeping with a colored woman, who bared their father's mongrel baby.

Timmy took a drag of grass, "If it weren't for me, we would be in a hell of a lot more trouble." He exhaled a cloud of skunk smelling smoke, "What the hell do you think Pa would do if he found out Dougie was messing around with his call girl? We'd be dead for not telling him; he would have shipped us off to those homo-infested boarding schools. That's our suffering Timmy, Dougie is finished with school. Pa had strict instructions; drop the damn money off for the nappy-headed half bread, but noooo, Dougie had to go and fuck the nigger bitch too. Her snatch must have been a God damn goldmine the way he was treatin her." Timmy took another pull, his eyes glossy. "All our asses would hang over the fireplace as trophies. I did what I knew was right." He took a swig of the moonshine, "These niggers want to take what's ours: our jobs, our fucking baseball careers, our country, this is a white man's country ain't no nigger needed besides free labor. Hell, them mother fuckers can't even vote." Timmy turned his vexation to Jonny. "Jonny this is your senior year and you're going to lose your major-league opportunity to that monkey David; he's the starting pitcher this year, didn't you get the memo? How does that make you feel?" Timmy harassed.

"I…I mean David can pitch his ass off, he's a cool kid. Besides, the team has a much better chance of winning state with him out front; have you seen the kid play? His arm is like a fucking rocket. He's going to be more famous than Jackie Robinson." he said with a smile.

Jonny stared off into the distance like the field was in front of him and he watched David throw the first pitch in the state's competition. His daydream only lasted so long, as Timmy went upside his head with an open palm.

Timmy kicked Jonny over off the chair, "You're a fucking idiot Jonny; this is bigger than some God damn state championship. These niggers are taking over, and that dumb ass thinking will allow them to run us over." Timmy kicked him in the chest. "Get your nigger-loving ass out until you get your shit together." Timmy spat on Jonny's converse. Jonny scrambled to his feet.

"Timmy, your brain is fried. You sit here and pretend to be one of us, but that silver spoon you were born with still shows behind all of the fucked up shit you say. You want to be a rebel so fucking bad, sitting in on the Klan's bullshit meetings to piss your dad off. Go fuck yourself, man, we are all trying to make it out alive, even David. You have a choice not to die in the fucking coalmines, but that's what happens to the assholes that get stuck in this shit hole!"

BANG! The door flung open. Timmy kicked Jonny down the stairs, "Jonny, even when you get your shit together… you're not welcome here you son of a bitch. I should come by later and have your mom lick my pole since your dad is too busy sticking his in men's asses, you prick!" He slammed the door shut. Daddy didn't budge; he wanted to hear more of Timmy's conversation. Jonny froze, looking at Daddy his heart dropped. Daddy aimed; Jonny, scared shitless, shook his head side to side, mouthing it wasn't me while crocodile tears fell from his face. Daddy lowered the barrel, happy that Jonny stood up for David; Daddy motioned the gun, telling Jonny to get lost. Jonny rushed to his car; he slammed his fist into the steering wheel enraged. He started the car and sped off, spinning the dirt with his tires. Daddy tiptoed closer to the door. Jonny made it to the end of the road and drifted the spinning the car around; the tires screeched loudly. He headed back toward the cottage and floored the gas pedal to 120. He hit a small hill, sending his car flying in the air. He was fed up with Timmy's bullshit, if Timmy couldn't wail on David, he randomly picked someone in the group if they didn't agree with his psychobabble bullshit of the day. Jonny felt forced to fit in. He was different; he could never consider himself a man until he took a stance against Timmy. The car flew through the air like a missile, going straight into the cottage knocking down bricks and shattering windows. Gasoline and oil leaked from beneath the car causing a small fire. Jonny's head bobbed into the steering wheel, knocking him unconscious. Daddy stood motionless like a deer in headlights. His parental instinct took over and he pulled Jonny's body from the car, dragging him away from the crash. Daddy sprinted into the woods headed back to Pete's; he didn't want the blow to fall on him. The car exploded; the force sent Daddy headfirst into a tree, he laid unconscious and his backside got caught by flames.

Momma with guilt in her heart wheeled Chayanne down in the waiting room; Chayanne's face was buried in a magazine. Momma took hold of the magazine; Chayanne snatched it away from her weak hands.

She reopened the magazine, "Why are you bothering me, don't you have a dance with death?" Chayanne's words cut like knives.

Momma sighed heavily in shock with Chayanne's brutality, "Ouch baby girl, words have a way of hurting people, too?"

Chayanne turned the page, "It can't be worse than you slamming your hand into my face." she snapped back.

"I was wrong to strike you, I'm sorry. I can't imagine what you're going through, all this has tainted your innocence, I'm sure." Momma apologized mournfully.

Momma clasped her hands together on her lap and sat back in her wheelchair. Chayanne's defense came down, along with the magazine she planted in front of her face.

"You have my attention," Chayanne said, crossing her right leg over her left. Her hands neatly clasped in front.

Momma smiled graciously, "How are you doing in all of this baby girl? I would like for you to use your own words and not Anthony's" she requested politely.

Chayanne cleared her throat, "I'm angry that you refuse to fight for more time with us. I'm angry that Daddy seems so lost in the world without you; the poor man couldn't even make us breakfast, he's like a stranger. I'm angry that you tell David not to fight back, look at what it has cost him now. I think men ought to fight for what they think is right, hell, look at wimpy Charles." she covered her mouth, embarrassed that a curse word slipped out.

Momma giggled; Chayanne was like a mirror to her. She nodded for her to continue, letting her know the slip of the tongue happens occasionally.

"The only thing consistent is Uncle Anthony; he cares for me like I'm the child he never had. He's always teaching me about business and money. I enjoy spending time with him when I'm not with Charles. I feel like nasty Mr. Henry needs to pay for his sin… I beg he get what he deserves…"

Momma bewildered, "What kind of man is Mr. Henry?"

Charles burst through the waiting room doors, "He's awake, he's awake!" He shouted jumping up and down in excitement.

Momma realized she left him alone; exactly what Anthony told her not to do. An uneasy feeling turned in her stomach as she rushed back to room 307.

16

UNSETTLED GOODBYES

Heavy black smoke cast out miles over the wooded area making it difficult to see; the blaze and smoke could be seen from town. The noise from the fire engine and the mist from the water woke daddy. His hearing muffed and his vision blurred. He wheezed as he tried to make out the nearby voices that talked amongst him. Sheriff Deputy Tomlin walked along the edge of the small dirt cliff—where Daddy was impacted by the blast—looking for clues. Tomlin demanded immediate answers; he didn't want anything leaked to the mayor or press. All of the mayhem in town made the future of his campaign bleak. Jonny was conscious in the back of the ambulance; his life flashed before his eyes. He couldn't recall how he got out the car unscathed; he deemed it as an act of God.

Daddy's ears rang, a deafening, high-pitch tone intruded his ears. His hearing returned in time to pick up on the last of Tomlin's discussion.

"Yeah, everyone deputy sheriff, all seven deceased including Senator Collins's boys. The Jonny was pretty lucky to get away, the high school team is really going to need him this year since uh David is uh... well, you took care of that." the officer reported with a bit of resistance.

Tomlin drew on his cigar; the raspberry tobacco leaves stuck to his lip, "Well, that Carter jammed his nephew up for thinking he deserved a seat at our table." he said bitterly, "I know he's sleeping around with that whore of mine, can't prove it yet, but I will." He paused, looking out trying to see through the smoggy ash, "The only way to hit a guy like Red is picking his loved ones off, one by one. Then, you let them dogs loose on a boy when he's by his lonesome. Good ole Tomlin method, it was used to tear the slave families apart; been in the family since the beginning of my family's wealth." He bit down on the cigar, "There ain't much resistance without numbers. We do it different down yonder where I come from; you bests believe I'm going to stick it to em real nice." he said whipping his pecker out, taking a piss right over the log where Daddy was hidden. "Well, I don't know how to piece this one together, I just know Senator Collins gone be pissed as a mad dog; both of his boys are dead. Now, I guess we have to cut the other one loose and pin the Parker murder on one of these knuckleheads. Give the zoo animals some resolution and close the case." he zipped his pants.

Daddy clenched his shotgun, wanting to take that son of a bitch out of his misery now that he knew the truth. Suddenly, Peter's advice started to sink a little deeper. The sheriff continued talking to the officer and headed in a new direction. Daddy used the heavy smog to start his escape; it wouldn't be long before he was discovered. If he got caught, he'd just be a pawn in Tomlin's pissing match with Anthony.

Momma wheeled her way to David's room. The colored community filled the hall holding flowers, balloons, and get-well cards; waiting their turn to visit David. Emotions swept over her as an immense amount of people poured into the hospital, showing their unity and support for him. She was obliged by their admiration.

Anthony approached her refreshed, "Damn it Evelyn, I told you not to let anyone in the room; here you go letting the whole riverside in the boy's room." Anthony teased—shocked at David's imprint on the community. Chayanne wandered from behind, attaching herself to his leg. "Well, hey you little hustler." he said, picking her up, "I think I have something for you." he reached, fumbling in his pockets. He pulled a crisp fifty-dollar bill out and handed it to her. "Now, all we have left to get is the penny candy and ice cream and my debt is settled."

She wrapped her arms around his neck, squeezing him tightly. "Thank you!" she said sliding out of his arms. She ran off to gloat to Charles.

Momma grabbed Anthony's arm, "I've decided to go back on the treatment. Baby girl made a point, highlighting my selfishness to refuse it. I see something that wasn't there before, and through these uncertain times, I know they need their mother more than ever." she dabbed the white corners of her mouth.

He placed his hand on her shoulder, gently squeezing it as a silent thank you. A tranquil feeling swept over them as they watched everyone uplift David from the hallway.

The sunset on Daddy, he slid on his belly down the rough terrain of the woods. He was a mile out from Pete's; he made it to the creek. He cupped his hands and scooped some of the clear water to sip it. His body was exhausted. He learned early on his ankle was dislocated; he couldn't bear to put pressure on it. He needed to keep pushing to get back to town to warn Anthony and check on his family, but his body yearned for a break. He propped himself on his side against a large tree that went down during the storm. His back was burned badly; the smell of burnt flesh followed him, he couldn't remove his shirt as pieces of it meshed into the open wound. Breathing slowly, he needed to relax himself from the pain. He couldn't go to the hospital with his injuries; his visit would lead Tomlin to question him and finger him for the crime. A coyote howled off in the distance as the moon appeared. Daddy's eyes enlarged. His adrenaline kicked in; he had to move quickly. Dehydrated and weak, he struggled to make it to the back door of the butcher shop. He tapped on the metal door with all the strength he had in him and faded in and out of consciousness.

"JAMES... JAMES... open your eyes... say anything if you can hear me." Peter panicked, pulling him into the shop and slamming the metal door behind.

Uncle Anthony waited patiently for everyone to clear out of David's room. Denise was the last to go, wishing him a speedy recovery. Anthony eyed her as she exited the room; his intuition told him she was the girl he'd run off to see.

"How are you feeling?" Anthony asked, pulling up a chair beside him. David gave him a thumbs up, still unable to talk. "You really gave us a scare... we are happy that you're pulling through okay. Dr. George said it would be maybe a month or longer before you're able to speak. That's a small price to pay, considering you have your life. I really want you to be optimistic; things will work themselves out in due time." He took a deep breath, "You're going to need a lot of physical therapy for your throwing hand. They shattered fourteen of your twenty-seven bones in your hand. Maybe we can condition you for first base or the outfield." A tear rolled down David's cheek—both his eyes were bloody red from his burst blood vessels. "You'll be able to play by the spring, so don't go gettin all emotional." Anthony wiped his tear while holding his back; he swallowed the dry lump in his throat. "You're stronger than you think, you'll heal in no time; you have to have your mind made up that you're healing more every day." he paused. "Everyone is doing just fine, if you were wondering; your momma is staying to complete her chemo treatment. I guess Suga put the screws to her about it—she was really torn up—whatever baby girl said sure as hell worked." He wiped the tip of his nose where a tear slipped. "Hell, I'm just rambling on; you need to get some rest. I'm sure you're tired from all your visitors... I seen the pretty, little young thing you messin around with. Just be safe and don't slip up and make a mistake you can't take back. You have a second lease on life, just make good of it." he kissed David gently on the forehead. David had a strange feeling on the inside about Anthony, but he nodded, reassuring Uncle Anthony heard his words. Before Anthony turned to leave, he looked back, smiled and said, "I'm proud of you and the man you're becoming. If I'm not around you for some reason, protect Suga like your life depends on it... I love you." David smiled weakly reciprocating the love he felt; before the door shut behind Anthony, David was asleep.

Charles was asleep on Chayanne's lap; she stroked his kinky hair like he was her pet. Her legs swung carefree in the air, not even close to touching the floor.

"Suga come and tell Momma goodnight before we take off." Anthony requested.

"Ugh, I didn't get to see David, all those people bombarded his room all day." she pouted, folding her arms tightly across her chest.

She placed Charles's head gently on the chair.

"You'll get your turn, I promise it's better. He heals before you see him in any kind of condition. You'll have nightmares for weeks. Remember that one Halloween about two years back when he was that scary monster and he made you cry?" he teased her pretending to be a monster going after her.

"That's not fair, I was a baby and didn't know any better... I'm grown now." she sassed, pretending not to be afraid.

"That's what you say now, but if you get a look at David, you'll go crying to your momma about it." he chortled at the thought. "Now come on and say goodnight." They walked, hand in hand, to the care unit where Momma was placed. Anthony waited his turn patiently in the hall to say good night.

"Night Momma, I'll see you in the morning, okay? I'll ask Anthony to take me down to the library to check out some new reading material for you." She kissed Momma on the cheek and skipped out of the room to find Charles. Anthony waited until she was out of sight to enter.

"Hey Evey, how you holding up?" A small smile stuck to his face.

Momma returned his smile, "You haven't called me that since we were children... I miss those days; things seemed a lot simpler."

"Yeah, I'd say so..." He looked away as tears built in his eyes. "I just want to say you did an amazing job raising those children. They are so strong and opinionated, that Suga gone cheat me out of my whole fortune one of these days."

He laughed, thinking of how Chayanne always smoothed talked her way into what she wanted, whenever she wanted. I think she's going to make a mighty fine career woman when she gets all grown." A sudden sadness came over him.

"Anthony? You making it seem like you're saying goodbye for something." Momma said, pushing herself upright. She patted the bed next to her for him to sit so she could dig into the real matter.

"Well, Evey, I think it's about time I run off and have a family of my own, it ain't fair that I take over yours. I hear New York is a pretty progressive place, especially for us colored folk. I just think it's about time for a change of scenery." he said staring off into the distance, picturing a fast-paced city life. "The painful memories are becoming a bit too overwhelming for me. Rebecca showing her face ain't making it any easier." He sat there, rocking his body subtly, seeking comfort within.

"So that's what this is really about... Anthony Reid, I may be getting old, but I'm not blind, cripple, nor crazy, you fixin to run off with her again." She threw her hands in the air, "I knew it was only a matter of time before she dug her claws into you. Is New York progressive enough for you to marry a married woman, or did you forget the laws banning us from marrying out of our kind?" she said calmly. She didn't blame him for following his heart, with David's near-death experience, she knew how short life could be. "At least send me a postcard every week. Baby girl is going to miss you, she's going to be kicking and screaming. You better promise to call that child every Saturday, lord knows my nerves are going to be shot." She grabbed his hand squeezing it tightly as tears dropped onto her hospital gown.

"I'm not sure how I'm going to tell Suga... maybe over ice cream next Saturday. I promise not to leave until things seem semi normal. I need to send out a search party for that husband of yours." He stood, rubbing his combed hair.

"Please find James, there isn't much I could do being bedridden through this process. I just need him to be okay." she said worried.

"I'm sure he's fine, just regrouping and blowing off some steam. This is the second time within months you and David are both laid up in the hospital. Just give the man some time and he will come around, I promise." he reassured her. "I have a nurse on duty watching David's room, I'm going to put Suga and her friend up in a hotel room tonight. I don't want her staying at the house alone, something she said about that old Mr. Henry gave me weird goosebumps." They both exchanged glances, thinking of Chayanne's words about Mr. Henry; they busted into laughter, thinking she was just being herself rambling on.

"Yeah, I don't know what's gotten into that child of mine. Ain't no telling what she done heard or saw Mr. Henry do that was abnormal to her. She thinks all folk live the way we do."

"Yeah that Suga boy... I'll be back to sit around with David after I get them settled in and put some food in their bellies." he said moving to the door. "I love you Evey, without you, my life would have been more hurt than what I know. I found my joy and peace with you; you're the best sister a man could hope for."

"I love you too, Anthony, you're the glue that keeps this family together. I will see you in the morning. Good night!" she said, fluffing her pillow and getting comfortable for her night's rest.. Anthony closed the door softly behind him.

CHAPTER

17

LET THE DUST SETTLE

Peter tended to Daddy's wounds nonstop for a week; he kept them well dressed and clean; he'd received medical training from his time served in WWII. He'd met young James the year he was discharged in 1945. Peter set up shop in the colored parts of town and had difficulty gaining business until Daddy stepped in vouching for his cuts of meat. Peter was intrigued by his charisma and salesmanship, so he gave Daddy a job. Daddy worked at Peter's shop until David was born; he loved working at the butcher shop but he felt financially inferior when it came to taking care of his family. This led him down to the dangerous coal mines. Daddy always felt out of place knowing Momma came from money; he was embarrassed that he could only put scraps from the shop on the table. Although Momma never complained, Daddy always felt like he was less man than she deserved.

To help Daddy cope with the pain, Peter took Jo to the pharmacist to get him some Percodan; Peter lied, saying he hurt his shoulder hauling a large steer into the shop; he was careful not to draw any unwanted attention. He stayed by Daddy's side until he was well enough to talk him through the details of the explosion. Peter checked in with Momma, using codes to inform her of his wellbeing. She was relieved to know Peter was caring for him since she wasn't in a nurturing condition. Her first week of chemo was hell on earth.

The sound of Peter scribbling his daily numbers filled the office. It was eight o'clock; an hour past closing on a Friday. The scribbles stirred Daddy awake. He rolled to his side careful not to disturb his back.

"Argh, this dang-old leg is itching in this cast again; what did you say you made this out of?" he asked, shelving a thin stick down the opening to relieve the itchiness.

"I told you about a million times now James; flour, water, and newspaper." he responded, not looking away from his work. "If I didn't know any better, I think the explosion knocked some sense out of you." he teased. "That reminds me, the Jonny fella, um, came looking for you again today, that's the third time this week..." he paused, scribbling in some more numbers. "I had to move your truck down by the coal mines; hopefully everyone can start snooping around there." he responded without looking away from his paperwork. "I'm going to head out soon, do you need anything before I go?" he asked, adjusting the small desk lamp.

"Maybe just a pain pill for the discomfort." he adjusted his position on Peter's office sofa. "I've suffered from worst burns in the mines; I remember when that fire broke out about ten years back." he replied reminiscing spending two weeks in the hospital; Momma thought he'd died with four others. The mine exploded, trapping them underground; Daddy was standing at the mouth of the mine when things went sour.

Peter nodded confirming Daddy's request for pain medication. He groaned like something else was bothering him. He reached in his top right drawer for the medication, tapping two pills from the bottle; he handed them to Daddy.

"What's eating you, Pete?" Daddy asked prior to swallowing the pills.

"I just can't get over that crook Tomlin framing an innocent boy to get the upper hand on Anthony, which he completely pulled out his ass with no proof. It pisses me off, if we were to expose him, it'll all get covered with conspiracy bullshit. Politics are always just that, politics; I'd be surprised if someone in the town don't clean his clock." He continued mumbling under his breath out of range for Daddy to hear. "Son of a bitch!"

"What now?" Daddy asked.

"I have a delivery tomorrow morning; you can't be here with all these people poking around for you. Nobody's been at your place for over a week now. I drive by every night—hoping to get someone—not a mouse in sight. I figured I go to the hospital tonight to see how David and Evelyn are doing for you. Hopefully, I can get in touch with Anthony; maybe he can put you up at his place until the burns heal so you won't be interrogated about them." he shrugged his shoulders, throwing possibilities out in the air. It wouldn't be long until the police start turning up rocks around his shop for James. Tomlin wanted to interview everyone that had a motive to eliminate the Collins boys; Senator Collins requested a deep, thorough investigation or he'd expose them and make the mayor clean house.

Chayanne sat at the foot of the bed, enjoying a cheeseburger and a chocolate milkshake. Her toes were wiggling with the widest smile on her face.

"Uncle Anthony, I wish you were always in charge." she said with her mouth full.

"Aw Suga, you're going to give me a cavity with your sweetness," he teased, "Charles, how's your hot dog and fries?"

Charles sat at the table underneath the window, "It's delicious, thank you Mr. Anthony." he responded with his eyes glued to his food.

Although the food was delicious, Charles had other endeavors on his mind. He knew soon they would have to set their plan for Uncle Henry in motion. He hadn't been home all week. It's the safest he'd felt since the last time he saw his mother. Henry was a cancer to his life and as he got older, the abuse would only be more elaborate. Chayanne looked over at Charles, knowing his wheels were turning in his mind. She knew that he was safe for one more night, but they would eventually have to follow through on their plan. She paused from enjoying her burger to study Charles demeanor.

She dipped her fry into her shake, "Uncle Anthony, what time are you going to sit with David tonight?" she asked, not taking her eyes off of Charles.

Uncle Anthony was tending to some bank work, he was a little more distracted lately than usual. "Uh soon, maybe in the next fifteen minutes. My lady friend, the nurse, will be getting off her shift soon." He bit down on the pencil as he read on.

"When are we going home?" she asked, wanting to know the timeline for taking care of Mr. Henry.

"Soon Suga, I promise. I need to tie up some lose ends, especially since the Klan is on a manhunt since the Collins boys were killed in the blast last week. All this death and no one to answer for it; makes you start wondering now, doesn't it?" he replied still focusing. She knew soon meant a few days or so. Anthony never tried to pull the wool over her eyes and that's what she appreciated most about him. "Why do you ask? Are you tired of the fancy-hotel living?" He looked up at Chayanne from his paperwork; "I just need to know you're safe when I'm not around. I need to know you are taken care of, fed, bathed, and loved. You've always been my favorite, baby girl; I see so much of me in you."

Chayanne distracted, "Yeah, I love you too Uncle Anthony; no one gets me like you." Uncle Anthony tapped his finger on his reddish-brown beard he let grow in over the week; he took a minute to realize what Chayanne was doing. Finally, the puzzle pieces started to arrange in his mind. He shook his head once he had the picture in mind; he was oblivious to Charles's abuse. He was in denial, not taking heed to the warnings she subtly whispered days prior; he thought Mr. Henry being weird was her sense of humor in describing him. In reality, he didn't want to hear the truth. He was now in tune with the silent stares and secret conversations Chayanne and Charles had. He put his papers down and walked over to the table, sitting on the opposite side of Charles. Charles was so zoned out he didn't even notice.

"Hey?" Uncle Anthony said placing his hand on Charles's shoulder to gain his attention. Charles looked at him shaken up. "You're safe... you're alright." he reassured him; "I'm sure it's been a tough year for you, losing your mother, I remember when my mother died…" he stared off into the distance, struggling to keep his emotions in check; "I was sad and angry, nothing made sense. I felt like I didn't belong in this world without her. Is that how you're feeling?" Charles looked up at Anthony, slightly nodding yes. "Why don't you tell me more about how you're feeling these days? Has moving with your Uncle Henry been easy?" he searched for verbal confirmation.

Charles's eyes darted toward Chayanne; he was afraid to answer. Her eyes widen in disbelief—she knew Anthony knew—how he figured out was unknown. Charles scratched his head in an attempt to buy more time.

Charles put his hands under his thighs, "I wish I knew who my daddy was, maybe I could live with him instead of my Uncle Henry." his nerves unsettled, "I don't want to move and lose Chayanne as my friend." he admitted honestly.

"You don't like living with Mr. Henry?" He pressed for the truth.

Charles looked down at his legs, nervous. "Umm… he does." the telephone rang, intruding on the conversation.

Anthony put up his index finger, "Hold that thought" he hurried to the phone.

Chayanne shot a look of relief at Charles. Charles leaned back fanning himself with his heart pounding. They continued talking in their code while Anthony was on the phone.

"Who came looking around, now?" he questioned the nurse.

"The sheriff deputy showed first; he wanted to talk to David, something in his energy just ain't right. I told him that his room is closed to outside visitors per the family's request; he pressed about it and then I told him visiting hours are done for the evening, either way. His breath smelled of moonshine; that's alarming, considering he's in uniform toting his revolver." Her voice distraught, she sounded afraid of him.

Anthony nodded along, "Umhum, then what happened?" he pushed wanting to know more.

"He rambled on under his breath saying how niggers need to know their place when authorities come around. He stumbled out of here. About a quarter till nine, some battered white lady came in looking for you. She said it was urgent to speak with you; she looked like a punching bag. I wanted to offer to treat her, but I didn't want to offend her. Something in my spirit isn't sitting right with them, Red. You need to be careful with what you're doing, I'd hate to see a good man go down." she explained distraught, afraid for him. Anthony tapped his finger to the phone like he was moving pieces on a chessboard; he was calculating his next move.

"Umhum, well alright. Your shift ends in about thirty minutes, still?"

"Yes, I considered working a double just to make sure you can stay out of sight and be safe."

"How is Evelyn? Have you checked on her since they came up?" he asked as his mind rambled.

"Yes, I checked on them both every fifteen minutes, as you asked me. I have other nurses I trust checking on them in between my fifteen, just to make sure."

Anthony rushed, "I'll be there in ten, you need to go home and get some rest before morning comes." He hung up the receiver.

He was on edge and restless; Rebecca was a cancer in Tomlin's life; since she stepped foot in town, destruction followed. He folded his lips, thinking tightly.

Anthony kissed Suga goodnight, "I'll be back first thing in the morning. You two take care of each other." He rushed to the door.

Anthony arrived at the hospital ten minutes before the nurse's shift expired. He hugged her tightly and thanked her; he knew the dangers that lurked nearby for helping him. He set up shop in David's room; he had to piece information together before time ran out.

The hotel door barely latched, Chayanne darted over to Charles.

"Oh man, that was so close." she said wiping the pretend sweat from her forehead.

"Yeah, I know; we need to get this plan moving along. Time is running out; people are starting to notice." he stressed the urgency.

"I think you're paranoid; we can't go causing more trouble in town right now, especially after the Collins accident. All fingers are pointed at my family. Everyone is still searching for Daddy; I figure he's long gone by now if he killed those boys, along with a few baseball players. Things weren't supposed to happen this way. How will it look like an accident if there has already been a fire?"

Charles thought about things for a minute, "Yeah, I guess you're right... I'm glad those boys are dead. They killed my momma; they don't deserve to live." he said angrily.

"Do you think the papers are telling the truth about that? I mean how could they not arrest Dougie for killing your momma? You said yourself, you've seen him dozens of times giving your momma money and hitting on her when she was with other men. How do they go from that to the other boys killing her?"

Charles calculated Chayanne's doubt; "Yeah, but they found the murder weapon at the fire. It took them four days to pull all the bodies out; when they found Timmy's body, he had the bat. Seems like they are going off facts." he stated, moving another piece into perspective in their mental chess match.

She was in deep thought, "Something just doesn't seem right, they still don't know how the explosion started; I think, maybe, we need a new plan."

"I agree, but what could possibly be better than what we drew up? If we get caught, they will throw us in jail for sure Chayanne; it has to be a better way."

"Do you think we could wait until all this blows over, when everyone forgets?" she added as a possible solution.

"I can't wait anymore; I can't keep living like this. I don't want to risk him finding out I told you and he hurts you."

They sat there, all night, bouncing ideas off one another in an attempt to find a solution. Nothing was better or even equivalent to the original plan they devised. They became frustrated and their eyes grew tired. Chayanne yawned and Charles was asleep before her head could hit the pillow.

Anthony woke the two by opening the shades on the window, letting the afternoon sunlight in. They moaned and groaned like vampires melting in the sun.

"What time did you two go to bed? It's well after three o'clock on a Saturday. Suga, I know you've been thinking about your ice cream fix all week, I'm surprised you were going to let the day get away." He was vibrant and lively.

"Oh, come on Mr. Anthony, five more minutes," Charles said pulling the covers over his head. Chayanne sat up Indian style, rubbing the sleep out her eyes.

She stretched her arms out, yawning for energy. "Did you bring some coffee with you, old man?" Chayanne asked, imitating Momma.

Uncle Anthony laughed, "Coffee? You trying to stay in your nine-year-old body forever?" he teased. "Come on get up and moving. We can go down to the diner for some breakfast or lunch. I need to talk to you alone Suga, so we will drop Charles at the hospital with Momma. She needs some company and someone to read to her while she's getting her treatment."

"Talk to me about what? Are we moving somewhere safer?" she didn't want the suspense clouding her day.

"Good things come to those who are patient. I guess you'll find out soon enough." he said, striking a match to light his cigarette.

She got up and headed for the shower, "Soon...soon all this soon stuff ain't ever got no time limit. Time waits for no one, and I can't wait for soon to never come." she fussed, closing the door. She started the shower, drowning out her complaints. Uncle Anthony peaked out of the window; he sensed someone was tailing him, but couldn't make it out.

They arrived at the diner; it was noisy and packed for a Saturday afternoon. They sat at a booth, anticipating the delicious food they were going to order. A pint-sized, dark-skinned man approached the table slipping Uncle Anthony a note, inconspicuously. Chayanne and Charles watched his facial expressions as he read it.

"Ahem, so what does it say? It's rude to have secret conversations in front of people?" Chayanne sassed.

Anthony crumbled the paper, "Oh you mean like the secret conversation you and Charles were having when I was on the phone last night?" he gradually mentioned.

She sat back in the booth admitting defeat. "I wish the waitress would come on, I'm hungry." she hissed, having a fit of hungry.

"Be patient Chayanne, remember it pays off." Charles teased, mocking Anthony's words from earlier.

Chayanne rolled her eyes at Charles and stuck her tongue out. She straightened up, catching a glimpse of Rebecca out the corner her eye. She approached the table with a pair of oversized sunglasses that barely hid the blue and purple bruises on her face; her lip was split, and a cut sat along her cheek. Chayanne sensed trouble was near.

18

THE LAST WORD

A nthony kept his cool in front of the children. His fury burned inside, astonished at Rebecca's unsightly appearance. His jaw compulsively clenched in.

He moved to the inside of the booth, "Sit down! You are drawing all kinds of unnecessary attention," he said, monitoring the chatter volume. She did as she was instructed. "Why the hell are you showing up in public places, knowing the consequences if we're caught? All it will take is one phone call to alert your beastly husband," he said through his clenched teeth, low enough for her earshot only.

He noticed the uneasy expressions on the children's faces. He tapped his fingers on the tabletop, waiting for her answer.

She sunk in the booth, "I can't keep waiting and living like this; I'm leaving for New York come morning. I wanted to make sure you're still on board; I will raise this child with or without you Red." she answered him at a whisper. Chayanne's eyes moved back and forth like she was watching a tennis match as the two adults exchanged heavy words at the table; she sensed the conversation was serious from the changing expressions.

He fired question after question, "You're fucking pregnant? When the fuck were you going to tell me? Don't you fucking think that's important? How do I know it isn't Tomlin's?" he tried to keep his composure.

"I just found out yesterday at my doctor's visit. Why the fuck do you think my face looks like this for fun? I haven't fucked him since we got here. He's questioning the term of the pregnancy; I just want to get out of here before the results come back. That's the proof he needs Red; that's all the reason he needs to take you out. I'm sure he'd claim it was rape; anything to put you behind bars and out of his hair. Let's just take the children and run, NOW! Evelyn will forgive you for looking after Suga."

A frustrated sigh escaped, "You couldn't stay away, could you? You like making things more difficult than they need to be?" He finally accepted Momma's warnings about Rebecca, but of course it was too late; his hand was already caught in the cookie jar. "God damn son of a bitch! I still have things to tend to here." He bit his bottom lip, drawing blood.

"The term results come back tomorrow afternoon; we need to be far from here as possible," she said, pushing for him to agree.

"Fine, it's not like I have any other choice; my child will not grow up without a father." His jaw muscles pulsed as he grinded his teeth. "This was your damn plan all along, to fucking pick back up from high school. You're so damn selfish, only thinking of you. What about my family, they need me too."

The waitress approached the table, breaking their whispering match.

"How nice, it's you two again!" she hissed, remembering Rebecca and Anthony from their first meeting at the diner. She looked at Charles and Chayanne, "Are these your children? They are so adorable..." she said admiring them, "Now, what can I get you?" she said with an attitude.

Chayanne pushed the menu away, "I lost my appetite... don't worry, it wasn't because you took too long to come get our order." she said sarcastically. The waitress's face went blank, she was blindsided by Chayanne's feelings.

"I'll take a tall stack of pancakes with warm syrup, scrambled eggs, and bacon... extra bacon, oh and some whole milk; I'm still trying to grow and I need vitamin D," Charles said, easing the tension at the table.

"I'll have the usual steak and eggs with a coffee," Anthony said, ordering without touching the menu.

"I'm... ahem leaving," Rebecca said, excusing herself from the table. "Nine o'clock tonight at the mill." she whispered in his ear before waltzing out the diner.

"Darling, are you sure you don't want anything?" the waitress asked in an attempt to win Chayanne over.

"Yes ma'am, I think I had enough sugar for today," she replied, referencing Rebecca's porcelain sheen. The waitress left the table. Chayanne shot Uncle Anthony a mean look. She was up to date with the nature of their talk. She knew he was leaving town and her heart shattered into a million pieces; the pain cut deeper than he anticipated because she didn't find out from him. The cutlery hitting and scraping at the plates where the only noise that filled the booth, as Anthony and Charles ate in silence. Anthony knew he could say anything to reverse the damage done.

Chayanne marched out of the diner behind Charles. She let him climb into the backseat first and she followed after. Anthony stood outside, smoking his cigarette. He wondered what he could do to fix things between him and his Suga. He didn't want to leave on bad terms; something in his gut was urging him not to leave her. He thought about Rebecca's word to just pack up and leave with the children. At least he'd know Charles wouldn't be violated anymore. He flicked the bud onto the ground and mushed it in the cement with his shoe; he blew the remaining smoke from his lungs. He started the car, pulled off heading in the direction of the hospital. The engine hummed, the wind blew through the windows, and the sun shined. Uncle Anthony tapped his fingers on the steering wheel; he often did that to cope with stress. He looked into the rearview mirror and adjusted it. Deputy Sheriff Tomlin pulled from a side road into view. His heart raced; he knew Tomlin was fueling with anger from the sight of Rebecca's face. Anthony wanted to strangle the life out of Tomlin and watch the life from his eyes fade. He'd never loathed something or someone so much.

Anthony lit a cigarette to calm his nerves, "Chayanne and Charles listen to me… Something is about to happen, something bad is about to happen…whatever happens DO NOT step foot out of this car, do you understand?" The bass in his voice sent chills through both their bodies. Chayanne never heard him speak in that tone; an eerie sensation took over her and her palms began to sweat. "I SAID, DO YOU UNDERSTAND? The question ain't rhetorical, dammit!"

They both answered in unison in a low tone, "Yes sir."

"Suga, I'm sorry I let you down today… that look on your face at the table broke my heart. I haven't felt that bad since Rebecca left me

15 years ago… I love you so much darlin, you are the twinkle in my eye. I feel like I created you and not Evey." he swallowed hard, puffing on his cigarette.

The blue and red lights flashed in his rearview and the short burst of sirens.

Tomlin's voiced rumbled over the loudspeaker. "Pull the vehicle over," he demanded.

Chayanne unclicked her seat belt and got onto her knees looking out the back window.

"Baby girl, sit down…" he said in a calm, but shaky tone. He feared for her life more than his own; he referenced the note from the diner from Peter:

> *Tomlin is out to get you; five little Indians until there were none. It is imperative we meet. I have more information. 7 o'clock at the promenade.*
>
> *~P*

Anthony gripped the steering wheel with both hands. His mission was to keep Chayanne and Charles safe, and to do that, he would have to swallow his ego and pride. Chayanne slid down in her seat, heeding Uncle Anthony's tone. Tomlin antagonized him with procrastination. She looked into Anthony's eyes in the rearview mirror; beads of sweat collected on his forehead. An apprehensive look filled his eyes as he watched Tomlin's every move in the rearview.

Tomlin flung his door open; the sound of his tactical boots clacked on the cement. He paused at the rear of the car, placing his index finger on the taillight. Anthony sat calm, predicting Tomlin wanted to psychologically instill fear. The squeak of his boots grew louder as he approached the window.

He spat his tobacco juice onto the open road, "Hey Chayanne, you pretty little thing you, it's been a while since we last saw each other, huh sweetie?" Deputy said waving to her and Charles in the back. Anthony bit the inside of his cheek, trying not to get roweled by his antics. Chayanne and Charles waived back with a half-smile, scared; the tension the two men gave off would have rippled for miles.

"Mr. Carter, do you know why I pulled you over, boy?" Tomlin asked, pulling his aviation shades down his nose to get a clear view of the smug look on Anthony's face.

"No sir, I don't," he replied, keeping it short so he could get on his way.

"Well now, I just don't believe that..." Tomlin replied, walking toward the back of the car, "Rebecca was seen leaving the diner where she was in your company." he said, pulling his club out and smashing Anthony's driver-side taillight. "I pulled you over for this busted taillight; a hit and run was reported at the diner where you were last seen, care to explain that?"

Chayanne and Charles covered their ears; they both let out a loud shrill of screams. Anthony shushed them, calming the commotion. "You and I both know that baby is yours." he said hastily approaching the driver's window.

"No sir, I am unaware of a hit and run at the diner, but I'm sure the mayor would have an issue with you sending law enforcement to tail me on companies time. I'd appreciate it if you issue my citation so I can get these children home sir."

Tomlin swung his club backhanded into the side of the car denting the door, "Is that a threat, you Red som of a bitch? You got that nigger lover in your pocket, don't cha?"

"Sir, I am unaware of the accusations you're making," Anthony responded, unbothered with his eyes still looking forward.

"You think you're untouchable, with your formal bullshit talk. Get out of the car," he said, yanking the door handle clean off the car door in an attempt to open it. Uncle Anthony opened the door from the inside and stepped out with his tall, well-built frame, intimidating Tomlin, who was a few inches shorter. Anthony looked down at his nose and saw his reflection in Tomlin's shades. Tomlin hit Anthony in the knee with his club, causing him to buckle instantly.

Chayanne sat up, looking out the small back window, "You motherfucker! You God damn motherfucker, I will kill you!" Chayanne screamed at the top of her lungs, infuriated at Tomlin.

"Suga calm down, stay calm." Anthony instructed.

"Did she threaten me?" Tomlin huffed, "I remove threats before they become promises." He unbuttoned the holster to his revolver. "Suga, that's familiar… Rebecca loves to use that word." Tomlin said with hurt in his voice. He drew the club over his head, going across Anthony's face. His head slammed into the car's side and blood splattered on the light blue paint.

"I'm going to kill you, you son of a bitch, cracker mother fucker!" Chayanne screamed as she climbed over the seats and crawled through the open door. Anthony put his arm out pushing her back inside.

"Baby girl, please don't." he instructed with a mouth full of blood.

"Oh, you send your little niggers to fight a man's battle?" Tomlin said, insulting him.

Anthony rose to his feet, he spat the blood from his mouth on the road, "I'm clearly more of a man here; your wife crawled into my bed every night on your double shifts. She cried about making the mistake to marry a weak sick coward like you. You don't have to wait for no God damn test to tell you that she's carrying my baby, once again. You can't even keep your dick hard long enough to procreate; you must get your rocks off fucking little girls or something, but you will never be able to fill all of her womb like I can. You're still fighting to win her over, to make her love and feel for you the way you feel for her. You're no better than her bitch-made stepfather who beat and raped her to get his nut off." he stated, staring him down with fire burning in his eyes. "You're better off killing me than competing with me, you twisted, sick son of a bitch. She will never love you how she loves me. You had to buy her, I had to meet her." Anthony smiled, saying his peace.

Tomlin drew his revolver, firing three rounds into Anthony's chest. The car caught the force of his body bouncing. The deafening, high-pitched tone from the gun made Chayanne's screams inaudible; she climbed from the car, grabbing at the spurting wounds on Anthony's chest. He reached for her weakly, with a smile on his face. Tomlin tossed a .22 pistol he kept for backup by Anthony's right leg.

He turned toward the open road and radioed dispatch, "GUN, GUN, HE HAS A LIVE WEAPON," he said firing shots into the air.

Everything slowed down, Chayanne's adrenalin ran high; her heartbeat drummed in her ears. Charles climbed over the seat to help Anthony. Tomlin ranted on his radio requesting back up, he failed to notice Chayanne gripping the .22, aiming at his direction. Anthony's blood dripped from her hands as her finger hugged the trigger. Hysterical with laughter, he turned slowly with his revolver on his hip. Chayanne's reflection in his glasses—she squeezed the trigger—firing one shot. Charles reached out to stop her, but the bullet had already exited the chamber, lodging itself into Tomlin's left temple. He collapsed, dying before his body hit the ground. The kick from the gun startled her; she dropped it, firing an accidental shot in Tomlin's torso. Her hands and dress were covered in Anthony's blood. She stood there frozen—tears covered her face and snot ran from her nose. Charles loud sobs fell upon deaf ears as the ringing from the gunfire still drowned their eardrums. Anthony mustered the strength to lift his heavy arm grabbing the bottom of Chayanne's dress; blood gurgled in his mouth, the light slowly draining from his eyes.

Blood dropped from his mouth onto his chin as he tried to speak; "Suga, I love you; put the gun in my hand, I did this…" He wheezed blood filled his lungs, "You tell everyone it was me."

She tried to make his words out; her hearing was drowned out. He reached in his pocket, giving her a small key. As her hearing came back, she listened carefully, "This is a key to a safety deposit box with your name on it at the bank." he gasped for air. "Everything you need is in that box… give me the gun!" he winced in pain, "Let the sheriff piece this together; you two never speak the truth about what happened today. The system is built to imprison you physically and mentally; they designed it to control your emotions and make you think twice about getting ahead in life. You two never leave each other and always fight for your beliefs. Never back down from..." his body went limp as he took his last breath. The light from his gray eyes disappeared; they stared blankly into the open air. A tear rolled down his cheek.

CHAPTER

19

THE THINGS SHE CARRY

Chayanne stood staring out the bay window that overlooked the garden Lilly loved to get lost in. She felt empty, remembering Anthony's last words. Her stomach tied in knots; his last moments meant more to her than her next breath. A monsoon of tears escaped her eyes; she stood silent. Her life changed forever that day; she never felt whole again. Her mind flashed back to being ripped from his cold body, kicking and screaming, as blood dripped from her clothes and fingertips. She laid there for hours, refusing to move or believe he'd left her. She begged for death, just to be reunited with him. She could not justify his absence in her heart; she felt robbed of life.

"Mommy... you okay?" Lilly's soft voice carried through the large family room.

Chayanne stationary, waived at Lilly; she wanted to be discrete with her emotions. Lilly was entitled to make her own connection.

"Why are you crying?" Lilly asked, sensing something was off.

Still peering out the window Chayanne answered, "Trauma is deeply embedded in our roots; we bury things and lie to ourselves so we don't have to deal with them because we don't know how to deal with them. As a child, Momma told me that crying is a weakness and showing emotion is dangerous; you relinquish control to others when you do so." she continued as her voice shook, "I will always cry for Uncle Anthony and I'm not ashamed of it. To witness…" she paused, fighting back her remorse, "To witness a man being shot in cold blood, by someone that is elected or paid to protect you, does something to you. It eats you alive; it makes you feel like your life too will parish any day now by the same hands that should bear mercy to your existence. That is the harsh reality we live in." she blew out a heap of air, trying to calm herself.

Lilly stood there feeling helpless; she felt the pain of Chayanne's bleeding heart.

"Mommy… can I be honest with you without you becoming upset?" Lilly asked, disheartened and nervous. Chayanne wiped her tears on her sleeves and the snot from her nose with the collar of her shirt. She gathered her feelings—placing them in her internal box—trying to gain composure.

She smiled, turning to face Lilly, "Of course baby, what do you need to get off your chest?" she replied, walking toward her, swooping her in her arms. Lilly wrapped her legs around her waist, resting her head on her shoulder crying. Chayanne rubbed her back coddling her. "What's wrong honey, tell me? I won't be upset I promise." she stated to reason with her. They reached Lilly's bathroom, Chayanne reached down with her free hand, turning the faucet on to run her a bath.

"I did it," Lilly admitted, quivering in her arms.

"You did what?" Chayanne asked baffled.

"I wrote the word nigger on Lexi's desk... I... I feel awful, I should have never allowed Mary Elizabeth to talk me into it. She said if I didn't write it... I was one too, and that means you are one too. It was before I knew that word was created to demoralize us. I never told you about it because I saw how upset Mrs. Dyer was with Mary Elizabeth; I just pretended like nothing happened. Mary Elizabeth and the rest of our friends didn't talk to me for a week because I didn't confess. I just feel so out of place there; I feel suffocated. I don't know who I'm supposed to be or who they want me to be." she sobbed in the comfort of Chayanne's bosom.

Chayanne sympathized with her, "If that's the way you feel sweetheart... imagine how that word made Lexi feel. Mary Elizabeth did what whites have done to us throughout history... they use us against one another. House slave, field slave, light skin, dark skin; if we are busy fighting each other, we'll never look in their direction to fix the real issues." She paused, sat down, and checked the temperature of the water with her hand. She sat on the edge of the tub to be eye level with Lilly. "You have to learn how to be strong and courageous," she said. "It's always easy to go with the crowd; going against the grain makes you special. It's important to find out who you are and not let anyone tell you who they think you should be. I think you owe Lexi an apology; you have to be accountable for your actions." She wiped the tears from Lilly's face and placed her in the warm bathwater.

"You don't think I'm a bad person?" Lilly asked.

"Just because you do a bad thing doesn't make you a bad person; we all make mistakes, it's the lessons we learn that help us grow to be better people. You're not bad honey, you were ignorant in your actions. Now that you're aware, you want to repair the damage you've caused, or at least attempt to; that takes courage and maturity. I'm proud of you for being honest with me, thank you for trusting me with your truth." She said, pulling Lilly's chin from her chest, smiling. Lilly smiled through her tears.

"How do you do that? You always know what to say; I wish I could do that." Lilly questioned.

Chayanne laughed softly, "It came from having empathy for others and understanding things outside of yourself. I guess I've always been this way, especially with your father." Her smile stayed in place as she thought about their childhood.

"So, what happened next in the story?" Lilly wanted her to continue.

Chayanne's eyes lowered to the floor; Lilly's confession momentarily distracted her ill feelings.

"Honey, I think I've had enough for today. I promise we will pick back up; I just need... need some time to process things. Do you understand?" she asked gently.

"Um... I guess so. I mean, I don't want you to cry anymore, so yeah, I can wait." she said, swirling her hand in the water.

Chayanne looked around, trying to figure out the best way to explain her feelings. She role played enough in therapy, and it was time she put it to practice.

"I never got over Uncle Anthony's death, it scarred my heart forever," she said with a shaky, sad voice. "Discussing the story with you brought back feelings I weren't prepared to deal with. I buried that day in the back of my mind and I don't want to feel or think about it. The smell of death still haunts me." she paused as the hairs on her arms stood up. "I'm having… it's just hard to move forward at the moment. My thoughts are paralyzed with his memories, so tomorrow we'll begin again, okay?"

Lilly nodded in comprehension, "I'm sorry you lost him, mommy, I could tell you loved him more than daddy. He must have really been your hero." Lilly tried to comfort her.

She cleared the lump in her throat, "Thank you for that," she said, ringing out the washcloth to wash Lilly's body. They enjoyed the silence of each other's company; life was getting back to normal for them, one day at a time. Chayanne wrapped Lilly in an oversized drying towel after the last of the water gurgled down the drain. She plucked her from the tub, carrying Lilly to her bedroom. She dressed her for bed, tucked her in, and kissed her goodnight.

Chayanne craved a distraction; she went down to her office to look over the Baxter case notes that were faxed to her that afternoon. The case notes read:

> An unarmed sixteen-year-old was gunned down by an off-duty police officer. Devin Baxter was accused of shop lifting by the shop's owner; Devin claimed he didn't steal anything and he purchased the sweet tea and skittles at the register. The shop's owner pulled Devin by the hood of his black hoodie as he exited the store. Devin pushed the owner off him, causing him to fall on the chip stand. Officer Gentry saw the scene and pursued Devin on foot. Witness testimonies say the officer drew his gun and called out after him to stop; Devin turned his hands, coming from his sweatshirt pocket,

*and the officer yelled "put down your weapon" and fired 6
shots. Devin was found unarmed on the scene with a bloody
receipt in his hand. A pack of skittles and a sweet tea was
found with his wallet that contained his identification card,
school I.D., eight dollars, and a metro train ticket.*

*The district attorney refused to bring charges to the off-
duty officer, saying he acted in the line of duty. The mother
is filing a wrongful-death lawsuit against the Atlanta Police
Department.*

Chayanne stopped reading and sat back in her chair,

Chayanne clicked her hand-held tape recorder, "Note, if enough
evidence is found, force the DA to prosecute, pull Devin's autopsy report,
find the 911 transcripts, and case the store for surveillance." she clicked
the recorder off.

She placed her hand on her chin; she'd seen dozens of similar case
files. This only fueled the fumes of her vexation.

She tossed the recorder on the desk, "AHHHHHHHHHHH!!!!"
she shrilled out in frustration; there wasn't a dollar amount that would
justify stealing a son from his mother. She slammed her fist on her
desk in agony. Uncle Anthony wasn't the first or the last to be lynched
systematically.

Chayanne yearned for relief; she approached the bookshelf where her
law books collected dust. She pulled a set of mock books that revealed
a large safe that was built in the wall. She turned the nob slowly,
32...7...26...13...5; a loud click echoed and the lock unlatched. She
pulled out the safety deposit box that Uncle Anthony left her.

She reached for the key that she wore as a bracelet on her right arm. The key slid into the keyhole, she twisted it, and the lock clinked open.

DING-DONG, DING-DONG, DING-DONG, the doorbell startled her. She looked at her desk clock and it was a quarter after ten. She rushed to the door, hoping the sound didn't wake Lilly. Who would have the nerve to drop by so late? She peeked through the wooden blinds that covered the windows next to the door. It was a package left on the doorstep; a white delivery van sped out the driveway, turning left out the gate. She flipped a switch on the light panel and the eight-foot-high gate closed slowly.

"Mommy, who is it?" Lilly called from the top of the stairs.

"No one honey, it's just a package. Go back to bed sweetheart. She said, unlocking the deadbolt to reassure the gate was fully closed. As she stepped out onto the stoop, the smell of rain greeted her. She picked the package up and looked around to ensure no one else was lingering outside her residence. An uncanny sensation sent chills through her body; she closed the door and locked it. She turned the on light above the entryway to examine the package; it was addressed to her with no sender. She took the package into the kitchen to find the antique letter opener Momma left her as a keepsake. She placed the unopened package on the counter and ransacked the drawers to search for it; she didn't come up with anything. "Maybe Lilly or Klara misplaced it," she thought. She used a pair of kitchen scissors instead. She cut through two layers of tape and a foul odor escaped. She doubled over, covering her nose with the back of her hand. She continued to unravel the box, curious to see what was inside. She cut the last strip, rushing to open it; she jumped back startled, dropping the scissors. The antique letter opener she was searching for was stabbed through a possum with a note attached:

~IT HAS HANDS BUT NO FACE; WITHOUT FINGERS IT POINTS, WITHOUT ARMS IT STRIKES, AND WITHOUT FEET IT RUNS...

~IF YOU LET THIS EXPIRE, YOU WILL BE IN THE BOX~

~You've been warned~

Chayanne puked in the kitchen sink. She turned the water on to wash the chunks down the garbage disposal. She had an indication as to why the District Attorney never filed charges. Her head rattled; someone was targeting her.

CHAPTER

20

A LETTER TO A WOUNDED HEART

Chayanne called Detective Walsh; she trusted him to handle her findings with care; she apprehensively awaited his arrival. She opened the safety deposit box from Anthony and loaded her silver magnum .57. She rapidly turned the lights out, making it hard to track her movements. She rushed upstairs to check on Lilly; she was sound asleep, once again. She debated on waking her; she wanted her insight, but she was afraid to bring her into harm's way.

"Fuck it, better safe than sorry..." she mumbled to herself, barging in. "Lilly sweetie, baby wake up... wake up." she pleaded, shaking her with her right hand with the gun tucked discreetly behind her back. "Baby, I need you to get up and come with Mommy."

Lilly groaned and rolled over; she shielded her eyes from the bright florescent hallway light, "Mommy, you told me to go to sleep, now you want me to get up. This is child abuse," she argued.

Chayanne giggled, Lilly reminded her of her own impersonations of Momma, "I know baby, I'm sorry, but this is really important; I want you to come to the office, I'm waiting on a friend. You have to stay in there, I'll bring you some hot cocoa."

Lilly pushed the covers aside, "Fine," she agreed, climbing into Chayanne's arm, clinging onto her. Chayanne cautiously returned to her office. Listening for suspicious noises. "Mommy, why is it so dark?"

"Shhhh, we're playing a game." she whispered. The sound of the doorbell frightened her; she sat Lilly down and aimed the gun at the door. She shielded the gun with her body and said, "Listen carefully, go to my office as quickly as you can and lock the door behind you. DO NOT open the door until I come to get you. Do you understand?"

"Yes mommy," she answered, running off down the hall.

Chayanne placed her right hand on the open side of the handgrip, holding it firm, but comfortable. She rigorously approached the door. The office door locked, she peeked through the blinds; Detective Walsh stood there waiting. She then cracked the door with the gun by her side.

"Holy shit!" he grabbed at his chest, "You scared the piss out of me." His voice vibrated through the doorway. "You're packing? I'm scared of you; I need to check my drawers to make sure I'm good." he chuckled, hoping to ease the heightened tension.

"Sorry about that, Daniel," she placed her hand on his back, rushing him in. "I just don't like to take chances." she smiled uncomfortably. "Come this way, please." she instructed, walking him to the kitchen.

Walsh trailed, immersing in Chayanne's sensual nature; her untamed hair flowed closely behind her. The casual attire fit her curves like a glove; her perfume was subtle. He knew she was fierce and unfriendly by the way she played her cards in the courtroom. Her power suits, pulled back hair, and uncanny mien were dead giveaways. She was a deliberate ball buster and sharpshooter; her faint, gentle voice over the phone disarmed his perspective.

"A weird delivery van dropped this off about ten minutes before our conversation. Is it possible to lift prints off the letter opener?" she asked, pointing to the open box. "Sorry about the smell, I locked all the windows." She mesmerized detective Walsh; he had a hard time hearing a word she spoke. She discerned his unprofessional behavior and kissed her clenched teeth, "Detective, you're on duty, in my home, on my day off; could you make this anymore awkward considering the time of night?" she squinted her eyes, sassing him.

He blushed in embarrassment, "I'm sorry Mrs. Parker... I."

"It's Carter Detective Walsh, just Carter." she interrupted.

"Oh...my apologizes." he replied, amused as he examined the contents of the box.

"Someone had to break in; the letter opener is my mother's—she purchased it in the 60s—her initials are engraved here." She reached over him, pointing to the handle.

He scribbled down notes in his small notepad, concentrating to remain professional. "Is anyone else home, your husband or children?" he asked to confirm Mr. Parker was out of the picture.

"My daughter, Lilly is locked in my office, my son, Ashton is away at school, and my ex-husband moved out three years ago, hence the name change. Context clues, Daniel, how did you get your badge again?" she sassed skeptically with her eyebrows raised.

The corner of his mouth turned up, "Is it okay if I speak with your daughter?"

"No Daniel, I want to keep her away from this. She didn't see anything, she was asleep." she reasoned.

"True, but if someone got in the house undetected, she may have been here to notice; on the phone you said the only person that has access to your house is your nanny. Your daughter could have been here when a mysterious man came knocking." he said, debating his reasoning.

"True... I got confirmation this afternoon that Dallas wanted me in the first chair; the firm will announce it publicly on Monday at a press conference with Miss. Baxter." Chayanne let her mind catch up to her ramble, "Lilly and I been here all day, which indicates someone knows that the family had an interest in requesting me for the first chair. Meaning, they're being fed inside information." The wheels in her mind turned as she strung clues together. "Lilly's been in school all week, finishing up for the summer. I urge you to interview Klara, she's been at the house all week; here is her address." he jotted it down on his notepad. "If she can't give you anything... then and only then, you can talk to Lilly, detective. Something feels off, the same day the case file was handed to me these riddles have appeared."

He commended her wittiness, "Indeed Ms. Carter... I see why you're toting that .357 around; you have a real knack for being a protector. I'm surprised you aren't on this side of the law." he said flirtatiously.

Chayanne overlooked Walsh's developing interest. She grabbed a trash bag and rubber gloves from under the kitchen skin and began to clean. Detective Walsh wrote his report in the kitchen at the breakfast bar.

"Ahem, may I ask you a question?" he asked, looking up from his papers inside his briefcase.

"Sure Daniel." she responded, throwing the last of the paper-towels in the trash bin along with the rubber gloves.

"Why did you call me?" he asked, inquisitively.

"You mean, outside of the harassing threats?" she sassed, "You're still one of the good guys. I pay close attention detective. In addition, I see you sit in on a lot of my cases without any involvement. It seems as though you're searching for something… can't really say what, but I have a good feeling about your morals." she answered without a second thought. "Now detective, if you don't mind doing your report at the diner or somewhere else, I have an eight-year-old child to put back to bed. If anything comes to mind, I will give you a call." she dismissed him.

He brushed over his neatly bearded face with his index and thumb as he chewed her words over in his mind.

He packed up his materials, "Yes of course, I don't want to intrude. I'll let you know if forensics pulls anything of interest off the letter opener." He moved swiftly to the front door with a new sense of confidence in his step. "Thank you for trusting me." he nodded.

She followed closely behind; he opened the door and vanished into the mist of the night. She locked up tightly and thoroughly checked the house with the gun in hand.

Chayanne tapped on the door lightly with her index knuckle, "Honey, open up, its mommy." She called, waiting patiently. She listened closely, no movement from Lilly. An immediate panic set in. She retrieved her keys from the glass bowl they rested in by the front door. She rushed back to the office, fumbling to unlock the door. Rushing in, she found Lilly sitting at her desk, reading her letter from Uncle Anthony.

June 27, 1963

> *Dear Chayanne, my sweetest Suga in life, I love you like you're my own. If you're reading this, I'm sure your heart is heavy, and you are filled with sadness. I wish I were there to hold you to ease the pain just a little more, DO NOT worry, my death wasn't in vain; we all have a greater calling in life, you will soon learn. I will address the frivolous things for a moment; I know it'll never replace me, but I have a trust fund for both David and yourself; David will get his right away, I know he will make the majors... that boy is mighty talented... you, my Suga, will not be able to touch yours until you have completed a four-year degree program in addition to completing law school (I have a feeling the finding in this box will propel your interest in getting vengeance—not just on Tomlin—but the entire justice system. I think you will oblige to practice law). I am leaving the land that's been in our family for two generations to your mother and father. The bank will be split it into equal shares for you all. My operating manager is aware and will continue to run the bank under my instructions left for him. I know this is all overwhelming and you don't fully understand how finances work, but in my absence, you will have an abundance of it. In the last week, I have gotten my affairs in order. I want to give you a heartfelt apology that I wasn't able to control my vice of Rebecca, catapulting things faster than anticipated.*

I'm human and I make mistakes Suga, all superheroes have weaknesses; my weaknesses brought about my demise. I don't regret it by any means, as it was my choice. I'm sorry it's affecting you to this degree.

Furthermore, I am aware of Charles's abuse. I have attached instructions on how to deal with Mr. Henry; it is imperative that you abided by my instructions as they are written. Do not deviate from that plan. I apologize that I wasn't able to take care of him before my departure.

There's important information on Deputy Sheriff Tomlin, the mayor, Senator Collins, and the Governor. It may look like a crime that was in the heat of passion, but I swear to you, it's bigger. Pay attention to the things that unfold this year. You are young, but you have wisdom; allow that to carry you forward when you look back on this letter years from now. I wish I were there to wipe your weeping little eyes; I am always with you, carry me in your heart, Suga. I love you, always and forever.

~Love your Uncle Anthony~

CHAPTER

21

UNINVITED GUESTS

Chayanne shuffled the papers and the contents of the box together, refusing to show any emotion in front of Lilly. She was a curious child, and Chayanne didn't want to kill that instinct by being overly emotional.

Lilly could sense the discomfort, "Mommy, are you upset with me?"

"No sweetie, everything is fine, I need you to go pour you a glass of milk and warm it for bed." Lilly hesitated, briefly wanting to engage about the letter, but she did as she was told.

Lilly poured herself some milk and her mother a glass of water from the carton in the refrigerator as she did every night before bedtime. She placed her colorful mermaid cup in the microwave for fifteen seconds.

Chayanne locked the box and its contents back in the safe. She inhaled deeply to free herself of the sadness; no one had ever touched those things outside of her and Uncle Anthony. As the years expired, the papers still smelled of his cigar smoke, it was the only thing she had left to make her feel close to him. Her heart weighted with emptiness, longing for his comfort.

Lilly stopped at the entrance to the office, "Mommy, I'm all set." Lilly interrupted her intimate moment alone.

Chayanne quickly composed herself, smiling and nodding at Lilly. "Alright honey, let me finish tidying up here and we can go up in a minute. Drink your milk at the bar top, okay?"

"Yes mommy." she replied softly.

"Honey, close the door for Mommy." she asked politely.

Lilly pulled the door up but she didn't shut it completely; she didn't want to be alone. Chayanne plopped down in her plush office chair and palmed her face. She was scrutinizing over every feeling; she too felt uneasy and vulnerable. Pitying herself, she dimed her office lamp and exited; she locked the door behind her. She was adamant about doing one last sweep through the house, but the sound of Lilly's talking to someone threw her off her game.

Chayanne wandered to the kitchen, "Sweetheart, where are you?" she called out frantically looking for Lilly.

Lilly jumped from the pantry, "I'm right here, mommy." Chayanne jumped, screamed in her hand, and loosened up once Lilly busted into laughter.

Chayanne returned the laugh, mirroring her daughter's emotions, "You scared me, silly. What were you doing in there, who were you talking to?"

"I was getting a little hungry while I waited for you. I was looking for a snack; I'm fine now, I'd rather go to bed." she expressed, grabbing the glass of water she poured for Chayanne. "Can you sleep with me tonight, mommy? I don't want to be alone." she asked, grabbing her hand, staying close to her side.

"Of course, sweetheart, we can have a sleepover in your room." Chayanne insisted.

Lilly's room was closer to the stairs, she could hear if someone came into the house. Chayanne drank the glass of water and placed the half-empty contents on the nightstand. She kissed Lilly's forehead once more before tucking her in and snuggling up alongside her. Her heart filled with grief and failure, she held her composure. She regretfully hadn't lived to the expectations Anthony had of her; she'd lost sight of her purpose, having children and getting married were never a part of the plan, she strategically constructed. She made herself vulnerable and weak. A walking target, the intruder entered her home and discovered intimate things about her and her family. She sighed heavily, feeling hopeless and compromised.

Lilly drifted off to sleep; her deep breath cadence confirmed that she too was exhausted. Chayanne laid next to her, afraid of the dangers that lurked outside their home.

Her mind took her to the day she wept in Uncle Anthony's lap for him to comfort her one last time. This broke something inside her; the love for her mother was never the same. She blamed Momma for not being well enough to protect him, but more importantly, to protect her or David. If Momma never refused treatment, David wouldn't have gone rouge, being strung up to a tree and barely hanging on for life. Momma put her own needs before her children's and that disgusted Chayanne as a mother. She bit the inside of her jaw; the metallic taste of iron seeped onto her taste buds. Her mind rambled on with hate until she dozed off. The gun was in one hand while her opposite arm wrapped around Lilly.

Dawn snuck in through the thickness of the thunderclouds. The house phone rang non-stop; the answering machine picked up and the ringing would start again. Chayanne hazily heard the ringing, but she couldn't move. As she opened her heavy eyelids, she noticed her vision was blurred and unfocused; she closed them. Her screams and cries as a child repeated in her subconscious; her limbs were unmanageable.

"Seems like all the men in your life just disappear," Momma whispered to her from the shadows of the room. "You could never protect or save them; you can't preserve life baby girl, you ain't God. Some things you have to live with. Now get up out that bed and go to the phone."

"Momma... I... I can't," she responded, her voice slurred. She used all her strength to reach out to the figure that stood in the shadows. Tears escaped her eyes.

"Mommy... mommy?" Lilly's voice trembled with fear; she shook Chayanne to wake her. "Mommy, please wake up." she whined.

Chayanne laid there, stuck inside her body, drifting, in and out of sleep. She reached for the water glass on the nightstand, but her first and second attempts were unsuccessful. She mustered up the strength to fight through the vapid disarray; she grabbed the glass and brought it to her lips. A powdery residue was stamped on the rim of the glass that she drank before bed. She dropped the glass; it shattered on the floor, bursting into tiny shards.

"Mommy... mommy please, please wake up," Lilly called, tugging at her arm. Chayanne rolled to face Lilly.

The bedroom door creaked; she pushed her body from the bed, pointing the loaded magnum .357 at the crack in the door. The figure of Momma in the shadow disappeared and chill bumps covered her body. She sat there, eyes enormous and her pupils dilated, still in a daze. She slowly stepped onto the area rug. Chayanne shifted her weight to stand; her head spun, the room moved in circles. unable to catch her footing, the side of her head smacked the corner of the nightstand, her body plummeting to the floor.

"MOMMY!!!"

The shrill of Lilly's voice was the last thing she heard before fading into the darkness.

The wind chimes that hung from her bedroom window sang their beautiful song every morning as a nice breeze greeted them. She was in love with its harmony. Uncle Anthony gave them to her for her ninth birthday. Now when they sang, they brought sadness to her heart. Her bedroom door squeaked open to a small gap; the hall was pitch black. Chayanne's stomach turned; the hairs on the back of her neck stood. She pulled her blanket underneath her eyes, afraid for what was to come.

"Momma... is that you?" her small voice called out.

A strong gust of wind entered through her cracked window and slammed the door closed; she was terrified, she pulled the covers over her head cowering in fear. Her heartbeat drummed in her ears rapidly. The distorted memories of the sheriff pulling her from her bed in the mist of the night while Momma screamed played on a loop in her mind. Her nail beds were sore from clawing their arms as they pinned her down forcefully on the wooden floor.

"STOP!" Momma yelled, "She's just a child."

"This is a scrappy little nigger here, sheriff." A deputy called out before taking his club to Chayanne's head, knocking her on conscious.

A blurred, bright light shined into Chayanne's eyes; she blinked rapidly, regaining her consciousness.

"Ms. Carter, can you hear me?" Detective Walsh asked.

"Detective, this woman has suffered head trauma, I strongly urge you to let her go to the hospital before questioning her." The paramedic hissed in agitation with his intrusiveness. "I am sorry Ms. Carter, he refused to wait in the hall."

Chayanne winced at the pain from her bleeding wound; she reached her glass-filled palm up to investigate the gash. The paramedic grabbed her with his muscular arm.

"I think you're going to need stitches; that hand of yours will only make things worse." he explained.

She rolled her eyes, snatching her arm away from him like an angry child, "Where is my daughter?" she asked with dry grogginess.

"You mean this brave little soul that saved the day?" the paramedic responded, pointing to the hallway.

Lilly sat on the hall bench with a blanket wrapped around her. Her face was covered in tears; a policewoman accompanied her.

"How long was I out?" Chayanne asked, looking up at Detective Walsh.

He scribbled notes, "It's hard to say, dispatch received an emergency call from your residence around 5:57 a.m. Paramedics and police were on the scene in ten minutes. The media arrived five minutes after." he responded, lackadaisically. His eyes were bloodshot and his suit was wrinkled.

"Long night, detective?" Chayanne pushed with her line of questioning.

"Indeed, it has been Ms. Carter." he said snapping his notepad closed. His pores reeked of scotch and cigars. "You aren't the only one that can't keep the demons at bay." He smiled weakly, exiting into the hallway.

Chayanne was uncertain of what Detective Walsh was implying.

"You were whimpering for Anthony while you were unconscious. Is he your husband?" the paramedic curiously implied.

Chayanne shot a cold glance, " He's my dead uncle you ass hole." she scolded him. "Are we finished here, sir?"

He blushed in embarrassment, unsure of how to recover from insulting her. "I think you should come down to the hospital to get stitched up. A doctor should have a look at those cuts on your legs and maybe do a toxicology screen." He looked back at Lilly, "I overheard your daughter telling the detectives about a weird man in the house and she thinks he did something to you." He said shrugging his shoulders, "I'm sorry if I offended you, asking about your uncle, I say stupid things when I get nervous." he smiled at her, shyly.

He removed the bloody gauze from her scalp, replacing it with a new one. Chayanne sat up, resting her back against the nightstand, vaguely remembering a figure in the corner. She disregarded the nonstop ringing of the house phone and rested her head on the edge of the nightstand; she listened to all the chatter in the house, trying to gauge what was real and what wasn't.

"Uh... I hate to bother you, but you do have a concussion; I don't want you dozing off to sleep. I need your eyes open, Ms. Carter." the paramedic demanded, " If you nod off, I have to take you to the hospital. Can someone tend to your daughter while you're away?" he asked, brushing his blond, shaggy hair away from his face.

"My daughter stays with me!" She said fiercely "I don't need to go to the hospital sir." she sassed.

He chuckled softly, "My name is Luke, and you don't have to refer to me as sir."

Chayanne looked him in the eye, " Luke... that was my grandfather's name."

He smiled uncomfortably, turning to put his medical stuff away in the EMS bag that laid on top of the glass. Something about him felt familiar to her: his smile, eyes, and nose. A washed expression swept over her; she thought she saw a ghost. Her intuition cranked up and she curiously studied him while he tended to her.

Luke felt her quietly studying him. "Is everything okay, Suga?" she heard him say.

Chayanne's face turned blue, "What the hell did you say?" she responded, posturing upright.

"I asked was everything okay, Ms. Carter? Maybe you fell a little harder than I thought." he said, shinning his light in her eyes again, waiting for her pupils to constrict. "Hey, I need the stretcher in here. We need to transport." he hollered to the medic team on standby in the hall.

Chayanne grabbed his collar, "That's not what you said, who the hell are you and how do you know me by Suga? Was that you standing in the corner? Was it you that drugged me?" Chayanne questioned him in a fit of rage.

Luke's face reddened, "I need 20cc of benzodiazepines," he demanded.

Chayanne completely caught him off guard with her line of questioning, "Baby girl, I don't know what you're referring to but I need you to release my shirt, or I will dose you with this sedative."

She cut her eyes, peering into his blue, model-like eyes, searching for answers. She released his collar, still studying him over. He looked away quickly, wanting to avoid eye contact. He hurriedly packed the rest of his things and stormed out the room.

Lilly watched nervously, "Mommy?" Lilly called from the hall, "Please don't leave me, I'm afraid." she confessed with a quivering lip.

"Everything is fine honey. Go put your shoes on, you're coming with mommy." she replied, never taking her eyes off of Luke.

"Ahem, Ms. Carter we do have some questions for you. We asked your husband to meet us down at the hospital. It's the procedure when a child is involved."

Chayanne leaped to her feet, pulling herself to reality. She read the DFACs worker's name badge. "With all due respect Victoria, I want to make this very clear to you... I am a highly respected attorney of the court; I am very aware of my rights. I also know the system loves taking our children and putting them on those pretty little adoption posters... I need you to use your common sense, and it seems like you don't have much. Take a look around; my child is well taken care of. I realize she placed an emergency call for her unconscious mother, but there was an intruder in my home. Do you know what that is, or would you like for me to spell it out for you? I suggest you use that clipboard and take some notes..."

Daniel stepped onto the battlefield, "And we are done here, Victoria. I am unaware of who contacted and the nature of the complaint, but please accept my apology for wasting your time. Ms. Carter will be transported to the hospital with her daughter. Please call Mr. Parker and inform him he is no longer needed." he instructed with caution.

Victoria stood with her mouth gapped open, eating all of the words Chayanne served her. The caseworker's ego had been dismantled in front of the entire room of wallflowers, with gawking eyes.

Victoria sighed and slightly shook off the shame, "Thank you Detective Walsh, my apologies Ms. Carter." she whispered like a timid child as she showed herself the exit.

"Well, I am happy to know you aren't suffering any brain damage from that fall." Walsh said, holding back his laughter.

Chayanne looked at him blankly, "Care to explain what that's about? Who called them?"

He allowed everyone to resume activities before responding in a low voice, "I'm working that out now. It seems like someone wants to tarnish or discredit your reputation before this trail leaks to the public. I'll be sure to let you know when I get the analysis back from the lab. It seems eerie, but I want to be positive before going to the chief."

"Daniel, the police department gunned down an innocent boy. You want to go straight to the devil... you're searching for answers for the attorney that is going to barbeque the entire department on the stand if the DA doesn't pick this back up. Did you leave your common sense in that bottle of scotch that you reek of?"

"Chayanne... I mean Ms. Carter; I don't think you should take this case, I really don't. Look at the danger you've been in, and you haven't publicly accepted it yet."

She chortled softly, "I don't run from fights; I don't care how big the bully is. Someone has to speak for the dead because they aren't here to speak for themselves. Besides, I know what it feels like to not have a voice and for people to gut you on the stand to dismantle your reputation."

"Ms. Carter, we're ready for transport. Please lay on the gurney." the medic insisted.

"I'll walk to the ambulance. I'm abled body, thank you!" she responded, turning her attention back to Detective Walsh. "No way the media will get me laying down on this one. This all seems so thought through."

Lilly appeared at the top of the stairwell, " Mommy, I'm ready to go." "That's awesome honey, can you go grab mommy's work bag?" she asked, never breaking her gaze from Detective Walsh, "I clearly have work to do." The corner of her lips curled up slightly, causing Detective Walsh to smile flirtatiously with chills running over his body.

"Well then Ms. Carter, I will be back to check on you shortly." He nodded his head excusing himself.

Lilly looked out at the sea of reporters through the rear window of the ambulance as they drove away; her worry clouded her.

"Mommy, who are all these people here for you? Are we famous?"

"No, we aren't famous." she said, patting the seat next to her, "Anytime something like this happens, some people are just curious to write a story about it. They want to know why someone broke in or how it happened. They want to know lots of things, but we are a private family. We don't share our information with anyone."

"Not even Mary Elizabeth?"

Chayanne's eyebrows raised; she pulled Lilly's chin up so their eyes could meet. "Sometimes, when people know your secrets, they can use them to hurt you. Mary Elizabeth knows you're black. Although she manipulates you to think otherwise; she used that to make you hurt Lexi and feel bad about yourself. How is that being a genuine, decent human—using racial slander to hurt others?"

Lilly began processing several situations where Mary Elizabeth influenced her to do things she didn't feel good about. "Yeah, I don't think you can be a decent human if you're constantly hurting others." her eyes lowered to the floor; she was ashamed she'd even brought Mary Elizabeth up. She twilled her thumbs and swung her legs.

"Are you ladies alright back there?" the medic slid the privacy window to ask.

Chayanne nodded to confirm that they were doing just fine. She requested to ride alone with Lilly to seek answers about the intrusion. She was afraid Lilly wouldn't be transparent and honest in front of anyone else.

She pulled Lilly close to her side hugging her; she kissed her forehead.

"I love you my little flower, you were so brave calling the police. I am proud of you."

Lilly looked up at Chayanne and said in a low whisper, "I didn't call, the man made me call."

THE MYSTERY MAN

Chayanne was puzzled. The ambulance breaks squeaked and came to a stop. The paramedics exited, closing their doors.

Chayanne asked discreetly, "What man?"

Tears filled Lilly's despairing eyes as she shook her head no. "I can't tell you, mommy." The opening of the hatch doors disrupted Chayanne's heavy gaze.

"Ladies, we have arrived. Please watch your step on your exit." the medic said jokingly.

Chayanne motioned her hand for Lilly to exit, letting her off of the hook temporarily. Lilly jumped down and waited patiently for her mother to exit; she didn't want Chayanne to be out of sight. Chayanne exited and Lilly clung to her leg immediately.

Chayanne paused, looking at the medic, "Hey, that Luke guy you guys were working with earlier... where did he go?"

He shrugged, "I don't know much about the guy, he got added to the team this morning… he gives off some pretty gnarly vibes." he explained, "Honestly, I'm glad he split."

Chayanne uncannily nodded, "Um… thanks!"

Chayanne turned her attention back to Lilly, "Honey, is everything alright?" she asked rubbing Lilly's soft curls.

"I just don't want anything bad to happen to you, mommy. I just need to stay close to protect you." she explained calmly looking at the ground, careful not to reveal her tear-filled eyes.

They walked swiftly in unison into the emergency entrance where she was greeted unpleasantly by Charles and Quentin.

"We've been waiting here for hours, what in the hell is going on?" Charles said angrily. Chayanne disregarded his temper as she silenced her ringing cell phone without looking at it.

"Excuse me, but don't use that tone with us." Lilly expressed with a matching angry tone, mimicking Ashton's demeanor when he dealt with Charles. "No one requested your presence, so you are free to leave like you did this family."

Charles stared at Chayanne with a vexed expression, "You're rubbing off on my sweet little girl too much. No wonder Victoria called me about your parenting."

Lilly rolled her eyes, "You were seriously born without a clue. I am standing right here. If you have something to say in reference to me, please address me," she placed her small hands on her hips, she was clearly over Charles.

"Lilly Parker, I did not raise you to be so unruly. You should be ashamed of yourself for behaving like this in public. I don't know what has gotten into you, but you need to fix it." Charles demanded sternly.

"That's the problem Charles, you didn't raise me at all you were too busy chasing after Mr. man pants over there. I decided my last name is Carter, I'd rather take after my Uncle Anthony." she said, walking away shaking her head disappointed.

Chayanne snickered, unable to control Lilly's outburst. The stain of embarrassment was all over Charles in his fancy, gray tailored suit. Quentin gasped, feeling the heat of Lilly's words.

"Lilly, get back here right now young lady." Chayanne called after her still snickering. "Charles, I am truly sorry, I don't know what has gotten into her lately." she apologized, showing all of her perfectly placed teeth.

"You must have bumped your head pretty good if you find that entertaining Chayanne. That was rude and she completely disregarded my feelings in this matter... When did you have time to kick up your ghostly past to tell our daughter? We agreed..."

Chayanne cut her eyes and shot a look at Charles that made him instantly recoil and shrink in the spot he stood; he swallowed his words.

"Charles, I'm sorry to inform you, but the way your chose to raise our children made them ignorant to their race and culture. Unfortunately, America isn't color blind. "I've omitted the past as long as I could... We've put plenty of fires out, need I remind you of how I saved your ass?"

"Oooooooh honey, I must say you are fierce, GAWD!" Quentin said, admiring how she scolded his fiancé. "Girl, I need to borrow that attitude. It's hard trying to get this man in check. Yes lawd, I wish I had a rewind button... Okay!" he snapped fiercely.

Chayanne observed, amused with Quentin's theatrics as he twirled in awe in the emergency room.

"Ms. Carter, we really need to examine you." a nurse called out.

A surprised look of hurt swept over Charles's face, "You dropped Parker?"

Chayanne disregarded Charles, "Lilly, you need to talk to your father with respect and dignity. Remember what I told you, you need to think for yourself." Chayanne said, chastising her, "When you're finished have your father escort you back to me, understood?"

Lilly sighed in frustration, "Yes mommy, I understand." she replied, slinging her body into the cushioned chairs in the waiting room.

"Honey your ex-wife is everything." Quentin expressed popping his lips. He took a seat next to Lilly admiring how beautiful she was. He'd never met her in person and was ecstatic to break the tension between her and Charles. "I so love that you take after your mother, she is something. Mmmmh, so Miss. Lilly, darling tell me about you, honey. What do you like to do?"

Lilly screwed her face up with an awkward smile, "How do you talk like that?" she giggled.

"You mean like this," Quentin replied in a high-pitched voice, "Or like this." he said in a low, sassy voice. Lilly chuckled at his entertainment.

"I like your animal print pants, what type of animal is that?" she engaged with him like her new best friend. Charles watched the two interact from a distance with his hand stroking his mustache. He paced around the waiting area, unsure of how to approach Lilly; this was the first time in a long time they shared words without a door separating them.

Chayanne's words cut Charles deep because they rang true, he was so concerned about his happiness and freeing himself from his past that he wanted his children to be ignorant of what they endured to be successful. He ran his palm over his deep, wavy hair anxiously. He watched Quentin and Lilly laugh together; he got a glimpse of a relationship he missed having with her. His emotions sank to his stomach, his eyes burned slightly from the tears that gathered. He walked through the exit sliding doors to rein himself in. He felt ashamed he'd abandon his children just like his mother abandoned him. He now understood the emotional turmoil he'd put his children through from Chayanne referencing the fires of the past. He took a seat on the outside bench to wallow in his sorrow; he lacked the courage to apologize to Lilly. His cell phone buzzed in his jacket pocket; he ignored the call. He submerged to find himself in solace.

Chayanne winced in pain as the nurse stuck the long, numbing needle inside the gash. She gritted her teeth to bear through it.

"Temperature and blood pressure are good. The doctor will be in momentarily to stitch you up, Ms. Carter. While the Lidocaine is at work, Detective Walsh wants to speak with you. Is that alright?" the nurse asked politely.

"Sure, send him in." she responded, a distraction was necessary. The iodine burned in her hands and thighs from her glass cuts.

Walsh walked in, "Thank you nurse," he closed the door behind him. "Ms. Carter... how are you feeling?"

"Daniel, you don't have to be so formal right now, lighten up a bit." she flashed a friendly smile, the pain medications started to take effect." I'm fine, I'll be happy when you unmask who's responsible."

His smile faded, "Chayanne, there wasn't a forced entry into the house; whoever sent that package, never left." his discomfort grew; he knew the next question could rattle her completely. "Is it possible that Lilly could have let this perpetrator in?"

Her face puzzled, "Why would you think she would let a stranger in?" she tapped her fingers in a slow cadence as she always did when she questioned new clients.

"We found traces of nitrogen fertilizer in your pantry from a man's boot, the same nitrogen fertilizer that matches your garden." He shifted nervously in his chair afraid to continue, "That's the thing Chayanne, I don't think this is a stranger to her... the team believes it's someone that Lilly has been in contact with prior to the incident. The evidence isn't adding up." he looked at Chayanne trying to anticipate her blow back.

She shook her head slightly, back and forth like she was calculating a difficult math problem, but the solution wasn't coming to mind.

"When Lilly called the Emergency Operator, was she calm or did she seem frantic?" she questioned, still shaking her head.

"I haven't personally listened to the 911 call. Why do you ask?" he pressed inquisitively.

"On the ride here, she said the man made her call, but refused to tell me who she was talking about. She tensed up uneasily like she was afraid." She tapped at her lip, "I have an uneasy feeling about that paramedic Luke. Lilly never took her eyes off of me when he was tending to my wounds. Something about him seems familiar, but I… I can't put my finger on it." she said, trying to solve the jigsaw mystery.

"I'll look into the paramedic, he seemed to be studying you very closely while you were unconscious," Detective Walsh said. "He was there before I arrived, and I can't say I've seen him around beforehand. He has a striking face of someone you couldn't forget."

"I feel a bit groggy from the meds, I need to lie down for a bit. Will you please check on Lilly for me." she asked, lying back on the bed and closing her eyes as her head hit the pillow. Her cell phone buzzed in her briefcase. Detective Walsh paused to inform her of the phone, he pulled back, allowing her to rest peacefully.

Detective Walsh walked swiftly down the hall toward the patient check desk; he turned over in his mind that Luke was one of the first on the scene. His walk turned into a swift jog; his shoes clacked loudly on the tiled floors. He reached the desk, panting out of breath; his stomach burned from the scotch he consumed minutes prior to the 911-dispatch call.

A grimaced look on his face, he struggled to speak to the nurse, "Excuse me… Um, the paramedic team that brought Ms. Carter in, are they still here?"

"Yes sir, they are parked on the side of the building. Are you okay?" the nurse asked, concerned about his physical state.

"Yeah, just had one too many drinks and no sleep. I'm just a little lethargic, that's all. Thank you for your help." He dashed out the doors, barely catching his breath. He jogged swiftly to the guys at the ambulance;

they were smoking and drinking coffee. Detective Walsh hunched over with his hands on his knees, panting.

"Sheesh, I'm sure I don't look out of shape, whew.

Gentlemen, let me catch my breath." he requested, holding one finger up. The three paramedics laughed.

"Just getting some facts together about the Carter residence and I need your help just in case I missed something." he paused, scanning the three of them. "Wasn't it four of you? You all arrived in two separate ambulances, correct?"

"Yes sir, it was four EMTs on the scene, but we didn't all arrive together." One of them replied with a heavy country accent.

"Well, where is the other guy...um" he patted his bearded chin as he thought. "Luke, right, isn't that his name?"

"Uh, he was around here somewhere on the phone, but I never worked with the fella. He was the first on the scene. All three of us here rode together. This is the unit we operate in." the chubby paramedic responded, snorting and spitting his tobacco out.

"Hmm interesting... did you all happen to catch his last name?"

"No sir, but he was parked right over there." the country paramedic replied, pointing to an empty parking space. He scratched his head wondering where he could have gone. "I don't know if his shift ended or not, but we haven't received any emergency calls. I thought it was kind of strange—a Paramedic working solo when we normally work in teams of two or three."

"Thank you gentleman for your time, if you all think of anything else that would be helpful, here is my card. When the mystery fella shows up, just give me a call, I'd like to ask him some questions related to the call." Detective Walsh handed the chubby paramedic his card, nodded his head, and walked off. He was disappointed he didn't pick up on Luke's scent before he disappeared.

He punched the air in frustration, "Shit, shit, shit, shit," he muttered under his breath. "Who the fuck is this guy?"

Charles looked at his Audemars wristwatch, noting the time was a quarter till 9 a.m. His agitation with his phone increased as it rang nonstop before his regular business hours. Unable to gather his thoughts in silence, he jerked his phone from the inside pocket. He had twenty-four missed calls and a full voicemail box from a Washington D.C. number. He paused running through his mental Rolodex of D.C. partners.

"Ah dammit, who is this?" he said, dialing his voicemail anxiously.

"Good morning Mr. Parker, this is Sheila West, a detective with the Metropolitan Police Department of the District of Colombia (MPDC). There has been an incident involving your son, Ashton Parker. We have attempted to reach his emergency contact Chayanne Carter since 5 a.m. but we never received an answer. You are listed as the backup emergency contact on his school forms. This is a very serious matter; please contact us at your earliest convince. Your son has... "

The woman's voice faded as Charles let the phone drop from his hand; it broke in two as it hit the ground. His heart raced in suspense, Charles hyperventilated. His mind traveled down memory lane—memories of David's body swaying over the quarry replaced with Ashton's face; memories of his mother's body lying on a steel slate replaced with images of Ashton. He held his chest as he stumbled into the emergency room, wheezing for air.

Quentin sprung from his seat, "Nurse, he has asthma. Please, he needs help right away. NURSE!" he screamed as Charles's body hit the tile floor; he couldn't get enough oxygen."

"I need medical assistance in the ER, code red; I need medical assistance in the ER, code red." the nurse repeated over the hospital intercom.

"Ashton... Chayanne, tell Chayanne Ash," he tried to explain.

The nurse put a mask over his face, "Sir, please don't speak." she barked at him. "I need you to calm down."

Lilly took notice from afar; she was unsure of how to respond or if to respond to her father's falling out.

She saw detective Walsh exit the double doors, she assumed he was coming from her mother's room.

She walked in his direction, "Mister police, can you take me to my mommy please." Lilly called out to Detective Walsh, who seemed to be in a rush. He hesitated, stopping in his tracks, looking over to Lilly. "Yes you." she confirmed she was talking to him, "Take me to my mommy." she asked reaching up for him to pick her up.

"Sure, I can take you to your mommy." he said, thrusting her up and cradling her in his arms. He wished it would soothe her weariness. She rubbed her red, sleepy eyes and rested her head on Detective Walsh's broad shoulders.

She was half asleep when they reached Chayanne's room. The doctor finished stitching her gash closed.

"You must be a doctor and a lawyer the way your phone rings nonstop, Ms. Carter." the doctor chuckled. "Don't be alarmed, but you will have a bruise around your right eye near the area of impact."

He hummed a small tune, cutting the suture. He left the materials on the tray and exited the room.

"Hey, look who I found." Detective Walsh said, setting Lilly down on the bed.

She smiled warmly, giggling through her closed lips, "Hi honey," she laid her head on Chayanne's chest away from Detective Walsh; she wasn't feeling social.

"Thank you for bringing her to me, Daniel. Did her father leave?"

"Oh... um, what does he look like?" he asked—squinting, looking into the distance—trying to think of anyone who resembled Lilly.

"Well built, gray suit, metrosexual, super posh, peanut butter complexion, brown hair." she spat out a list of characteristics of Charles.

"Oh... yeah, he's having an asthma attack or something. He's in the care of the doctors."

Chayanne blushed, showing her discomfort, "Well, I suppose we should go check on him." Her eyes uneasily danced around the room.

"Mmmmh, that's interesting," he smirked, "I've never witnessed you in an uncomfortable situation; you're so well composed."

He lowered his head, looking at her out the corner of his eyes. "It's... kinda cute."

Her eyes darted to meet his, "Really?" she said with a goofy, relaxed look. "How about now?" they shared a lighthearted laugh.

"I don't want to overstep, but what happened between you two?"

"He found love with someone else... I am happy for him. I think we got married because of childhood familiarity." she clarified.

"Well, I guess I can check this off as a first date since you're finally opening up." He fist-pumped the air in celebration.

"Wishful thinking Detective Walsh." she busted into laughter until tears trickled down her face. Lilly turned in her sleep, causing the roaring laughter to quiet down.

"Wow, that's cold... am I not your type?" he teased, smiling and flirting with her.

She pretended to check him out, "I wouldn't say that," she looked down shyly, "I've had a few boyfriends growing up here and there, but never anything like I had with Charles. Honestly, I don't think I know how to date, or if I want to." she confessed.

"I'm either on fire or it must be those good old drugs they're giving you for pain. You're difficult to crack; you're so stern and serious. It's nice to see an easier side of you." he said, satisfied with the small talk they were having. The buzzing of her cell phone disrupted them.

"Daniel, you mind grabbing my palm pilot out of my bag? It has to be the partners at the firm about the case. I'm sure my house was all over the news this morning. I think Lilly and I need a little retreat at the Four Seasons until I can get an upgraded surveillance system installed."

Her mental to-do list brought her back to reality.

"Well, I could be your personal bodyguard, if needed." he laughed, grabbing her phone as she requested. "All I require are home cooked meals; I wouldn't charge you... hell, it would keep me out of the bars late at night." he said, handing her the phone.

"Thank you, I am truly flattered." she smiled, taking her phone out his hands. Her playfulness ceased when she noticed she had 56 missed calls from D.C. and 5 missed calls from Ashton.

"Daniel, will you give me the room please? I have an emergency." she requested with a serious and stern tone. He nodded and pointed to the hall mouthing he would wait for her. She held her hand up acknowledging him, but she wasn't really listening. The door barely closed; she began playing the messages.

"Good morning Ms. Carter, this is Sheila West with the MPDC. I am calling in regard to Mr. Ashton Parker; there has been an incident..."

Chayanne redialed the number before the message concluded. Worry filled her; she died to know if Ashton was safe.

TAKE THE BAIT

Chayanne tried Sheila's line multiple times and got her answering machine:

"You've reached the desk of Sheila West; I am currently away from my desk at the moment. Please leave your name, number, Case I.D. and a detailed message at the beep and I will return your call as soon as I am available. Sorry for the inconvenience. Wait for the beep"

Beep.

"Good morning Miss. West, this is Chayanne Carter, I've received several calls regarding my son, Ashton Parker. I have called his dorm phone numerous times and I am not getting an answer. I was in an accident myself, so I do apologize for the delay in returning your call. I am a worried mother so please call me as soon as you receive this message."

Chayanne ended the call; seconds later, the same D.C. number called her.

"Hello... Hello this is Chayanne Carter."

"Hello, Ms. Carter, this is Sheila West from the MPDC..."

"Yes, I am aware is my son okay? Is he hurt?"

Sheila cleared her throat, elongating Chayanne's suspense, "Ms. Carter, your son is in police custody... They are stalling, waiting for evidence to come in from the crime lab. They are gunning to charge him with sexual abuse in the first degree and murder in the second degree of a classmate that attended the university. The only reason he hasn't been arrested is the results aren't in for the autopsy report and the rape kit. He's been in an interview for 36-hours without his phone call. The crimes happened this past weekend after a fraternity house party off the Georgetown campus. This case has aired live over the news here in D.C.; we picked Ashton up with a mob of angry classmates outside of his dorm building. He suffered a black eye and a busted lip when the officers picked him up for questioning. He's still considered a minor according to Washington D.C. laws. You're listed as his emergency contact."

Her voice monotone she explained.

Chayanne quickly went from a concerned mother to the woman she was highly known for in the courtroom: ruthless and unforgiving.

"Miss. West, in order for the department to arrest Mr. Parker, a case would have to be built against him with compelling evidence or a signed confession stating he committed the crime. Either way, he shouldn't have been interviewed without a parent or attorney present; he can only be detained for questioning for 24 hours if he wasn't charged with anything. If they have a judge's signature, he can only be detained for 36 to 96 hours... I must say, I'm highly disappointed. This should be unfavorable when placed in front of a judge. I need to speak to my son, will you put him on the phone?"

2 00

"Ms. Carter, I am a domestic violence detective; simply put, I push papers. Your son begged me to get in touch with you since they brought him in. The only thing he is guilty of is underage drinking and unfortunately, being at the wrong place at the wrong time. Three of the Omega frats gave witness testimony against Ashton, saying they saw him leave with her. I've personally read the case notes and... Ms. Carter, I am disconnecting the call. I will be in touch shortly." she abruptly hung up the phone.

Chayanne gathered Lilly's dead weight in her arms, collected her briefcase, and headed for the door. The nurse met her on her way out.

"Ms. Carter, the doctor recommends you stay..."

"To hell with the doctor's requests, I need to get on a flight to D.C. immediately."

"Chayanne, everything okay?" Detective Walsh inquired, walking swiftly behind to keep up with her pace.

"Daniel, I will be in touch; I hope you have a break in the case soon. I have to leave town, family emergency." she replied, speed walking down the hall; she pushed through the doors to the waiting area, Quentin sat next to Charles receiving an asthma treatment.

"Who drove? I need to go straight to the airport." she demanded without hesitation. Detective Walsh came crashing clumsily through the heavy wooden doors. Charles inhaled, pointing to himself.

"He has ten more minutes on this machine." Quentin pleaded.

"Screw that, my Ashton is in trouble; I need to go NOW!" Daniel interrupted, "You need a ride to Hartsfield Jackson?"

She nodded walking to the sliding doors to exit. Detective Walsh followed.

"Chayanne, can you wait for me? I need to be there; I am his father." Charles protested through his steamy mask.

"Charles there isn't a choice between my life and my children, things may be different for you, but they are all I have. There is no damn machine or treatment that would stop me. I will fight, tooth and nail, until my last dying breath ...I will see you in Washington." she spoke to him without the courtesy of looking back.

It dawned on her; the news reporters were waiting behind the iron gates for Ashton. They used the media to get the upper hand. Unfortunately, Ashton wasn't from a troubled background, on some bullshit, IVY league scholarship as a one way out of the ghetto. She was immensely angry by the time she reached the passenger door of Detective Walsh's blue GT Mustang painted with racing stripes. He jogged to open the door and disposable coffee cups and papers blew out on the cement. He struggled to retrieve his litter. Chayanne looked away; she didn't want to embarrass him any further. The last conversation she had with Ashton played over in her mind; she could place him at the party, but when did he leave? The pieces in her mind moved; she needed to read the police reports to pick out the facts.

Momma's voice whispered to her, "You can't save them all Chayanne."

"Would you like to stop at your place to pack a bag or two?" Detective Walsh insisted.

Chayanne waved him off, "No, straight to the airport. I can pick up whatever is necessary when I get there. Materials can be bought, but

I can't buy another son." she responded, staring out the window as she tried to smothering Momma's voice. He looked her over; for a woman that endured a hectic night, she was still wrapped tight. She didn't seem frazzled or distraught; that put his radars on. She's endured much worse in her life and he was anxious to figure out what she's experienced. He sensed she was locked deep in thought, so he put a muzzle on his small talk. The sound of the V-12 engine roared down 285 South toward the airport.

The detective folded his hands and leaned forward into the table.

"Ashton, we know you want to go home; you've been here close to two days. We know you're hungry and tired; we know you want your mammy. All we want to know is what happened? Simple, just tell us what took place after the Omega house, and we will set you free." The old, white-bearded detective said trying to coerce a confession out of him. He knew they were on borrowed time; it was only a matter of time before the chief barge in demanding for him to be cut loose.

"I told you sir, I just want my phone call. I don't want to speak without my attorney or parents present. Anything I say could be used against me in the courtroom and my mother is a lawyer; you have denied my medical rights to see a doctor. My eye is blackened, my lip busted, and I think one of the officers dislocated my shoulder. Until I get what I need, I can't help you. I've repeated this same thing to everyone that's been in here several times. You can keep starting your tape recorder over and over, for a confession that you'll never get because I DID NOT DO IT!" Ashton huffed hot air, sitting back in the metal chair. He was exhausted, doing the same dance with different detectives. He knew the holding time was expiring; how soon he had—no idea because the analog clock in the interrogation room was broken. The detectives rushed his door in at 3:17 a.m. He was thrown in the interrogation room at 4:47 a.m. He caught a glimpse of the first detective's watch that escorted him in. At that time, the clock on the wall was three hours behind the original time.

The officer clicked the recording tape off. He sat on the edge of the table as close to Ashton as he could. He looked down at him like morning garbage, "You think you're a smart nigger, don't you? Going to your fancy Ivy League college, blending in with the white boys. I'm going to nail your ass to the wall for this one boy. You just wait; forensics is finding your nasty juices all over that girl. You're a nasty motherfucker for ejaculating all over her face the way you did; did your daddy teach you how on your mammy?" he laughed, putting a cigarette between his lips.

Ashton chuckled along with the officer; He was aware the officer wanted to get a rise out of him. He wanted him to be angry and make a random outburst, just like Chayanne warned him in his early adolescence. He knew he was prying on the stereotype of what an average, black man was said to be.

"Did I say something funny to you, boy?" he said abruptly in the midst of lighting his cigarette.

"You made a joke sir; I was merely indulging in a laugh with you," Ashton responded with a smirk. "I find it interesting that I had your intellectual intelligence when I was eleven. It's sad to see some people never push through to accomplish more in life." Ashton said, mocking him.

"You better watch it nigger; you're seconds away from me blacking that other eye; someone needs to knock you off that high horse." He inhaled his cigarette and took a long draw to calm himself. "I wonder how many peckers your mammy had to suck to pay for that Ivy education of yours? I'm sure they splattered her good just like you did Kendal Fisher, yeah? I'm sure it felt good putting your little nigger dick in some pure, white pussy; I bet my last dollar it's the best thing you ever stroked."

"Detective, it looks like you live on your last dollar; my mother told me to give to the poor, not rob them." Ashton grinned hard, staring the officer down with his gray eyes. The officer puffed his cigarette and chuckled; he stared back into Ashton eyes and blew smoke on Ashton's face, causing his eyes to water. Ashton blinked rapidly to clear his eyes from the cloud of smoke. The smoke cloud cleared and the detective put the cigarette out Ashton's cheek.

"AHHHHHH, you son of a bitch!" Ashton yelped in pain.

"Yeah, that's the temper I knew you had in you, boy," he said satisfied, stroking his white beard and patting his oversized belly. He exited the interrogation room, pleased with his malicious behavior.

Ashton jumped to look at his face at the two-way mirror; the smell of his burnt flesh nauseated him. His energy ran low since he refused to drink or eat anything they offered, not sure if they would plant evidence to make their case. His anger ran high—he wanted to deck the cop right in the face—he barely contained his temper. He sat back in the chair and rested his forehead on top of his arms; he jumped when the door swung open. Miss. West brought a phone in the room.

"Your mother is unavailable; if you have someone else to dial, I recommend doing that." She handed him a black rotary phone with a note taped on the bottom of it. "You have five minutes." she said, closing the door behind her. Ashton ripped the note from the bottom and rushed to unfold it.

Contact successful!

He crumbled the note in his hand, happy that his mother knew his circumstances. He picked up the receiver and dialed out. The phone rang; a knot grew in Ashton's throat. He was nervous to explain his predicament but he wanted to call someone he figure would calm him. The phone rang a few times; his hopelessness began taking over, the phone clicked.

"Hello?" A woman's voice said softly.

"He...Hello, this is Ashton is my Uncle David home?" he asked frantically.

"Oh honey, it's so good to hear your voice. Your uncle is out coaching the boy's baseball game today. Should I have him call you back?"

"Um... tell him I need him come to pick me up, I'm at the MPDC station."

"Ashton, what's going on? Why are you at the police station? Have you called your mother?"

"Aunt Linda, I can't really talk much right now; please tell Uncle David where I am as soon as possible. Does he have his blackberry with him?"

"Yes baby, he does, you go on and call him. I'm going to go down to this park and let him know he needs to get in the car and drive over there. Oh honey, I hope they treating you okay?"

The white-bearded officer put his finger on the hook switch and disconnect the call, "Times up! Who gave you this phone?"

Ashton sat back in his chair, cutting his eyes at the officer.

"Are you deaf, boy?" He yelled in frustration.

"Detective Michaels, that will be enough, you are excused." A man called from the hall. "Go home detective, I want to see you first thing in the morning." The man ridiculed him in a low tone that was inaudible to Ashton.

"Captain, the kid was about to crack. I was just doing my…"

"Michaels, do you know who the hell this kids' parents are? You're in here treating him worse than the motherfucking gang kids that you constantly bitch up to. The tapes were rolling the entire time behind the glass you dumbass. How the FUCK am I going to explain to his mother that his face has a God damn cigarette burn on it? How the hell would we be able to convict anyone with this shit? Did you miss the whole Rodney King bullshit? You's one stupid motherfucker, makes no damn sense. Using the word nigger, I ought to whoop your ass if I didn't have this damn uniform on. Get your white trash ass out of here you dumb son of a bitch. His holding expired eighteen hours ago. I don't need any blowback in this department; it's already bad enough we have a dead girl on our hands. Just get out of my sight." He let out a moan, frustrated. Michaels, disappeared down the stairwell. "I'm convinced everyone has lost their damn minds around here. I'll never make the damn ballot for mayor with this bullshit." He collected himself, entered the interrogation room, and shut the door behind him.

Antsy, Chayanne and Lilly waited for takeoff. Lilly was happy to get away, she felt safe. Chayanne on the other hand was distressed; she knew every second mattered and she was more concerned with him being released. Memories of David's neck flooded her mind. She cursed herself for letting Charles talk him out of going to Morehouse or Howard at an early age.

"Mommy, why is daddy invited on this trip? Ashton doesn't even like him." Lilly questioned, peaking over the back of her seat.

Chayanne turned in her seat to look at Charles; he was boarding through the aisle with Quentin waltzing behind him, making his presence known. Chayanne faced front, putting her Versace sunglasses on to relieve the light off her bruised eye that darkened as the day progressed.

"How ironic Chayanne, you refused to wait for us, but we made it in time to sit next to you." Charles gloated satirically, mocking her. "Would you look at that, we even got seats right across from you," He fell into the seat letting out a relieved sigh.

Chayanne shook her head; she definitely planned to see her therapist the minute she got back. She coached herself through her emotions silently; it was foreign for her to see Charles interact with someone else in a romantic setting. Yet, she was happy he could live in his truth in modern day; she was determined to adjust accordingly.

"Honey, let's switch seats," Chayanne suggested to Lilly. Lilly looked past her mother and frowned immediately.

She looked up at Chayanne, "Mommy, seriously?" she asked sarcastically.

"Pleaaaase?" I'll buy you room service when we get in tonight." Chayanne pleaded, sweetening the deal.

"Fine, as long as it comes with ice cream," Lilly said unhappily.

Chayanne settled into her window seat reclining as far back as the seat allowed. She hadn't felt the pressure of drowning helplessly since the day she stood on the asphalt where Uncle Anthony took his last breath.

A tear dribbled down her rosy cheek; she gritted her teeth together to fight against the unstable, emotional tide that rose.

"Passengers, this is your captain speaking; we are gearing up for liftoff. Please pay attention to your cabin stewardess that will direct you to our safety guidelines. Refreshments will be offered shortly. Thank you for flying Delta Airlines."

"Psssst, Chayanne... Chayanne, are you going to eat your complementary peanuts?" Charles whispered across the aisle as the flight attendant gave safety instructions—trying to lift her mood. Chayanne tossed the small packet of peanuts to the edge of Lilly's tray without responding. She pulled her blanket out its packaging and wrapped it around her torso. The lights dimmed; the aircraft backed out of the loading area and prepared to hit the runway.

CHAPTER

24

THE STAGES OF GRIEF

The onyx casket lowered into the ground slowly; the town's people threw red and white roses to say their finally goodbyes to Anthony Reid Carter. His body was finally laid to rest, six months after being stored in a freezer at the county's morgue. An extensive investigation had to be completed before the county approved his burial. Momma wept loudly, unable to contain her emotions; she hadn't fully come to terms with parting with him. She pretended he had ran off with Rebecca and took baby girl along with them since she'd been missing since his death. She knew for sure someone had drug her and Charles into the woods and slaughtered them like prize cattle. No one had an explanation; the colored part of town combed all the surrounding woods and streams in search for them. Momma endure six months of agonizing nights; she was burying two of her true loves, although one was in the casket. Daddy and David posted posters all over town of Chayanne; even in the white parts of town they received a citation for every flyer. Still, no one knew anything about the disappearance of Chayanne Carter-Rice and Charles Parker. David stood watching Uncle Anthony being lowered into the grave, stricken with grief; in his heart, he felt his sister was still alive. His tears fell unwillingly, he hated life didn't make sense without his annoying, sassy, and privileged little sister. He rubbed his lower neck where his rope scars lived. He wanted anything in his path to pay for his grief.

"Fuck this bullshit!" he muttered, undoing his black necktie storming off across his grandmother and grandfather's grave. Daddy, who sat in the back of the funeral crowd, was the first to notice David's unacceptable behavior. He excused himself from conversing with Peter. Peter sensed David's frustration and was aware they hadn't gotten along much since he dangled lifeless in the quarry; he grabbed at the coattail of Daddy, but missed him by a hair as he narrowed in on David. He had to jog to catch up to him.

"David... David, I know you hear me calling you, boy!" he snatched his suit jacket by the collar, jerking him off the ground. His patent leather dress shoes slid, tossing up dirt. He reacted instantly pushing daddy's hand and freeing himself from his suit jacket. David hit a growth spurt and he spent most of his time moving lumber down at the lumber yard. He saved his pay for a private detective; he was adamant that Chayanne was still alive, and he felt her energy near. He vowed to himself he would rather fight ten toes standing than die a coward. He danced with death, and he wasn't afraid to die.

"Get the fuck off of me!" he said, bucking up and taking a stance against Daddy. He could smell the moonshine on Daddy's breath.

"What did you say to me? You think you're a man now because you have some height on you and some bass in your voice, nigga?" Daddy cocked his fist back, waiting for David's disrespectful words. David pushed his chest out and his chin up, daring Daddy to hit him. The attendees for the funeral gawked in suspense. Momma paid no mind, like she had been for the last several months. She ignored the reality she lived in; she blamed Daddy for the disappearance of Chayanne and the death of Anthony.

She uttered, "If you'd just been there and not off on your selfish mission, they would be here; I wish it were you that God took away from me, not them."

She couldn't stand the sight of him; she would sleep in baby girl's room, just to feel near to her. Her internal guilt ate at her about David; if she stayed with her treatment to begin with and talked to him, he wouldn't have spiraled out of control, sneaking out and lying. She sat crying. She wished cancer would have canceled her out; at least she would be with them.

Peter rushed across the yard, grabbing daddy's cocked arm, "James, that's enough; it's a yard full of people here to celebrate your brother's and daughter's life. Why would you rob them of their goodbyes? You need to go sleep that moonshine off, brother. You don't want to do something you'll live to regret. David is just making sense out of all this, like everyone else. We all deal with our demons differently." Peter whispered in a low tone, only Daddy could hear his words. Daddy relaxed and jerked his arm away from Peter. He stumbled off in the opposite direction. David aggressively snatched his grass-covered jacket off of the ground, bunching it up in his hands. He looked Peter in the eye and continued walking.

"Hey David, you mind if I walk with you? We haven't had much time to talk. I don't see you down at the boardwalk or church much anymore." Peter wanted to know what was going on, this wasn't the family he'd admired and gotten to love.

"Yeah, whatever man." David responded nonchalantly, not really caring much for company.

"So how ya been, man? Are you getting that arm ready for spring baseball?" Peter placed his hand on David's shoulder.

"I haven't really thought about training much; the hand surgeries went well, I guess; it's been too many distractions." David walked faster to politely remove Peter's hand from his shoulder.

"So, what's really going on, David? Your parents treating you okay, son?" He couldn't hold his burning curiosity, he wanted David to be transparent.

"What do you mean by okay?" his voice hit high pitched then dropped.

Peter laughed, "The puberty thing, that used to bug the hell out of me." David joined in on the laugh, nodding his head in agreeance. "Are you getting the attention and compassion you need with everything going on?"

David stopped in his tracks; the chagrin feelings flooded him, "Peter, we don't talk about our feelings where I come from. We do as we need as the day progresses. All these questions about what I'm feeling ain't going to get my parents to be who they were before all of this. Momma hates and blames Daddy for everything that's happened, and he drinks himself half-crazy to not feel her rejection. They sold the house to pay for this funeral and most of the citations for putting Chayanne's missing poster up on the wrong side of town. They used the rest of the money to pay the hospital for Momma's treatment and my surgery. We had to move back into Uncle Anthony's place; that put me in a different school district to play baseball. The scouts barely make it down to the colored part of town to see the kids play. Uncle Anthony left us nothing, but his bank is still standing; his advisors said that the bank doesn't belong to Momma. So, when you ask me how I'm feeling, I can only give you the facts for you to get your own feelings. I just stay to myself, working in the lumber yard. I don't bother anyone and I don't like when people bother me. Now if you will excuse me, I have to get to work."

David walked off into that chilled, gloomy day in December a changed man. Peter stood with his chin in hand, letting the condensation build in front of him. His brows wrinkled and tears collected in the corners of his eyes. His nose and cheeks redden as his heart sank from his chest.

PROVE IT

Chayanne yelled for a taxi, holding on tightly to Lilly's hand outside the Ronald Regan airport entrance. She rushed to get to Ashton. Chayanne was disappointed in Charles's mindless, childlike behavior while Ashton's life was in danger.

"Hey Chayanne, wait up." Charles called out as he and Quentin tried to catch up.

Chayanne glared, pursing her lips, she closed the taxi door. Her look confirmed he hadn't handled the situation appropriately. He was relieved to know Ashton was in holding as opposed to turning into a human popsicle on a morgue table somewhere. An overwhelming sadness clouded him as it dawned on him, he lost his best friend.

Quentin bumped into Charles hysterical with laughter," Oh my, those ladies were hilarious, darling. Wait where is Lilly and Chayanne, I thought they were holding a cab for us?" he cuffed his arm underneath Charles's arm. "Why the long face, lover?"

"I think this was a mistake." Charles turned to face him. Quentin's face went white as he grabbed at his chest through his open shirt.

"What... what do you mean, mistake?"

"My son needs me, my daughter despises me, my... Chayanne is pissed at me and I'm just laughing, having the time of my life with you, ignoring that my family's life is blazing on fire. I never knew my father, and I don't want my children to know I exist and not have a relationship with them. I fucked everything up; I left her to live some fantasy I dreamt up, not considering all the hardships and crazy shit we've been through. It made our bond what it is. I feel guilty, I betrayed her..."

"Baby... baby, you can't feel guilty for being happy." Quentin ignored Charles's conviction of remorse.

"Quentin, I was cheating on her with you for two years; all those late nights and fake ass work trips; I'm parading you in front of her like a prize pig I won at the county fair. Chayanne has always been my best friend before my wife. Before she became the mother of my children, some things are aligned the way they are, and we can't change that... It just dawned on me; she's a single mother like my momma was. I am gallivanting through life without a fucking care. That's fucked up of me to do to my best friend. It was a mistake bringing you on this trip; my son revolts me because he comprehends the damage I've caused. Parading you around in front of them isn't fair, lover." He rubbed his head in frustration, "Go check us in at a hotel, we will talk more tonight. I just have to fix things."

"Charles, you always do this thing." Quentin sassed, "You have one foot in and one foot out. If I am going to be your husband, you need to allow me to take my place."

"Your place is with me, not my family. They have to accept you when they are ready. We can't force a relationship upon them, that's not how it works." he fussed back.

"I don't know how long you expect me to keep playing the sidelines, I'm a priority in your life, act like it. Chayanne knew you were cheating on her because I sent her the damn email the first time after the holiday party. That woman ain't dumb nor hurt; she's playing you."

The fire in Charles's eyes burned, "You fucking what?"

Quentin stood on the edge of the curb, wailing his arms for a taxi. "Charles, you can go to hell, first class. When you get there, call me." He opened the door aggressively, dropping his designer purse and clumsily fumbled into the taxicab. He rolled the window down halfway, "The truth hurts lover, but I'm sure you will learn to cope. I will be at the Four Season if you decide to finally pick me over all your drama. Tootles!"

The taxi driver pulled Chayanne and Lilly to the entrance of the MPDC building.

"That's four dollars and ninety-five cents." He slid open the bulletproof divider that separated the back and front of the cab.

"Thank you!" Chayanne replied, placing a ten-dollar bill in his hand. "Keep the change, come on Lilly let's go." The weight of it all began to sit on her shoulders; she took Lilly's hand and marched into the entrance of the police department. The air was musty and thick; the thunder clouds loomed over, threatening a catastrophic storm. The thunder roared when they entered the building. Her head was held high and her black sunglasses were planted on her face. Her hair was pulled back loosely, covering her fresh set of stitches. She cleaned the dry blood from her face in her palm mirror on the ride over. Her three and half hours of sleep for the day hadn't refreshed her; she was operating on fumes of adrenaline. She reached the front desk of the station like a coiled rattlesnake ready to strike.

"Excuse me, is Sheila West available?" she asked politely. The doughnut-eating desk clerked looked up at Chayanne and looked down at Lilly.

"She's in an interview with the captain, you can come back later, miss." He responded looking back down at his magazine.

"Ahem, I don't care if she's in a meeting with George W. Bush, I need to speak with her." She pulled up her shades revealing her black eye. The clerk looked up, startled at the bluish-black bruise that neighbored her eye.

"Of course, you need to file a report. Give me one second." he said moving as fast as he could manage.

"Mommy," Lilly whispered tugging on her arm.

"One second honey, let me handle this. Chayanne requested, not taking her eyes off the clerk, moving through the glass cubes. Lilly, let her hand go and ventured off into the lobby area. She walked right into David's arms and picked her up and embraced her in his long, lean, and muscular arms. She clasped her arms around his neck, hugging him.

"I missed you too, sweetheart. The last time I saw you, you were barely taller than my knee." He teased.

"It's only because you're a giant, Uncle D. You're like nine feet tall, aren't you?" she laughed.

He joined in, "Well of course not, I'm only 6'5. It only seems like I'm a giant because you're so tiny." He tickled her.

"Ha ha ha ha ha ha ha, Uncle D stop, I have to use the potty."

Lilly's laughter alarmed Chayanne, pulling her attention toward the noise.

She put her head down as soon as she noticed David, "I don't have the time." she mumbled to herself.

"Miss?" the clerk called for her attention, "Miss West, we'll see you now. Just go through the glass doors over there, through the metal detectors, and I will buzz you in. I hope they nail the son of a bitch that did that to your eye. I hate to see women battered; just know you're safe now." Chayanne smirked and pulled her shades down off her forehead. She walked toward the metal detectors leaving Lilly in David's care; David watched in awe as she gained access. He'd been there for an hour and still hadn't gotten access to Ashton.

She cleared the metal detectors, disappearing into the thick of the police station. She wandered past Miss. West's empty office; she went up the stairwell toward the interrogation rooms. Two officers stood outside the interrogation room; Three officers observed an interview from the two-way mirror. Chayanne got in earshot of their conversation undetected.

"I heard Michaels is going to be on a month's suspension for the way he interrogated the kid." One of the officers gossiped.

"Yeah, I wondered who fucking turned the camera on then reported it to the captain upstairs. That's fucking bizarre; I'd be pissed. No one says anything about us jacking the dipshit neighborhood kids up. We mace them, tase them, kick the shit out of them, pistol whip them, but this Ivy league nigger gets royal treatment, I don't get it?" the taller officer said, gossiping.

"The captain's running for mayor; we don't need a headstrong nigger in office. Once he's gone, I'm sure they will put Neil, the D.C. Chapter KKK leader, in there temporarily; he made lieutenant a few months back. Then, it'll be open season to pick these fucking thugs off. You know my brother can't even get a fucking job. This city is so filled with these fucking porch monkeys. It's sickening; how is a real man supposed to live?" The other officer laughed.

"Man, Neil as Captain? Yikes! If this happened under his watch, this kid wouldn't have made it in. I'm surprised all he got was a black eye and busted lip for raping and killing that poor white girl. If I were on that detail to pick him up, I probably would have choked him out. They rarely look into those claiming the suspect died of natural causes during an arrest. Dennis got off on a choke out last month; he put in his report the victim had asthma and took off running on foot, when he actually choked the motherfucker out." They both laughed then hurriedly dispersed; the captain approached the door.

"You two shit heads stop gawking and get some God damn work done for once. I'm still waiting on the reports from you both that were due last month. If I see you two around this door one more time you will be taking a leave of absence without pay. You crooked bastards; get the hell out of here!" He sipped his coffee; the lip of the cup disappeared behind his white, tobacco-stained mustache; he watched the officers go back to their desk. "Miss West, go ahead and take care of that mystery woman. Tell Jerry's lazy ass to send this fella's uncle up so we can release him; I can't believe this God damn circus around here.

God knows I can't imagine the hailstorm his mother is going to bring to us. Any word on her yet?" he asked. Sheila left the room and walked past Chayanne, pretending to casually look at a bulletin board waiting for her to pass. Sheila's kitten heels descended the stairs; she cleared the last step. Chayanne took action.

She walked into interrogation room and the captain sat at the table with his back to the door. Ashton's head swayed; he could barely keep his eyes open.

"This is how your department treats minors, captain?" Chayanne said with aggression. Her voice shook them both; the captain spilled his hot coffee on himself. Ashton jumped, not really knowing if she was a mirage or real.

"Ahem, um Miss, I think you have the wrong room." The captain turned in his seat peering up at her; he tried to soak the coffee off of him with napkins.

She leaned down inches from his face, "Captain, this is my son, tell me exactly what's your plan is here or I will slap a civil suit on this place so fast, your great-grandchildren couldn't run for mayor if they wanted to. I don't want any bullshit, captain, I want the cold hard facts!" Her face scowling, she dared him to call a bluff. Dozing off, Ashton stood from the chair on high alert. He recognized that tone and it meant business; he saw steam escaping her ears.

"Well Ms. Carter, no one told me about your arrival, I do apologize. Have you been waiting long?" he asked, cowering in his chair.

"I don't want the small talk. On what grounds did you have to bring my son into custody?" she questioned, removing herself from his airspace. The chatter and whispers grew in the hall; she used her left foot to close the door.

"Ms. Carter, I would be more comfortable speaking with you in my office."

"Do you think my son had that luxury? He's on display like a zoo animal. Your officer and detectives are peeking through the two-way mirror, slaughtering his reputation based on race. Where are the facts? Your department is going off witness testimony of three, drunken frat boys. Captain, were their blood-alcohol levels taken at the time of their statements? Were the "frat boys,"" she said using air quotations as she spoke, "finger-pointing so they could be cleared from such charges? Were they asked for DNA samples?" she paused so he could catch his thoughts. "I've been here a good twenty minutes and I can tell you've walked into some deep shit!" She walked to sit with Ashton on the opposite side of the table. She crossed her legs, removed her glasses, and folded her arms across her chest. "Here we are, captain... explain please?"

"Mom I swear I..."

"Ashton Anthony Parker, I am not speaking to you. You are to speak when spoken to." He swallowed hard, shrinking into his chair; his feelings of despair faded.

26

PERCEPTIONS

Charles walked into the front entrance of the MPDC with his chest poked out through his half-buttoned shirt under his blazer. He strolled in letting his ego go unchecked. He spotted David, Lilly, and Linda in the waiting area and strolled over to them. They were engaged in talk with Lilly to distract her and they were witnesses of trauma shaping a fragile mind.

"Hello Linda, hello David, nice to see the family support." Charles's voice bellowed.

"Ahh Charles, nice of you to finally join us. I didn't know we would be graced with your company. David expressed smugly.

Sheila butted in from behind the desk, "Uhh, Mr. Carter, the captain would like to speak with you now." Sheila called, motioning him to join her.

Charles intruded, "I'm his father, I think I should be the one to speak with the captain on my son's behalf." Charles stood surveying the waiting area for Chayanne. "Linda, is Chayanne in the bathroom? She should be here for this; she's the lawyer." Charles huffed.

Linda rolled her eyes giggling, seeing through Charles's charade of theatrics; Chayanne played the mother and father roll in her eyes. They walked over to the desk; Lilly was in David's arms.

"Wow, you're much taller in person than you are on the television set," Jerry murmured to David.

David chuckled, "I get that a lot."

"Jerry, captain said Mr. Carter and the others will have to wait." Sheila looked around, "Umm, the mystery woman... where is she?"

Jerry scratched his receding hairline and shrugged, "She was instructed to sit in your office. Maybe she had to use the restroom, I don't know."

Shelia rolled her eyes, "Any word from Ms. Carter? Captain is very adamant about her arrival."

"Sheila, that woman hasn't stepped foot in the building, I would know. It's just been these folks here and that battered lady with the little girl... That little girl in Mr. Carter arms." Jerry paused for a second to process his thoughts. "Oh... oh my maybe, maybe that was her." He looked perplexed. "Well, how'd she get the black eye? Oh hell Shelia, you figure it out." Jerry gave up trying to think and went back to reading the comics in the morning paper. Sheila fussed at Jerry for being incompetent and lazy.

"Lilly, what happened to your mommy's eye?" Linda whispered looking suspiciously at Charles.

Lilly cupped her hands and proceeded to talk normal in a soft voice. "The man was in our house, he hurt mommy and made me call the ambulance for her." She pulled back and put her fingers to her lips to inform Linda it was a secret.

"What man?" she mouthed, pointing at Charles while he stood amused at Sheila and Jerry fuss.

Lilly shook her head no.

"Mr. Carter, this way." Sheila instructed, ignoring Jerry; she cursed him under her breath. She would be responsible to deal with the captain's rage. Her nostrils flared and her small arms flailed as she stomped down the hall furious.

David handed Lilly off to his wife and walked to the same direction Sheila was headed; Charles followed closely behind. David's four extra inches camouflaged him.

"Sir, you aren't made of glass, I can clearly see you," Sheila said without looking back once at Charles. "I have children of my own and I know when someone is trying to pull one over on me. You have to wait in the hall while Mr. Carter speaks to the captain, is that clear?"

"Ashton is my son, the captain should want to speak with me!" Charles exclaimed, wanting to insert himself as Ashton's hero.

"Listen, judging by your tailored suit, you're a businessman; when the boss gives an order, that's what you follow. I don't have time to go stand in the welfare line because of what you say. You don't pay my salary, so just respect the rules. You're lucky I'm allowing you back here, Mr. whatever your name is."

"I'm Mr. Parker, you left messages on my voicemail, remember? I'm not even sure how David got involved with this."

"Oh, you're Mr. Parker," she said in a sarcastic tone, smiling.

"What is that supposed to mean? Oh you're Mr. Parker?" He mimicked her in a snooty high-pitched voice.

Sheila laughed uncontrollably climbing the stairs, "Ashton described you perfectly." She hollered laughing.

Charles followed behind with his attitude in hand. He had an idea what Ashton may have told her; he wasn't vague in expressing how he felt about him face to face.

The officers crowded interrogation room 3. The crowd ooed, watching through the two-way mirror intensely. They were having a field day at the expense of their captain.

"Hey, clear this out!" Sheila demanded, "If the captain catches you all were gawking at him while he's cleaning up your bullshit, he would flip." She barked, letting her Latina accent come on strong. "Get back to work." The crowd dispersed and the men muttered under their voices amongst one another. "NOW!" Shelia yelled sternly. They all moved like a fire had been lit; they scrambled over one another, fumbling back to their desks.

The crowd stopped when they took notice of David, "Hey, that's David Carter from the Boston Red Sox!" A random officer blurted out. They all bombarded David like a pack of wild dogs. The chatter grew; the men asked for his autograph. David was pinned to the station wall nervously. The last time he was surrounded by that many whites he was lynched. He felt the walls caving in on him, so he panted for air trying to remain calm. Charles panicked and headed for the stairs to make his way back to the lobby area.

Sheila, angered that her command was disregarded, climbed on a nearby waiting bench and whistled loudly. The captain came rushing out to see what the fuss was about.

"What the hell is going on out here? Everyone, get back to your desks and do some damn work. You all are making so much ruckus, I can barely hear myself think." He massaged his temple to calm his madness. "Come on, son," he said, waiving David into the room. "Sheila, I will deal with Jerry later." he said shooing her. He closed the door and offered David the chair next to him.

Ashton's face lit up like Christmas lights when he saw his superstar uncle. "Uncle D, you came." His excitement was smoldered out by Chayanne's cold glance. He knew she was pissed and he feared what was to come after they left the station.

"Um yeah, I was explaining to your sister here, Mr. Carter. I haven't reviewed the report thoroughly; Ashton was picked up for a witness statement, not questioning."

"Captain, what about the fact that your guys tried to coerce Ashton into a false confession, have you given that a thought? Black men are accused of crimes they didn't commit, locked away for years, and no one believes them. Look at the Central Park Five case a couple years ago; I for one second don't believe those boys are guilty, but our judicial system is color blind. It's black or white, and we all know black ain't in… captain?" David remarked sarcastically, folding his arms and sitting back in his chair.

Chayanne annoyed began grinding her teeth and swallowing her words. David didn't know how to leave the spotlight; he commanded the room unapologetically.

The captain attempted to reason, "Listen, this is a shit show, I can't deny that. I just want to make amends; the department cannot handle a lawsuit right now."

Chayanne sat up and clasped her hands on the metal table, "His name was released as a person of interest on Georgetown campus. To start a riot outside his dormitory is a mystery I'm certain I can solve. Your men then tried to convenience him they were taking him in for his safety—that they were responding to the campus security complaints. When he refused and asked to call his mother, they slammed their iron fist, taking him in because he was the only black boy to attend that frat party. Are you asking us to look the other way? That's the confusing part; you're saying all that just to say nothing captain, you're talking in circles. It's an election year; you want to be voted to take the democratic seat as mayor. A smudge like this in the black community in this city? You can kiss that ticket goodbye. Let me inform you; just because you take a seat at the white's table doesn't make you one of them, you're still outvoted by many on a daily basis. Real change happens when you punish the men who have wronged my son who sits here with a black eye, a busted lip, and a fresh burn on his face. You'll leave and another white supremacist will fill your chair; and next time, a little black boy won't be so lucky to have a Sheila West fend for him while his mother is states away, providing for her family." She gasped for air continuing her rant. "Now, since there aren't any charges to be filed currently until you've done a T-H-O-R-O-U-G-H investigation, I am taking my child to receive medical attention. I am then taking him home. If your investigation turns up any evidence pointing to my son as the suspect, here is my card. Please feel free to follow up with me as his attorney."

"Ms. Carter, we ask that Ashton not leave the state until the investigation is complete. Your brother lives not too far from the city, couldn't Ashton reside there until all the dust is settled?"

Chayanne cleared her throat agitated, "Captain Mitchell, I am no fool. I want you to take to my words kindly, GO FUCK yourself if you think my son isn't coming home with me. He has rights and until you can bring suitable evidence to a judge about your murder case, he doesn't have to stay. You are better off going to play in traffic if you think I am going to willingly comply with that bogus request. I understand you're on a political hot seat; the Governor will not back your seat with an open murder case on a white innocent college girl; but I will be dammed if another innocent black life is taken by force or caged like an animal because he reigns superior genetically. Get a fucking grip and check into reality!"

"NO Ms. Carter, you get a God damn grip!" he said slamming his hands on the table, standing to his feet. "Your family's reputation is well deserved, I'll give you that, but if you think for one minute that you can turn this system on its head, you got more than that blacked eye coming to you. Your family is always so hot-headed, beating on your damn chest like you're King Kong at the top of the fucking Empire State building. Why do you think your Uncle Anthony was killed, huh? I hope you don't for one second think it was because of some cheap motel love affair with a white woman. This kind of change that you talk of, ain't ever going to happen if I don't make my way to the senate, and so what if I have to turn my head once or twice to sacrifice a few black lives to save millions of black lives. Keep on with your mission, little girl, and that small target will continuously grow on your back. You've been around long enough to know what they do to the ones that make ripples in their ponds, not playing by their rules." He collected his folders and stormed out the investigation room, leaving the door open for their exit.

CHAPTER

27

CLOSURE

Lilly sat and dangled her feet deep in thought. The propellers of her life had just turned on; she felt uprooted and complacent, barely grasping the straws of her reality. She couldn't fathom how her mother wasn't unraveling after she was attacked and dragged to another state, all in the same breath. The overwhelming sensation of anxiety crept in the back door and swallowed her whole. She wanted to ball up and weep her feelings until she felt empty. She stood and paced around the small waiting area, hoping she could escape herself if she paced fast enough.

The buzzing of Chayanne's palm pilot agitated Lilly. She pulled it out and noticed it was work calling her mother. Lilly looked around dubiously at her Aunt Linda who was engaged in conversation with Jerry about baseball. Lilly ignored the call and turned the palm pilot off; she knew Chayanne couldn't handle another distraction, her life was already in shambles. She dug through the briefcase to look for something to color on; she needed something to occupy her time while she spent the beginning of her summer vacation waiting for another thing to happen.

Her mind flashed back to the shrilling screams she let out as her mother fell unconscious on the floor. The man in the black ski mask grabbed her from the bed as she kicked and screamed. Lilly fought as hard as she could until the man slammed her small body against the accent brick wall that hung her mother's expensive painting. Lilly hung on the wall by her collar on a picture hook; she stared into his blue-glassed eyes filled with hate.

"You coward!" Lilly spat in his face.

He gripped her throat and let her body dangle, "Listen you little shit, you do exactly as I say and your mother lives. One wrong move and I'll slit her fucking throat in front of you, letting her blood spew all over your face. You'll watch her gurgle her fucking blood, gasping for air. Your family has already taken enough from me, so there won't be any hesitation to kill that bitch." he said in anger with his hand clenched tightly around Lilly's throat. Her face turned blue and her body made a loud thud when it met the floorboards. She coughed and wheezed, gasping while grabbing at her neck. He grabbed her foot and dragged her to Chayanne's room to the telephone.

"Lilly, honey, did you hear what I said?" Charles asked for the third time, grabbing her arm gently.

"STOP!" Lilly screamed; Charles snatched his hand away, frightened by her reaction. He thought he'd done something to hurt her. He played tennis in his mind, contemplating on whether to walk away or be her father.

He stooped down, eye level to Lilly, "What's going on with you? Are you alright?" He could sense how petrified she was.

"I just want to go away with mommy. I don't want… I don't want her to die." She slowly confessed, allowing her tears to pour out of her.

Charles rubbed her back, trying his best to soothe her; her words struck him in a manner he wasn't prepared for. He sat beside Lilly, taking her hand into his. They sat in silence, allowing it to mend the awkward void between them.

"What happened to provoke you to say that, honey?" He asked without thinking.

"Why do you always have to use words I don't get?" she snatched her hand away and slumped back into her chair. "This isn't business Charles; you don't have to talk to me like that. I'm not one of your interns or associates." she shot at him nastily. "If you gave the same effort of being my dad, maybe we wouldn't be like this."

Her words hurt, but he knew they only hurt because they were true. His financial presence didn't equate to being a real father. The only father he somewhat knew was Uncle Anthony, but he pushed him out of his mind, hoping her could escape his past.

"Lilly… I'm sorry for not being the father that you believe I'm capable of; no one taught me how to be a father and mine wasn't around; I was a shameful secrete of his." With a dry throat and dejection, he continued, "My mother died when I was young and she didn't really teach me how to parent. She would put cartoons on, give me a bowl of cereal, and deadbolt herself in the room with random strangers. She would polish off a bottle of gin after she powdered her nose with flour and tell me to go stand in the closet because I looked too much like my father. She said she hated me for coming along and ruining her life. She dreamt of being a fancy-colored model, but her freedom was restricted when she had me. I only ever knew love from the way your mother taught it to me." He looked down at his lap, trying to collect himself; it was hard for him to talk about his feelings because they weren't a simple calculation to solve like his work. Lilly looked over at him; she unfolded her arms from her chest and softened her callus for him; she was amused, she wanted to hear more of his story.

They were pulled from their heartfelt moment from the sounds of Chayanne and David bickering in a low tone when they entered the lobby with Ashton.

Charles stood and wiped the wrinkles out of his pants. He put his palm out for Lilly and grabbed Chayanne's briefcase, "Let's go see what all the fuss is about." She accepted his hand willingly after being drawn closer to him by his vulnerability.

Charles and Lilly approached the small group quietly at the front of the lobby near the glass exit doors.

"David, I am tired; I don't have time for you to play Daddy David right now. Let me check into a hotel, get some sleep, and we can discuss this later!" she hissed.

"Fine, you go and get checked in, but the kids are coming with Linda and I. Judging from your eye, you can barely protect yourself."

"If you wanted to be a father so bad David, why didn't you have any kids of your own? Exactly, you were selfish just like Momma wanting to live your life in the damn limelight!" She stormed through the exit door and the rain engulfed her as she flagged down a taxi.

Charles let Lilly's hand go and ran after her with her briefcase in hand. Lilly tried to run after them, but David picked her up. She cried and fussed, wanting her mother. Ashton tried to go after her as well. David grabbed his shoulder and applied a small amount of pressure to stop him.

Linda stood in embarrassment; her eyes lowered to the marbled floor. She was certain Chayanne knew she was infertile. His mouth twisted in shame; she couldn't even be a woman right.

David sneered at her reading her thoughts, "Come on, we have to get Ashton seen by a doctor," he said, snarling at Linda.

"Uncle D, I want to go with my mommy. I need to protect her, you don't understand." Lilly fussed, trying to free herself from his strong arms.

"Listen here, you need to cut the act; your mom is one hell of a woman. She can protect herself. We need to get you fed and put down for a nap. I've heard about the night you two had, and your mother is being foolish and selfish with her work, putting you all in harm's way. She's not thinking straight and she needs to sleep her nonsense off." he said angrily.

On his command, they all stepped into the rain and jogged toward his white Range Rover that was parallel parked on the curb; they noticed Chayanne and Charles being driven away in the taxicab.

"I don't know why you insisted on climbing in here with me. Where is Quentin?" Chayanne said in suspicion.

He hesitated to answer, "I don't know, we disagreed and he left. I'm here where I should be." he responded not so sure.

"Are you looking for me to validate you choosing your son over your lover?" she shot back at him.

"Why do you have to do that? Why do you have to be like that to me? This is why we don't have a friendship anymore." he scolded her, poking his lip out. He stared out the window huffing.

She sighed; she knew she was moody from her lack of sleep, food, and coffee. "I'm sorry, I'm just tired... I shouldn't have said that."

He placed his hand on her blue jeans, "Don't worry about it. You're right; you didn't have the luxury to walk away like I did. I'm sorry for that." He inhaled deeply, "I'm sorry that I led you on that last night we spent together. That was cruel; I wasn't sure if... if I wanted to leave you, I..."

"Charles, it's fine; you don't owe me an explanation. You've expressed how happy you two are and it shows when you're with him. I'm happy for you... for both of you." She placed her hand on top of his. "Our relationship journey has ended; but that doesn't mean we can't be friends and co-parent. The kids need you in their life." She smiled warmly, looking into his eyes with sincerity.

"What if I... wanted to," he hesitated, he didn't want to say what his heart felt; the building chaos had reminded him why he fell in love with her as children.

"Are you choking on your words? Spit it out already," she said as the taxi came to a squeaky stop in front of the Ritz Carlton hotel. The rain pattered on the tin roof of the car.

"I just want to be around more; you know for the kids, and I want you to be comfortable with that." he lied.

"Absolutely, I've never taken that away from you. I filed for joint custody for you last year and you never followed through. I knew you wanted to be in their lives, but I thought you'd given up. You and Quentin are family; we're just an extended family now. The kids will come around. I noticed you and Lilly in the lobby talking; it made me feel something I haven't felt in a long time… like things are really going to be okay." She reached over his gapped legs for her briefcase and smiled, flashing her perfect white teeth and dimples. She grabbed the handle to exit the car. Charles leaned over, just missing her lips. She put her briefcase over her head. "Did you say something?" She asked loudly over the traffic; her face puzzled.

"No… no, I think Quentin checked in at the Four Seasons, I thought you were going to stay there? He said embarrassed, trying to cover the tracks of his missed attempt.

"No, I've been here plenty times, I prefer the Ritz over the Four Seasons. In D.C., the room service and hospitality has always exceeded my expectations. I'll call you later." She closed the door before he could respond and waived him off with her free hand. He frowned feeling unsettled as the car pulled off; he knew she was over him. He slumped in the seat, breathing her lingering scent in.

The taxi driver adjusted the rearview mirror looking down at Charles. "Wow, that's tough, to let a good one walk out of your life like that."

Exasperated, Charles gazed out the window listening to water slosh beneath the tires. He questioned his love for Quentin with what he felt for Chayanne.

Chayanne waltzed into her hotel suite feeling light in the midst of events that had taken precedence in her life. She finally received the closure her therapist was so adamant about her getting. The romance was finally dimmed; a weight lifted off her shoulders. She jumped into the bed; the feathered duvet hugged her body, she cried happily. The feeling of self-love and worth was all she needed in that moment. Her soft whimpers released the built-up tension she had remaining for him inside of her.

A soft knock at the door pulled her from her joy. She looked at the time; she hadn't informed anyone of where she checked in. She walked barefoot over the soft printed carpet slowly to the peephole of the large white door; she observed for a few seconds.

She opened the door slowly, "Detective Walsh, what are you doing here?" she asked from the small crack in the door.

"You just left in such a hurry, I just wanted to make sure you got settled in okay. I've been calling you all morning. I have a lead on the mystery fella." He responded nervously adjusting his small black tie.

The door creaked open; she stepped aside inviting him in. His broad shoulders bumped in between the door and the doorframe closed softly behind him. "Wow!" He said looking around the room, "You didn't spare any expense, did you?" He laughed anxiously.

She looked him over wondering why he took a flight all the way to D.C. to check on her, she cleared her throat restively. "What lead do you have? It must be a good one if you booked a flight to come all the way here. It couldn't have waited until I came back in town?" She studied him closely, looking for an indication of his real reason for visiting. His gaze finally landed on her.

He smiled and his dimples protruded his scruffy, closely-shaved beard. "Okay, you got me, I just wanted to gaze into your hazel eyes and lose myself inside of you. I just can't seem to free my mind from the thought of you. Your beauty, your stern serious looks, your edgy persona to not let people in, but most of all, I've been wanting to do this." he said, pulling her into his iron chest; before she could manage to object, his warm, soft lips met hers. He kissed her roughly with a burning desire, in a way she'd never been kissed before. She pulled away from his firm grasp smacking him with force; a snarling glare printed on her face as she stared at him. He grabbed his jaw, checking to see if she draw blood.

"Well... I apologize for misreading the situation, Ms. Carter. I thought we had some unspoken chemistry and I acted on my own feelings instead of waiting for you to make a move." he explained in embarrassment as he moved toward the door. Chayanne trailed behind, her wetness leaked through her silk panties; the trail of his lingering cologne aroused her. She bit down on her bottom lip fighting the urge to rip him apart. He grabbed for the door handle and opened it to a small crack. Chayanne pushed her weight against the door and slammed it shut; he turned his head toward her, their eyes met. She pushed him into the door and pressed her body against his. She could feel his heart dance in his chest with uncertainty; her hand pressed against his chest as the other slid slowly over his tight abdomen, down to the front bulge of his trouser and his upper thigh. He refused to break eye contact as he stared intensely in her eyes, daring her to make a move. Her eyes became a pool of seduction, drawing him toward her. He closed his eyes and rested the back of his head on the door as his sense of touch heightened. Chayanne's hands wandered all over his body, caressing him to arousal. She unbuttoned his shirt and kissed his bare, smooth chest. The warmth of her mouth opened his eyes; he looked down, watching her flick her tongue over his nipple, before suckling it. Her small, petite hands unbuckled his belt and pants, finding their way into his boxers; his stomach muscles flexed and his body was tense. One hand stroked, rubbed, and caressed his penis while the other laid on his chest. She watched him like a night owl watches it prey as he gave into her pleasing him. Her every move pushed him closer to ecstasy. She nibbled on his earlobes softly; her tongue made a trail to his lips. He gasped, inhaling her breath like a drug; she rubbed her lips across his open mouth. Her eyes were glued to his.

"Fuck me!" she whispered sternly, demanding him to obey her command. She could feel the pulse in his cock growing with every stroke of her hand; he was on the verge of ejaculating into his boxer when she stopped. He bit down on his lip in frustration, wanting to release his sexual tension in her palm. Chayanne walked backward to the bed and Daniel followed closely in her footsteps. He reached for her; she swiped his hand away with a smirk on her face.

"Come on Daniel, act like you want me. I told you to fuck me, not make love to me." she teased.

He lunged forward to grab her and devour her. Chayanne moved to the side and flipped him over her hip, landing him onto the bed.

She burst into laughter, "I told you I could protect myself. I guess you just have to see for yourself."

"Is this foreplay to you? I never met a woman so challenging in the bedroom." Daniel said, frustrated at the twisted game she was playing.

"I want you to make me want you, to make me want to give into you," she laughed at his response. "I am very attracted to you Detective Walsh, but that physical attraction will only carry me so far with you. If you can't entice me to move past that… then you don't deserve to feel my intimacy, it's that simple." she said shrugging him off.

He slammed his fist down into the plush mattress; he was a frustrated cat trying to catch a mouse. He jumped off the bed and started after Chayanne once more. She stood in an offensive stance, waiting for him to attack. He felt like an adolescent chasing his crush on the playground as he watched her dance around. He pushed the green, cushioned armchair with his foot toward her wanting to throw her focus off. She dodged the chair still locked in on him. He grabbed her wrist firmly. He tussled with her and maneuvered his weight over her small body; Chayanne was turned on with the struggle. With two moves, she had him pinned against the window; her hand pressed firmly against his throat. She smirked then bit her lip seductively as she pulled him in by the nape of his neck. She parted her lips and kissed him. He wasn't falling for anymore of her tricks, he desperately wanted to insert his dominance over her. He cupped her thighs and picked her up. They reversed positions; he pinned her body against the window. She wrapped her legs around his waist, relaxing into his arms. She kissed him roughly and passionately. She pushed her fingers through his short, wavy hair as their tongues tangled; she closed her eyes allowing the pleasure to sweep over her. It had been more than two years since she felt a man's touch. Daniel slammed Chayanne onto the plush mattress; his body weight pressed on top of her. He kissed on her neck, returning the favor, unbuttoning her pants. He slid his hands in her panties, dipping his finger inside of her pool of nectar; she bit down on his lip, satisfied by his touch. He caressed and massaged her clitoris with his middle finger. She thrust her pelvic into his finger, yearning for more. He paused to pull her jeans and panties around her ankles, revealing her bare pussy. He plopped back onto her; she reversed, mounting herself on top of him. She slid his rock-hard penis in her sticky opening until all eight inches were fully emerged in her. She exhaled, gripping her fingernails into his pectorals. She rocked her hips slowly, allowing her throbbing pussy to adapt to the shape of him.

The blaring of the hotel phone startled Chayanne, her eyes popped opened; she didn't realize she dozed off. Her vagina throbbed in her jeans. She sat up with a hazed headspace, shaking her thoughts off.

"Hello?" She answered sleepily, rubbing her eyes.

"Chayanne, this is Gary, your paralegal. I've been trying to reach you all morning. The media is a massacre with allegations of Ashton killing murdering a young college woman." He was frantic and distressed; she could tell by his tone. "The partners are not happy with this situation; especially since you haven't picked up or returned any of their emails or calls. They feel slighted; you were supposed to be in the office. They publicly announced the firm taking the Baxter's case that you've been deliberating on all weekend. This is just chaotic; I went by your place to check on you since you weren't answering and your street was filled with a sea of media, pushing to get through your gates. I could barely drive down the road for Pete's sake. It just so happened that Detective Walsh came poking around at the office; he wanted to know any specifics about the Baxter's case. He said that you'd been attacked by an intruder." Gary breathed heavily, trying to wrap his head around all the overwhelming stream of events. She could hear him panting over the receiver. She chuckled to herself, replaying the many times she had to witness Gary and his minor panic attacks. He was always worked up over the slightest things.

"Gary, just breathe, things are going to be fine. Don't worry yourself to insanity, its only Monday. We have a lot of work to do before the week is out. I will touch bases with the partners; stay by your phone and check your emails for updates." she responded calmly, reassuring him.

"I called half the hotels in D.C. before I found you. Jesus Christ, I don't like this feeling."

"Gary…Gary, I will handle this. Meanwhile, I need you to go down to the police station and request to the evidence on the Baxter's case."

"Yes, Ms. Carter," he said sighing with relief.

"Gary, it's just Chayanne." she responded, laying the receiver on the hook softly.

She looked around the room, reminiscent on her short-lived dream. She ran her hand through her hair and winced in pain when she hit her patch of stitches. This reminded her of the kind of day she was having.

She collected herself, organizing her tasks mentally; her chest felt tight and her heart pitter-pattered frantically. She finally inhaled, sinking into reality. The silence of the hotel room and traffic fourteen-floors down were the only things that comforted her.

CHAPTER

28

THE FRAT PARTY

David pulled the SUV in his gravel driveway that stretched a mile long over his eight-acre stretch of land. Lilly sat quietly in the backseat, watching the gloomy clouds. The others chattered amongst themselves, occasionally asking her to chime in. She really wished she had gone with Chayanne—she yearned to be comforted and reassured by her mother that things were okay. David could sense her dreariness as he observed her through the review mirror.

"Lilly, what would you like to do today to officially kick your summer vacation off?" David asked interrupting Linda's and Ashton's conversation.

Lilly shrugged her shoulders, gazing out of the window. Ashton looked over at Lilly annoyed that her damper mood was taking away from their family time with David.

"Uncle D, how long has it been since we been out to see you?" Ashton butted back, conversing with David.

David turned his attention to Ashton, "Maybe four or five years or so, I haven't seen much of you all since your parents separated. Your

287

mom's been in her bubble; I've asked her to send you two out over the summer a few times, but you know your mom and how close she likes to keep you all to her. I was surprised she agreed for you to come all the way up here to Georgetown."

"I don't think she had much of a decision really," Ashton sighed. "My dad said since he was paying for my tuition, I had to go to the Ivy League school of his choice. My mom wanted me to go to Morehouse back home, but my dad thought an HBCU wouldn't look good on my law school application. He doesn't understand that I don't even want to be a lawyer; he's always painting an image of me that's not me." Ashton looked out the window, his mood now mirroring Lilly's.

"Aw, come on guys, why the long faces? I want this to be a happy vacation; considering the circumstances." David said in a goofy voice, attempting to lighten their moods.

The car finally came to a stop in front of the huge farmhouse porch. David placed the SUV in park; he looked over to Linda slightly nodding his head for her to be excused.

"I'll go find us some lunch in the pantry; I have to whip something special up for you two since it's been so long." Linda said nervously smiling. She closed the door behind her then disappeared into the darkness of the house. Once she was out of sight, David started his interrogation of the children.

"What's really going on here?" he asked, turning around in his seat to put his eyes on their faces.

"What do you mean Uncle D?" Ashton asked nervously.

"I can sense something in the water ain't clean. I want to know everything that's happened since the last time I saw you two." David looked at them both with suspicion. Ashton sat back into the seat, not wanting to be the one to say anything. He knew Chayanne liked information to stay in the house. Lilly ignored the question, still looking out the window lost in her reality.

The rain splattered violently against the tin roof. Neither Ashton nor Lilly had much to say.

"Lilly!" David said sternly, snapping her out her daze. She turned her head, slowly looking at him. "How did my sister get that black eye?"

Lilly squinted her eyes and pursed her lips.

"Uncle D… she was attacked." She shook her head as if the answer was obvious.

"By who?" Ashton asked, intrigued that Lilly actually answered.

"Someone broke into the house last night and attacked her. I called the police; we were at the hospital until mommy got a call about you." she answered, rolling her eyes annoyed that Ashton dragged them miles away from home. "What did you do? Why did we even have to come to get you?"

"Why don't you stay in a child's place and mind your business." Ashton shot back, embarrassed by his sister's question.

"Now I see why you got the burn on your face. You can never manage to do as your told. That's probably why Charles sent you all the way here, so he didn't have to deal with you being disrespectful to him." She crossed her arms, glaring at Ashton.

Ashton lightly touched the tender cigarette burn on his cheek, "Shut up Lilly, you don't know what you're talking about. You think you're so smart, but you're just a stupid little girl."

David reached into the backseat and grabbed Ashton by his collar, coldly staring him in the eye, "ABSOLUTELY NOT! You will never speak to your sister or any woman for that matter like that." Without breaking a stare David instructed Lilly, "Sweet pea, go help Aunt Linda with lunch. Your brother and I have some things to discuss."

"Okay Uncle D," Lilly responded, leaving the car as quickly as her little body could move. The door slammed behind her; she hightailed her small frame up the stairs into the house.

David loosened his grip on Ashton's collar, "I apologize for my reaction, but I wasn't raised to disrespect women. If your grandmother were here today, you would have been picking your front teeth up off of the floor. That is your sister, and you are her protector at all costs; you wouldn't want another man disrespecting her, so why should you?"

Ashton lowered his eyes to the floor, "So, I'm just supposed to let her talk to me like that?"

"She's a little girl, you guide and teach her. You don't need to tear her down more than this world will. That ain't going to solve nothing, just add to the list of problems us black folks already have."

David turned forward in his chair; he reached down, grabbing his cigar. He rolled it between his index finger and thumb; he put it between his teeth, biting it firmly. He adjusted the rearview mirror toward Ashton and studied him briefly. He sparked his lighter, putting the flame to the tip of the cigar. He puffed; smoke filled the cabin of the truck. David turned the A/C on to clear the smoke.

"What was your relationship to the white girl they claimed you hurt?" David asked, peering at Ashton while taking a long draw on his cigar.

Ashton eyes danced around the car while he hesitated to answer, "We... were friends Uncle D, what else would you expect?"

David waited for Ashton to focus his eyes back on the mirror, "Were you two fuck buddies or was she your girlfriend?"

Ashton's face blushed, he was embarrassed to admit the truth, so he sat quietly, staring back at David through the mirror.

"Ash, you don't have to lie to me. I was young once and probably did a whole hell of a lot crazier things outside of having my fair share of white women, especially when I played professional ball," David admitted, wanting to ease Ashton's mind.

Ashton swallowed hard, looked down toward his lap, and twirled his fingers nervously, "We were dating; we were planning to celebrate our three-month anniversary at her parent's summer cabin in a couple weeks." He paused, holding back his tears. He sucked his running nose and dabbed it with his bloody sleeve. "We planned the trip so we could finally go all the way with one another." He paused choking on his sorrow, holding back his tears. He took a deep breath before continuing.

"We were joking that morning about running away together because our families don't understand who we are as individuals; they only see us for what they want us to be." He whipped his eyes with the back of his sleeve, hoping David didn't notice he was hurting. "She understand who I was as a person, and that was special to me. I've been with plenty of other girls, but I never felt the way I did for her." He changed his tone and uttered under his breath, "No one would ever believe that because she was seeing the asshole Scott Wiseman, the All-American Rugby player, for appearances."

"Hmmm… interesting… go on." David instructed him, still puffing away at his cigar.

Ashton paused, unsure if he should proceed with his version of the truth. David picked up on his hesitation.

"About the party, Ash, at the frat house, why would they blame you if you didn't do it?"

"Can I get some water Uncle D?" He requested with his voice crackling.

"Reach in the back, there is a cooler behind you. I was at the ballpark with my… uh, with the little league team, so uh yeah, just get a Gatorade or something out."

Ashton turned and reached back to open the cooler and grab a bottle of water. He returned face front, sighing heavily before he continued. "I went to the Omega's frat party with a few fellas I room with. I know Scott lives there, it's his fraternity; I got wasted on a bottle of Old Tom Gin and a joint my roommate was holding. I knew Kendal was going to be there with him and I had to numb myself." He took a sip of water to compose his idling hatred for Scott. "Ahem, I saw them standing off in a corner together when I first got there. She was smiling and having a good time; she was his arm candy in the limelight. I got lost long enough to down a half bottle of gin. I talked to my mom about my dad's stupid wedding and she told me I needed to respect his wishes and move on. She wanted me to stop holding grudges against him because it affects Lilly's feelings."

"Charles is getting remarried? When did they get divorced?" David blurted out; he was so shocked that he choked on the cigar smoke.

"You didn't know Uncle D? My dad left and never came back, he chose his queer life over us." Ashton fingered his red, soft, and curly hair frustrated, huffing through his clenched teeth, still furious with Charles. "They never separated, all he left was the divorce papers on the table for her to sign. I came home from school, and they were on the breakfast bar spread out for her. She didn't even have a clue he'd filed for it. I wanted to burn the papers to ashes along with the house, but the nanny came home with Lilly from the park. I shredded the papers in mom's office, she didn't know what was going on; she was so busy working on a case I don't think she had time to notice he wasn't around. He's such a fucking coward." Ashton kissed his teeth, shaking his head with fury.

David grabbed the water from Ashton's hand trying to soothe the burn in his throat. "I had no idea." He said clearing his throat choking, "your mom gets in these moods where she wants to shut the world out. I had no clue that Charles liked... men." His voice squeaked into a high pitch surprised at the news.

Ashton balled his fists, "Yeah, me either... I found out he was cheating with Quentin, his temporary assistant. He invited Lilly and I to dinner at a fancy restaurant to break the news about the divorce; he didn't know I saw the papers. He got up to take Lilly to the bathroom and I hacked his work laptop to see if my gut feeling about him seeing another woman was right. Instead, I found nudes of Quentin throughout his emails and different messages about hotel meetings. I smashed his laptop, flipped the dinner table, and walked home. He pulled up an hour later with Lilly and tried to confront me; he told me I had to intern at his office to pay for the damages. I lost it and attacked him. He had me committed to a psych ward for 72 hours, claiming I was bipolar and suicidal. I lost all respect for him that day. He couldn't face me like the man he was trying to teach me to be. What a joke, I was surprised to see him at the station today; he wants to pretend to be a caring, loving, and devoted father when it's beneficial for him."

"Ash, I had no clue man. Why didn't you call me or reach out to me when all of this was going on?"

"Mom wasn't convinced that he was gone for good. She didn't want to taint our family's image; honestly Uncle D, I think she's in denial. Lilly's told me she started seeing my therapist three times a week. Lilly says mom is like a zombie most days; her brain is on autopilot. It's kind of strange because I didn't see that today at the station; I saw the mom that I've always known: strong and courageous. I don't play that shit, and I'll knock a motherfucker out over my kids." Ashton laughed at the thought of Chayanne going off on the captain. "It's just been a lot Uncle D. It wasn't my intention to keep you at bay, but I had to listen to mom; she's the only parent and protector I have." He rested his head on the headrest staring up at the ceiling.

"I can relate Ash, my old man and I butted heads quite often. I too felt the same about him as you do Charles. Seems like things have been pretty tough on you lately. I'm sorry I didn't do more to reach out to you and Lilly during this rough patch. I was waiting for your mom to come around after she stormed out of here with you all that Thanksgiving I last saw you guys. I'll do better with checking in going forward." David said, attempting to console and empathize with Ashton. "So, back to the frat party, after you talked to your mom, then what?"

Ashton stood in the doorway of the den with half a bottle of Gin in hand. He grimaced at the sight of Kendal and Scott making out in the corner together. He stumbled out the den into the kitchen where beer-pong was being played. The crowd up roared in a cheer as Sommer Rose sunk the Ping-Pong ball in her opponent's last cup. She raised her hands above her head in celebration. As she looked over the crowd, she noticed Ashton. She waved at him with a slight smile. Ashton smiled and waved back. Their friendship had been sparse since he'd spent all his free time sneaking around with Kendal over the last semester; he'd only seen Sommer in the few classes they shared before the semester ended. The crowd chanted for an encore, enticing Sommer to play again. She disregarded the majority and walked off into the crowd; Ashton followed her until he was close behind. She weaved in and out the crowd of people, looping back into the den. He followed her in, closing the sliding, barn-like door behind, blocking the loud music and cheering from the other areas. She walked toward the mantel, fingering her long, black, silky, and straight hair behind her ears.

She turned smiling to face him; "I haven't seen you since the semester ended. What's been going on? Are you going home over the break or are you taking more classes?"

He placed the bottle of Gin on the coffee table, his drunken haze made him notice how attracted he was to Sommer; her tight, slanted Asian eyes and her light caramel skin were appealing to him. He walked around sitting on the sofa buying himself time to admire her glow.

He smiled and wiped his glossy gray eyes, "Yeah, I am staying during the summer to take extra classes. I would like to graduate early; plus, I have a few things I'm working on here, nothing major, just an internship. I want to change my major next year to journalism, but my dad will most likely freak and threaten to take my college funds away. What about you? I didn't expect you to be hanging around after finals. I thought you were um… going to visit your dad's home country in uh… shoot wait… Okinawa, right?"

She blushed chortling, "Yeah, that's right… um my parents separated over the last semester, so I'm kind of on a hiatus here on campus. My mother has been at my dorm trying to hunt me down and drag me back home. I've been lucky enough to dodge her, but I don't know how long I can avoid her." Her eyes dropped to the floor. "I'm just not ready to accept it yet. I knew it was coming, but I don't know a life without them coexisting. It's just been really tough; my dad is pissed I failed my exams. I'll be on academic probation during the fall semester. I kind of want to drop out and say fuck it." She folded her arms and leaned back on the mantel."

He scratched his head, mulling over what he could say to soothe her discomfort, "I understand wanting to lose yourself, but you shouldn't carry the weight of your parents split on your shoulders. I know I did that, and it landed me in a mental institution for 72 hours."

She was shocked; her face was in awe, "Why didn't you tell me your parents divorced? We used to be so close and you never told me. What happened to us?"

He shifted in his seat nervously as she sat down beside him, placing her hand on his knee, "Umm… Ahem, well I'm not sure; we were always good friends; I guess I kind of got lost with in this semester and some personal shit, I guess." His voice cracked as her hand slid up his thigh. "Are you uh, not dating Steven anymore?"

"He broke up with me a little after I got the news about my parents. I started drinking heavy to cope. He told me I was sloppy and unattractive. Plus, he was planning to hook up with his high school sweetheart over the break."

She reached over Ashton to grab the bottle of Gin; her perky breast propped up in his face. He swallowed hard with his eyes fixed on her breast. He inhaled her sweet fragrant perfume. She sat back, twisted the cap off the Gin, and tossed her head back to pour the flavorful liquor into her mouth. She closed her mouth and the Gin spilled over, trailing its way down her neck. She guzzled as her mouth was still full. Ashton watched amused; his penis slightly stiffened in his boat shorts.

She barely finished swallowing, "Ash, do you think I'm attractive to be Black and Asian? Steven always said he could never take me home to his parents because they'd just die." she laughed, taking another huge gulp from the bottle.

"I think you're drop-dead gorgeous; I don't think your looks have anything to do with him taking you home. It's more so Steve is from the whitest suburb on the planet and this is probably the most he's been exposed to other ethnic groups. You had to have something right if he converted to dating you."

He relaxed a little more, sinking back into the sofa. The doobie he smoked with his roommates took his body on a high. He giggled; his eyes were hazy and red.

"Man, I'm so fucking wasted." he confessed in laughter.

Sommer rubbed his soft curly hair while she admired his deeply embedded dimples.

She licked her lips as her mouth salivated, "Ash?"

He rolled his head to the side making eye contact with her, "Yeah?"

"Can I kiss you?" she asked with a straight face.

Ashton touched her cheek, pulling closer to her lips. His lips met her wet mouth; she melted, dropping the open bottle of Gin on the floor. Their breaths were heavy as they passionately kissed; she pulled her body on top of his, mounting him while engaged with his lips. His hands roamed over her, groping her plump ass; his erection grew with every feel.

She pulled away, "Someone is excited." She unbuttoned his plaid button-down, kissing and sucking on his neck.

He tilted his head back enjoying the warmth of her mouth. "Fuck Sommer, I want you so bad," he whispered.

She kissed down his chest, licking over his steel-cut chiseled stomach until she reached the top of his shorts. His penis threatened to bust through.

She looked up into his eyes seductively, "How bad do you want it?" She teased, using the tip of her tongue to trace her full, luscious lips.

He licked his lips, folding them in. He thrusted his pelvis, encouraging her to keep going, "Suck it," he pleaded on the edge of the sofa.

She unbuttoned his shorts; he lifted to allow her to pull them to his ankles. His penis bulge through his boxers; she entered her hand through the opening to pull it out. She rubbed it on her lips; his pre-cum oozed out slowly. He gasped and his eyes enlarged; he anticipated her to wrap her mouth around his pulsating penis. She ran her tongue up the base, flicking the head with her tongue before taking all of him. He clenched the sofa fabric tightly, feeling the pleasure of her mouth. His hips thrusted slowly, moving him in and out of her mouth; her hand stroked him as he pulled out. He gripped her hair in his hands and built momentum, prematurely erupting in her mouth and on her lips.

Sommer giggled, "You must have really been excited," she said, wiping her mouth.

Ashton was embarrassed that he didn't make it to two minutes, "Sorry, I should have warned you; it just got away from me" his face flushed red.

She stood and pushed him back on the couch. She lifted her skirt and pulled her silky, moist panties aside. She straddled him and rubbed her sappy wetness on the tip of his penis. He was aroused once again. She rubbed his tip on her opening and slid down cautiously.

"Fuck, you're bigger than I expected." She confessed, inhaling deeply. She allowed all of him to disappear inside of her. Her cushioned thighs met his; he gripped her hips and pushed her back and forth in a rocking motion; she gyrated on him, giving him what he wanted. Her hands pushed his chest, giving her more leverage over him. His penis hit the back of her throbbing vagina, sending her in a tailspin of euphoria; she amped up her gyration, now bouncing and causing his thighs and her butt to smack together. Her moans grew louder and louder and she uttered out his name; her climax lurked close by. Her nails dug into his shoulders as she sped her motions. He hit her g-spot until she couldn't hold on any longer.

"Oh my... oh I'm about to... ffffffffuck, I'm cumming, I'm cumming!" she whimpered, her body shook uncontrollably as she released her juices on his hard penis. His boxers were covered in both of their cum. Ashton, still engaged in the act, flipped her over. He was deeply embedded in her warmth; he took control and placed her legs on his shoulders. Her vagina sucked him in. He slowly pushed and pulled, in and out in rhythm to her soft moans. He stared deeply into her eyes with every stroke. He wanted to hold on to his next eruption a little longer as he lost himself in the feeling of her fleshy fruit.

His moans were in tandem with hers as he picked up his rhythm, stroking harder. Her hands were around his hips, pulling him roughly, "Harder, fuck me harder," she demanded, moaning in bliss. Their thighs smacked violently as he went harder. "Don't stop, please don't stop, I'm cumming, I'm cumming..." She screamed aloud, gripping his thighs as she trembled helplessly.

Sweat dripped down his torso. He kept the rhythm, going faster and harder.

He thrust deeper inside her; the pulse in his penis thumped harder. He pulled out, exploding his load on the sofa, "FUCK, FUCK, FUCK!" he grunted lowly, putting his half-stiff dick back into her. He pumped short and quick before collapsing his sweaty body on her breast.

He looked up at her as she looked down at him; both smiling shyly at each other.

"WHERE THE FUCK IS HE!!!" Kendal screamed over the music in a mewling voice.

Ashton disregarded Kendal's cries, assuming she was looking for Scott. Sommer pulled Ashton up by his chin to kiss him. Both very much engaged in each other.

Sommer giggled in between their pecks, "Keep kissing me like that and we're going to go for another round."

Ashton giggled, kissing her passionately once more. Neither saw Kendal standing with her mouth gawked opened, witnessing their romance through the open sliding door.

"ASHTON ANTHONY PARKER!!!" Kendal screamed. She lunged forward to smack and punch him. Ashton fumbled to pull his shorts up, tripping over the coffee table landing on the floor. Kendal turned her aggression on Sommer. She jumped on her, pulling her hair and scratching her. Sommer fought back, balling her fists and hitting Kendal in the face. She grabbed her hair and slung her to the floor.

"You stupid fucking cunt, how could you Sommer...you fucking whore... you fucking mulatto bitch, I will kill you!" The crowd blocked the entrance, watching in awe as the two tussled around on the floor.

"What the fuck is going on in here?" Scott's voice bellowed over the stereo; he pushed toward the front of the crowd. "Cut the music," he yelled back to his frat brothers.

The shattering of the glass coffee table made his fight to get to the front more critical. Both Sommer and Kendal laid out, barely conscious.

"What... what the fuck? Kendal, what the fuck are you doing?" Scott's eyes darted around the room, looking for clues to piece together what happened. His eyes landed on Ashton, whose pants were falling off his ass, helping Sommer to her feet. He dusted the glass off of her. "Yo

Ash, what the fuck bro? What happened?" Scott asked, standing over him as he kneeled to clean the glass off of Sommer.

"Dude, can you back the fuck up? I think you need to talk to Kendal about what's going on." Ashton replied, standing up meeting Scott face to face with his chest hulked. The music cut from the other room; everyone stared in silence.

Scott quiet looked down at Kendal and then Sommer: his face turned up. He looked back to Ashton, pushing him into the mantel.

"Are you screwing Kendal, bro? I thought we were cool." Scott exclaimed with his nostrils flaring; his face was red with anger.

"Dude, I'm telling you, don't put your hands on me. You need to talk to your girl and leave me out of this." Ashton warned.

"I'm not stupid bro; this looks bad," Scott said angrily, swiping his bang out his face.

"Scott, stop!" Kendal said, coming to pull on his jeans.

He brushed her hand away, nudging her hard with his foot, "What the fuck is this shit, Kendal? Are you screwing around with Ashton behind my back?"

"Scott, can we talk in private?" she said in a low, muffled tone, looking at the gawking crowd.

"Everybody, get the fuck out of here... NOW!" Scott yelled with clenched fists.

Ashton brushed past Scott, grabbing Sommer's hand; they quickly headed for the exit. The crowd dispersed.

Lilly tapped on the window with her index nail.

"Uncle D, lunch is ready. Aunt Linda wants you to come in now, she told me to tell you the phone is for you." She reported quickly, hurrying to get out of the rain.

David's cigar went out, he was so immersed in Ashton's story, he'd lost focus. He scratched his head, puzzled because he wasn't anywhere close to getting the answers he sought. Ashton hurriedly escaped the car seconds after Lilly departed from the window. He sighed with relief; he was off the hook, temporarily.

LET'S MAKE AMENDS

Chayanne typed fiercely at her keyboard; she had tons of emails she needed to respond to. She stopped clicking clacking at the key to take a sip of her coffee to revive her tired eyes. She rubbed her temples to relive the headache that had been nagging her since the D.C. flight. She looked down, peaking at the bedside clock that read 3:36 a.m. She'd been submerged in work non-stop since Gary called early that afternoon. She looked over at the cold dinner she never touched; she didn't have much of an appetite due to the recent drama that unfolded. She pressed the send key on her last email and closed her laptop. She stretched her limbs while sitting, dimmed the lights, fluffed her pillow, and sunk into the cozy California King bed. Her eyes heavy, she began drifting off. She heard a light knock at the door.

"You have to be fucking kidding me." she complained through her gritted teeth. She hastily flung the covers off her and stormed to the door. She looked through the peephole and rolled her eyes, letting out an annoyed hiss. She unchained the door and opened it to a small crack.

"Yes, Charles?" she questioned

"Don't treat me like a stranger, let me in," he said, pushing past her. "Were you sleep?"

"I don't think it matters if I was; you still decided to knock on my door at wee hours of the morning." She pursed her lips in agitation. She closed the door and retreated back to bed. "What do you want? I swear I see you more now than I did in our last year of marriage."

"You don't have to always go for the jugular, you know. Just be cordial and casual; we were friends once."

"Wasn't it you that told me to move on with my life? How could I possibly when you pop up every five minutes?"

He sat on the sofa and shot a dirty look at her, "There you go with the pushing off thing you do."

Chayanne sat up in the bed, getting comfortable once more. "Here you go—showing up at my residence unannounced all hours of the night like you used to—so what's your point?"

The long silence filled the gap in between them, "Ahem, well I was out jogging, hence the black jogging suit, and I ended up catching a taxi down to campus. A few of the fellas who Ashton rooms with let me in. I spoke with the boys briefly about the things that have been going on surrounding this Kendal thing... they claimed Ash has been acting different lately—disappearing and not going to class. Then, out of nowhere this eerie feeling I don't know how to describe came over me. I thought to myself, what if he really did it? What if the apple didn't fall to far from the tree?"

Chayanne adjusted uneasy at Charles speculations, "Why don't you just ask him if he did it? We can drive over to David's and drag him out of bed in the middle of the night, just like the police did, and interrogate him. We are his parents, we should know when he's lying, right? She said in a sarcastic tone.

"See, I knew you wouldn't understand. I don't know why I even try." he huffed. Charles got up from the sofa and headed toward the door. "You make it impossible to talk to you. It's like a part of you died with Anthony on the road that day. You do and say enough to be relevant, but you're barely alive. I think the divorce just gave you the excuse to give up completely." He grabbed for the door handle.

"That's a sad picture you've painted of me, Charles. I have to admit, it's casted by your own reality. You died when your mother was found in the quarry, you weren't reborn again until you found out who your father was. You branded yourself as someone I never had a friendship with; your million-dollar golf club memberships and your late nights rubbing elbows with the good old boys. No matter how much money you make, no matter how many million-dollar empires you build, the harsh reality is you will never be good enough to be one of them. You will never fit in your skin; you will never be any lighter. You can pretend as much as you want, but it'll never change the truth. Your own daughter doesn't even know she's black dammit! I lived in your fairytale for twenty-one years of my life." She spat back, her words were like daggers piercing Charles's pride. "The more you vowed to never be like him and abandon your children for your own selfishness, the more you became him, so yes Charles, you are absolutely right, the apple doesn't fall far from the tree. You've forced Ashton to move away from home and attend an Ivy League school that wasn't even in his top five. You used your money the same way your father used his. He bought you off and now you've done the same to our son."

Charles hand dropped from the knob on the door, he mentally licked his wounds before muttering, "How long have you known about Quentin and I, Chayanne?"

"The truth finally comes out. This is what this is about?" She shook her head in disappointment. "I actually thought you wanted closure and have a real grown-up conversation about how to help our son out of this mess he's in. I should have known it will always come down to your self-centered bullshit." she said, kissing her teeth and adjusting her pillows to lay down once more.

"Please Chayanne, will you just answer the damn question!" He asked angrily; his back still turned to her.

"I know Quentin wasn't your first, although he thinks he is if that could put things into perspective for you." He cringed, hoping she thought Quentin was his first as well. "To answer your question, Quentin emailed me the day after the holiday party and spared no expense giving me the juicy details of your love affair. He explained how he coaxed you for months, waiting for you to make a move on him. You finally cracked that night playing into your weaknesses. He said if I really loved you, I should set you free to live your truth. I knew most of your moves before you made them. I've always been steps ahead Charles, always." She sighed, anticipating his next question. "When we were in our junior year of college and I ended things with you when Momma died, I knew you were sleeping with Professor Atkins... he was your first. That's the real reason I left that summer for home. I didn't know how to confront you or what to even say; my mind kept flashing back to your Uncle

Henry and how he hurt you, but I saw the way you looked at Professor Atkins with fire and compassion the—way you never looked at me."

Charles swallowed hard; he was a specimen in Chayanne's microscope. He was clueless on how much she actually knew. He hung his head, shaking it side to side, too embarrassed to admit she was right, "I made a mistake with Quentin. I know it's a little too late, but I am sorry, I never should have left. This whole thing just made me realize what's important and I... I want to come home to be there for you and the kids."

Chayanne put her hand to her mouth holding her laughter in. Her face reddened as she giggled quietly. She knew Charles was playing the wounded deer role; she fell for it too many times not to know.

She quickly composed herself to respond, "I appreciate your apology, not that I needed it after this long. I've accepted you for who you are, and I'm not interested in being an itch you have to scratch every now and again. You made a choice to be with Quentin, so you have to live with that. All the back and forth isn't healthy for me or the children. You are more than welcome to come stay at the house, if that's what you want to do to be around the kids, but I can only be a co-parent and a supportive friend."

His heart sank into his stomach; he never thought she would have the courage to reject him. Her ragged friend she saved on her doorstep for an ice cream bar. He moved away from the door and sat back in the spot he warmed on the sofa.

"I need to get some sleep; I have a heavy week ahead of me. The firm is picking up the Baxter case that's been all over the news and guess who's the lead attorney." She sighed heavily, flopping back on the pillows." She was already exhausted from thinking about the case. "I'm taking Ash home tomorrow and he won't be returning here for the fall semester. I suggest you get on board with him choosing a different school to attend. I'm thinking after all this chaos, he should take a year off; I can't even imagine what he's going through right now. David was so adamant about keeping them. Argh, why is this my life?" She palmed her face with both hands, distraught by all the chatter in her mind.

Charles palmed his chin taking her words in, "You're taking the case on the cop that gunned down that fourteen-year-old boy at the convenience store over a bag of skittles and a sweetened tea? Do you really think you need to be in the spotlight with our son having a case of his own?"

She pulled the covers up and over her head, she adjusted herself to a comfortable position. "Did you forget why I became a lawyer? Arrrrgh!! She bellowed in frustration. This case is the exact reason, if you needed to be reminded; everyone isn't privileged to get the kind of justice we did. I'm sure you can still smell the burning rotting flesh; that smell lingers in my nostrils as a reminder of the vengeance we served. Every time I walk through those courtroom doors, I smell that smell, serving my purpose for slaughtering the system as it is. I don't try to bury our past or pretend like it never happened; I use it as my ammunition. The battle is staying alive long enough in the streets until those changes happen. The war is won in the courtroom; that's how real change is made. As for our son, I've been waiting for charges to be filed against Ashton and the truth is, they don't have a case. The hearsay of those frat boys will be thrown out before the case could make it to a grand jury. Until then, I have a job to do Charles. I can't put my life on pause and check out the way you do."

"How do you explain the bruises and black eye then? I'm sure it's because you don't know how to leave well enough alone." He pushed, curious to know the truth.

Chayanne yawned, "If I knew we were having a sleepover at gossip hour in the morning, I would have come better prepared. Someone broke in last night; the police are on it. That's all I know."

"Bullshit, someone randomly breaks in the day your firm decides to take on one of the biggest media cases Georgia has seen? The same day your son gets accused of murdering a classmate? That doesn't seem coincidental to you Chayanne? Someone is gunning for you big time baby and you don't want to let off the gas! You know if you slam dunk this case, they are for sure going to make you partner."

"Good night Charles. If you aren't crashing on the sofa, please let yourself out. I'm sure you don't want to go back to the mess you created with Quentin anytime soon." she stated, shutting her heavy eyes.

Charles rolled his eyes because he knew it was true. He'd been arguing with Quentin since he gotten to the hotel room. He grunted and turned the table lamp off and laid back on the couch. His hands folded behind his head as he stared up at the ceiling, wondering what the next day would bring.

Ashton breathed heavily as he slept on the sofa in his Aunt Linda's study. Oddly, it was the only place he could sit still long enough to get some rest. On his chest rested an open book titled Behold a Pale Horse by Milton William Cooper.

Linda, not knowing Ashton was asleep, barged in, "David, I don't understand why you are choosing to go back with them after everything that's happened to you there."

David uneasy, rubbed the small scars that kept his neck company, "There is no way in hell that I will let anything happen to my sister while the world is crumbling around her. Dammit, if I knew Charles was any less of a man, I would have suggested we high-tailed it with the wind long before now. She can't be there alone with the kids. Did you see her face or am I the only person standing here with eyes?"

Linda softly closed the door to the study, not wanting her voice to carry, "I already played second fiddle to your baseball career and now your child that you decided to have outside of our union. We have a lot of work to do in our marriage David, and it's not going to get done when your hundreds of miles away from home. Our marriage is in the toilet, if you leave for Georgia, you might as well flush it, dammit!" She snarled angrily. "You asked to work this out, my bags were well packed when your mistress had the audacity to bring your two-year-old child to our doorstep. A child I knew nothing about because my husband was too ashamed to admit he couldn't keep his damn dick in his pants." Linda's bottom lip quivered, her brown doe like eyes watered, "You've done the one unforgivable thing that broke my core David; you got another woman pregnant after you made me infertile with all of the STDs you brought back from the road. I never once asked for any of it for fuck's sake; I should have listened to my gut and left you high and dry when the Mets traded you. I knew you were a cheater then and it wasn't worth keeping your promises." She covered her mouth with her small fragile hand to help gag her painful sobs. She rubbed her short hair at the nape of her neck with her free hand, wishing to soothe the knots in her stomach.

David slumped over, sat on the edge of her desk in the study. He sighed, taking her valid arguments in. He stared blankly into space as the wheels of his mind turned to find the best solution for all. Linda stood by the bay window, staring out allowing her tears to flow freely. Ashton, now awake, stirred and pretended to be asleep. Moments of silence passed, he let out a coughed to make his presence know.

David jolted from his thoughts, "Oh Ash, I didn't know you slept in here," he admitted embarrassed. David hoped that Ashton missed most of the information Linda spilled. Linda stormed out of the study, embarrassed that Ashton was exposed to their marital issues. David squirmed, knowing there would be hell to pay in a future conversation with Linda. The door slammed, startling Ashton to sit upright.

"Uncle D, is everything cool?" he asked, pretending to not have eavesdropped on their conversation.

David hesitated to answer "Yeah...yeah, everything is fine." He lied. "Hey Ash, do you want to take the truck with Lilly down to campus to grab some of your clothes? I have to admit, you look a little rough wearing those same clothes several days in a row." He asked, wanting to get him out the house so he could tie loose ends with Linda. David adjusted his glasses while he waited for Ashton to respond.

"Things got a little crazy on campus after the story about Kendal leaked. I can be quick in and out, but not so much with Lilly. I could maybe drive her to the hotel with mom before heading to school."

David mulled over Ashton's concerns, "Yeah, your right. Leave Lilly here. The last thing I need to do is worry your mother with a drop off. I'll figure a way to entertain her for a while."

"Are you sure Uncle D?" He pushed for reassurance.

"Yes Ash, but no funny business; there and back, do not stop and kid around with your buddies. I don't need anyone catching wind that you're on campus. I have half the mind to take you myself."

"I'll be fine, no extra stops, you have my word," Ashton said, jumping up to grab the keys that dangled between David's index and thumb. He rushed out of the study brushing past Lilly in the hallway and down the stairs.

"Watch what you're doing, ding-dong breath," Lilly said with attitude and sass. Her patience wore thin since she hadn't seen or heard from her mother. She'd only called Chayanne's palm pilot sixteen times in the two hours she'd been awake. She called to the hotel and left four messages with the front desk. She was having a hissy fit and set in to let Uncle D know about it. Lilly marched down the long, overly decorated hallway, taking notice of herself in the mirrors that lined the side of the hall. She thought out of Uncle D and Aunt Linda, who were so vain. She made her way through the entrance of the study. She observed David's demeanor before barging in. He sat on the edge of the desk, staring down into his palms and interlocked fingers. His energy was heavy and thick, like a dark, smoldering smoke cloud.

"Ahem Uncle D?" she said softly, waiting for his acknowledgment before continuing.

A few minutes passed before David felt Lilly's presence, "Oh Lilly, I didn't even hear you come in. What's up doll, what do you need?" he said attempting to be bubbly.

Lilly pursed her lips then but down on the inside of her lips contemplating if she should walk away. " Is everything good uncle D? I heard Aunt Linda storm outside to her workshop where she builds furniture. She was crying." Lilly said pushing for the truth. She was tired of everyone hiding things from her.

"We disagreed, that's all. When you get married, you'll understand; it's not as simple to keep the peace as you would like for it to be." He sighed, looking down at the patterned rug as if he were looking for answers to his issues.

She nodded, seeming as if she was interested in what he had to say. "I'm sure a bouquet of roses or her favorite flowers would help, somewhat. That's what Klara's boyfriend Luke does when he makes her cry; she smiles and pretends like nothing ever happened. It might work for you as well." She paused, allowing him to take her words in before getting to the real reason she came to bother him. "Can you take me to the hotel to my mom?"

David kissed his teeth teasing, "Um, maybe I can figure something out. Are you having a little separation anxiety?" he asked curiously.

"I'm not sure what that is Uncle D, but I just need to know if my mom is okay. I mean it's not like everyday life when some man is out to get you or hurt you." she stated, making her argument as to why they should go.

A look of concern appeared on David's face; he rubbed his beard at the validity of Lilly's case. "Well, I suppose you're right; and I myself haven't heard from her all morning." He agreed, looking down at his wristwatch that read 1:28 p.m. "I would have thought she would have made her way over by now. Let's head into town to see her and pick up some flowers for Aunt Linda. What do you say?"

Lilly, who was happy her concerns were heard, smiled and nodded.

Ashton pulled into the parking lot of his dormitory. He made it to campus in half the time it would normally take. He barreled down the expressway, nearly causing a few major accidents as he dodged in and out of lanes. His heart raced as he parked his uncles' truck in half empty lot. Most of the students from his building cleared out the night of the frat party. Ashton was anxious to catch Sommer before her mother dragged her back home, kicking and screaming. He hurriedly exited the truck, jogging swiftly onto campus in the direction of the female dorms. He couldn't help but take notice of the damages that were done to his building the night Kendal turned up dead. The windows were busted, the front entrance was unhinged, and beer cans and bottles lined the lawn. His heart fluttered, thinking of all the things that could have happened to him if the police never picked him up. His thoughts turned as quickly as his legs churned; he gained speed as he sprinted across campus, not wanting anyone to get a glimpse of his 6'1 frame. His mouth opened and sweat beads brimmed from his brow; his breath was heavy. "In through your nose, out through your mouth," the words of his high-school cross country coach played in his subconscious as he gathered his breathing into a cadence. He made it to her building out of breath; he stopped at the bottom of the stairwell hulled over, panting for air; his throat was dry. The sound of his heart pounded in his ears loudly. He was unable to hear the rustling of the bushes that neighbored the stairs.

"I knew you'd come here; you're so predictable, Ashton." Steve affirmed aloud.

Ashton took a deep breath and stood upright to face Steve, who was a few hairs taller. Aston took notice that Steve wasn't the well-manicured Steve he had come to know over the last two semesters of school. His hair was wild; his eyes were reddened and glassed over. His beard grew beyond a five o'clock shadow. His light-blue lacrosse button down was halfway untucked. He had small, red splatter stains on his rolled-up sleeves and chest area. Deep red scratches were embedded on his arms. His pants stained with dirt and grass and he reeked of puke and booze.

"Yo Steve, I don't know what you're on, but you need to back the fuck up!" Ashton demanded, his internal deference radar alarmed him.

"You were supposed to be my boy Ash, then you went behind my back to steal my girl." Snot dripped from Steve's nose; his eyes were watery. "You know how embarrassing that was for me, huh?" He asked rhetorically, "To have my frat brothers laugh in my face about Kendal fucking some coon ass nigger behind my back." Steve dug into his left pocket as he moved toward Ashton. He pulled out a small velvet felt box. "I just asked her parents for her hand in marriage. I knew she had a year left here, but I didn't want to leave for New York without her knowing how I felt." He opened the box taking the ring out, flashing it to Ashton. "Never in a fucking million years would they have accepted a proposal like this from you. If they'd known about you, they would have disowned her and put her out and away. They probably would have made her transfer. You ruined her just like your kind ruined everything in this country with your minority bullshit. I'm sure you wouldn't have fucking qualified through admissions if they didn't have a quota to fill. You're fucking scum Ash; you're the scum of the fucking earth and you stole the one thing from me that I actually cared about." He used the back of his hand to clear the snot from his nose. He couldn't hold the flood gates of his tears any longer.

"Steve, what happened to Kendal?" Ashton inquired, confused about what took place.

Steve sucked in his tears, "My life is over Ash. There is nothing left for me here." He paused catching his breath, "She chased after you and Sommer after you left. She was so torn after finding you two together, she cried and called out for you with so much passion and love in her voice. It didn't matter how many times I broke up with her or cheated on her, I've never heard the pain in her voice the way she had for you." He swallowed hard. "I let her go after you like the dumb bitch I knew she was. I tried to let it go man, I tried to not let it bother me. I drank more and turned up with my frats toward the end of the summer. I thought, fuck her I'll find another dumb blond in New York. I did a few lines of coke off some chick's ass and boned her raw. She ran out my room crying; I was being too aggressive choking her and holding her down. I said fuck it, that's what most of the bitches say anyway when they want to get in my dad's wallet." Steve shrugged it off and removed a flask from his right pocket. He took a swig of the contents and stumbled forward. He sniffed, wiping his nose and the rest of the powder residue the snot didn't take away. "My buddies gathered me around the mantel and told me how much of a bitch Kendal was and I couldn't let her get away with what's she's done. They told me they refused to go to school with a jungle bunny's whore next year and if I didn't settle it... they would. They pleaded and pushed for me to go and smack the shit out of her to punish her for all she's taken from my pride and reputation. They said after I was done beating the living shit out of her, to call and drop the dime to her parents; to explain why I refused to marry a whore like their daughter. The fucked-up thing is my parents already paid for the wedding, psh, go figure." Steve got quiet as rage grew within, "I called her to pretend I wanted to console her. I asked could I come and keep her company, she told me... only as friends." Steve licked his jaw, causing his tongue to protrude it outward. "A fucking friend, after three years of dating? That pissed me off even more. A few of the frats came with me, I was too fucked up to drive. I got over to her place and I couldn't keep my cool. I was angry; she played me, and I felt like a fucking fool, you know. I knocked over a few things, so what, big deal. I smacked her around a bit, I pulled her skirt down and showed her what a real man felt like. I knew you would never take her back if she was pregnant, so I let a few off inside of her, no big deal. She cried she screamed. She told me she hated me and could never love me the way she loves you; that did it for me. I stormed out the house, calling her all sorts of names, but she was alive when I left; so that means you killed her. I realized my beef wasn't with her, it was with you. It's how your kind comes along and takes things from us and don't think you owe us anything. Kendal is dead and I'm still furious at the world; I'm still angry with you." Steve cleared his nose, harking up a glob of spit and lodging it on Ashton's face.

Ashton stepped back, wiping the slimy contents from his eye and the side of his face. Enraged, he wiped his hands on his shirt and lunged toward Steve. Ashton was seconds away from ripping Steve apart, the cocking of the pistol caught him dead to rights in his tracks. Steve had the barrel of a semi-automatic pistol pressed against the front of Ashton's face, adjacent to his nose. His finger hugged the trigger; his palms were sweaty.

Sommer screamed for Ashton as she came flying out the building toward the feud.

JUST ANOTHER NI**A

L illy sat back, enjoying the breeze flowing through her golden-brown hair as David raced down the street in a shiny, blue, two-seater convertible corvette. The V-12 engine roared as he mashed on the accelerator to enter the freeway. Lilly put her hands in the air, mimicking the excitement of a rollercoaster ride. She felt like she was flyer and free of her worries for the moment. David put his aviator shades on then blasted the radio to set his free spirit mood into drive. The sun beamed through the clouds, shinning a little light on their day.

"Uncle D?" Lilly called out over the radio. David downshifted into fifth gear, sinking Lilly further into her chair. "Uncle David!" she screamed out once more. David turned the radio down and looked over at Lilly to acknowledge her; her reflection mirrored in his glasses.

"Do you have a garage full of cars so you can be like Uncle Anthony?"

David's face turned sour, "What do you know about him?" he questioned.

"I know he cut you down from the tree the Collins had you hanging from. He saved your life and he told you to never settle, but you married Aunt Linda. Do you wish you could be like him?"

David rubbed his chin, and then the scars on the back of his neck. "Your mom told you that? he said in distaste.

"She told me his story and made it clear why she does the things she does, being a lawyer and all. I was just curious if you are the way you are because of him too."

David cleared his throat; he never thought too much about Anthony or why he was the way he was, although he had a lot of Anthony's bad habits. "I have to be honest, Lilly; I haven't thought about him much since I've grown up. I've just been submerged in my baseball career… I guess I owe that to him too, the only reason I was as good as I am are because of the nights he took me out to the field to practice. We used to spend hours out there; he drilled me on the weaknesses that hindered him from making it to the majors." He smiled down at her. "Mmh, good question."

"Do you think what happened to Uncle Anthony will happen to Ashton?"

David frowned, "Do you know what happened to Anthony?"

"Sheriff Deputy Tomlin shot him in the chest. He knew Uncle Anthony and Rebecca wanted to run off together. My mom was there; she saw the whole thing and told me although she got her revenge, it never brought Uncle Anthony back."

"What revenge?" David asked confused.

"She shot Sheriff Deputy Tomlin, duh Uncle D. You were alive back then, how couldn't you know?" she said with sarcasm.

David swallowed hard; the speed of the car slowed. He had no idea what really happened that day. He was helpless laying in the hospital. The same helplessness he felt in that moment.

"Lilly, we are going to detour to Ash's school, is that cool with you?"

Lilly rolled her eyes and slumped back in the seat, "Just like Ashton, always stealing the attention. Can't you check on him after you take me to mom's?" she said, trying to reason with him.

"It's on the way to the city, I promise it won't be long. I think your mom would like to see you both. Wouldn't you agree?"

"Not at all, if Ashton wanted to see mom, he wouldn't have come all this way to school. He would have stood up to Charles and went somewhere else; he came here to escape home and now that he has, everyone is trying to reel him back in. Gee, I read his journals he has locked away in his closet." She said sticking her finger in her mouth pretending to gag. "He wastes so much of my time never really saying what he wants... he's just like dad, he thinks he knows it all." she professed in frustration.

"Why are you so upset? Do you not get enough attention?"

"You wouldn't get it; you wouldn't understand anyway." she said muffled looking out the open window.

"Try me?"

"Luke promised to handle Ash and he didn't; he's a liar like everyone else. He told me the truth about everyone and promised he wasn't the same. He lied and hid things just like the rest of you." She crossed her arms and poked her lip out.

David pulled off the expressway in the direction of the Georgetown campus. "Who is Luke and how do you know him?" he asked perplexed, thinking she was talking about an imaginary friend.

"Luke Carter, Uncle D, he goes by LC. You know him, he said he knows you and mom. Why do you all pretend like you don't know anything?" she said with conviction. "Ugh! Maybe that was another one of his lies." She rolled her eyes annoyed that David was dragging her to check on Ashton after she confessed she didn't want to.

"Did your mom tell you that? Uncle Anthony never had any kids, not that I'm aware of, hell apparently. I'm not up to speed on a lot. Your mom had him over for coffee or something?"

Lilly grunted even more agitated, she shook her head side to side, "Never mind forget I mentioned it. I told you, you wouldn't understand. No one ever listens to me, anyway!"

David had stop listening to Lilly when he pulled from the expressway, his attention was drawn to the flashing lights of the metro police cars and ambulances that surrounded the west wing of the campus. His heart sank in fear that Ashton had gotten to campus and was spotted. He pulled around to the men's dormitory on the east end of campus. He spotted his truck; a little relief swept over him thinking Ashton was inside on the opposite end of chaos. He pulled in and parked next to the truck in the lot.

He opened the driver's door, "Come on, let's go check it out." he said, nudging Lilly to undue her seatbelt to tag along. Lilly complied against her will and followed David to the vandalized building. Just as they made it to the entrance, they heard a ring of gunshots let loose. David grabbed Lilly and retreated in the building, hiding in a vacant dorm room closet.

Chayanne slept well into the afternoon; she was awakened by the opening of the hotel room door.

"Housekeeping!" A woman called out, knocking on the door as she entered.

Chayanne woke in a haze, "No, no, I don't need housekeeping today. Maybe tomorrow." She said waiving the woman off with one hand, rubbing her the eye that wasn't bruised with the other. The cleaning lady complied and left, closing the door behind her. Chayanne looked over at the sofa where Charles was. He vanished, just as she expected him to do after being rejected. His attention was pulled away by the sound of the toilet flushing. Charles emerged from the bathroom, drying his hands on a small, white hand towel.

Chayanne's nasty glare startled him in his tracks, "Sheesh, if looks could kill."

"Why are you still here?" she asked sternly.

"Is that seriously your question? Come on, get up, your phone has been going off like a fire alarm. We need to go rent a nice sized truck to move Ash's stuff back home."

Chayanne looked surprised, "You're not going to fight me on this?"

"There is no need to, you made a valid argument for him to be closer to home. You've put a few things into perspective for me, so yeah, let's not dwell on it." He teased. "I went down to the lobby and picked you up some toiletries and a few things to wear. I got coffee and breakfast, but you slept way past your prime, so it's cold now. We can grab something for you on the way out."

Chayanne smiled warmly, "Thank you!" her voice hoarse.

"Ah, you don't really mean it; you hate my guts and have every right to do so."

"No, sincerely, thank you! I missed this part of you for a long time."

"Exactly what part is that?" He pushed as he basked in her gratitude.

"The part where you're actually my friend and not trying to fill your own interests."

He smirked softly and nodded, walking back to the sofa where the white pages laid open on the coffee table. Chayanne rolled out bed to tend to her chiming palm pilot. She scrolled through the mountain of missed calls. The flashing message light on the room phone caught her attention. She phoned the front desk.

"Front desk, how may I help you?'

"Messages for Carter room 1402."

"Yes Ms. Carter, please hold."

The sound of elevator music greeted her ears while she waited. She continued scrolling through her phone, now checking emails. An email marked urgent from the firm caught her attention.

"Ms. Carter, are you still on the line?"

"Yes!" She answered distracted

"You have four messages from a Lilly Parker, urging you to return her call at your brother's residence. Would you like the number?"

"No, I have it thank you!"

"You have a message from Mr. Gilbert, a managing partner at your law firm. He said his news is urgent and to please return his call on his personal line. Would you like that number?"

"No, I have it thank you!"

"Very well, lastly, you have a call from a Daniel Walsh, he has an urgent matter that needs your attention as well. He wants you to page him when you can. I'd assume madam you have his number as well?"

"Got it, thanks!" she said putting the receiver on the base.

She scammed through the email from, the firm:

Given the latest news on your personal matters, at this time, we have decided to sever our relationship with you. We believe your personal matters are imposing on the firm's reputation. We have highlighted below the firm's code of ethics in which you are in violation of. Please return your office keys and lobby fob upon arrival to clear your office space.

Chayanne mumbled through the rest of her unread emails, reading them aloud. Charles drawn into her concerned look, wandered to the bed side.

"What is it?" He questioned impatiently, wanting to know what was going on. Chayanne still entangled in the contents of the email ignored his thirst for details.

She rested her hand on her chest with disbelief, "The firm... they let me go because of the accusations surrounding Ashton with this girl's murder. The nerve and the unjust prejudice. The girl's parents contacted the firm; apparently the father is golf buddies with Mr. Gilbert, per Gary's email. I can't believe all this is..." She clenched her fists with hurt in her eyes as she looked at Charles, "They fired me through an email… after everything I've sacrificed for those greedy bastards… That's all I'm worth, a fucking 363-word email with a generic separation letter attached." Her voice shook Charles's core. He coiled away, afraid she may unreasonably lash out. "By God, they built a fortune off my work alone. I'm an underpaid attorney because I don't have a piece of meat that dangles to qualify me. I damn sure can't get equal pay because of the color of my skin. ARRGH!" she shrilled, reaching her boiling point.

"Chayanne?" Charles whispered to let his input resonate. She looked possessed staring at him; her green eyes enlarged, filled with despair. "Honestly, you aren't a lawyer for the money, but for the cause. You're the voice that our people don't have in the courtroom. You're the game changer here, don't let this petty bullshit of whose dick is bigger get you down. Metaphorically speaking, I'm sure you would win given the set of balls on you." He chuckled to lighten the mood, "You're made for something bigger; something more meaningful than sitting around, breathing life into someone else's shit. We promised each other that day Anthony took his last breath that we would always remind each other of our purpose and I'm here doing just that. All of what we're going through is rebuilding what got us here; don't let those yellow belly mother fuckers see you hurting. You've become their competition. Make them regret letting you go; your reputation alone will get existing clients to side with you. You can practice law with someone else's firm or even your own." He stood in silence for a few moments, "I say start your own firm… there's no better day than the present. I believe in you and so does your win rate. I pay attention, you're still slaying the dragons and putting them to rest. Don't be the typical stereotype of the bitter black woman; that's what they paint y'all as. Come out guns blazing and take them for the clients you have."

Chayanne listed to Charles rant with care, "You're right; my ego got a hold of me for a moment. It was unexpected, that's all, I live in a world of certainty, so it's hard to let the uncertain take over at times." She swallowed hard, breathing her remorse in to gather her mental. "Thank you for helping me through that. I would have been in therapy first thing in the morning trying to unravel those things. I guess this friendship has its perks." she said hugging him.

"That'll be five-hundred dollars," he teased jokingly. "No seriously, how much do you pay your therapist per session? I need to hire one for all the baggage I'm carrying on the daily."

"You should know how much it is, you're the one they bill." She busted out in laughter. "I guess you didn't read all the stipulations in the divorce papers, buddy."

Charles's face went blank, "Seriously, how did you pull that off?"

"Honey, you just said I'm the best the courtroom has ever seen, now you're eating your facts." she laughed her way into the shower to get ready for the remainder of her day.

She thought long and hard about the things taking place in her life, as the soothing stream of water washed over her. She felt calm and relaxed, she knew it was a storm brewing within, but she was unsure of when the havoc would be released.

Charles knocked softly on the door, "Hey, you need to wrap it up in there. Something weird is happening down on campus. I don't think we'll be able to get in there; they have police choppers and all. It's a story that's unfolding minute by minute on the news. We might have to leave Ashton's things." he said kissing his teeth, "I just bought him that damn Macintosh." he said to himself.

Chayanne stopped the shower and wrapped herself in a robe. She dried her hair with a drying towel and exited the bathroom. Her eyes immediately found the TV. A feeling grew uncomfortably in her gut. She rushed over to the phone and dialed David's home phone. The phone rang until the answering machine picked up. Her heart raced as she tried again.

"Hello, Carter's residence." Linda's sweet voice came through the receiver.

"Linda, it's Chayanne, where is David and the kids?" she asked frantically.

"Is everything alright?" she deferred, answering out of concern.

"Linda please, are they there?"

"David and Lilly were headed to you over two hours ago. That's a twenty-minute drive. Maybe they stopped for breakfast; have you tried his car phone or his cell?"

"You said David and Lilly were headed to me... where is Ashton?"

Linda sighed, recalling the disagreement she had with David earlier that day, "David let Ashton take his truck on campus to pick some of his things up and for a change of clothes."

Chayanne's face turned pale and her heart beat rapidly as it drowned in her chest. She felt her tongue swell and she was unable to speak.

"Chayanne... is everything alright?" Linda kept repeating, waiting for an answer. She could hear her breathing on the other end of the phone. "Chayanne... Chayanne?

"Turn on the news," Chayanne commented before hanging up.

Her fingers were moving faster than her thoughts as she misdialed David's cell several times.

"Hey, hey, calm down." Charles instructed "What did she say? Are they there? Are they safe?"

Chayanne finally calmed her nerves to dial the right number. The phone rang until the voicemail was answered. Chayanne pressed redial, hoping to get David or anyone of her children. After the eighth time, she grew weary and nauseous. The room started spinning; she jumped up and rushed to get dressed.

"Chayanne, they are saying it's a gunman on the campus." Chayanne rushed to the TV to listen to the news reporter.

"Swat is just now arriving on the scene to aid local authorities in detaining the unknown gunman. The Dean stated that most students departed yesterday to leave for summer break. The campus is filled at forty percent capacity with students that are taking classes over the summer. The Dean stated students protested violently into the earlier hours of the morning due to a student death that took place on campus. He believes one of the students took the protest a bit too far. This story is still unfolding..."

A rain of gunshots caused the news network to break the broadcast. Chayanne turned the TV on, hoping to catch the unfolding events on another channel. She found nothing as most networks cut the footage. She rushed to the door.

"Chayanne, what the hell?" Charles lashed out.

"Ashton… Ashton is on campus dammit, we have to go Charles, we have to go!" she screamed, fighting her tears back.

Charles rushed after her to the elevator in disbelief. Chayanne danced impatiently, waiting for the elevator to come up to their level.

"Fuck it, I'm taking the stairs," Charles exclaimed, heading toward the stairwell. Chayanne followed close behind. He bumped into a housekeeper's cart, knocking it over as he flung the door open to descend the twenty-eight flights of stairs.

They crashed through the lobby exit out of breath and fumbled onto the street to hail a taxicab. Charles's arms flailed tirelessly, trying to stop a cab driver. Chayanne was at the street corner with her back to Charles, waiving for a cab too. Both were so focused on the task at hand that they didn't notice Quentin approaching.

"You fucking scumbag, I knew you were with her." Quentin yelled over the noisy traffic and car horns. He smacked Charles with full force from behind.

Charles caught off guard, spun around throwing an elbow to Quentin's face, "WHAT THE FUCK MAN?" Charles yelled angrily, turning to face him. Blood spurted from Quentin's nose; Charles surprised to see him kneeled down to apologize. "What… what were you thinking? Why would you strike me?"

"You son of a bitch, you broke my nose." he winced in pain applying pressure in an attempt to stop the bleeding. "I knew you were with her." He held his head back shaking it side to side. "Can you go get help?"

Charles looked around for the nearest payphone. He took notice that a concerned Chayanne was headed in their direction. "Oh no, I don't want to deal with miss missy, you can forget about it. Charles, handle her!"

Charles stood up towering over Chayanne's small frame, "I think I broke his nose."

Chayanne grabbed Charles's Nike hoodie pulling him close to her, "I do not give two fucks about miss man over there, our son is in trouble. Pick a side and stop straddling the fucking fence!" she said through her clenched teeth. She let him go, pushing him back to Quentin. She went back to the edge of the curb to flag a taxi.

Charles stooped down next to Quentin, "Listen, Ash is in trouble, I have to go... plus I..."

"Fucking great, the problem child raising hell again. You need to send his little ass to a boarding school! I'm sick of this shit, Charles!"

Charles rolled his eyes in annoyance, "No Quentin, I'm sick of your shit. Always nagging, whining, bitching and complaining about Chayanne. You want me to put on a front that we're so happy, but the truth is you're happy with the money. You're not interning on someone's clock anymore! You're forcing me into marriage so you can take Chayanne's place won't make shit different. My children come first, and I lost sight of that living out some twisted fantasy with you." Charles noticed a taxi stopped for Chayanne, "I'm over this shit!" Charles dropped his ring on the sidewalk next to Quinten. He looked at him sternly, shaking his head in disappointment. He leaped and ran to hop in the cab before Chayanne closed the door. Quentin sat remorseful of his actions; he felt

Charles was putting on a ruse for Chayanne, like he's done many times beforehand when he was a secret.

David and Lilly heard noises coming from the hallway as they stayed hidden in the closet of the abandon room.

"Lilly, did you close the room door behind you?" He whispered to her.

Lilly tried to see if David had a look of fear on his face, but she was unable to make it out from the small crack of light that beamed in from the bottom of the door.

"No!" Lilly responded in agitation.

Five more rounds were let off, Lilly hugged her legs and rocked, wishing she was with her mother.

"Everything is going to be okay Lilly, I promise." David reassured her.

"Everything would have been okay if you took me to mom instead of dragging me here."

"I'm sorry, I should have listened to you. Instead of dragging us into this mess. I knew I shouldn't have let him take the truck... I guess my embarrassment outweighed my judgement."

"How long have we been in here? Your legs are smushing me." Lilly complained.

"I don't know, I can't see my watch; it's not enough light." David put his watch closer to the crack of light, still unable to make out the time.

"Can we just go back to the car?"

"I don't know where the gun shots are coming from, they sound close."

"Ugh, how do we know Ashton hasn't left yet? It was noise in the hallway." Lilly said, twisting the doorknob and opening the door.

They were greeted by a breeze of fresh air.

"Lilly, get back in here" David said, grabbing at her top.

She broke free from the closet and ran into the hallway, disappearing from David's sight. "God dammit! Jesus fucking Christ, is this what having children is like? No wonder I've never wanted them." David said aloud, confessing to himself. He grunted, pulling himself off the floor from the tiny closet. He ran into the hallway to look for Lilly.

Lilly ran up to the second floor in search of her brother so she could get on with her day. She had a great memory and knew this is where they left Ashton when they drove for a million miles to drop him off to school. The halls were deserted; it felt like the scary movies with Michael Myers that Ashton forced her to watch. The agonizing feeling of fear grew intensely as she neared Ashton's room. She thought to herself how she'd feel if she found him dead. Her stomach turned, making her feel nauseous.

"Lilly...Lilly... where are you girl?" David whispered.

Lilly tiptoed into David's dorm, bypassing the carved word DIE NIGGER on the door. She snooped around, looking for Ashton in the common area. She went into his bedroom and her heart dropped to the floor.

"Lilly? Oh my gosh, you're alright," Chayanne said relieved. She stooped down to give her a warm. "I was afraid something happened to you." She smiled and kissed her forehead and hugged her again. Chayanne looked around confused, "Where is Ash and David?" Lilly shrugged as a pool of her tears collected on Chayanne's shoulder. Chayanne picked Lilly up and headed back to the hallway; she collided with David.

"Um, excuse me..." David swallowed the rest of his words when he realized it was his little sister with a look of evil on her face.

Chayanne was about to lay into David and tear him a new one. Charles interrupted, running down the hall toward them.

"All the action is on the other side of campus, some crazed kid with a firearm. Maybe Ashton pulled on campus and before he could get in to refuge somewhere else."

"Why don't I just take Lilly back to the house and wait for you all there?" David interjected.

"You're pathetic! Your standards as a man are shot to hell! Ugh, Pa really did a number on you. How do you want to run away from a situation you created, David? I don't know how you got it in your twisted fucking mind to let a teenage boy drive himself back into danger, ALONE! Linda told me you let him take the car and you were bringing Lilly to me. You really disgust me; all that protector crap, but soon as real trouble comes around, you're like a ghost, nowhere to been seen and nowhere to be found. Coward!"

"Guys, come on!" Charles pleaded. "You two always want to go for the jugular. We don't have time for this shit, we need to find Ashton and get out of here... maybe we should split up, it's a lot of ground to cover." Another stream of gunfire let lose; they all crouched down against the walls.

"Psh, coward huh? We are all crouched down like some fucking Vietnam soldiers and best part of it all, we're unarmed, Chayanne. If we run into a gunman, how the hell do you plan on fighting a bullet?" David remarked in a nasty, condescending way.

"Well David, I'm happy to know that you aren't a father! When your children's lives are on the line, you leave no rock unturned. I thought Momma taught you that when she never stopped looking for Charles and I. She bankrupt her damn fortune that Nana and Papa left her to find me. That should have taught you something, but you were too busy chasing tail to notice. You ran away then just like you're running away from everything now. That's why you decided to play pro ball and not finish school, to run away just like you always do."

Charles threw his hands in the air with annoyance, "Can we please not have a repeat of Thanksgiving. I don't know why you two have so much animosity with one another. You have your own stories but try to discredit each other at any turn."

"Well Charles, I see you living mighty fine off the fortune Uncle Anthony left little miss princess over there. So you didn't have to result in leaving your family to make decent money. I refused to die in the God damn coal mines like Daddy. I had a choice: a life of luxury or a life of scowling on my damn belly, barely making enough to survive. So you God damn right, I chose to leave." David hissed.

"I see your damn talent is the only thing God blessed you with because it wasn't the brains you ass hole. Senator Collins is Charles's father! He paid Charles off a shit load of money to keep his secret. I don't think Senator Collins wanted any more bloodshed in our small, dung hole of a town. You sit there thinking you know it all on your high and mighty horse, but you don't know SHIT! Uncle Anthony left you things, but you squandered it on the things he did: women, clothes, cars, and everything else. You wanted to be him, but didn't have his smarts or wits. So go ahead, sit there and pretend like the world is out to get you one more time… don't worry, we will wait since the sun rises and sets on your small-minded ass." Chayanne said maneuvering herself off the floor with Lilly still in her arms. "Truth is David, I have the life you want and dream of. I have a life of purpose. When you're all washed up and the fans don't wear your jersey anymore… what will you have left? It's clear your marriage is hanging on by strands. Linda called me a few times over the last month about divorcing procedures, but you know everything, don't you? Now if you will excuse me, I have a child to find." Chayanne walked away, disappearing into the shadows of the stairwell.

Charles shook his head in disappointment, "With all this chaos and hate around us, y'all can't unite? That's your family! When we were growing up, the only reason I wanted a family was because of y'all; I never knew what it was like to be loved the way your parents loved you two. At the end of the day, money, fame, passion, or a career isn't going to stop that from being your sister David. You're wrong to many degrees and so is she, but she has a reason… you allowed her son… our son to get wrapped in another situation. She's traveled miles and lost her job at the firm over this, and you've allowed the fire to grow beyond a remedy. If anything happens to Ashton, you can bet your last dollar she'll never speak to you again." Charles sighed, picking himself off the ground. He extended his hand to help David up. David grabbed the olive branch and accepted Charles's hand; he pulled him up with force. They jogged out the building. The sun blinded them as they exited; they saw Chayanne holding Lilly, heading into the east wing of campus cutting across the fresh green lawn. David and Charles jogged after them.

"You two, stop right there and get on the ground!" Charles and David spun toward the voice confused." SWAT had their rifles drawn and the barrels pointed at them. They looked at one another terrified for their lives. They noticed SWAT was raiding all the buildings and putting people on their faces.

"GET THE FUCK DOWN, NOW! GET ON THE GROUND!" students and faculty wiped their tears sobbing.

Charles and David lifted their hands above their heads, complying with the officer. They dropped to their knees in sync. Their hearts raced; time moved in slow motion and everything around them seemed to pause. They knew this was one of many ways black men were lynched. Charles put his head down and closed his eyes, taking in all of the vibrant life that surrounded them; he was afraid that he may never open his eyes again.

"Fame can't save you now David. You will still and always be another nigger to them."

Chayanne made it to the barricades of the east wing; the police blocked it off and further instructed the crowd to stay back. She glanced over the crowd, frantically searching for Ashton's face. She began moving through the crowd disrupting the bystanders.

"Ashton?" she called out with her heart fluttering. Ashton!" Her hands trembled on Lilly's back. "Ashton!" she called once more, still scanning the crowd.

Chayanne bumped into a woman with tears pouring down her face; she looked down, noticing the woman's faculty badge.

"Ashton Parker was a student of mine for Economics last semester. I remember meeting you during open house. He's a brilliant young man. I know Ashton didn't harm Kendal and he's not the monster media is painting him to be. I will pray for you and your family." The professor pointed in the direction past the barricades.

Chayanne turned her head as two paramedics wheeled a covered corpse with a blood-soaked sheet into the back of the ambulance. Chayanne dropped to her knees and buried her face into Lilly's hair sobbing; she squeezed Lilly tightly.

"No God... please no... please, please, please, not my baby, not my baby." She repeated over and over, rocking back and forth with Lilly tucked into her arms.

Book II coming soon to a bookstore near you!

CPSIA information can be obtained
at www.ICGtesting.com
Printed in the USA
BVHW031118130322
631356BV00005B/70